# PRAISE FOR M[...] W9-CFN-896

"*Empress of Earth* is a gourmet feast for those who like science fiction. The mystical technology is so well conceived and exhaustively thought out that by the end one finds oneself convinced that it is real. . . . Plan on losing sleep because you won't be able to put it down."     —*Wilson Library Journal*

"Scott's space drive and description of space piloting alone would mark her as an expert . . . This is the stuff of which 'sense of wonder' is made." —Debbie Notkin, *Locus*

"*The Armor of Light* is at times breathlessly exciting, a truly remarkable action novel."
—*Rave Reviews*

"Melissa Scott has created a fascinating world and culture, and filled it with believable characters and an intriguing story. . . . All in all, *The Kindly Ones* is an absorbing book."
—*Aboriginal SF*

"Winner of last year's Campbell Award for Best New Writer, Scott weighs in with an ambitious novel of the world Orestes. . . . Scott is still a writer to watch."
—*Publishers Weekly*

"Melissa Scott, one of science fiction's most talented newcomers; for two years running she has been nominated for the John W. Campbell Award for Best New Writer. Her first two books were innovative . . . the stuff of science fiction: starships and distant worlds, new societies and captivating interstellar politics."     —*The Baltimore Sun*

# MELISSA SCOTT

BAEN BOOKS

## MIGHTY GOOD ROAD

This is a work of fiction. All the characters and events portrayed in this book are fictional, and any resemblance to real people or incidents is purely coincidental.

Copyright © 1990 by Melissa Scott

All rights reserved, including the right to reproduce this book or portions thereof in any form.

A Baen Books Original

Baen Publishing Enterprises
260 Fifth Avenue
New York, N.Y. 10001

ISBN: 0-671-69873-7

Cover art by Tom Kidd

First printing, May 1990

Distributed by
SIMON & SCHUSTER
1230 Avenue of the Americas
New York, N.Y. 10020

Printed in the United States of America

*Oh, the Rock Island Line, it is a mighty good road*
*Oh, well, the Rock Island Line, it is the road to ride.*
*Now if you want to ride it,*
*Got to ride it like you find it,*
*Get your ticket at the station for the Rock Island Line!*

# CHAPTER 1

The Memorial glowed in the somber light that mim-
icked Earth's setting sun, or the reddened light of fires.
It was a disturbing light, to anyone who'd spent any
time on the orbital stations of the Loop, and deliberately so. At the center of the pool of light were the
statues, twice life-size, a man and a woman crouching
together, their bodies arched protectively over the huddled shape of a fallen child. The pale stone stood out in
high relief against the blackened metal that sealed off
what had once been the entrance to the Cross-Systems
Railroad's Platforms Four and Five. There were flowers
at the woman's feet, real flowers, already wilting a little
from the heat of the lights: an extraordinary expense on
any station, but especially here.

Gwynne Heikki shivered, seeing the frail bundle,
and glanced for reassurance back over her shoulder
toward the bustle of the still-working platforms. Signs
flashed above the entrances, the mass of the most recent arrivals ebbing away through the multiple customs
barriers. Few appeared to notice the statues, or the

1

other signs of the disaster, the charred softiles, bare metal, melted wires hanging in tatters, that were still carefully preserved on the memorial wall. Nor did they pay much attention to the man who sat cross-legged on the floor tiles just outside the band of light that defined the memorial, protest banner dangling limply over-head. The green circle stood out sharply against the black background, three interlaced gold "R"s inscribed on its surface. They stood, Heikki knew only too well, for the Retroceders' creed: *Remember, Repent, and Return.* Remember that the railroad has failed once, repent of your dependence on it, and return to the planets from whence you came.

Heikki shook her head, and turned away. Popular though that creed might be in the Precincts, for the planets not yet connected to the Loop by a spur of the railroad, it was hardly practical. Settled space depended utterly on the Loop as its economic and political center, and the Loop in turn was dependent on—more than that, was created by and existed only because of—the railroad, the network of permanently open warps that allowed virtually instantaneous travel between the Loop's stations, the thirteen Exchange Points. But the railroad in its turn was dependent on the Papaefthmyiou-Devise Engine, and that, Heikki thought, was the weak point that the Retroceders could and did exploit. After all, a PDE had failed once, here on Exchange Point One, and the station was still recovering from the disaster a hundred and fifty years later. Despite the engineers' assurances—and they swore it could never happen again, that it had been the strain of trying to open a fifth warp in an already crowded system that had caused the PDE to fail—not one could be entirely certain that they were right.

Heikki shook herself then and turned away, annoyed at having given Retroceder propaganda even that much consideration. She stepped onto the slidewalk that car-ried arriving passengers toward the center of Point One, swinging her carryall deftly out of the way as barriers rose to either side. The flexible carpet picked up speed, and signs flashed overhead, warning riders to use the handrail to either side. Heikki balanced easily, shutting out the hum of the machinery and the shop displays flickering past outside the barriers. She should deposit the draft from the ProCal job as soon as possible, now that she had access to Loop banks and the better exchange rates they could offer. Even if she had to search a little to find an open console, she'd still have plenty of time before her next train left for EP7.

The end-of-strip lights flashed overhead, breaking her reverie, and a moment later a dulcet mechanical voice repeated the warning. She stepped from the slidewalk as soon as the barriers went down, disdaining the slow-down strip or the grab bars. To her left rose the massive arch that joined the Station Axis to the Travellers' Concourse, the gleaming, gold-washed metal engraved with the names of the people who'd died in the disaster: Exchange Point One wanted to be certain no one would ever forget her losses. Heikki made a face, and looked away, adjusting the strap of her heavy carryall.

Outside the arch, the Concourse was crowded, as always—Exchange Point One was still the unofficial capitol of the Loop's Southern Line—but Heikki wove her way through the crowd with practiced skill, heading for the massive staircase that led to the Concourse's upper level. After several weeks in the Precincts, and in the open air, working sea salvage on Callithea, the noise and the faintly chemical smell of an over-worked ventilation system were almost pleasant: this was home, or close to it. Heikki allowed herself a faint, lopsided smile, and took the upward stairs two at a time, dodging a group of giggling tourists whose clothes marked them as inhabitants of the Danae cluster. The first four uni-bank consoles were occupied, lights on and doors blanked. The fifth was empty. Heikki started toward it, then checked, abruptly understanding why. A group of neo-barbarians crouched in an alcove less than three meters away from the cubicle's door—probably between trains like any other travellers, Heikki knew, but neo-

barbs had a deservedly bad reputation on and off the
Loop. In the same moment, she saw a florid, soberly
dressed man whose high-collared jacket bore half a
dozen variations on his corporate logo, obviously hesi-
tating to use the same cubicle. He saw her glance, and
sneered slightly. That was enough to make the decision
for her. This was EP1, the Travellers' Concourse of
EP1, not some planetary spaceport. If the neo-barbs
were stupid enough to start something, the securitrons
would be on them in an instant.

Even as she thought that, the group in the alcove
stirred uneasily, scowling down the length of the Concourse and murmuring to themselves. One of the Point's
security teams, a half-armored human and his mechanical enforcer, was making its leisurely way along the
walk. The neo-barbs pushed themselves to their feet,
the single woman tugging nervously at her greasy skirt,
the three men hastily collecting their heavy, shapeless
bags, and started back toward the station axis. Heikki
waited a moment longer, then stepped into the cubicle,
ignoring the veiled annoyance of the florid man. As she
latched the door, lights faded on inside, while the clear
material of the door darkened to opacity behind her.

Like most people who did business both on the Loop
and in the Precincts, she did her banking through
Lloyds/West, with its well-earned reputation for being
able to handle any local currency at an acceptable rate.
She settled herself in front of the console and keyed
Lloyds' codes into the machine. The screen blanked,
the internal mechanisms clicking to themselves, and
she leaned back in the little chair to fish her data lens
from the outer pocket of her belt. She fiddled with the
thick bezel, adjusting the setting to match Lloyds' privacy codes, then squinted through it as the prompt
sequence appeared. She keyed in her personal codes
and the serial numbers for the local draft that was the
payment for her latest job. Viewed through the lens,
the string of numbers was perfectly bright against the
dark background; when she opened her other eye, she
saw only a blank screen. The machine considered briefly,

then signalled its willingness to accept the draft. Heikki fed the embossed datasquare into the port, and watched through the lens while numbers shifted on the screen. The exchange rate was better than she'd expected, almost two Callithean dollars to the pound-of-account. Nodding to herself, she touched the keys that would accept the transaction. The machine beeped twice, and recorded the transfer of 13,128.49 poa, less service fee, from the negotiable draft to the account of Heikki/ Santerese, Salvage Proprietors. Even after twenty years in the business, Heikki still smiled a little, seeing the name.

She shook herself then, slipping the data lens back into the belt pocket, and touched more keys to close the terminal and retrieve her access card. The cubicle door swung open, plastic fading again to transparence. The florid man was still waiting for a cubicle, his face prim with disapproval. Heikki hid a grin, and started down the Upper Concourse, still heading away from the station axis. It would be almost five hours, by the exchange points' standard time, before she could board the train that would take her to Exchange Point Seven, and there was no point, she added silently, in spending that time in the station's common waiting rooms.

A few meters further along the concourse, a sign flashed invitingly above a General Infoservices multiboard. Heikki paused, glancing over the charges engraved on the plate beside the tiny numeric keyboard—as on most exchange points, the basic locator service was free, but further inquiries were assessed at an increasingly exorbitant rate—then fished her data lens out of her pocket. After a moment's thought, she twisted the bezel to the Explorers' Club's standard setting, and held the five-centimeter-thick cylinder over the multiboard's screen. Within the charmed circle of the lens, the chaos of colors and shapes vanished, to be replaced by the Club's greeting and the location of its nearest members' lounge. As she had hoped, it was on this level of the concourse, perhaps a quarter-hour's walk from the multiboard. She slipped the lens back into her pocket and turned away,

unconsciously lengthening her stride. The disapproving
glance of a dark woman in a maroon corporate uniform
reminded her that she was no longer on a Precinct
world, and she shortened her step to something more
appropriate for the exchange points.

The Club lounge was a small place, a sort of alcove off
the main walkway that not even dim lighting and carefully sited distortion units could make spacious. There
was, however, a bar and an autokitchen, and the two
dozen tables were arranged around a four-seater newsvendor. It was not particularly crowded, only a few
men and women tucked into the corner tables, barri-
caded behind their printed flimsysheets. Heikki slipped
her membership card through the sensor gate, and
seated herself at the empty newsvendor. There were
some new options available—a general fiction listing,
for one—but she ignored that, and punched in the
personal codesequence that would give her a custo-
mized precis of the day's news. The machine murmured to itself for what seemed an interminable time,
then spat sheet after sheet of closely spaced print. At
the same moment, the service charge appeared discreetly in the corner of the screen. Heikki winced, but
tore off the last flimsy, and headed for a table by the
wall. An order pad was set into the polished surface.
She touched the keys that would bring her a 'salatha
gin—a sequence so familiar she hardly looked at the
pad—and settled back to scan the flimsies.

Nothing much was happening on the political scene,
either in the Loop or in the Precincts, and she lifted
the sheets to allow the Club's human waiter to set the
tall glass in front of her. The Loop's Southern Extension
was accusing the Northern Extension of more than usually Byzantine dealings in the bidding for the new FTL
depot; there had been Precincter riots on Bacchus;
there was trouble between neo-barb incomer-workers
and the eco-fundamentalist settlers on Hauser, in the
Tenth Precinct—but that particular problem had been
simmering for the past three years, standard. Neither
side was likely to listen to reason at this late date.

Heikki sighed, and made a note to put Hauser on her personal watch list when she got back to EP7: it was not a place to be accepting work, just now.

The technical news and markets were more interesting, including an article culled from a scholarly journal describing the exhumation of an ancient Lunar waste-disposal site. Heikki had advised on several similar projects, though always in-atmosphere, and read through the article attentively, noting technique. The next article was culled from an unfamiliar source, the *Terentine Argus* of Precinct Six, with a screaming headline, *Local Business Under Siege from Off-world Magnate; Insiders Baffled.* Heikki stared for a moment at the glaring type, wondering what had possessed the compiler to slip this piece of trash into her file, and then saw the first line of the story. *Local salvage proprietors Four-Square confirmed today that they are the object of a breach-of-contract suit by the Iadara-based crysticulture firm Lo-Moth, following FourSquare's refusal to complete its search for the LTA craft lost on Iadara eight months ago.*

Heikki's eyebrows rose. Salvage proprietors did not break contract even with mid-rank firms like Lo-Moth; or rather, she amended grimly, one broke a contract in the full knowledge that one was also breaking one's career and company. Something must have gone very wrong, to force FourSquare to give up like that. . . . She skimmed quickly through the article, but it said nothing more about the reasons for the breach, concentrating instead on the suit and the possible legal consequences for FourSquare. The dateline on the article was nearly two weeks old.

The final flimsysheet was less than half full, and contained only a single entry. *Lo-Moth of Iadara announced today the settlement of its dispute with Four-Square, salvage proprietors, Terentia, in exchange for all data collected by FourSquare during the term of its employment. Lo-Moth is presently accepting bids (licensed proprietors only) for completion of the project abandoned by FourSquare.*

"Holy shit," Heikki said aloud, and winced as the red light flashed above the orderpad. A moment later, numbers streamed across the little screen: the Club's monitor program assessed a fine of ten poa for immodest language. Heikki made a face, but pressed the acknowledgement button silently.

"Oh, dear, Heikki," a too-familiar voice said, and a second, equally familiar voice added, "Slip of the tongue?"

Heikki looked up slowly, allowing herself a slight, lopsided smile. Piers Xiang and Odde Engels, known without much fondness as the Siamese twins, smiled down at her, the expression particularly at odds with Engels' hard-edged blondness.

"What's up?" she said in return, and did not offer them a chair.

To her surprise, however, the two men lingered, Xiang's green eyes flickering sideways in what might have been a reproving glance. "I see you've seen the news," he said, in the clipped Havenite accent he'd never been able to erase.

"Which news?" Heikki asked warily.

"About Lo-Moth." Xiang paused, round face suddenly serious. "May we join you, Heikki?"

Exchange point etiquette required that she say yes—though 'pointer etiquette also decreed that the question should never have been asked. Heikki hid her annoyance, and gestured to the chairs that stood opposite. "Make free."

"We heard you spent time on Iadara," Engels said. He did not reach for the orderpad, and Heikki did not offer it to him.

"Staa, Eng," Xiang murmured. To Heikki, he said, "I assume you and the Marshallin will be bidding?"

"I only just heard about the opening," Heikki said. "We haven't spoken."

"It is, from all accounts, an excellent opportunity," Xiang said.

Heikki hid a sigh, recognizing both the ploy and her own imminent capitulation. "I haven't seen much about the job," she said aloud, "but Iadara, now. It's an interesting planet."

Xiang leaned forward a little, folding his hands neatly on the tabletop. In that position, he looked rather like a young and somewhat naive monk of some ascetic sect. Heikki, who had seen the act before, eyed him with concealed dislike. "Lo-Moth lost a lighter-than-air craft that was carrying some important research cargo, on a flight over the—I gather unsettled—interior. The locator beam went off the air, and the crash beacon did not fire. Lo-Moth is, not unreasonably, curious."

Heikki leaned back in her chair, her dislike of the Twins fading in the face of an interesting problem. "Crashed in the interior? And a research cargo—so it probably went down in the 'wayback. The weather's very bad there, there's a central massif that sets up a bad storm pattern during the planetary autumn. The storms have been known to—" She caught herself before the monitor could respond, substituted a more modest word. "—interfere with beam transmissions before now. But of course, that wouldn't explain the beacon. I take it no one's walked out?"

Engels shook his head silently. Xiang said, "I understand they don't expect anyone to do so."

"They wouldn't," Heikki said, and allowed herself a grin. "There's an indigenous primate, nasty job, semi-bipedal and tool-using—probably well on its way to intelligence. They're fairly territorial, the orcs, and they find humans a pleasant addition to their diet."

"Don't try to scare us, Heikki," Engels said.

Heikki spread her hands, opening her eyes wide in innocence. "Oath-true, Eng. The Firsters—the first settlers—were just lucky they landed in the Lowlands. The orcs don't come down there."

Engels frowned, and Xiang touched his shoulder. The blond man settled back in his chair, lips closed tight over whatever it was he had been going to say.

"Still," Heikki went on, the mockery fading from her voice, "orcs and bad weather—that shouldn't be enough to make pros break contract. Who is FourSquare, anyway?"

Xiang shrugged. "I don't know the company, myself. They were—still are, I suppose—licensed in all the proper ways, so. . . ."

Heikki nodded thoughtfully, as much to herself as to the Twins. Something had gone very wrong on Iadara, that much was obvious—something political, possibly; companies had been paid to break contract before now; maybe something technical that wasn't being reported for fear of scaring off other companies that might bid for the job. Almost without wishing it, she found herself adding up the costs of the job, framing an acceptable bid.

"Then you will be bidding?" Xiang asked softly.

Heikki allowed herself a rather wry smile. "I'll have to talk it over with Santerese, of course. But it does sound like an interesting problem."

Xiang returned a crooked smile. "And also a difficult one," he said, without much hope. Heikki's smile broadened, and Xiang sighed. "Which is, of course, what makes it interesting."

"Precisely," Heikki agreed, and wished they would go away.

Engels' eyes narrowed as though he'd read the thought, and he leaned forward a little, as though he wanted to prolong the conversation out of sheer perversity. To Heikki's relief, however, Xiang rose gracefully, shaking his head at Engels. "It was good to see you again, Heikki," he said aloud. "I'm sorry to rush, but we have to catch a train."

"Nice talking to you," Heikki said, to their retreating backs, and knew Engels, at least, heard the patent insincerity in her voice.

When they were out of sight, Heikki fished her data lens out of her pocket, tilting it so that she could read the chronodisplay that flashed in the heart of the lens. She had a little more than three hours to kill before her train left for Exchange Point Seven: not enough time to do any useful research into this possible contract, and too much time to fill. She touched the pad again, ordering a second gin, and stared into space, hardly seeing the hurrying waiter.

Trouble on Iadara—no, she amended quickly, not necessarily trouble, you can't jump to that conclusion yet, but a problem to be solved, and on Iadara. . . . She had not been on that world in more than twenty years, but to her surprise the memories were still startlingly clear. She could almost taste the dank air of Lowlands, heavy with salt and the peppery smell of the perpetually encroaching clingvines, could feel the kick of a sailboard crossing the dirty bay, see the sunlight flaming from the long low roofs of the crystal sheds on the sands just outside the city line. She had learned to drive heavy-load vehicles on those sands, and flown her first aircraft over the scrubby backlands; it had been Iadara she had left to work in salvage. It would be strange to go back there now, her parents dead, her brother gone who knows where, to work for the corporations the family once had scorned.

She shook the thought away, forcing her mind back to business. If they bid for the job, they—she—would have the advantage of knowing the planet: it would help, but not that much. They would still have to make a canny estimate, and impress whoever was doing the hiring at Lo-Moth, before they got the job. She touched the orderpad again, summoning the waiter, and when the man appeared, asked him for an intersystems messageboard. The waiter bowed and vanished, to return a moment later with board and stylus. Heikki thanked him—the Explorers' Club did not permit gratuities—and punched in the familiar codes. After a moment's thought, she began to write.

*M. Santerese, sal/prop, UMC RQ5JB/P19.22051, greetings. Do me a favor and check the bid listings for Lo-Moth, no numbers known, out of Precinct 10/Iadara, then meet me at the Club on the far concourse. I'm on the 1805 out of EP1. Thanks, love. G. Heikki, sal/prop, UMC RQ5JB/P19.22053.* She read the message through a final time, wincing a little at the transmission charge displayed in the upper corner of the screen, but there was nothing she could cut without offending her partner. She sighed, and pressed the transmission codes, watching the message fade from the screen. There was no acknowledgement, and she had expected none. She sighed again, setting the board aside, and reached for her drink instead.

Salatha gin was an Iadaran drink: the taste brought back more memories, less pleasant ones. Iadara was a divided world, split like almost every Precinct world between the first settlers—who had to be generalists, jacks-of-all-trades, simply to survive the first years—and the second wave of specialists, come to exploit the particular resources discovered by the first wave. In Iadara's case, the second wave had been crysticulturalists, corporate employees importing a corporate, 'pointer, ethos completely foreign to the Firsters' ways of thought. Heikki had come to Iadara just turned fourteen, newly admitted to the ranks of the almost-adult; her mother had worked as a consultant for Lo-Moth itself. Ten years a consultant, Heikki thought, an unconscious echo of her father's constant complaint, ten years a consultant to one firm, and then offering contract work, begging her to take it, but she never gave in, never gave any of us that security. They had settled in Lowlands, the largest—the only—city, a hot, dirty place cooled only fitfully by the wind off the too-distant fields or by the seasonal storms. It filled every tenth-day with workers from the crystal fields—neo-barbs, many of them, another local grievance, that off-worlders could be hired so cheaply—a tide of people that ebbed and flowed with the rhythm of the growing stones, black sheep, too many of them, shipped off to sinecures where they could do no harm. They tended their putative business when they felt like it, or when they had to, and spent most of their lives in the clubs and private houses inside the charmed circle that was Lowlands' inner range. The fourteen-year-old Heikki had taken a long look at them and theirs, and with the cold certainty of the adolescent had thrown in her lot with the Firsters. She had eaten their food and learned to drink their liquor, learned their lisping dialect, accepted corporate scorn and parental reproof, and never been one of them. These days, she had to admit the folly of the attempt, but she did not—entirely—regret it.

Cold thoughts make hot choices: the Iadaran proverb made her grimace, and push her drink away unfinished. She touched the orderpad a final time, calling up and verifying the list of charges, and stood slowly, the carry-all a sudden weight on her shoulder. *Maybe we shouldn't bid on the job after all,* she thought, but the outrageousness of that idea steadied her. If half of what Xiang had said was true, it would be an interesting problem, and interesting problems usually brought healthy fees.

She walked a little further down the concourse, barely seeing the brightly-dressed crowd, and turned after a few moments into the bow of an observation bubble. It was filled with tourists, perhaps half of them 'pointers, the rest planetsiders, all exclaiming and hanging back from the front of the bubble, where floor and walls alike were made of clear armorglass. Heikki ignored them, and made her way silently through the crowd until she could rest her hands against the cool surface of the glass. The bubble did not look out into space—not even the architects of Exchange Point Four, the most structurally ambitious of the stations, would have dared so to compromise an exchange point's integrity—but onto the immensity of the Main Concourse. Directly opposite, several hundred meters away, the concourse wall ran with color: the most imposing lightfall in the Loop, responding instantly to every sound made on the concourse below, the noises translated to light that blended in a display more gorgeous than the most active aurorae.

Heikki stared into the lightfall, letting her mind go blank. The solid wall cut off the sounds from below, but she had been on EP1 often enough to guess at some of it. The rippling background light, yellow and oranges spiked now and then with blossoms of acid green, was the sound of human voices, the 'pointer linguaform spiced now and again with pitched languages and the drug-deepened voices of FTLships' crews. Another, more brightly colored pattern, deeper greens and blues with a flush of lavender, moved in counterpoint across the lighter background: music, Heikki thought, and craned her neck until she found the musicians, a group of four seated just outside an expensive-looking restaurant.

The lightfall was a famous landmark, the one thing every visitor, even those who had only an hour or two between trains, had to say she'd seen. It was also, Heikki thought, one of the very few famous sights that lived up to its reputation. She edged back a little, letting others get between her and the open wall, watching the crowd as well as the spilling light. They were much the same as any group of travellers, the subtly-shaded, soberly-tailored clothing and brilliant facepaint of 'pointer fashion mixing with the looser, lighter styles that prevailed planetside. There were even a pair of neo-barbs, their elaborate crystal-and-copper jewelry at odds with their coarse homespun trousers and fraying tunics. They were cleaner and younger than most of their kind, but the rest of the crowd gave them a wide berth. They edged forward together to stare wordlessly at the technological marvel, then left as silently as they had appeared.

Heikki followed them a few minutes later, retracing her steps along the crowded upper corridor, then down the secondary stairs that led to the slidewalk and the station arch. It was still a little more than an hour before the train could leave—it took several hours for power to build up again in the cells, and for the crystals to return to the resting state—and she hesitated for a moment at the end of the slidewalk, wondering if she really wanted to spend that time shut into the train's tiny capsule. She shrugged to herself, and reached into her belt for the disk that was her ticket. There was nothing else to do, unless she wanted another drink, and there wasn't time for that. Sighing, she resettled the carryall, and shouldered through the crowd to the accessway that led to platform three.

The ticket machine whirred gently to itself as she inserted the disk, and then the padded barrier swung back. The disk did not reappear. Heikki sighed again, and touched the button that would route the costs to her tax file, then stepped through the opening. A moment later, the barrier fell back into place with a dull thud.

The platform was crowded, men and women—predominatly 'pointers—milling back and forth between the string of capsules and the dozens of vendors, mechanical and human, that were crammed into the arches against the stationside wall. Most were tape-and-game dispensers, but Heikki counted four different newsservice kiosks and at least three preprinted bookstores, as well as a brightly lit Instapress. All were busy: the actual act of travelling between Exchange Points might be virtually instantaneous, but the preparations for each translation could take several hours while the crystals relaxed, the capacitors regenerated, and cargo and passengers were moved on and off the train. A multi-Point trip, one between two stations not directly connected, could take six or seven hours; if one were travelling from the Loop—from any of the Exchange Points—into its parent planetary system, the trip could take days. Even with the new generation of FSL taxis, "fast sub light" remained something of an oxymoron. It was no wonder that the multi-system businesses tended to concentrate management and sales functions in the Loop, and leave only production facilities planetside. That shift of power was the real reason for the Retroceders' popularity, Heikki thought, and it's not that unreasonable. Of course they, the planetsiders, want back the power they lost—but you can't reverse four generations of change.

Lights flashed overhead, and a chime sounded, signalling that the capsules were open for boarding. There was a general rush for the train. Heikki lifted her eyebrows as an acrimonious voice rose over the general noise of voices—it belonged to a thin woman in a planetsider's loose robe and the Retroceders' triple-R pin, haranguing strangers in an unfamiliar linguaform—

and chose a capsule as far from the stranger as possible.
The door swung open under her touch, and she slung
the carryall into the empty compartment. The capsule
rocked a little as she climbed aboard, settling under her
weight, then steadied as she shut the door behind her.
With any luck, she thought, lowering herself into the
forward-facing seat, she wouldn't have to share the
capsule.

Automatically, she tucked the carryall into the space
beside the seat, suddenly aware of the way the capsule
swayed in the light lifting field. The high-bowed boats
that crisscrossed Lowlands' silty harbor moved just like
that at anchor. . . . She pushed the thought away, and
reached back into the carryall for a workboard. Scowling to herself, she began to scribble down the information Xiang and Engels had given her, making notes for
Santerese. After a moment, she leaned back, studying
the faintly glowing screen. The locator beam failed, she
thought, and then the crash beacon. The odds against
that being accidental— She cut off that thought with a
frown. No, it was still possible that it was merely an
accident—planetsiders, especially in the Precincts, were
notorious for running without working safeties, just to
save a few poa—but still, a double failure like that
sounded unpleasantly like deliberate sabotage. She and
Santerese had dealt with a couple of jobs that turned
out to be sabotage, and neither had been easy.

The sound of a chime put an end to those thoughts.
Automatically, she returned the board to its place in
the padded carryall, then drew the safety webbing across
her body. She settled herself more comfortably against
the cushions, feeling a familiar tension tightening her
muscles, and willed herself to relax. Santerese claimed
blithely that she was never worried before a train ride;
Heikki, who had seen her partner go pale each time the
trains lurched into motion, was only half grateful for the
lie. Sten Djuro, the firm's third member, claimed that
the first trip through the open warp left its print in
every fiber of the body, and that the tension one felt
wasn't fear, but a sort of physical memory of passage

through the unreality of the warp. Well, he should know, Heikki thought—Djuro had been an engineer-crewman on FTLships before he left that for the asteroids and then for salvage, and knew more about the theories of the Papaefthmyiou-Devise Engine than either of the others—but the explanation wasn't particularly helpful.

Overhead, red lights flashed on the ceiling board, and the chime sounded again, deeper and more insistent this time: last call, and clear the platform. The roving vendors would be retreating to the shelter of the arches as the vacuum shields slid into place—not much use in the case of catastrophic failure, and everyone knew it, but regulations still required them. Outside the capsule's bubble window, the light turned blood red as the platform was sealed. The PDE was running up to power, the full power necessary to move the train's mass through the permanently open warp. Heikki could feel the capsule wobble as the field's grip weakened. Ahead of the train, the barriers that sealed off the warp would be folding back, a gap too empty to be real replacing the comfortable grey of the massive doors; beyond that, the crystals that created and held the warp would be crackling, sparks snapping between them and out into the unreality of the warp. And at the heart of it all, the twinned central crystals, one on EP1 and one on EP5, would be glowing blue-white with the power they had absorbed from the cells, ready to unleash it, to fling the train capsule by capsule across the gap between stars.

Then the train lurched into motion, each capsule jerking forward separately. In the same instant, the shutters came down over the capsule's windows. Heikki swore softly, half in exhilaration, and flattened herself against the yielding cushions. The capsule bucked once, crossing the "threshold," and then she hung for an interminable moment outside all reality. Then the capsule was through, reality returning to body and mind, and the shutter lifted to show the familiar platform of Exchange Point Five's Station Axis.

Overhead, the lights faded from red to normal-white as the capsule slowed in the clutching gravity field. Heikki touched the tractor, and waited while the safety netting reeled itself back into the housing. She stretched then, and leaned forward to look out the now-unshuttered window. She could just see the notice board and its flashing message: *This train is proceeding to EP7. Transfer to platform 2 will begin in 15 minutes.* She sighed, and reached for her workboard again, calling up the newsservice article on the lunar waste dump. She read it through twice more, paying solemn attention to each word, before the train was finally shunted onto the station's second track, positioned in front of the warp that led to EP7.

There were no vendors on the platform outside her window. Heikki frowned, and then remembered that Exchange Point 5 restricted them to the outer station. Instead, a double row of dark red rubiglass pillars stretched along the platform's face, casting weird shadows across the last hurrying travellers. It was a severe and somber architecture—typical of EP5, Heikki thought. For some reason, it and EP6, the other major FTLport, where most goods were brought into the Loop from the Precinct worlds that fed them, seemed to favor an aggressively functionalist design.

The warning sounded, and a few moments later the platform lighting went from white to red. The pillars glowed eerily in the changed color, and then the shutters closed and the train lurched into motion. Translation came almost at once, jolting away breath and thought, and then the capsule was through the warp, and sliding up to the platform on EP7. Heikki reached sideways a little stiffly and pressed the release. The safeties retracted into their housings, while in the same moment the door folded back, letting in the bright lights and the noise of home. She seized her carryall and levered herself out onto the platform, balancing herself almost absentmindedly against the rocking of the capsule, enjoying the familiar chaos of a newly-arrived train.

As a resident, she was entitled passage through the priority gate. The duty officer barely gave her a glance as he scanned carryall and papers, then waved her through the dissolving barrier field. "Thanks," Heikki said, to his unresponsive face, and headed down the length of tunnel that connected the Axis to the main body of the Exchange Point. There would be jitneys available on the concourse.

There was a queue at the jitney stand, of course, and it was obvious that the ten jitneys pulling to a stop in a neat line would not be enough for half of the waiting crowd. Heikki swore to herself, and pulled the lens from her pocket. The chronodisplay read 1829: she could take a float, or be late. She swore again, silently this time, and joined the queue at the float platform. It was shorter—the floats were expensive, and only carried passengers across the open inner volume of Pod One—but even so she was still ten people away from the head of the line when the attendant shook her head.

"Sorry, full up. The next float will be along in five standard minutes."

Heikki grimaced, and bit her tongue to keep from saying something immodest. To her surprise, however, it was only a few minutes before the next float swam gently up out of the lower levels, and into the platform's grabbing arms.

"Let the people off, please," the attendant chanted, barring the entrance with her body. Heikki schooled herself to wait, one hand already on the cash card in her belt. Finally, the last of the passengers had left the float. The queue moved forward. The attendant took Heikki's card, snapped it through the reader, and returned it to its owner in a single smooth gesture.

"Move to the front, please, dam-i-sers, move to the front."

Heikki did as she was told, edging along the row of seats until she could go no further. She was in a good position, near the middle of the car, between two window braces and just opposite the floor window's widest point, and she felt some of her impatience ease. It had been a long time since last she'd ridden the floats through Pod One.

The float lay steady in the platform's arms as the last passengers filed aboard, and the attendant closed the heavy door. The seals sighed into place, and then the arms snapped back. The float lifted slowly, light as a bubble, falling upward into the open volume of the pod. There was an awed murmur from the ring of passengers, people shifting in their seats to try to see in all directions at once. Heikki smiled, suddenly overwhelmed by a strange, fierce happiness. If EP1 was all metallic grandeur, an architecture of massive columns and gleaming arches, and EP5 a severe marriage of form and function, EP7 was air and fire. The open center volume of Pod One—unique in the Loop—was broken here and there by the glittering, multi-color webs of filament and slag crystal, spun by an artist who called herself Spider. Beyond those sculptures, more lights, blue-white, pink, fire-red, acid-green, and eye-searing purple, glowed through the crystal walls that enclosed the Pod's working levels. Above and below, at the spherical pod's twin poles, the crystals of the light traps glared and sparked, running together into a single mass of color. The float rose faster now, the multi-colored bands of metal that marked the different levels blurring into each other. There was another murmur, first time riders glancing nervously around them, and then the float swung neatly over into the down-drawing beam. Glancing back, Heikki could see the distant mouth of the projector, thought she saw the crystal glowing red-black in its depths.

The float fell gently toward the farside platform, slowing as it came closer to the attractor. The platform's arms swung up and out, and the float glided between them, landing against the platform with a dull thud. The seals released with a hiss, and the passengers began to get to their feet, reaching for bags and carrycases as the hatch swung open. Heikki followed them out onto the farside concourse, blinking a little in the strong light of the pole crystals.

There were plenty of jitneys available on this side of the pod. Heikki lifted a hand to summon the nearest, and swung herself into the passenger compartment as soon as the door popped up. "Explorers' Club," she told the voicebox mounted on the forward wall, and ran her cash card through the sensor. The jitney's computer beeped twice, and the door closed.

The jitney deposited her at the entrance to the Club in record time. The cast-glass panels, patterned with a stylized representation of Loop and Precincts and the uncharted stars beyond, opened at her touch, the Censor verifying her membership. Inside, she deposited her carryall on the conveyor that led to the checkroom, and headed for the main room. The corridor lights grew dimmer as she made her way past the print and film libraries, then brightened again, blued now by the reflected light of the pole crystals, as she turned the final corner.

Light blazed beyond the tinted glass wall, a pair of floats rising and falling through the central volume. The same light, softened only a little by its passage through the greenish glass, spilled across the dozens of tables, across faces and sober, rich suits. Heikki blinked, half blinded, and a voice at her elbow said, "Dam' Heikki?"

Heikki glanced down at the grey-haired man in Club livery, nodded automatically. In the same moment, a familiar voice called, "Heikki!"

Grinning foolishly, Heikki said, "I see my party, thanks, maitre." Still grinning, she made her way through the maze of tables toward the voice.

Marshallin Santerese rose from her seat, her smile belying the formal gesture. "Welcome home, Heikki."

There was someone else at the table with her, but Heikki ignored that for the moment, reaching instead to take the smaller woman in her arms. They embraced, holding each other longer and more closely than was considered modest—but that was the Precincts' prejudice, not the Loop, Heikki thought, and rested her cheek against Santerese's braids.

"Lord, doll, it's good to see you." That was Santerese's private voice, too soft to carry beyond Heikki's shoulder. More loudly, she said, "I got the information you wanted, the bid specs and all, and I brought Malachy down to draft us a contract."

Reluctantly, Heikki released her, and nodded to the man still standing politely by the table, a rather amused half-smile curving his lips. The lawyer was wearing a severely cut evening suit, the short jacket molded to his still-slender form. The trousers, despite the dictates of this year's fashion, were not full enough to disguise slim hips and elegant legs. The cord of a data lens stretched across his flat middle, and a plain gold fob marked the presence of a palmcorder in the jacket's left-hand pocket: certainly he'd come for business.

"You're looking good, Malachy," Heikki said aloud, and lowered herself into the remaining chair. "So, what did you find out, Marshallin?"

Santerese looked up from the orderpad, then fumbled in a pocket of her own day suit. "Here are the specs," she answered. "I don't know if it tells you anything new."

"Excuse me, Malachy?" Without waiting for his answer, Heikki reached for the viewboard that lay discarded on the table, and fitted the datasquare into the port. A moment later, the screen lit, but no letters appeared on the glowing surface.

"It's protected," Santerese said, unnecessarily.

Heikki nodded, already adjusting her data lens to their private setting. Within its circle, text sprang into existence. She scanned the formal paragraphs quickly, but it contained little more than what the Twins had already told her. The LTA had gone down in bad weather, all right, just as she'd suspected—it had been one of the worst storms of the winter season, in fact, bringing down several other craft. It had been flying from the main research station at Retego Bay to Lowlands, on a course that took it near the edges of the central massif. She stared down at the board, not really looking at the glowing letters in the circle of the lens, seeing instead a wall of clouds lurching up over the wall of greenery that marked the slope of the massif, moving faster than she had ever thought clouds could move outside of a viewtape. The Firsters with her had sworn, and scrambled, one turning the scanning radar groundward, looking for a clearing, the pilot swinging south, to lay the latac parallel to the prevailing winds, the engineer hurrying to bleed gases from the envelope, ready to collapse it as soon as they could land. They had found a place at the last possible minute, and the adolescents of the crew had scrambled outside, stakes and mallets in hand. They'd tied the latac down with double chains, the rising stormwind whipping dirt and bits of leaves about their bare legs, the envelope hissing as it folded down on top of the basket. They'd made it back inside just as the first rain fell, and huddled shivering together while the rising winds lashed the grounded ship, making it shudder and tremble against its moorings. At the height of the storm, thunder sounding almost instantaneously with the lightning, the latac had lifted a little from the ground, and she'd heard the pilot whispering, *hold, damn you, hold.* . . . over and over again. When the storm ended, and the engineer began to refill the envelope, they'd gone back outside to find that three of the starforged chains had snapped.

She looked up, shaking aside the memory, and Santerese said, "Where'd you hear about this one, anyway?"

"The Twins," Heikki answered, and nodded when Santerese laughed.

"Are we bidding out of spite, doll, or is it a decent job?"

Heikki glanced sideways, and saw Malachy's imperfectly concealed frown. She suppressed her own laughter—the lawyer was 'pointer enough to be appalled by the thought of filing a bid for any but the most businesslike of reasons—and said, more seriously, "No, I know Iadara. The only thing I'm worried about is the chance of sabotage."

"Does sound bad, doesn't it?" Santerese leaned back with an abstracted smile as a waiter appeared with a platter of tapas. "I think we should build a risk factor into the contract."

Heikki nodded, reaching for one of the little pastries.

Malachy said, a touch of disapproval in his voice, "That sort of clause is always tricky, to write and to enforce."

"That's what we pay you for, darling," Santerese said.

Heikki suppressed a chuckle, said indistinctly, "I think it's warranted." She swallowed, and added, "And I'm sure you can draft something that will stand up in court—if it has to."

"God forbid," Santerese murmured, and grimaced as the table's monitor flashed. The fine for invoking a recognizable deity was only five poa; she acknowledged it with a sigh, pressing the button beside the orderpad, and went on, "There's only one problem with the job, though, doll. I'm promised to Pleasaunce at the end of the week."

"Pleasaunce?" Heikki frowned.

"PAMCo, Pleasaunce Automatic Mining Company— the sea-mine that went aground," Santerese said.

"I didn't know that had come through."

"Oh, yes." Santerese smiled. "The owners did some looking at what it was going to cost them, doing it themselves. Even with the shipping, I can get it off for less, and save the cargo. Pleasaunce is pretty low-tech."

"When do you leave?" Heikki asked.

"The end of the week." Santerese shrugged. "It should take a week to a ten-day, so I could join you on Iadara, if necessary."

Malachy cleared his throat reprovingly. "This contract," he began, and Santerese broke in hastily.

"It's just the standard form, darling, with the hazard clause added. Nothing more."

"Surely that's quite enough," Malachy answered. He

pushed himself to his feet, and the women rose with him. "I'll have the form sent to you in the morning."

"Thank you," Heikki said, but the lawyer was already on his way. She reseated herself, shrugging, and reached for another pastry.

"I've set up an appointment for you tomorrow," Santerese said. "Charged them for a full consultation, too."

"They paid that?" Heikki stopped in mid-gesture, her hand frozen above the platter. She made herself continue the movement, took and ate another of the cooling pastries.

Santerese nodded, her smile no longer amused. "That's right, doll. And they didn't even ask about haggling."

"No one pays full price," Heikki said. "Not when they're putting it out to bid."

"Lo-Moth is."

There was a moment of silence. Heikki stared at the half-emptied plate, wondering if she'd made a mistake after all. *We don't have to put in a bid,* she thought, *but I as good as told the Twins we were going to. I don't want to back down to them—though we could make it an unreasonable offer, I suppose, something Lo-Moth couldn't accept.*

"Jock Nkosi's back on station," Santerese said suddenly, and Heikki looked up.

"Is he, now? He'd be a help. And I'll want Sten, Marshallin."

Santerese lifted an eyebrow. "I could use his help too, you know."

"Not on Pleasaunce," Heikki answered, and Santerese laughed.

"All right."

Heikki smiled back, but the expression faded quickly. "I'll want local help, too, a pilot and a local guide, and hire for a heavy-duty aircraft—not an LTA. Did the sheet give any idea of a budget?"

"No." Santerese shook her head, black braids swinging. "Doll, the man I spoke with—Mikelis, his name was—didn't seem to care."

Heikki swallowed a curse. *It sounds like trouble*, she thought, *but then, trouble's usually profitable—and besides, I told the Twins we were bidding*. "When's the appointment?" she said aloud.

"Fourteenth hour," Santerese answered.

"Well." Heikki pushed aside her glass. "I might as well hear what the man has to say."

"It couldn't hurt," Santerese agreed. She was smiling, and, after a moment, Heikki returned the smile.

"I'm beat, Marshallin. Shall we go home?"

# CHAPTER 2

Heikki dragged herself awake, aware at first only that something had changed. Santerese was gone. Not long gone, she thought—the sheets were still hollowed beside her—and then heard the sound of voices from the outer rooms. One was Santerese's business voice, her expressive range flattened to something closer to 'pointer taste. Heikki swore under her breath, and pushed herself out from under the covers, reaching for the wrap and the remote that lay on the chair beside the big bed. Precinct prudery, she thought, with a mental shrug, but tugged the wrap closed anyway and stepped out into the business rooms.

The lights were on in the suite's main room, but the status cube was empty; in the tiny kitchen, the coffeemaker clicked quietly to itself. Heikki nodded to herself, and went on into the workroom. The media wall was blaring, multiple windows displaying half a dozen news-and-information channels. Santerese, headphones clamped to her ears, gestured vaguely toward the remote lying just out of reach on the other workstation.

27

Heikki grinned and reached for it, fingers moving on the touchface. The sound faded until the newsreader in one corner mouthed inaudible information, the stock numbers in the window behind streamed past in eerie silence. Other windows displayed multicolored tables: arrivals and departures from the Station Axis, shipping schedules for the FTL port, local and mean times and the ambiant temperatures for pod and Point. Heikki took in the information with a glance, and settled herself at the workstation opposite her partner, careful to stay out of the cameras' range.

Santerese smiled a greeting, her eyes barely moving from the screen in front of her. *Pleasaunce*, she mouthed, and Heikki nodded.

"Coffee?" she asked, quietly.

Santerese covered the mike again. "Yes, please."

Heikki grinned, and went out into the kitchen. When she returned a moment later, carrying the steaming mugs, Santerese was busy at her keyboard.

"—makes a difference, certainly. It will require some specialized equipment, and you will have to pay the shipping and the tech costs—" She broke off, listening to a voice in her headphones, and shook her head. "I'm sorry, you knew your situation when you decided to wait. There's no way I can do it, otherwise." She listened again, and sighed. "Very well, I'll hold." She touched buttons on her board, and leaned back in her chair, shaking her head. "The mine's slid off the shelf it was lying on—which is what I was afraid it would do all along, damn it."

Heikki gave her a sympathetic glance, and slid the second mug across the table. "Is it serious?"

"No, not really." Santerese took a sip of her coffee, staring at the images crowding her screen. "Not if it doesn't fall any further, that is. It means a rush job after all, and some deep-dive equipment, with staff. I was hoping to get away without it, that's all. Do me a favor, doll, see if there are any ships leaving for Pleasaunce from anywhere this side of the Loop."

"Sure," Heikki said, and switched on her own

workscreen. She tied herself into the Lloyds/West shipping net, and began punching inquiries; while the screen cleared and filled, she said, "What happened?"

"Tidal shift—" Santerese began, and broke off, reaching for her keyboard again, reopening the audio channel. "This is Santerese." She listened for a few moments longer, then nodded. "As I told Fost, the consulting fee will still be applied, but there will be additional charges. I copied that to you already, it should be on your screen. Good. Well, I'm finding that out right now. Please hold." She cut the sound again, and looked at Heikki.

Heikki said, "I show a single freighter leaving today from EP5, scheduled to arrive on Pleasaunce a little after planetary midnight on 225. The next ship is the mailship you were planning to take."

"Thanks," Santerese said, and touched keys. "There is a ship leaving today—what time, Heikki?"

"Leaves from Dock 15 at 1750."

"Which I can catch with some difficulty," Santerese continued smoothly. "It will reach Pleasaunce Port in six days; I assume it's another seven or eight hours' flight to the wreck site? Yes. So there you have it." There was another long silence, and then Santerese nodded a final time. "Very well. I will copy my schedule to you as soon as I've confirmed it. Goodbye. Idiot," she added, to the fading screen, and reached for her coffee. "Is there really a cabin, Heikki?"

"I'm afraid so," Heikki answered, and reached for her own mug. They had both travelled by FTL freight before.

Santerese swore.

"And I've already reserved it," Heikki said mildly.

"You don't love me at all," Santerese muttered. "Christ, what about the trains?"

"Also already reserved," Heikki said. She glanced at her own screen, then touched the keys that would transfer the information to Santerese's station. "You've got six hours to get yourself together."

"Four," Santerese corrected. "I'll need a couple of

hours on EP5 to file the shipping papers. Why do I do this to myself?"

"Because you love it," Heikki answered, but the other woman was already gone. "And we can always use the money." There was no response from the outer room, and she raised her voice. "Can I contact anyone?"

Santerese's head reappeared in the doorway. "See if you can get hold of Corsell—leave a message if you can't—tell him what happened, and to try and catch the freighter—what's its name?"

Heikki consulted her screen. "*Sea Comet.*"

"I hope it's not an omen," Santerese muttered. She shook herself. "If he can't, tell him—" She stopped abruptly. "I don't know what. The next ship is the liner?"

"Yes."

"Tell him to catch the damn freighter." Santerese vanished again.

Heikki grinned in spite of herself, and turned her attention to the screen. She tied herself into the Loop's central communications system—Corsell maintained quarters and a message-service subscription on EP5 —and left Santerese's message, then closed down her station and returned to the main room. Santerese looked up from her half-filled carryall with a preoccupied smile.

"Have you seen my breather?"

"In the far wall?" Without waiting for a response, Heikki crossed to the storage wall, and pressed the hidden catches. The mask lay with the rest of their underwater gear, and she handed it and the thin pressure suit to Santerese.

"Thanks." Santerese fitted both items into her case, and sat back on her heels, frowning a little.

"Have you made arrangements for deep-dive stuff yet?" Heikki asked.

"I thought I would talk to Jorge personally, on my way to the Axis," Santerese answered. "I already reserved a minibell, but for a ten-day from now. I just hope he can supply me."

"There's one good thing about this," Heikki said,

after a moment. "You might be able to join me on Iadara after all."

"That's true, isn't it?" Santerese pushed herself to her feet and reached for the carryall. "Damn, we were going to go over the figures—"

"It's all right," Heikki said, and bit back a laugh. "Don't worry about it, Marshallin, I can handle it."

Santerese had the grace to look somewhat embarrassed. "I know, doll. Sorry."

"I'll contact you through the company of Pleasaunce if the bid goes through," Heikki went on, "and we can make plans from there."

"All right." Santerese slung the carryall across her shoulder, and glanced around for a final time. "I think that's everything I need. Let me know what happens with Lo-Moth."

She started toward the suite's main door, a small woman in a severely tailored day suit, the weight of the carryall balanced against one rounded hip. The narrow skirt, slit for walking, showed a glimpse of brown thigh. She had her hand on the latchplate when Heikki said, "Marshallin?" There was a note of laughter in her voice.

"Oh, God." Santerese turned back, half laughing, half embarrassed. They embraced, not quickly, and Santerese said again, "Let me know about the bid."

"I will," Heikki answered. "Be careful."

"You, too," Santerese answered, and released her hold, reaching again for the latch.

Heikki stood for a moment after the door had closed behind her, trying to marshall her own thoughts. The Pleasaunce job was well under control, despite the inevitable chaos of the hurried departure; it was up to her to bring in the Lo-Moth bid. Sighing a little, she returned to the workroom, her fingers busy on the remote.

Sound returned to the media wall, the newsreader's voice rising above the rest of the noise. Heikki listened with half an ear as she settled herself back at the workstation, and emptied that window as soon as she had heard enough to satisfy herself that the Loop was not on the verge of any major catastrophe. She replaced the newsreader's vacuously handsome face with tables of shipping charges, and turned her attention to the screen in front of her. If she was to meet with Lo-Moth's representative this afternoon, she would need to have a rough bid in hand.

As she had told Santerese the night before, she would want local help for this job, people who knew the back country as she could not. A guide and a local pilot, she thought, and Jock Nkosi, if he'll take the job. Full union rates for him, of course, and three-quarters for the locals—no reason to be stingy there—plus a hazard clause to add forty percent of scale if we find evidence of sabotage. Djuro, as usual, would have his choice of union rates or a percentage of the profit.

She ran her hand across the shadowscreen, watching images flicker past on the monitor. Once she had found the file she wanted, she turned back to the keyboard, her fingers dancing across the controls. An instant later, a map of Iadara's eastern hemisphere sprang to life on the screens, the scattered settlements traced in red, the terrain indicated by ghostly washes of color. She studied that for a moment, one finger idly tracing the most likely flight path across the shadowscreen. On the monitor, a green line appeared, moving with her hand. It crossed the thick jungle that edged the central massif: not promising terrain for a search. She eyed it a moment longer, then flattened her palm against the shadowscreen. The line vanished.

It was also not country to be crossed in lighter-than-air craft—as witness the accident itself, she added, with a grim smile. They would want a good scout-flyer, one of the sturdy, long-range machines that were common on Iadara, and then, if they found anything, a heavy-lift powercraft to land by the wreckage. From the look of the land, it would be a week's search at the very least, and who knew how long to recover wreckage. . . . So, she thought, her fingers busy again on the keyboard, three weeks' pay at the least, plus option, rental for the aircraft, and then maybe for a jungle crawler if we do find it, plus food and fuel. . . . She glanced thoughtfully at the charts on the media wall, then filled in numbers. Forty-three thousand pounds-of-account—we'll call it K45 to be sure, she thought, and made the adjustments. I wonder, can I get poa these days, or will we have to take the local scrip, and worry about the exchanges? In the old days, everything had been calculated in a private corporate currency, with all the problems that entailed. But that was twenty years ago, she told herself. There's no harm in asking for poa.

She looked at her figures again, head tilted slightly to one side, then touched keys, transferring the rough figures to her standard bid form. She made a few final changes, then dumped the completed bid to a datasquare, at the same time reserving a copy for herself. The diskprinter whirred softly, and extruded a neatly labeled square. Heikki left it in the bin, and ran her hand across the shadowscreen, shifting nets until she was tied into the Exchange Point's main mail system. In the confusion, Santerese had forgotten to tell her partner where Lo-Moth was, and where they were to meet. On the whole, not surprising, Heikki thought, and keyed first her mailcode and then the codes listed for Lo-Moth's main office.

The screen shifted to the search pattern. Heikki leaned back in her chair, fully expecting to receive the usual white-screen "engaged" signal, and a request that she leave a message. Instead, the contact lights flashed, and a dark woman, her face painted in a severe geometric mask, appeared on the screen.

"Dam' Heikki? Could you hold one moment, please?"

"Certainly," Heikki answered, by reflex, too taken aback by the old-fashioned courtesies to do anything more.

"Thank you," the woman said, and vanished. The screen shifted to a started holding pattern, soft swirls of green and blue, then, almost before the pattern had fully formed, vanished again.

"I'm sorry to keep you waiting, Dam' Heikki. How may I help you?"

Heikki studied the woman for an instant. In the twenty years she'd been in salvage, no corporation, large or small, had ever showed Heikki/ Santerese this much courtesy. They must want something very badly, Heikki thought, but said aloud, "I'm calling to confirm my appointment. With Ser Mikelis."

The woman glanced down at a lapboard. "Yes, Dam' Heikki, I can confirm that, for fourteen hundred. Our offices are in Pod 2, business suite 273. I can have an escort waiting on your arrival, if you'd like." It was less an offer than a command.

"That will be fine," Heikki said, achieving a proper boredom with an effort, and cut the connection. She sat staring at the empty screen for a long moment, her coffee forgotten on the table beside her. This is not the way the corporations deal with the independents, she thought again. They had my name, my mailcode, not just the personal contact code, on their hot list, pulled it out of the automatic answering queue and gave it to a human being to deal with. And that, she added silently, is when I start to worry.

Almost without thought, she keyed Sten Djuro's codes into the machine. She owed him warning of a possible job anyway, but, more than that, she wanted him to use his connections among the FTL community, to see what he'd heard about Lo-Moth, and FourSquare. The screen pulsed softly to itself for some minutes, but she did not cancel the contact. At last, the screen brightened a little, but no picture took shape. Djuro's harsh familiar voice said, "What is it?"

"It's Heikki, Sten."

"Ah." The screen cleared abruptly, and the ex-engineer's lined face filled the screen. "What's up?"

Over the little man's shoulder, Heikki could see the single room he lived in, as bare and unfurnished as though he still lived in freefall. A slate-blue sleeping pad lay near the far wall, disarranged by his waking; there was nothing else, not even a teacup, on the spare white mats.

"We're bidding on a job," she said aloud. "Do you know anything about a company called Lo-Moth?"

Djuro shook his head.

"They're a crysticulture firm, based on Iadara, Sixth Precinct. It's a typcial crysticulture world, hot, humid, and a lot of sand." Heikki took a quick breath, pushing away the too-vivid memories. "Anyway, they lost an LTA there a couple of months ago, and they're taking bids to find it."

"No locator, no beacon?" Djuro asked. The wrinkles tightened around his yellowish eyes, an expression that could be either humor or suspicion. Heikki shook her head, and had the satisfaction of seeing the ex-engineer frown. "Wait a minute, didn't somebody default on that one, a precinct firm, a week or so back?"

"That's right." Heikki smiled. "See if you can find out anything about that, would you? Official or unofficial, I don't care. I'm meeting a man named Mikelis at fourteen hundred, and I'd like to know a little more before I talk to him. It sounds like an interesting job."

"That's one way of putting it," Djuro said, rather sourly. "All right, Heikki, I'll ask around."

"Thanks," Heikki said, and cut the connection. Left to herself, she studied the various menus for a moment, her hand sliding easily across the shadowscreen, then selected the Exchange Point's business library. At this hour, there would be a dozen librarians on duty, and the surcharges would be correspondingly high—but with luck, she thought, the information I want should be available with ordinary callcodes. At the idiot prompts, she keyed in requests for Lo-Moth's shareholder reports and precis for the past three years, and then, after a moment's hesitation, called up the more expensive FortuneNet yearly report. As the screen began to fill, she shunted the information to the hardcopier, and leaned back in her chair to consider her next move.

She had friends in the corporations, people for whom she'd worked, people with whom she'd studied, years ago, people she'd done favors over the years. The question was, was this the time to call those in? No, she decided slowly, not yet. I can find out enough on my own. She shut down the workstation and most of the media wall, and reached for the sheaf of paper lying in the copier's basket.

By the time she had finished reading, the media wall's remaining window displayed the time as 1242. Heikki sighed, and set aside the last of the closely printed pages. She had learned nothing world-shattering from the morning's work: Lo-Moth was reasonably respected by its peers, made a steady though not spectacular profit for its shareholders, and had only the usual difficulties with its workers. In truth, the only oddity was that the company was able to maintain an office suite in the point's exclusive Pod 2, and that was explained by the fact that Lo-Moth's major shareholder—their holdings amounted to a controlling interest in the company—was the Loop conglomerate Tremoth Astrando.

1243 now, and the appointment was for 1400: it would take her most of the hour just to reach Pod 2. She swore softly, and left the workroom, to begin pulling clothes from the wall units with practiced haste. She dressed quickly, skirt, sleeveless tunic, multi-pocketed belt, a long scarf wound like a turban over her unruly hair, bright gold rings in ears and nose, then shrugged on the tailored jacket with the spiral collar that was the badge of business on the Loop. She caught up her data lens and tucked it into the slim outer pocket of the belt. She clipped its cord into the powercell concealed in yet another pocket, and saw the red test light glow briefly in the heart of the lens. As she slid her feet into the brightly painted station slippers, she heard the suite's private door sigh open.

"Heikki?"

Djuro's voice: Heikki let herself relax, her hand moving away from the latch of the compartment where she kept her blaster, to pick up the c-plastic knife she habitually carried in a thigh sheath. Even corporate security generally failed to pick up the special plastic, and she did not like to travel completely unarmed. "What's up?" she called, and moved out into the main room. "I don't have a lot of time, Sten—" Her voice faded, seeing the expression on the little man's face. "What's up?" she said again.

Djuro grimaced. "I don't entirely know, Heikki. I did what you asked, and I'm getting answers I don't like."

"Oh?" Heikki stopped in the act of tucking the datasquare containing the bid figures into her belt. "What sort of answers?"

"They say—and I grant you it's 'pointer gossip—that FourSquare was paid a lot of money to break the contract." Djuro shrugged, his expression bleak. "I heard that from Tabith Fang, and Jiri, and Thurloe. I'd've called you, but I wasn't sure I wanted to put that kind of talk on the net."

Heikki nodded. "Probably smart. Do you think it's true, then?"

"I don't know," Djuro answered. "Fang doesn't get this kind of thing wrong, but Thurloe—he's a gossip, and Jiri's just crazy. I don't know. I'll keep asking, if you want."

"Yeah, I do, thanks."

"Heikki."

The woman paused, her hand on the doorplate, looked back over her shoulder with a lifted eyebrow.

"If it's true, there's serious trouble," Djuro went on. "I don't think we should bid."

"I agree," Heikki said, and kept her voice deliberately mild. "If it's true. But I want to hear what Lo-Moth has to say. For God's sake, Sten, it's a preliminary meeting."

Djuro shook his head. "You're the boss, Heikki," he said, not happily.

"That's right," Heikki answered, with a nonchalance that would have pleased Santerese, and pushed open the door of the suite.

She rode the spiralling stairs up to the corridor level, where Pod 19 joined the Exchange Point's support lattice. About a hundred meters from the stairhead, a roving jitney slowed invitingly. Heikki hesitated for an instant, balancing expense against time, then lifted her hand. The jitney slid to a stop, and she levered herself

into the cramped compartment. "Pod 2, suite 273," she
said to the computer box, and to her surprise there was
a clicking noise from the machine.

"Pod 2 is traffic-restricted," the voicebox informed
her, its artificial tones without inflection. "Transport is
provided to the main level entrances only."

Heikki's eyebrows rose. "Then take me to the second
level entrance."

"Acknowledged." Lights flashed across the voicebox's
black surface, letters and numbers moving too fast for a
human eye to read, and the jitney pulled smoothly out
into the center of the corridor. Heikki leaned back
against the cushions, trying to erase her sudden worry.
Sten's contacts don't necessarily know what's going on,
she told herself, he said as much himself, but the words
seemed to ring hollow in her mind.

The jitney made its way down the corridor, then
through a connector tunnel, this one lined with holo-
panels displaying a simulated starfield, and finally out
into the brilliance of the Ten-Twenty Connector. It was
crowded there. The jitney was stopped for several minutes, beeping futilely, in front of an interactive theater,
before the press of people eased, and the machine was
able to proceed. It was a relief when the jitney reached
the descender and was able to swing off into the maze
of express corridors. Light flooded the tubes from strips
set into ceiling and floor, a dizzying brilliance. Heikki
shielded her eyes, wincing, until the sensors kicked in
and the jitney's windscreens darkened.

They grew light again as the machine slowed and
turned onto a short spiral ramp that led down into a
pool of cool light. It diffused from the flat ceiling and
the pale, ice-green walls, glowed in the business plaques
that were projected at ten-meter intervals along the
corridor. The windscreens faded, more quickly than
they'd gone dark, and Heikki caught her breath. Heikki/
Santerese did not generally deal with the top-rank corporations; this was a class above what she knew.

The corridor widened at last into a wide turnaround,
the central island filled with enormous and expensive

plantlife. Heikki's eyebrows rose as she recognized Terran palms and Aliot flowering groundvines among the profusion, and she hastily schooled her face to its most neutral expression. The jitney swung around the island then, and slid to a halt in front of a marble-pillared door. It could be trompe-l'oeil, of course, Heikki thought, as she slid her paycard through the sensor and levered herself out of the cramped compartment, or at least cast stone built up from powders, but somehow she didn't really believe it. It took an effort of will to keep from tapping the pillar like a yokel as she passed it, to see what it was really made of.

The open lobby was as filled with greenery as the island, and surprisingly crowded, though the clustered plants did much to absorb the sounds of conversation. Heikki allowed herself a single slow glance, her eyes sweeping across the room, then started toward the central podium. Most of the people were of the secretarial classes, data clerks and system monitors, marked by their too-fashionable clothes and the badges that clasped their collars. There were a few executives, however, the richness of their impeccably tailored coats and trousers visible even at a distance, and a single programmer stared disgustedly into his data lens, his face turned deliberately and offensively into the high side of his collar.

The young woman seated behind the podium's triple keyboard looked up sleepily at Heikki's approach, heavy lids lifting slightly to reveal slit pupils. The cat's-eye lenses, Heikki knew, were a recent fashion.

"Can I help you?"

Heikki returned the lazy stare, lifting an eyebrow at the lack of title. "My name's Heikki. There should be someone meeting me."

At the sound of her voice, pitched a little too loud for 'pointer convention, she saw several of the lounging figures straighten, heads turning into their collars. Corporate touts, all of them, she thought, and allowed her lip to curl in open contempt, set to wait and watch in the entrance lobby, ready to report any interesting or unusual arrivals to their employers. Well, boys and girls, here I am. Make what you want of it.

"Gwynne Heikki?" The cat-eyed woman's metallic voice gave no hint of emotion.

Heikki nodded.

"Just a moment." The woman swung sideways in her chair, and touched keys on a different board. Out of the corner of her eye, Heikki saw a man in a neat, very plain suit straighten abruptly and start toward the podium. As he came closer, she could see the thin wire running along his cheek from the plug in his ear.

"Dam' Heikki. I'm Pol Sandrig. Director Mikelis sent me to meet you."

"That was kind of him," Heikki said, and put out her hand in greeting. Sandrig took it with a deferential little half bow.

"If you'll follow me?"

"Of course," Heikki murmured. Sandrig was not quite what she'd expected: the cloth of the suit was much too good for a high-ranking secretary, but a person of higher status should not have been sent on such a menial errand. Of course, Mikelis might be sending him in order to convey a message to his rivals—everyone knew the floor lobbies were full of touts, and staged their meetings accordingly—but that didn't explain what that message might be. She eyed Sandrig warily as he moved ahead of her through the maze of corridors. No, not a secretary, she thought, and I don't like not knowing what this may mean.

Sandrig paused in an inner lobby, where another woman sat at a multi-board podium, and said something in a low voice, his mouth half hidden behind his collar. As was polite, Heikki took a half-step backward, making sure she did not hear. The woman—she was older, her face unpainted, and there was a slight bulkiness in the breast of her otherwise perfectly tailored jacket that marked her as a private securitron—nodded, and touched keys. Sandrig glanced over his shoulder then, and smiled.

"Director Mikelis is waiting," he said. "This way, please."

Mikelis's office was a two-room suite in the heart of the office complex, the outer room carpeted and lit in tones that reflected palely from the polished, almost-white wood-grained furniture. Yet another woman sat behind an electronic desk, a second, dark-haired woman in a brocade suit leaning over her shoulder. As the door opened, the dark-haired woman straightened, frowning, and Sandrig said quickly, "This is Gwynne Heikki, Electra."

"Ah. Good."

The woman at the desk touched a button, cooing into her filament mike, "Ser Sandrig and Dam' Heikki are here, Director."

The inner door slid back instantly, and a voice from the desk speaker said, "Come in, please."

Sandrig gestured politely, and Heikki stepped into the inner office. To her surprise, both Sandrig and the dark-haired woman followed her, the latter still frowning moodily.

Mikelis's office was almost aggressively plain, the lighting frankly artificial, curtains drawn across the media wall, the plain desk littered with printouts and a crooked stack of datasquares. Mikelis himself was equally plain, a stocky, grey-eyed man in a dark suit trimmed at collar and cuffs with nailhead opals. He rose politely at their entrance, but his eyes were still on the workboard lying on the desk.

"Dam' Heikki, I'm glad to meet you. I'm Rurik Mikelis. If you wouldn't mind waiting just a moment—"

"Of course not," Heikki said, and took the seat she had not been offered. To her surprise, none of the 'pointers seemed offended by the gesture—Mikelis, in fact, looked almost relieved. He stooped over his board for a moment longer, fingers busy on a hand-held shadowscreen, then flipped off the workboard. He re-seated himself behind the desk then, sweeping papers and datasquares indiscriminately aside.

"Thank you for inquiring about the bid, Dam' Heikki," he said, "and for being willing to give us a consultation. You've met Pol Sandrig, my research liaison, and this is Electra FitzGilbert, director of operations."

The dark-haired woman gave a curt nod. Heikki smiled back, deliberately overpolite, and murmured, "Delighted to meet you." Behind the platitude, however, her mind was searching. Director of operations: she would be the person responsible for the lost ship, while Sandrig was at least partly responsible for its cargo. An interesting combination, she thought, and folded her hands neatly in her lap.

"I understand from Dam' Santerese that you're generally familiar with the course of events," Mikelis went on. "Before we go into any more detail, however, I would have to ask you to sign a bond of silence."

"Of course," Heikki answered. "And while I'm looking at your terms, perhaps you'd like to look at our rough-estimate bid? Based of course on the first information we have."

"Yes, thank you." Mikelis slid a viewboard across the table, the screen lighting at his touch. Heikki fished the correct datasquare from her belt and laid it on the desk, then turned her attention to the viewboard. The lens setting blinked in the upper corner; she slipped her data lens from her belt, adjusted the bezel until the numbers matched, then squinted through the lens. Letters sprang to life on the screen: it was a standard form, pledging her to silence regarding the subjects discussed at this meeting—time, date, and place were specified in excruciating detail—for a year and a day, and named a heavy fine for breaking the agreement. She nodded, and reached for the stylus clipped to the board.

"This seems reasonable," she said aloud, and scrawled name and verification code at the bottom of the form.

"Excellent," Mikelis said, and even FitzGilbert looked a little less thunderous. "So, to business, then. As you know from the various reports, we lost a latac—an LTA—over the back country, on what should have been a routine flight from Retego Bay to Lowlands. Under normal circumstances, we'd expect to have a record of the course from the automatic locators, or at least to be able to home in on the beacon after the craft went down. The locators failed in-flight, and the beacon did not function. The latac was carrying a new crystal matrix, which was potentially extremely valuable. But I should let Electra tell you about the latac, first."

*What, no mention of FourSquare even now?* Heikki thought. She looked at FitzGilbert, who grimaced.

"The crew has not walked out, which, coupled with the mechanical failures, begins to look like sabotage to me. Mik tells me you lived on Iadara—then you know what the set-up is."

Heikki nodded, suppressing her impatience. Mikelis —or one of his underlings—would have gone through her records as a matter of course; the point hardly seemed worth making. When something more seemed to be expected of her, she said, "There's triple redundancy in the locators, or there was thirty years ago, and the crash beacons are the type used all over the Loop and the Precincts. I'd have to agree, it's suspicious."

"Iadara's weather is peculiar," Sandrig murmured. "Electrical storms alone—"

"Do not affect the beacon, damn it," FitzGilbert retorted, and made no apology for her immodest language. "The beacon should've gone off."

"What did you do when the latac failed to come in?" Heikki asked. She had used the Iadaran dialect word out of old habit, and Mikelis gave her a rather startled glance.

FitzGilbert scowled again. "Not one hell of a lot, at least not at first. There was a storm brewing—we assumed that brought the latac down, and that delayed us. Like Pol says, the weather's something fierce. We do lose a lot of transmissions, and we did think that it was just normal interference cutting out the locator. When the latac didn't dome in, and we didn't get a beacon signal, we sent out a search flight, working from both the projected flight path and the wind data we'd gotten from station blue—that's the nearest recording point, weather station blue northwest. And we didn't find a damn thing. That's when I started getting worried, and I pushed the panic button." She nodded to Mikelis. "That's why it's on Mik's plate now."

"So you'd be hiring us not just to find the wreck," Heikki said, "but to tell you why it went down."

"Yes," Mikelis said, and added, before Heikki could speak, "I accept that it's going to cost us more for that."

"I'm afraid it will," Heikki murmured, but in spite of herself felt the stirrings of a salvage operator's curiosity. Hijacking or sabotage, one or the other, and from FitzGilbert's story the two possibilities were evenly balanced— She curbed her enthusiasm sharply. There was still the matter of FourSquare's attempt at the contract to settle, and the question of the cargo; better to deal with the lesser of the two first. "I take it that the cargo—you said a crystal matrix—was something fairly small and portable?"

"Yes." Sandrig leaned forward in his chair, his hands sketching a cube perhaps half a meter square. "About so big—I don't know if you're familiar with crysticulture, Dam' Heikki?"

"Only with what everybody knows. And I've seen the fields."

"Ah, this is something different. It was the matrix— the seed for first-stage growth—for what we hoped would be the universal center crystal." Sandrig managed a sudden, deprecatory smile. "We hoped! But the indications were promising."

Heikki nodded. Anyone who spent time on the Loop knew that the great stumbling block to intersystems trade and to the expansion of the Loop lay in the way in which the Papaefthmyiou-Devise Engines were constructed. The Engines "folded space"—which was not what really happened, of course, but was the closest undisputed analogy—around an FTLship or Exchange Point, warping hyperspace until the points of origin and destination lay side by side. At the heart of the Engines were the crystals, the common crystals focussing the energies from the generators onto the crucial center crystal, whose interior geometry was crudely analogous to the "geometry" of the hyperspace it manipulated. Each of these center crystals had to be grown specifically and exclusively for the Engine in which it would eventually be mounted; the PDEs that drove the startrains had two such crystals, mirrored twins, to hold open a permanent fold in space.

Mikelis nodded as if he'd read her thoughts. "The failure rate for growing center crystals runs between sixty and seventy-five percent—for the common crystals we lose maybe one in a hundred as too flawed for use. A universal matrix. . . ." He let his voice trail off.

"A universal matrix—a matrix that would fully and truly reflect the geometry of hyperspace—could be used in any PDE," Sandrig said. "It could be grown in mass lots—and you heard what Mik said, common crystals have a one percent failure rate, and they're grown from a universal seed. More than that, it would make it possible to build FTLships quickly and cheaply. Shipbuilders wouldn't be held up while they waited for an unflawed crystal, they wouldn't have to make expensive last minute changes to accommodate the center's peculiar resonances." His voice took on an almost evangelistic fervor. "It might even eliminate the problems with the startrains' PDE, allow us to put more than three terminals into an Exchange Point. After all, the problem seems primarily to be one of interference. . . . But can you imagine, an infinite number of Exchanges within each point?"

"It's been tried before," FitzGilbert said. Her voice was not unkind, but it broke the spell. "They'd only just started testing, Pol."

Sandrig looked away, blushing fiercely.

"I do have one more question," Heikki said, into the sudden silence.

"Of course," Mikelis answered, and seemed grateful for the change of subject.

"What happened to FourSquare?"

The question was verging on the immodest, but Heikki was not prepared for the vehemence of FitzGilbert's response. "You tell us, you're one of them. We signed a contract, made a first payment, then they backed out, said they couldn't handle the back country, that we hadn't given them all the information." Her smile was a baring of teeth. "This when they'd been in contact with local talent from the beginning, even if we hadn't been honest enough to give them all the details—"

"Electra." Mikelis's voice held a warning. "It's a reasonable question." He looked back at Heikki. "What Electra's said is perfectly true, though. We hired them in good faith, and they broke contract without offering us any rational excuse. When they refused to turn over their survey tapes—which will be made available to the winning bidder, of course—we sued, and eventually obtained the material. Does that answer your question?"

*I suppose it will have to,* Heikki thought. "I think so, thank you," she said aloud, and glanced down at the viewboard. Lab and analysis fees—we'll have to add a clause to the final contract allowing us to send back to the Loop for molecular work, if we need it, she thought, at Lo-Moth's expense—and money to cover the hire of extra ground equipment. . . . She touched keys on the calculator inset beside the screen, and nodded at the new total.

"Bearing in mind that you are hiring us to find out why the latac crashed, as well as to locate the crash site, I've added recovery expenses and the costs of a Loop analysis to our estimate. The new total will be K49, pounds-of-account."

"Do you think that's necessary?" Sandrig asked. "Loop analysis, I mean. After all, we have excellent facilities on Iadara."

FitzGilbert sighed audibly. Heikki said, with caution, "If it is a matter of sabotage, I think you would be better off getting a completely independent analysis."

"Oh, of course." Once again, Sandrig flushed to the roots of his thinning hair.

"If you feel it will be necessary," Mikelis said, "I see your point."

"Then you have our bid," Heikki said, and the director nodded.

"We will be in touch with you, Dam' Heikki. Thank you very much for coming." It was an unmistakable dismissal, and Heikki rose to her feet just as Mikelis added, "Pol, would you see Dam' Heikki to the entrance?"

There was a jitney waiting at the level entrance: Lo-Moth was expensively efficient in the small matters, it seemed. Sandrig walked her to the craft and handed her in with punctilious courtesy, wishing her good luck on her bid. Heikki thanked him, but wondered, as she folded herself into the cramped passenger space, if he was really eager to see her win the contract. He seemed remarkably unwilling to face up to the possibility of sabotage, or an enemy within the corporate ranks. . . . Hold it right there, she told herself. You have absolutely no evidence that there is an inside agent, or even that there was sabotage. It could have been a hijacking, even an accident; leave the speculations for when—and if—you get the contract.

"Pod 19, suite 2205," she said aloud, and leaned back as the jitney creaked into motion.

When she finally reached her home suite, she was not surprised to find Djuro waiting for her, feet propped up on the table that held the status cube. "I ran into Jock Nkosi while I was making your inquiries," he said without preamble. "He asked if we had anything going, and I told him about the Lo-Moth bid—in confidence, of course. Was that all right?"

Heikki nodded, shrugging herself out of her tight jacket. "Yeah, that's good. If we get the job, I want him."

"I told him that, too," Djuro said. "You want a drink? I've made a pitcher."

"Thanks," Heikki said, and subsided into the chair that stood waiting for her. It tilted back, programmed to the proper angle; she kicked off her own slippers and rested her bare feet on the low table. "Did you find out anything more?"

Djuro appeared in the kitchen doorway, a tall glass in each hand. He gave one to Heikki, saying, "Not really. Nobody reliable seems to know anything more, so I tried to get back to Fang, but she's left already—off on a three-monther, out past Precinct Twelve."

"Fang's a miner?"

"Yeah." Djuro reseated himself, sipping cautiously at his own glass. "She doesn't usually make mistakes. So what did Lo-Moth say about it?"

"They just said that FourSquare broke contract for no good reason, and then made difficulties about handing over the tapes," Heikki said slowly. "Which does sound suspicious to me."

Djuro nodded thoughtfully. "Yeah, if you have to break contract, you don't give your employer that kind of trouble, not if you want to keep your license."

"I wonder. . . ." Heikki let the sentence trail off, and swung herself out of the tilted chair. She grabbed the remote from its place by the door to the workroom, and stepped inside, running her fingers across the touchface. The media wall lit, filled abruptly with names and numbers that vanished and were replaced by others at the touch of a key. She flipped hastily through the data base, not bothering to put the data through to a workscreen, but without result.

"Well?" Djuro asked, at her shoulder.

"I thought maybe if FourSquare'd been bought out, they'd've made arrangements to reconstitute themselves under a new name—after the old company lost its credit and licenses, that is. But the Board doesn't list any new applications from them." Heikki looked down at the remote, and made an adjustment, sending a new list of names flashing across the screen. "I guess now the question is whether they did go out of business."

"Yeah, there it is," Djuro said, after a moment. Heikki touched the key that would freeze the data, and they both stared at the glowing letters. "FourSquare, declared license-void 005/492, declared disbanded 105/492. That settles that."

Heikki nodded, though privately she was not so sure. Still, she told herself, it does mean there's no evidence of anything wrong beyond incompetence, and that's something.

"If they offer the job," Djuro went on, "will you take it?"

Heikki looked at him in some surprise. "Of course," she answered, and was surprised in turn by her own certainty. Why do I want this job? she wondered, and put the question angrily aside. "Why the hell shouldn't we?" Her voice was harsher than she'd intended, and Djuro shrugged.

"Just wanted to be sure. I'll be off now."

Heikki nodded. "I'll let you know as soon as I hear anything."

There was no word from Lo-Moth for the next ten-day. Heikki occupied herself with the routine business of operating from an Exchange Point, and kept an eye on the news reports from Pleasaunce. Santerese did not appear in them, though she did dispatch a brief message saying that she had begun work. All in all, Heikki thought, I shouldn't ask for more. Djuro reported that at least two other companies, including the Twins' co-operative, had put in bids on the job, but no one was offering odds on the eventual winner. Heikki grumbled, but resigned herself to waiting.

When the message finally arrived, it was at the end of the business day, too late to send a formal response. The media wall lit and windowed, codes streaming across its obsidian face. Heikki answered the prompts, filling in the security codes, then waited while the screen went blank and the hardcopier linked to the wall whirred to life. Sighing, she went to read the sheets as they came off the machine: as she had expected, Lo-Moth had copied her standard contract into its corporate format, but, to her surprise, there were no significant changes. She frowned, read it again, dumped the original to the legal analysis program, and leaned against the edge of the desk, waiting for the results. After nearly a minute's consideration, the program spat its response: *no significant changes.* Heikki's frown deepened, and she settled herself in front of the workscreen.

She tied herself into the communications net, and keyed in the codes that would reach Malachy's secretarial program. She dumped a copy of both contracts to him, and added a quick note, asking him to go over the language and make sure that Lo-Moth hadn't changed anything important. Only when the codestring indicated that the message had been accepted did she touch Djuro's code.

It was several minutes before the screen lit, and when it did, the camera was turned carefully to the white-painted wall. "Yes?"

"It's Heikki, Sten."

"Ah." The camera did not move. "What's up?"

"We got word from Lo-Moth," Heikki said, and could not keep the pride from her voice. "We've got the contract, if we want it. I've got Malachy looking over the terms now."

"Didn't they do what you wanted?" Djuro asked.

"It's practically our contract, copied onto their format," Heikki answered. "That's why I want Malachy to look at it. Do you know where Jock's staying these days, or if he's taken another job?"

"No, he's still looking," Djuro answered, and swung the camera back toward himself. Heikki blinked, dizzied by the sudden movement, and saw the little man fasten the last clasp of his jacket. "He's staying on the hostel level here, but I don't think he'll be there now. He's probably at Victoria's."

"We can track him down there," Heikki answered. "Meet me—unless you have other plans."

Djuro shook his head silently.

"It'll take me about an hour to get there," Heikki went on.

"I'll be there," Djuro answered, and cut the connection.

It would take somewhat less than an hour to reach Dock Seven, and Victoria's, but there was a certain code of dress observed in the dock pods that could not be broken with impunity. To ignore it was to proclaim oneself an outsider, fair game; to follow it was to state quickly and clearly who and what one was. Heikki kicked off the station slippers she was wearing, rummaged in a wall bin until she found the tall arroyo-leather boots she usually wore planet-side, and worked the clinging leather up over her knees. She left the two front slits of her skirt unbuttoned, freeing the sheath at the top of each boot, and transferred her knife from the thigh sheath to the boottop. Then she reached into a second bin for the jacket she kept for venturing into the docks. It had the standard 'pointer collar, left side higher than the right, an electronics pad sewn into the stiffened material, but it was tailored more sharply, broad in the shoulders and nipped in at the waist, and the fabric was visibly expensive, an unpatterned blue-black tree-wool. She shrugged it on, feeling automatically for the electronics in collar and cuffs, then went back into the bedroom for her blaster. She slid a fresh cartridge into the charging chamber—half-power, a stun cartridge, all anyone ever carried on any space station— and slipped it into the top of the right boot. It was not that she expected to need it—in all her twenty-five years in salvage, she had never yet had to use it, or the thin-bladed knife she carried in the left boot, on any Exchange Point—but it was a part of the uniform, part of the romance of salvage. She grinned, too aware of the ironies in that view to do more than enjoy them, and started for the door.

She took the stairs to the connecting level and walked the length of the tube to the minitrain station. The other passengers, recognizing the clothes, gave her a wide berth until the Docks change-station, and then she was swallowed in a crowd of similarly dressed men and women. The corridors connecting the dock pods were brightly lit, high-ceilinged tunnels with padding on the floors and halfway up the slightly curving walls. People moved quickly along the center of the corridor, the harsh light flaming from exotic Precinct clothing and flamboyant spacer dress, but here and there eddies formed in the relative shadow of the padded walls. Once it was a group of neo-barbs, mostly women this time, clustered about the platform of the sonic drill that was their sole means of support; then it was a trio of spacers, standing close together, heads turned into their collars as they talked. Light flashed from biolume bracelets as they gestured.

A slidewalk ran down the center of the tunnel that led to Docks Five through Nine. It was crowded, knots of men and women in spacers' bright clothes leaning against the groaning grab bars, while other people, carefully suppressing any immodest language, pushed past them to hurry down the moving strip. Heikki hesitated for a moment, then, with some reluctance, stepped up onto the walk. By the time the slidewalk had carried her the three hundred meters to the entrance to Dock Five, a number of adolescents—'pointers, mostly, out for a spree in the frowned-upon dockside clubs—had stepped up onto the walk, and Heikki advanced her left leg a little, letting the skirt fall back to expose the knife tucked into the cuff of the boot. The nearest 'pointer hesitated, and there was a little swirl of movement as the group rearranged themselves, giving her a wider berth. Heikki allowed herself a cold smile, and looked away. Most of the trouble in the docks was caused by touring 'pointers; the real dockside crime tended to be silent, nonviolent, and deadly only when it had to be.

The slidewalk ran out between Docks Six and Seven. Heikki walked the last fifty meters to the entrance to Dock Seven, disdaining the slidewalk's continuation, and turned into the dock corridor. Behind her, the gang of adolescents stopped dead, glancing first at the brightly lit directory board, and then at the glittering signs that lined the head of the corridor. I hope to hell they're not going to Victoria's, she thought—but Victoria will know how to deal with them, if they are. The thought was more than a little satisfying, and she was smiling when she stepped through the mirrored door.

It was very dim in the main room, especially after the brightness of the tunnels, but she made her way to the bar with the ease of long habit. It was not particularly crowded yet, and Victoria himself was manning the bar. He stepped forward as Heikki came into the wedge of light in front of the bar, his generously painted mouth curving up into a genuine smile of welcome.

"Heikki. Where've you been, dear, and where's the Marshallin?"

"Pleasaunce," Heikki answered, and seated herself comfortably on the nearest stool. "And I'm just back from Callithea."

"Another one of your archeological specials, or routine business?" Victoria asked, and leaned heavily against the bar. He was a big man, despite the corsets and padding that provided the shape beneath the satin and sequined evening gown, and his heavy makeup could not entirely hide the lines at the corners of his eyes and bracketing the sensual mouth. He looked like a dowager who resolutely refused to give up the habits of her youth—and it was, Heikki thought, a fair summation. "Salatha gin?"

"Please." Heikki accepted the drink as it appeared seemingly from nowhere, and shrugged when Victoria waved away the proffered cashcard. "That can't do your business much good."

"Oh, the next drink's on you, dear, never fret." His eyes narrowed as the door opened again, and the group of adolescents Heikki had noticed on the slidewalk came in, clustering together and murmuring into their collars at the strangeness of it all. Victoria sighed, and shook his head. "Excuse me," he said, and ran his fingers across the touchplate embedded in his enormous bracelet. Heikki grinned, and swung around on her stool to watch. A moment later, a short-haired woman in a black leather bodice and trousers that fit like a second skin slouched forward to meet them, her white-painted face set in a forbidding scowl. A heavy chain swung menacingly at her waist.

"Yeah, help you?" she growled, with patent insincerity. The adolescents exchanged glances, and said something too soft for Heikki to hear. Then, as abruptly as they'd appeared, the group retreated. As the door swung shut behind them, the leather-clad woman grinned, the expression transforming her almost elfin face, and came over to the bar, pulling her orderpad out of her waistband by its chain.

"Was that all right, boss?" she asked. "And I need a bottle of joie-de-vivre for upstairs, while I'm here."

Victoria nodded, touching buttons on the bar, and a moment later the frosted bottle rose through the serving hatch, steaming gently in the sudden warmth. "Neatly done."

The woman smiled again, and disappeared, balancing the bottle easily in one hand.

"Who's she?" Heikki asked.

"Happily married—to a freighter tech, I believe—with two kids," Victoria answered.

Heikki laughed. "I hadn't seen her before, that's all."

"You haven't been in recently," Victoria answered. "Lord, my dear, I think it's been two months."

"I've been working," Heikki said again, and added, before the other could ask, "All routine." She took a sip of her gin, and leaned forward. "And I'm afraid it's partly business that's brought me now. Is Jack Nkosi here tonight? Or Sten?"

"Sten's not in yet, if you're meeting him. Jock's upstairs." Victoria lifted painted eyebrows. "Flirting with the waitresses. Do you want him?"

"I've got some business with him," Heikki answered. She started to stand up, but Victoria waved her back.

"I'll send a message. He'll be distracting them all night, else."

"Thanks," Heikki said, and waited while the other fingered his bracelet again.

After a moment, Victoria nodded. "He's on his way. You don't know how glad I'll be when I can finally retire, dear, and let someone else take over."

"There's no one else like you, and you know it," Heikki began, but Victoria continued as though she had not spoken.

"You know what I'm really looking forward to? Not having to put on this damned corset every night." He gave an impish smile as a warning buzzer sounded, and reached out to hit the monitor's override button. "And I will say what I want in my own place, thank you very much."

Heikki returned the smile, but Victoria's eyes were already on the staircase that curved down from the bar's upper floor. "And here he comes, looking like a cat in cream."

Heikki turned on her stool, and couldn't restrain a laugh. Nkosi was a big man, made bigger by the bulk of the leather coat he wore slung across his shoulder, its color and textures dulled by the rich brown of his skin. Two of the waitresses—and one of the waiters, who should have known better—were hanging over the railing, the younger girl calling something that Heikki could not hear. Nkosi lifted his hand in laughing answer, and moved toward the bar, arms spread in greeting. Heikki, who did not as a rule like being touched, submitted to being lifted off her stool, whirled in a dizzying embrace, and set neatly back where she belonged.

"And that is also a mighty fine jacket you have now," Nkosi said, as though their last meeting had not occurred five standard months ago. "Tree-wool? Yes—"

"Now, dear," Victoria said, and he was smiling, "I can't have you assaulting the customers as well as corrupting my staff." He slid a tall drink across the counter toward the newcomer.

"Have there been complaints?" Nkosi asked, with a grin.

"I'm not waiting for the paternity suits, dear," Victoria retorted.

"Outrageous," Nkosi said. "I always take precautions, do I not, Heikki?"

"I wouldn't know," Heikki answered, and Nkosi continued as though she had agreed with him.

"One would think you were jealous, Victoria. Most unworthy of you."

"I could be jealous," Victoria said, "if you ever paid any attention to me."

"If I thought there was a chance you would consider me, Vickie, I would be on my knees in an instant," Nkosi answered.

Victoria shook his head, smiling. "Someday, dear,

I'm going to take you up on that offer, and then where will you be?"

Heikki laughed. "Sten said he ran into you about a ten-day ago, and you were looking for work?"

"And I still am," Nkosi answered. "The job he mentioned came?"

Heikki nodded. "I'm just waiting for the contract to go through our lawyer. It looks as though it will be pretty much a standard air search and wreck analysis— it's been long enough since the crash that even if it was sabotage or hijacking—"

"Sten did not say that that was a possibility," Nkosi murmured.

"—there shouldn't be any problems, and there's a danger bonus built into the contract in any case," Heikki finished. "Yeah, there does seem to be a good chance it was one or the other. Does that make a problem?"

Nkosi shook his head. "Not in the least. It should add spice."

*Well, that's typical,* Heikki thought. She said aloud, "I can offer you union rates, plus your share of the bonus if we earn it. How does that sound to you?"

Nkosi didn't seem to hesitate. "I am willing, the pay sounds good. Yes, I will go. What are the atmospheric conditions like?"

That was also typical, act first and think later, Heikki thought, and suppressed a grin. "Do you know Iadara, Sixth Precinct?"

"No."

"It's semi-tropical, in the settled areas, with a bad weather pattern through the interior—"

"Which of course is where we're going?"

"Of course." Heikki smiled, rather thinly this time. "It rates about a four on the Antraversi scale, up to a six in the storm season."

"Not bad." Nkosi nodded. "We can handle that, no problem. When do you want to sign papers? And when do we leave?"

"I'm waiting for the contract to come back from the lawyer," Heikki answered.

"Heikki?" That was Djuro's voice, and Heikki repressed a start. "Sorry I'm late," the ex-engineer continued, "but I got a call from Malachy. He's cleared the contract."

Nkosi beamed down on the little man, and Heikki said, "That's good news."

Djuro nodded, and edged forward between two of the tall stools to lean easily against the bar. "I checked the shipping schedules, too, and there's a freighter leaving for Iadara in six days."

"So." Heikki paused, considering. "If the money comes through from Lo-Moth in time, we'll reserve cabins. You did say a freighter, Sten?"

"Yeah. I doubt there'll be any trouble getting space." Djuro paused for a moment, frowning, but then seemed to think better of his objection.

"That's settled, then," Heikki said firmly. "Jock, come by tomorrow morning, we'll draw up an agreement and I'll give you copies of the information that we have so far."

"Excellent," Nkosi said, and nodded to Victoria, who had withdrawn discreetly to the far end of the bar. "Then if you will all excuse me, I will return to what I was doing."

"God help us," Victoria said, and put his finger on the override.

"You're not happy, Sten," Heikki said quietly.

"I just—I've got a bad feeling about it, that's all," Djuro said. "But I'm not backing out on you, don't worry."

"I didn't think you were." Heikki forced a smile, pushing away her own sudden unease. "Come on, I'll buy you dinner."

# CHAPTER 3

The money arrived as promised, within ten hours of Lo-Moth's receiving the signed contract, and with it came the survey tapes from FourSquare. Heikki raised her eyebrows a little at the unusual promptness, but reserved passage on the freighter and on the connecting trains for herself, Djuro, and Nkosi. Together, the three reviewed FourSquare's data, and by the end of the week, Heikki had decided that the tapes were essentially useless.

Djuro, scanning the figures on his own workscreen, nodded. "Yeah, the numbers just don't match. We'll have to do it all over again."

"Which won't hurt us any," Heikki answered mildly. "Don't worry, I took that into account when I made the bid."

Djuro grunted, acknowledging the hit. "Still, it's a pain not to be able to trust their work."

Heikki shrugged, and Nkosi looked up from his own board—which displayed a complicated game pattern—long enough to say, "No problem. We'll just fly a few extra passes—up near the mountains, that should be exciting."

"That's one way of putting it," Heikki said. She stared at her own maps, colored now with the bright red lines of the prevailing weather patterns. At least they were arriving on Iadara during the summer's calm, not storm— but that just meant that the weather would be difficult, not immediately dangerous. "We'll have to make friends with someone in meteorology," she said, still frowning at the map, and Djuro looked up quickly.

"Why not bring someone in from the Loop? At least we'd know they'd be reliable."

"I've thought about it," Heikki said. "I think what we'd gain in reliability we'd lose in local knowledge. No, our own program's pretty sophisticated; with that and the local mets, we should be all right."

Two days later, they left Exchange Point Seven for Iadara. They travelled by startrain to Exchange Point Six—halfway across the Loop, despite its number—and then Heikki sent the others on ahead on the FTLport while she supervised their container through Customs. She had done this a hundred times before, and never yet had it gone smoothly. This was no exception: by the time she reached the entrance to the FTLport, container floating behind her on its grav disks, shepherded by a pair of union handlers, her temper was growing short, and she glowered impartially at both the handlers and the lanky steward, frowning over her manifest. To Heikki's surprise, however, the steward seemed concerned only that the crate's mass match the numbers she had been given in the shipping order. Once that had been confirmed, she saw the container aboard without trouble, and turned to show Heikki to her cabin. "Unless you want your partner to show you," she added. Her tone made her preference clear.

Heikki glanced up the boarding tunnel, and saw Djuro's wiry figure just inside the circle of the hatch. She hid her frown, and shrugged. "That's fine with me," she said, and the steward nodded.

"Rec room and passengers' mess are on the same level, unless you want meals in your cabin. Times and the surcharges are posted for that. Engineering and control are off-limits—no offense—and you should remain in your cabin any time the red lights are on. Otherwise, enjoy your voyage."

"Thanks," Heikki said, but the steward had already turned away, her mind fully focussed on the next piece of cargo to come aboard. Heikki shrugged to herself—she was used to the vagaries of FTLships' crews—and started up the tube toward the hatch, her single carryall balanced on her shoulder.

At the top of the hatch, Djuro came forward as though offering to take her bag; at the same time, he said, "We've got company."

"Oh?" Heikki waved away the offer of assistance, her eyes suddenly wary.

"Yeah. Electra FitzGilbert, her name is—she works for Lo-Moth."

"I've met her," Heikki said. "She's the director of operations, was the director for this particular flight. She belongs on Iadara, not in the main offices—she may just be going home."

"Do you really think so?" Djuro asked, and Heikki smiled.

"No. But what else can we do? Show me my cabin, Sten, and then we can talk."

The cabin proved to be about what she had expected, small and spartan, with most of its space taken up by the bunk and the limited-access console wedged into one corner. At least it had its own bath, Heikki thought, tossing her carryall onto the mattress, and the bunk, at least, was reasonably large. "Relax, Sten," she said aloud. "Even if FitzGilbert is going back to keep an eye on us, what harm can it do? We're honest—and if she isn't we'll deal with her."

"I hope to hell you're right," Djuro said morosely, and looked instinctively for the monitor.

Heikki smiled. "It's good to be back in the Precincts, isn't it?"

Djuro flushed slightly. "There are times," he said, "when a person can't remember where he is."

"Let it ride for now," Heikki said, lowering her voice. "Which cabin is she in?"

"Two upship and across the corridor. They aren't numbered. I'm in the one in between."

Heikki nodded. "I'm going to unpack, then. I'll see you at dinner."

"Right," Djuro said, and closed the cabin door behind him.

The freighter left dock on schedule, but Heikki, rereading the tapes she'd received from FourSquare, was barely aware of the shifts of power. She looked up when the bulkheads around her seemed to lurch as the ship went from dock gravity to its own generators, but then returned to her reading. The faint thrum of the engines deepened as the tug cast off, but she heard that only as a counterpoint to the Iadaran wind. Of all FourSquare's data, the only useful tape had been the record of the locator's automatic transmissions: it showed routine readings for LTA status and weather alike, then the rising temperature that often preceded Iadaran storms. The LTA had dropped a few hundred meters—normal precaution, in case they were forced to land—and then the transmissions had ceased. Heikki stared at the strings of numbers, seeing instead one of the massive silver-enveloped ships soaring against the brassy Iadaran sky. She could almost see the heat rippling up off the jungle, could hear the first faint hiss of a rising wind. . . . The crew would have been worried, certainly—back country weather was nothing to fool around with, everyone knew that. She pictured them talking to each other, Firsters murmuring back and forth in their lilting accent, and then the decision to drop lower, perhaps swing off course toward one of the safe-harbor clearings every back country pilot knew about. . . .

She stopped abruptly. I don't even know if the crew were Firsters or Incomers, she thought, with some surprise. And it might make a difference. She sighed then, and set her workboard aside. The chronometer on the console showed nearly 1900 hours by ship's time: almost dinnertime, for the passengers. She touched keys, checking the schedule for the first FTL run—it wouldn't happen until well after ship's midnight; she could afford to eat a decent meal—and then touched the button that would project a schematic of their planned course and present position on the main screen. After only a moment's hesitation, she blanked the workboard, locked her tapes into her personal strongbox, and started toward the passengers' mess.

The larger cabin was surprisingly comfortable: whatever money had been budgeted for the paying passengers had been spent on its fittings. A galley console filled one narrow end of the room, and a much larger media center took up perhaps two-thirds of the long inner wall. At the moment, its green-black surface was broken into facets, each one showing either the ship's projected course or an elaborate relative-times chart. They meant nothing, of course, but the room's sole occupant had not bothered to adjust the controls. Electra FitzGilbert looked up as the door sighed back, and gave a curt nod of greeting. Heikki was too well-schooled to show her dismay, but she felt her heart sink. *Where the hell's Sten?* she thought, and said aloud, "Good evening, Dam' FitzGilbert."

"Dam' Heikki." To Heikki's surprise, the dark woman did not return to the workboard propped beside her tray, but blanked the screen and set it aside. "The dinner isn't bad at all."

*A typical oblique 'pointer invitation,* Heikki thought. *I wonder exactly what she wants?* "Thanks," she said, and turned to the menu displayed on the galley screen. It was typical FTLship fare, heavy on the ubiquitous grains and shipgrown vegetables, but healthy and satisfying. Heikki considered the list for a moment, then touched keys. A moment later, the serving hatch slid open, and Heikki collected the steaming dishes and slid them painfully onto the recessed tray. There was a small bar as well, but she settled for a pot of tea instead—alcohol and FTL travel did not mix well—and returned to the table. FitzGilbert was watching her from under lowered lashes.

"Your partner was in," she said, after a moment.

"Oh?" Heikki hesitated for a moment, then decided that there was no point in refusing the overture point blank. "Did he eat?"

FitzGilbert shook her head. "He went off with the big man—he said he knew someone aboard?"

Nkosi would, Heikki thought. Pilots tended to have friends—or friends of friends—scattered across known space, precincts and Loop alike, and Jock was not the sort to miss any chance of renewing connections. "I'm not surprised," she said. "Pilots do know people, and Sten used to be in FTL engineering." It was a concession, she thought, but a cheap one: anyone could check Sten's records.

"And you, you're Iadaran?" FitzGilbert asked.

*Not subtle*, Heikki thought. *Not subtle at all.* "I lived on Iadara—with my family—for about twelve years."

"With your family," FitzGilbert repeated. "And your mother worked for Lo-Moth."

It was not a question, but Heikki shook her head anyway. "She was an independent consultant, under contract to Lo-Moth." I'll answer about three more questions, she decided silently, and then we'll see.

To her surprise, however, FitzGilbert did not seem inclined to pursue the subject. "You've reviewed the tapes? Ours and FourSquare's?"

"Yes." Heikki poured herself a cup of tea, watching the other woman curiously. She could not decide if FitzGilbert were deliberately skirting the edges of insult, or if she were simply naturally ungracious. I'll treat it as the latter, she thought, at least until proven otherwise. "There are a couple of questions I'd like to ask, since you were the operations director involved. If you don't mind talking over dinner, of course."

FitzGilbert scowled, but said, "Might as well get it over with."

"Gracious of you," Heikki murmured, and saw the other woman flush.

"What did you want to know?" FitzGilbert's heavy brows were still drawn together, but she was making some effort to be conciliatory.

"The latac crew," Heikki said. It was a little frightening, she thought vaguely, how easy it was to slip back into a linguaform she hadn't used in almost thirty years. "Who were they, regular employees, free-lancers, or what, and how well did they know the back country?"

FitzGilbert took a deep breath, her voice becoming more professional. "They were regular flight crew, of course—Firsters, so they knew the area pretty well. The area they were supposed to be flying over, anyway! They were well off course, or either our flights or FourSquare's would've found them. What more do you need to know?"

"How many aboard?"

"Five—pilot, back-up pilot, systems op, engine techs." FitzGilbert shrugged. "The usual crew."

"And you think, as ops director, they're all dead?" Heikki could not keep the edge of distaste from her voice, and saw FitzGilbert wince, her color deepening again.

"They didn't walk out," FitzGilbert said, in a voice too harsh to be anything but false. "Either they were part of a planned sabotage, or they're dead."

*Maybe I underestimated you,* Heikki thought, and let her own voice become conciliatory. "What do you think the odds are? When I was on Iadara, Lo-Moth was well-respected. People didn't try things like that."

FitzGilbert looked down at her emptied plate. "I don't know."

"You're the ops director," Heikki said. "They were your people."

"They were Firsters, I told you. And I'm not." FitzGilbert's voice was deceptively matter-of-fact. "I don't know what they'd do for me. No, I'd've thought, that lot wouldn't be in on a hijack—but you know as well as I do that's the way things are done, ninety percent of the time."

Heikki nodded. "I know. And you're saying you don't think this crew would've gone along with that?"

FitzGilbert shook her head. "No."

"So we'll work on that assumption, anyway," Heikki said, and saw FitzGilbert's face ease slightly. "Four-Square's tapes don't seem to be much use. I'd rather work from the original material you have—fresh copies, if possible. We might be able to pick up something they missed."

"I'll see to it," FitzGilbert said. She glanced down at her emptied plate, pushed it aside, grimacing. "If you'll excuse me?" It was hardly a question, despite the faint rising inflection.

Heikki nodded as automatically, and turned her attention to her own plate. She did not look up until she heard the door sigh shut behind the other woman. Then, sighing, she reached for the shadowscreen that sat in the middle of the table, and ran her fingers across the surface, getting the feel of the controls. The media wall flashed and shifted, until at last she'd found the chronodisplay: two hours until the FTL run. She killed the image, leaving the wall blank, and leaned back in her chair. Not much point in going back to her own cabin yet—there was always the chance that either Djuro or Nkosi would show up—but there didn't seem to be much use in staying, either. She pushed aside her almost untouched dinner, poured herself a second cup of tea, and curled her fingers around the warmed ceramic cylinder.

And what am I supposed to make of FitzGilbert? she demanded silently, staring at the other woman's empty plate. I wish to hell I knew if she was meaning to be insulting, or if she's just inept. Still, I think she did care that the latac crew is—probably—dead, which is one thing in her favor. . . . She put the thought aside, and reached for the plates. After a moment's search, she found the disposal chute and slipped them in, hardly hearing the machinery whir up to speed to return scraps and plastic plates to reusable components. I'll leave things as they are, Heikki thought, and hope we don't have to work too closely with Dam' FitzGilbert.

Back in her cabin, Heikki settled herself on her bunk, propping her workboard in front of her, but she could not seem to concentrate on the preliminary search pattern she had mapped out before leaving EP7. Her eyes kept straying to the chronodisplay, its numbers moving inexorably toward the time of translation. She kept at it, doggedly, but knew her work was worthless. When the buzzer finally sounded at the half-hour mark, she switched off her board and set it aside, then stretched out unhappily on her bunk. After a moment's hesitation, she reached for her remote, and ran her fingers over the shadowscreen until the console's main screen was tied into the display net. As was customary on passenger ships, the captain had tied the display to part of the visual security system; the picture shifted slowly, and at random intervals, from one corridor or working compartment to another. In the control room, glimpsed only briefly before the duty tech looked up at the camera, frowned, and cut it from the circuit, the ship's full astrogation team hunched over the consoles, comparing the readings from the buoys at the edge of the Exchange Point's parent system with the numbers already plugged into their equations. The picture wandered then through the corridors, catching a steward manhandling a balky emergency suit back into its locker, then switching to the special-cargo hold, where a woman in a flat grey cap was running a mass pulser over the last layer of crates. One view showed only indistinct figures crossing the corridor, just out of the camera's circle of focus: the system stayed with the shot for what seemed an interminable time.

Then, as Heikki had hoped it would, the system switched to the drive compartment at the center of the ship. The Tank—the reinforced housing for the ship's crystals—loomed in the center of the picture, almost filling the compartment; the dark-goggled engineers, busy at the consoles at its base, seemed almost ant-like by comparison. Light, a light so hard and white that it seemed almost solid, or at best as slow-moving as glacier ice, glowed behind the test-ports, seemed to turn the narrow line of the calibration bar to white-hot steel. Heikki blinked and reached for the shadowscreen to dim the image, even though she knew that the camera was already shielded. Before she could make the adjustment, however, a familiar three-toned chime sounded and the picture went dead. At the same time, the room lighting went red: five minutes to translation, and all non-essential personnel were to stay in their cabins. Heikki grimaced, and braced herself against the edge of the bunk. Sometimes, she thought, sometimes I think it would be better if they left the cameras on, let us watch the purposeful confusion—at least I hope it's purposeful; Sten always swears it was—and take our minds off what's really happening, off the fact that space and time, reality itself, are being bent around us, are being persuaded to ignore, however briefly, the laws that usually define the universe—

The red lights dimmed slightly, marking the surge of power that initiated translation. Heikki swallowed hard, feeling the first uneasiness beginning at the pit of her stomach. The sensation grew rapidly, until if she closed her eyes she could feel herself, the ship, and everything around her tumbling end over end, somersaulting lazily, each individual cell, each molecule, trying to turn itself neatly inside out. She kept her eyes open, staring at the red-lit ceiling, hoping translation would end before she was sick. Then, at last, the sensation peaked and began to fade even more rapidly than it had grown. Heikki drew a ragged breath, blinking eyes that watered from the constant light, and shifted slowly to a more comfortable position. The lights flickered again, brightened, and a moment later shifted from red to the normal spectrum. Heikki pushed herself upright, leaning against the lightly padded bulkhead, and ran her fingers through her sweat-dampened hair. The intercom clicked then, and a steward's voice said, "Post-translation check. Everything all right, Dam' Heikki?"

Heikki reached to the console to thumb the intercom switch—her hand seemed steady enough, but she did not want to risk the shadowscreen—and answered, "Everything's fine here, thanks." *This time, anyway,* a small, pessimistic voice whispered, but Heikki contrived to ignore it.

"Good-oh," the steward answered, and cut the connection.

Heikki ran her hand through her hair again, and fumbled with the shadowscreen until she'd recovered the chronometer display. It was late, by ship's time, and later still by her own internal clock. Even so, she pushed herself up off the bunk and made herself shower, washing away the fever-sweat of translation, before allowing herself to sleep.

There were three more major translations before the ship settled into the almost imperceptible microhops that would position it at the entrance to the Iadaran Roads, and Heikki faced each one with the same dour resignation. There was no chance that she might become acclimated—it took years of constant exposure to build up any tolerance at all, and some people never did—and by the time the ship swung into the Roads she was even glad to see Iadara's disk on the viewscreen. It was a bright planet, the rich green of the forested islands almost perpetually obscured by swirling patterns of cloud. Nkosi, watching on the large screen in the passengers' mess, shook his head at the sight.

"My God, those are fast-moving systems. What is the weather like under them?"

Djuro, who was closest, fingered the shadowscreen. Heikki said, mildly, "You were warned, Jock."

The screen split, one half still displaying the disk as seen by the forward sensors, the other displaying strings of data from the meteorological stations. Nkosi whistled thoughtfully, and stood up to compare the two pictures more closely.

"The average windspeed seems to be thirty to forty-five kph, the humidity looks miserably high—"

"Not everywhere," Djuro interjected, with a dry smile.

"—and, Jesus, look at that temperature differential." Nkosi looked up, one finger tracing a line of cloud on the sensor view. "There must be some pretty big storms in there."

Heikki nodded, looking up at the displays. "That's the Ledoma River Plain—the area report will be from weather station red north central. You'll almost always find some storms along the line of the river."

"Wonderful," Nkosi murmured, and turned his attention back to the displays.

Heikki continued staring at the picture, remembering the storms. When the thunderstorms came rushing down out of the hills, as they did almost every day in the long summer, the sky would darken, and the air change slightly, in a way you could not define, but only feel. The wind would come then, little tendrils of air licking at your sweaty skin, a touch that swelled to a breeze and then to a wind that seemed crazy-strong, strong enough to lift you off your feet, so that you ran into it, arms outstretched, yelling for it to carry you away. And then the thunder came, and the adults, and then the pelting rain, and you ran for home, to be scolded when you got there, and to hear the old saying quoted one more time, as you towelled your hair dry; *summerwind makes dogs and kids crazy.*

She shook herself then, putting aside the too-vivid memory; they would do her no good now, would only distract her from the present day. With a frown, she reached for her workboard and called up the paperwork that had to be completed for the landing, concentrating on the details of shipping certificates and import licenses.

Somewhat to her surprise, the freighter landed as scheduled, and the stewards did their best to minimize the chaos of unloading. There was equipment to spare, but no human beings: she and Djuro and Nkosi together jockeyed the anti-grav buoyed crates through the glass walled corridors to the customs station. The inspection there was perfunctory, one tired blond skimming through the disks while another ran an ineffectual looking scanning rod over the sealed crates. Neither seemed to find anything of interest. The first clicked keys on his waist-slung keyboard, adding his own certification codes to the collection of papers, while the second peeled iridescent stickers from the roll hanging at her belt and fixed one neatly to each of the containers. It was all done with only the most necessary exchange of words. Not at all like the usual precinct planetfall, Heikki thought, and her eyebrows lifted in spite of herself. Usually, planetary customs were, if not thorough, at least more than mildly curious about strangers, especially on a world as far from the usual passenger runs as Iadara. Either they received orders from Lo-Moth to pass us through, Heikki thought, or there's something else going on. She thanked them anyway, with the punctillious politeness she always used when dealing with customs, and joined the others in easing the crates out through the last narrow doorway.

There were autopallets for rent on the far side of the barrier, and Nkosi said, "I will get one."

"Do that," Heikki agreed, and stood for a moment, squinting into the sunlight that streamed in through the clear, blue-tinged bricks that formed one wall of the terminal. "What do you think?" she asked, after a moment, and saw, out of the corner of her eye, Djuro's mouth twist briefly.

"It was funny—not like customs at all. Of course, what can you smuggle in that they can't already buy? I bet security's a lot tougher, going out."

"True," Heikki said, but her tone was less certain than her words. Still, what Djuro said was true: corporate worlds, especially one-product worlds like Iadara, tended to be fairly lax in what they allowed on-planet. *And I expect he's right,* she thought, *security will be tighter when we leave. After all, they wouldn't want to risk losing any of their crystals to the black market.*

"Dam' Heikki?" The voice had a 'pointer crispness, and Heikki looked up sharply.

"That's me. Are you from Lo-Moth?" She heard crisp footsteps behind her, and realized that customs had finished with FitzGilbert.

"Yes, that's right. Ah, Dam' FitzGilbert, it's good to see you back." He looked back at Heikki, with a wary, professional smile that included all the off-worlders. "I'm Jens Neilenn."

"Pleased to meet you," Heikki murmured. "My assistant, Sten Djuro, my pilot, Jock Nkosi."

Neilenn managed a polite greeting for both of them, though Nkosi's handshake nearly overwhelmed him. The Iadaran was a little man, in his middle forties, with bright eyes webbed in a net of wrinkles: permanent middle management, Heikki guessed, and content to remain there.

"Director Mikelis asked me to act as your liaison," Neilenn went on. "I've taken the liberty of arranging rooms for you at the corporate hostel, but if that doesn't suit your needs, I can make other arrangements first thing in the morning."

Morning? Heikki thought. Surely that was morning sunlight outside the transluscent wall. . . . And then she remembered. The spaceport was built to the west of the city, along the east-west axis that would protect it from the worst of the winds. She was looking into the sunset, not the sunrise her body had assumed it to be. "That'd be fine," she said, and saw FitzGilbert frown.

"Why there?"

Neilenn gave her an uneasy look. "I thought it would be more convenient, if Dam' Heikki wanted to talk to the people in meteorology. . . ."

"She can talk to them from headquarters," FitzGilbert said. "You can arrange that, can't you?"

"Wait a minute," Heikki said. She smiled at Neilenn, made herself hold the smile as she turned to FitzGilbert. "I'd just as soon leave things as they are. There are people—not just corporate people—I'll need to see in the city."

FitzGilbert hesitated for a moment, then nodded reluctantly. "If that's what you want, fine. But the headquarters complex is much—nicer—than the hostel."

Heikki kept smiling, perfectly aware of the other woman's real meaning. The hostel would, of course, be perfectly comfortable, even luxurious; Lo-Moth could afford nothing else, for the sake of its own pretige. But it was still in Lowlands, still on Firster territory, and therefore, by definition, inferior. "I'm sure it'll do fine," she said, and looked to Neilenn. "I'd appreciate your help in arranging transport."

"Of course, I'll have the car brought round," the little man answered hastily, and fumbled with a touchpad sewn into the pocket of his jacket. "Dam' FitzGilbert, your car is at the door."

*And that,* Heikki thought, with an inward grin, *puts us in our place.* FitzGilbert nodded perfunctorily, and strode off, her long straight coat snapping behind her like a flag. *An interesting woman,* Heikki admitted, reluctantly, *maybe even a striking one . . . but I'd give a lot to know why she's angry at the world.* "Let's get moving," she said aloud, and stooped to adjust the antigrav unit attached to the nearest crate. The crate rose under her expert touch, and Nkosi slid the autopallet forward neatly, centering it beneath the crate. Heikki touched controls again, returning the crate to a weight that would keep it stable on the pallet, and stepped back as Djuro repeated the process with the second and third, smaller, crates. The entire procedure had taken little more than a minute.

"Dam' Heikki, sers, the car's here." Neilenn blinked nervously up at them.

"Will it be able to take our equipment, or should we arrange for storage here?" Djuro asked.

Neilenn glanced at the pallet. "Oh, we can tow that. Just a minute, I'll arrange it." Without waiting for an answer, he scurried across to a multi-screened kiosk, and ran his hands across its shadowscreen. The screen above lit, displaying the face of a man in a hat badged with Lo-Moth's logo. There was a brief conversation, conducted in a voice too soft for the off-worlders to hear, and then Neilenn blanked the screen and came back, a faint and satisfied smile on his face.

"All set," he said. "If you'll follow me?"

The heat beyond the aqua-glass doors was stifling. Heikki winced, the sweat pearling on her body—this was the part one always forgot, the damp heat of the afternoon—and heard Djuro swear under his breath. She glanced back, and saw him pull the hood of his shirt up over his thinning hair.

"Here we are," Neilenn announced, and pointed to a vehicle drawn up against the edge of the low walkway. It was a typical ho-crawl, squat and broad-beamed, a closed passenger cabin mounted awkwardly in what would normally have been the front of the cargo well. It was the sort of dual-purpose craft that was common on the precinct worlds, slow and unspectacular, but immensely durable either on or off the existing roads. At the moment, it was configured for on-road travel, its wheels, six sets of three soft tires, each group arranged in a triangle, retracted into the wells while the idling fans kicked up a low-lying cloud of dust. Lo-Moth's logo was painted on the side of the front-mounted engine housing.

"You said you needed a tow, ser Neilenn?" That was the driver, levering himself out through the window of the driver's pod so that his forearms were resting on the cloth-covered roof.

"That's right," Neilenn answered, but the driver didn't seem to hear him, staring instead at the off-worlders.

"Heikki? Is that you, then?"

Heikki frowned, trying to place the suddenly familiar face. "Dael?" Time had dealt kindly with him, done little more than thicken an always stocky body, and add a scattering of white to his sun-bleached hair. They were much of an age, had become good friends in the two years just before she had gone off-world.

"My God, it is you." Dael pulled himself all the way out of the pod, still disdaining the use of the door, and

Heikki couldn't help smiling at the compact strength of the movement. He moved around the nose of the ho-crawl, swinging his hips clear of the hot engine block, and came forward to greet her, at the last moment changing what might have begun as an embrace into an extension of both hands. Feeling suddenly awkward herself, Heikki took his hands, very aware of unfamiliar callouses. From the expression on his face, Dael was feeling the same awkwardness.

"My God," he said again. "How long has it been?"

"Years, I think," Heikki answered, and saw a sudden withdrawing in his face. "It is good to see you, Dael."

The tension vanished from his smile, and in the same instant, Neilenn made a soft, unhappy noise through his teeth. Heikki glanced toward him, recalled to the business at hand, and saw, behind him, a bank of clouds rising out of the southeast. They loomed up over the low-roofed port buildings, their solid shapes turned a bruised purple by the full light of the westering sun. The wind was changing, too, she realized in the same instant, swinging around so that it was blowing from the heart of the rising storm.

Dael had seen it, too. He eyed the clouds appraisingly, then glanced at the equipment-filled pallets. "We better get loaded up and on the road before that breaks. I'll drop the wheels."

Heikki nodded, and Nkosi said, "I will take care of the hookup—if that suits you." He was looking at Dael as he spoke. The Iadaran looked warily back at him, glancing sidelong at Heikki for her verdict before answering. When she said nothing, he nodded twice, a little too vigorously.

"Thanks. I appreciate the help."

Nkosi nodded, and moved toward the towpad.

"Does this happen often?" Djuro asked, and jerked his thumb back over his shoulder at the swelling clouds. Heikki bit back a laugh, and Neilenn cleared his throat.

"Almost every afternoon," he said, and frowned up at the sky. "Though this does look a little heavier than usual, I must say. We should be moving out."

"What about the pallet?" Djuro asked. "Will it be secure?"

Neilenn looked at the driver, who nodded. "If the weighting's right, it should do." He glanced back toward Nkosi, still inspecting the towpad, and called, "Stand clear."

Nkosi straightened, and Dael leaned back into the ho-crawl, manipulating the controls one-handed. Servos whined, clearly audible even above the noise of the fans, and the wheels came down until they just brushed the paving. He cut the fans then, and the ho-crawl settled heavily, the suspension sighing in protest.

"It should do," he said again, staring at the numbers on his narrow repeater screen.

Djuro looked as though he would protest, and Heikki said quickly, "It'll be fine, Sten."

The little man grimaced, but said only, "Then let's get going. It looks as though that storm is coming fast."

Dael levered himself back into the ho-crawl and popped the main door. Neilenn lifted it the rest of the way, and gestured for the off-worlders to enter ahead of him. Heikki started toward it, and Dael called, "Why don't you ride up front with me?"

Neilenn's back stiffened, and Heikki said hastily, "I'd like that." She looked back at Neilenn, forcing a smile so as not to offend. "I used to live here, I knew Dael when I was a kid."

Neilenn swallowed, visibly remembering that she was a company guest, and nodded. "As you wish."

Heikki nodded, and reached in through the well's half-open window to trigger the interlock. It was a gesture of old habit, so old that she could no longer consciously remember the reasons for it—and then she did remember, all the old stories about bandits and the need to keep jungle vehicles secure against them, back before the company had tamed Iadara. Neilenn laughed, the sound making him seem suddenly younger.

"Are you a Firster, then?"

Heikki hesitated, the door already half open under her hand, then shook her head. "Not really."

In the same instant, Dael said, "Near as makes no difference, she is."

Heikki looked at him in some surprise, an old anger stirring in spite of herself. Twenty years ago, that admission—that acknowledgement, that claim of kin-ship—would have meant so much more, would have made such a difference. . . . She killed the thought, and forced herself to smile again at Neilenn. "I told you, I grew up here. I ran with a lot of Firster kids then."

Neilenn nodded, clearly a little embarrassed by his own unprofessional behavior, and stooped to follow the off-worlders into the passenger compartment. Heikki ducked into the well, settling herself comfortably on the narrow bench seat at Dael's side. The Iadaran gave her a companionable smile, his hands already roving across the simple controls as he adjusted power plant and brakes.

"All secure back here," Neilenn's voice said from the overhead speaker, and an instant later, Djuro said, "I'm still not comfortable about the tow, Heikki—"

"The tow's all right," Heikki answered. "Our crates should be secure against rain, if that's what you're worried about."

"Whatever you say, boss," Djuro answered, but he did not sound fully appeased.

Dael grinned, and eased a lever backward. Gears groaned, a deep sound of metal against metal, and engaged. The ho-crawl juddered forward, bucking once as its wheels jolted onto the metalling of the main road.

Heikki leaned back against the worn padding, staring out the windscreen at a landscape at once strange and painfully familiar. Many of the old landmarks were gone— Goose Green, for one, the old spacers' bar, no longer flaunted its string of gaudy show lights along the main highway. Instead, its low-lying, barrel-roofed building had been replaced by a series of sleek towers, many bearing the logos of Precincter shipping firms. A.T. Leigh's was gone, too, but the Good Times Chandlery had actually expanded, a third—or was it the fourth? —flat-paneled khaki-colored prefab wing jutting out from behind the sand-scarred main building. But the land was just the same, sandy here on the edges of crystal country, bound in place by the ground-growing native clingvines and by more deliberate plantings of imported feather grasses. The latter grew in clumpy stands, man-high or a little taller, a few stalks already sprouting the plumes that would eventually spread their fluffy, pale-pink seed a little further into the relatively fertile midlands between Lowlands and the upthrust central massif.

The road swung wide to avoid a sand wallow, its edges marked by frayed, once-red warning flags whose thin poles were bent into graceful arcs by the still-rising wind. The ho-crawl was pointing inland now, so that she could see the first trees of the midforest, the nearest perhaps two hundred meters from the roadbed, a gnarled, low-growing chaintree with oily, almost-black leaves. Beyond the forest, the mountains of the massif were no more than a smudge on the horizon, indistinct as smoke. That was where the latac had gone down, somewhere up beyond those hills, on the plateau of the 'wayback, and she was conscious of a faint, almost pleasant excitement, contemplating the job ahead.

"I was sorry to hear about your da," Dael said, and Heikki recalled herself to the immediate surroundings.

"Me, too. I suppose accidents happen—but that doesn't make it any easier."

"Especially not so soon after your mother died." Dael kept his eyes on the road ahead, and the clouds that had almost reached the zenith. "I looked for you at the funeral."

Heikki knew she blushed, and was annoyed by her own reaction. There was no reason to be ashamed, none at all, but still she found herself answering the unspoken question. "I was on Embros, off the main net, when it happened. They—the local authorities—

weren't able to contact me until it was too late. He was buried before I could find a ship going off-world."

Dael nodded sympathetically. "That happens, too, but it's a shame." There was a silence, and then he said, "Do you hear anything from Galler, these days?"

Heikki bit back the sudden pulse of anger. Dael of all people should know better than to ask that question. . . . She kept her voice steady only with an effort of will. "Who?"

"So it's still like that, is it? Well, your business, not mine."

"Yes," Heikki said, and saw Dael's quick sidelong glance, half of apology, half of sympathy. They were silent again, for longer this time, neither quite knowing what to say to the other. There was nothing between them but their work, Heikki thought, sadly, and shook her head at her own longings. *If that's all there is*, she told herself, *then make use of it*. She glanced at the instrument panel to be sure the intercom was off. "Listen, Dael, you know—or you've heard—what I'm here for."

"I've heard." Dael glanced sideways again, but this time his expression was unreadable.

"What's the talk? What are people saying?"

"They're saying a lot of things," Dael answered, "and damn few of them make good sense." Heikki waited, and after a moment the Iadaran sighed. "Of the sensible ones. They say the wreck should've been found a long time ago. They say it's a bit late to be calling in experts, when the crew's probably dead and eaten. They say the Widows and Orphans is planning to sue for the heirs, that's what they say."

"So there's no talk that the crew might've been in on a hijack," Heikki said, interested, and Dael shrugged.

"Not in my hearing, anyway. But then, nobody would talk like that, not while I was around, not even if it was true and half FirstTown was snickering up their sleeves at the company. I work for the company now, and they don't forget it."

*And they don't let you forget it, either*, Heikki thought.

She said aloud, "It's still interesting to hear. Thanks, Dael."

The wall of clouds had passed the zenith, and the first layers were already overspreading Iadara's sun. The light curdled, became sickly, unnatural, tinged with a yellow-green like an old bruise, and then the heavier clouds reached the disk and the sunlight vanished completely, as though a switch had been thrown. Lightning, a distinct and jagged line, forked through the sky above the city's clustering buildings; the thunder was drowned in the growl of the ho-crawl's engine. Heikki frowned and leaned sideways a little, looking out the side window so that she could see beyond the skyline. The city buildings dwindled there to nothing, a few low domes mingling with the scrub and grass. On the horizon, a stark line showed between the trailing edge of the storm and the clear sky beyond. Heikki's frown deepened, and Dael said, a new, worried note in his voice, "Switch on the U-met console, will you?"

Heikki did as she was told, finding the familiar inset screen-and-keyboard without difficulty. Even as she keyed it on, Neilenn's voice crackled in the intercom speaker.

"Dael? What's the weather doing?"

"Channel five's the metro-port now," Dael said, to Heikki, ignoring the voice from the passenger compartment. Heikki nodded, and touched keys to tune the machine properly. The screen glowed and displayed a rough map of the city and the port and the roads between them; a moment later, a second image, this one the ghostly, multi-colored reflection of the clouds overhead, was superimposed on the brighter map. Two sections of the clouds glowed brighter, yellow, and Dael spared them a few seconds study before he answered the intercom.

"Nothing yet, just potential."

"Good," Neilenn said. "Keep me informed."

"Right," Dael answered, but the intercom was already off. He glanced again at the console display, then forced his attention back to the road.

"I'll watch," Heikki said, and the other nodded, not taking his eyes from the road ahead. Heikki fixed her eyes on the shifting display, watching with some alarm as one of the two yellow spots grew brighter. The local weather station was monitoring the winds in the clouds above, highlighting areas that could produce the dangers—tornadoes, wind shear, devastating hail—for which Iadara was infamous. The pattern stayed steady, bright yellow but not yet shading into the red that would mean real danger, and began to drift off to the south, fading a little as it went. Heikki allowed herself a small sigh of relief, a sound that was drowned in a crack of thunder that seemed to come from directly overhead. She blinked, and the rain poured down.

"That's that, then," Dael said, raising his voice to be heard over the rush of water.

Heikki nodded—the rains usually signalled the passage of the storm's most dangerous phase—and leaned back against the cushions. Outside the windscreen, the rain swept in almost solid sheets across the roadway. Dael slowed the ho-crawl, fighting to see between the blasts of wind-driven water. Lights flared on the control panel as the remotes kicked in and faint lines appeared, projected on the windscreen: a directional grid, and then the linear outline of the road ahead. The ho-crawl rocked sideways with the force of the wind, and Dael muttered something profane under his breath.

Then, almost as quickly as it had risen, the storm began to ease. The wind dropped, and the rain began to fall again, rather than being blown horizontally against the ho-crawl's sides. The lightning faded, and the banks of clouds began to look less solidly threatening. By the time the ho-crawl drew up at the entrance to the corporate hostel, just outside the 5K Road that was the city's legal limit, the rain had stopped altogether and weak sunshine was beginning to throw beams through the shredding clouds.

"Here we are, then," Neilenn said, over the intercom, and Dael looked sideways at Heikki.

"I hope I'll see you again, now that you're here."

Despite the polite words, his tone was less than enthusiastic, and Heikki could not hide a crooked, comprehending smile. It had been too long, they had both changed, had nothing really in common any more. Better not to have met, than to have met like this, when the only tie between them was their work for Lo-Moth. She said aloud, "Definitely, if we can find the time," and was ashamed to see the fleeting relief in the other's eyes. She looked away, and reached for the interlock, pushing herself up and out of the well in the same smooth movement.

Djuro and Nkosi were already out of the passenger compartment, and Djuro was checking the crates on the tow. He looked up at her approach, and nodded grudgingly. "Everything looks all right. The seals are tight."

"Good," Heikki said, though she'd expected no less, and looked at Neilenn.

"Your rooms are already reserved and confirmed as of this morning," the little man answered. "There will be a corporate systems Accesscard waiting for you at the desk, as well as the information you requested from the central office. I have also been instructed to inform you that a local expense account has been set up for you, with a five thousand poa line of credit. Ser Mikelis asked me to make clear, however, that this was intended for incidental expenses rather than employment or equipment rental or anything of that nature. For the latter, you need only call the Bursar, and she'll issue the order. Your projected expenses have already been placed in her accounts."

"Thank you," Heikki said, and saw Nkosi staring open-mouthed. She frowned at him, and he hurriedly adjusted his expression, but for once she couldn't blame him. Lo-Moth was being unusually generous. . . . She put the thought aside, annoyed with herself for borrowing trouble, and turned her attention back to Neilenn.

"There's just the question of where to store the equipment, then."

"Kasib will see to that," Neilenn said.

Heikki turned, to find herself face to face with a tall, unsmiling man in a high-collared, short-sleeved tunic and loosely woven trousers. The collar button was printed with Lo-Moth's logo. The man touched his forehead politely, still unspeaking, and Neilenn said again, "Kasib will take it."

Djuro said, "I'll give you a hand."

"Oh, that won't be necessary," Neilenn said, and in the same moment, Kasib said, "I can handle it."

Djuro opened his mouth to protest, and Heikki said quietly, "I think he can manage, Sten."

Djuro's mouth closed abruptly. After a moment, he said, "Whatever you say, boss." He was silent as they made their way into the suddenly cool lobby, and while Heikki collected room keys, information packet, and the promised disks from the desk clerk, who made a production of summoning a scout to lead them to the suite. She glanced warily at Djuro as she turned to the hovering scout, but the little man's expression was remote to the point of mutiny. She suppressed her own annoyed response, and nodded to the scout.

"You can take us up, please."

The scout led them through the expensively furnished lobby, and past a first bank of lifts to a second, more secluded row of cars. There was a card sensor in place of the usual panel of buttons, and the scout cleared his throat. "Dam' Heikki—?"

Heikki handed him one of the cards she had received from the clerk; the scout passed it across the reader face and handed it back to her with a flourish. Heikki said nothing, and the scout looked away.

Lo-Moth had assigned them a comfortable suite of rooms near the top of the building, bedrooms, mini-kitchen, mainroom and workroom. Comfortable, but hardly luxurious, Heikki thought, scanning the working space, and could not help feeling a certain relief. Lo-Moth was finally behaving the way it should. She tipped the scout, and saw the door closed and locked behind him. Djuro still glared at her, but said nothing. Heikki smiled, crookedly, and rummaged in her carryall for the minisec she always carried. She keyed the general search, and then, when that triggered no alarms, tried the more specific common frequency search.

"No bugs," Nkosi said, and grinned. "Not that I really expected any, in a place this expensive."

Djuro muttered something inarticulate.

Heikki ignored them both, and readjusted the minisec's controls so that it shifted from active to passive security, putting out an inaudible field guaranteed to disrupt most of the bugs commonly used in the Loop and Precincts. Only then did she look at Djuro.

"Sten—"

"Why did you let them go off with our equipment?" Djuro demanded. "Damn it, Heikki, they were just looking for a chance to search it."

"I know." Heikki shrugged. "At least, I think I know. Maybe we're misjudging them." She could hear how doubtful her own voice sounded, and sighed. "And if they do—they'd've found a way anyway, Sten. You know that."

"They might damage something."

Nkosi made an odd sound that might have been a snort of laughter. Heikki said, "I doubt it. If they do—we call them on it, Sten, get repair plus the nuisance value, and if necessary, we break contract. We'd have a good argument that they violated the contract first, at any rate." She paused, staring out through the workroom door at the enormous window that dominated the mainroom. The storm had almost vanished over the western horizon, was little more than a distant line of clouds. The sun streamed across a broad swath of perfectly manicured lawn, drew faint curls of vapor from the vanishing puddles at the edge of the metalled access road. "What I'd really like to know," she said slowly, "is why they want to search the crates."

"It doesn't make good sense," Djuro agreed. His anger had vanished almost as quickly as it had risen.

"Oh, I can think of quite a few reasons that Lo-Moth might want to search us," Nkosi began, and Heikki smiled sideways at him.

"But do any of them make sense, Jock?"

"That I cannot promise," Nkosi answered.

"So you're saying we should ignore it, Heikki?" Djuro asked.

"For now, yes." Heikki's smile widened. "Maybe I'm wrong after all, and they're just being polite."

"To an independent?" Djuro murmured.

Heikki ignored him. "If not, think of it as giving them the rope to hang themselves."

# CHAPTER 4

Heikki spent the next few hours at the communications console, arranging for the rental of a fastcat, an on-road machine lighter and faster than a ho-crawl, and eminently suited for city travel. After the encounter with Dael, she was reluctant to run into anyone she'd known from the old days, and was glad to rely on the relative anonymity of the communications net. Only contacting the Explorers' Club's local representative required a face to face meeting—ostensibly, she wanted to check what her membership could bring in the way of local privilege; actually, of course, she wanted to tie in to whatever local networks the local representative had managed to infiltrate, and that required a personal touch—and at least the name was not one she recognized.

Ionas Ciceron was listed in the city's business and services index as a private meteorological consultant, with an office in the Portside district. That area was inexpensive but respectable; Djuro lifted an eyebrow at the address.

"Problems?" Heikki asked, and kept her voice calm with an effort.

Djuro shook his head. "Weathermen—especially poor weathermen—don't usually act as Club Reps, that's all."

Or belong to the Club in the first place, Heikki thought. "Yes, but . . ." she began, and Nkosi grinned.

"Nothing has been normal yet on this planet. Why should the rep be any different?"

"Classist," Heikki said, to Djuro, and shook herself, hard. "The 'cat's waiting. Let's go."

She left the two men at the expensive end of the 5K Road, where the equipment rentors generally kept their show lots, and turned the 'cat back toward town, threading her way through the minimal traffic to the Portside district. This was one of the newer parts of Lowlands, where the low, mostly one- and two-story buildings were finished with dull bronze-colored insulating tiles. The streets were broad, but empty, most workers hiding inside, out of the morning heat. Once she had found the Frozen Pool—it was actually a broad black-metal sculpture of a pond crammed with the local wildlife, birds and various small amphibians, even a fish caught in the act of leaping half out of the mirror-bright "water"—it was easy to find Ciceron's office. She worked the 'cat into one of the narrow parking slots, and made her way into the building.

The lobby was cool and quiet and empty, blank-walled except for the dull grill of a mechanical concierge. Heikki crossed to it, and pressed its almost invisible button.

"Gwynne Heikki, for Ionas Ciceron."

For a long moment, there was no answer, but then at last relays clicked, and she heard the faint indistinct hiss of an open channel.

"Dam' Heikki," a voice said, from a speaker set somewhere in the ceiling. "I'm so sorry, I didn't expect you so early. Please, do come up."

"Thank you," Heikki said, and waited. A minute or so later, servos hummed, and an almost invisible section of wall slid back, revealing a moving stair. A new voice—the building's computer, Heikki guessed—said,

"Please take the stair. Movement will stop at your floor. Enjoy your visit."

Heikki bit back her instinctive answer, and stepped onto the stirring stairway. It rose, slowly at first, then faster and more smoothly, curving up and around a massive central pillar. Heikki could see other offices, the ones on the lower, more expensive floors, each with its shaded-glass frontage and a human secretary visible behind it to prove the operation was worthwhile. As the stairway approached the fifth level, it began to slow down, slacking off tread by tread. Heikki clutched at the handrail to steady herself, and was looking down as the machine ground to a stop and she stepped off onto the mirror-floored landing.

"Good morning, Dam' Heikki."

She looked up quickly—she hadn't seen anyone as the stair approached—to see a small man standing in an open doorway at the far side of the stairwell.

"Ser Ciceron?"

The little man bobbed his head in acknowledgement. He was a perfect miniature of a man, Heikki thought, bemused. His head barely reached her shoulder—and she was not exceptionally tall herself—but he was so strikingly handsome, and carried himself so gracefully, with an assurance long unconscious of his size, that it was she who was outsized, not he who was diminutive.

"Do come in," Ciceron continued. Heikki smiled, and stepped past him into the office. It was a typical business property, reminding her of the suites she and Santerese had rented for years, but the media wall had been half blocked off by an elaborate cloud chamber, only a third of its surface visible from the working desk. Heikki could not help raising an eyebrow at that, and Ciceron smiled crookedly.

"I do rather more simulations work than anything else, Dam' Heikki. Despite my other responsibility."

"I beg your pardon," Heikki said automatically, and settled herself in the client's chair. "However, it is as Club representative that I've come to see you today." Deliberately, she left other possibilities dangling, knowing that Ciceron would know what she had been hired for, and saw the little man's smile broaden briefly.

"Of course, Dam' Heikki. How can I be of assistance?"

"I need recommendations," Heikki said bluntly. "I expect you know why I'm on planet."

She waited then, curious to hear his response. After a moment, Ciceron nodded. "The missing latac. Yes, I heard they were hiring off-world to find it."

*That*, Heikki thought, *was an odd turn of phrase.* "Locals couldn't handle it?" she asked, and allowed a note of contempt to seep into her voice.

Ciceron frowned. "They didn't try."

"The Firster problem?"

"No."

Ciceron's voice changed subtly, and Heikki swore to herself. She'd missed it, whatever it was, and he knew she knew less than he did now. She kept her face expressionless, and said, "I need a pilot, one with back-country experience, and a lot of it—someone reliable. And I need a guide, also reliable, preferably someone who knows the massif well."

"What would you mean by reliable?" Ciceron did not reach for his workboard, but steepled his fingers above the desktop. There was amusement in his voice that did not reach his eyes.

"I want people outside Lo-Moth politics." Heikki's tone added, *of course*.

"So you do think it's sabotage."

"I don't know yet," Heikki answered, and then, because that was no answer at all, said, "I'm not ruling out any possibilities." She waited then, and when Ciceron said nothing, added, carefully casual, "Is that the local talk, sabotage?"

Ciceron's mouth twisted as though he'd bitten into something unexpectedly bitter. "That's the talk, certainly. But Lo-Moth blames the crew, and the crewfolk blame the company."

"Do they now," Heikki said, almost to herself. That was a possibility she had not fully considered, and one that did not, at first glance, make a good deal of sense.

After all, the crystal matrix was—potentially—the company's ticket to the first ranks. . . . Even as she articulated that thought, however, she began to see other scenarios, rivalries within Lo-Moth's ranks, between departments and between parents and subsidiaries. It was plausible enough, but she put the thought away as something to be tested later, and turned her attention back to the little man behind the desk. "Would you recommend anybody?"

Ciceron nodded. "For the guide, yes, without reservation. There's a woman named Alexieva, licensed surveyor, who has her own company outside the Limit." He held up his hand, forestalling Heikki's question. "She was part of the team that did the ordinance survey, the reliable one. She was a section chief, I think. But there's not a lot of survey work these days, so she does some guide work. She's good. Or anyone she recommends, of course, but she's the only one I really know is good."

Heikki nodded back. "Contact code?" she asked, and Ciceron slid a card across the table. Heikki took the featureless square of plastic, feeling the familiar roughness of the data ridges, and tucked it into the pocket with her lens. "Now, what about a pilot?"

Ciceron hesitated. "The best pilots are Firsters," he said after a moment, his voice completely without expression.

"I do the hiring," Heikki said, and when he did not respond said, "It's in my contract, I have a free hand."

"Ah." Ciceron's expression did not change, but his voice was fractionally warmer. "The best pilot—" He stressed the word. "—is a kid called Sebasten-Januarias."

"What's wrong with him?"

Ciceron smiled thinly. "One. He's very young. Two. He's a Firster—*real* Firster, trouble to the core when it comes to Lo-Moth. Three. . . . No, three's just a part of one. He's *very* young."

Heikki's eyebrows rose. "All this, and you'd still recommend him? He must be one hell of a pilot."

"He's the best I know. If you weren't working for Lo-Moth I'd recommend him without reservation."

"I'll bear that in mind," Heikki said. "Do you have any other names?"

"Pell Elauro," Ciceron answered promptly, "and Liljana Kerry." He reached into his desk again before Heikki could ask, and produced two more cards. Heikki accepted them, and lifted an eyebrow.

"Don't you have one for the Firster, Sebastian—"

"Sebasten-Januarias," Ciceron corrected her. "No. He works out of a bar called the Last Shift. By the airfield—"

"I know it," Heikki said, and was rewarded by a look of surprise from Ciceron.

"Not many off-worlders do."

Heikki allowed herself a genuine, if somewhat crooked, grin. "I grew up here, Ser Ciceron. I'll try Sebasten-Januarias first, thanks—if he's the best."

"He is." Ciceron nodded twice as if in punctuation. "He is."

"Good enough," Heikki said, but made no move to go. "I'm also going to need some meteorological analysis done, confidentially. Lo-Moth will be doing most of the sim and scan work, but I'd like an independent verification. Can you handle that for me?"

Somewhat to her surprise, Ciceron neither smiled nor frowned at the possibility of work. "Yes." He nodded to the cloud chamber blocking the media wall. "As you can see, I've got the equipment."

"Are you interested?" Heikki asked bluntly. "If you're not, I'm sure you can recommend someone who has the time."

"It's not that." Ciceron shook his head as though coming out of a dream. "No, I can handle the work—I'd be glad to handle the work."

"Rates?"

Ciceron reached into his desk again, withdrew a slightly larger card that shimmered faintly, light sparking as well from the metal threads woven through its surface. "Everything you need is on this."

*I'm missing something*, Heikki thought, and bit her

lower lip in frustration. *I'm missing something, political or professional, and I don't know what it is.* She put that knowledge aside with an effort, filing questions to be asked later, of other people, and took the card. "I appreciate your help, Ser Ciceron."

Ciceron bowed slightly, an antique gesture Heikki had not seen in years. "My pleasure, Dam' Heikki."

Heikki made her way back to the fastcat quickly enough, but sat in the cab without touching the controls, fingering instead the cards tucked into her pocket. She didn't really want to go into First Town in search of Sebasten-Januarias, though she knew perfectly well that that was the easiest way to find any Firster. After a moment's thought, she pulled out Alexieva's card, and adjusted the data lens to the standard setting. Letters sprang into existence within the thin plastic, giving the woman's full name—Incarnacion Alexieva Cirilly, with the middle name, the business name, underlined—and beneath that the various contact codes. The office address was for a quarter on the opposite side of the city: she would almost have to go by the port, and the Last Shift, to get there. Heikki sat for a moment longer, eyeing the 'cat's communications panel, and wondered if she could call Alexieva first. She frowned at her own weakness then, and tucked card and lens back into her pocket and punched on the engine. There was no point in talking to Alexieva until she knew whether or not she would be asking the surveyor to work with a Firster. Better to deal with Sebasten-Januarias first and get it over with, especially if it meant meeting someone she knew. And besides, she did want to see First Town again after all these years, in spite of all the people she might meet, who might remember— She slammed the 'cat into gear, focussing on the act of driving, and swung the machine out onto the road, heading for First Town.

First Town hadn't changed much, in the years since she had left Iadara. The roads were still rutted, drifted with the fine dust; the tall, thin houses still stood almost bare on their tracts of land, their stark white paint either faded into the bleached silver-brown of the wood itself, or violently new and bright, never anything in between. There were crawlers in the yards, or the occasional 'cat, sometimes stripped to the frame with tallgrass springing through the empty engine well. Faded clothing hung on frames outside, bleaching in the sun; an equally faded woman leaned from her third-floor window, calling to the pack of children in the dust below. A fruit tree stood beside one smaller house, incongruously green and blossoming behind its protective cage. Its owner scowled as he sprayed the dust from its leaves, daring it to die.

Closer to the airfield, the buildings stood further apart, but the space between them was filled not with gardens or children's playgrounds, but with rusted machines and heaped wires, or nothing at all but the dust and the ubiquitous sere grass. A group of Firsters, most of them so muffled in headscarf and loose sun-cheating coat, four meters of sunblocking fabric pleated into a gaudy patchwork yoke, as to be indistinguishable by age or sex, sat on the broad steps of one house, passing a stoneware falk from hand to hand. So afaq is still common here, Heikki thought, and shifted her leg so that she could reach the slim blaster tucked into the top of her high boot beside her knife. The group did not move as the 'cat slid past, but in the mirror she saw one of them throw a stone after her, not purposefully, but with an old and pointless despair.

The Last Shift was just outside the airfield perimeter, where the buildings changed from tall houses to the squat shapes that marked machine repair shops throughout the Precincts. The neighborhood was busier, a few men and women gathered outside the shops, or busy in the open bays, sweltering despite the wind scoops on the roofs. There were a few other vehicles in the vacant lot next to the Shift, a pair of battered 'cats tucked against the airfield fence, and an enormous ho-crawl pulled up next to the building itself, the roof of the driver's well just brushing the overhanging eaves. Heikki edged her 'cat up next to the others until its blunt nose almost touched the fence, and swung herself out of the cab. The heat was scorching, the sudden weight of sunlight a hot wind against her skin. She could feel eyes on her, not from the blank-walled bar but from the shops to either side, and ignored them.

The Shift was exactly the same as it had always been, miraculously cool and dark after the glaring heat outside. Through the green sundazzle, Heikki saw the bar's familiar shape, and, less clearly, the maze of wovewood tables that filled the central room. Most of them were empty now, she saw as her sight cleared, and those that were filled held mostly the retired or the unemployable, bent over drinks or shallow falks. They looked up as she passed, were still watching her as she leaned against the bar and touched the bell that called the bartender. Its sonorous note sounded through the space, filling the air, drowning out the lack of conversation, and faded slowly. After a moment, the bartender appeared from the back room, wiping his hands on his faded shirt. He hesitated, seeing who had summoned him, then came forward reluctantly.

"Can I help you?"

"I hope so." Heikki kept her voice scrupulously neutral, attempting neither to hide nor to emphasize the liquid off-world vowels. "I'm looking for someone, a pilot. I was told he worked out of here."

The bartender's expression shifted subtly. "Who would that be, that you're looking for?"

"The name I was given is Sebasten-Januarias. Mine's Heikki, I'm in salvage, based in the Loop."

The bartender's expression eased even further, and he nodded. "If you want to wait, I'll find him. Would you want something to drink?"

It was early to be drinking, but Heikki nodded anyway. "Field punch, please." She glanced over her shoulder, toward the row of semi-private cubicles set along one wall. Most were empty, the sound-proofing curtains pulled back to expose the stained cushions and chipped glass table-tops. "I'll be over there."

"I'll see if I can find him," the bartender said.

Heikki bent her head politely, and took the drink he slid toward her, offering her paycard in return. He accepted it, flushing, and ran it easily through the scanner. She took it back without looking at the total already fading from the display window, and started toward the nearest of the cubicles. She settled herself against the dirty cushions and waited. The bartender vanished again, and the conversations slowly recommenced.

The punch was tartly sweet, deceptively mild to the tongue. Heikki sipped it with wary respect, but even so found herself finishing the last of it before she had intended. She was not drunk, not nearly, but she could feel the liquor warming her stomach, warning her to have no more. She stared down at the glass, cupping her hands around it to hide its emptiness, and heard the door open. She looked up, hoping it would be Sebasten-Januarias, but it was only a boy barely into his teens. Then the boy turned toward her, visibly looking for someone, and Heikki fought to keep her expression steady. Ciceron had said he was young, certainly, but this was ridiculous. He looked all of sixteen, at a generous estimate, a skinny, brown-skinned boy with the enormous headscarf of a Firster adolescent wrapped around his head and shoulders—

"Dam' Heikki?" The boy stopped just outside the cubicle, dropping one end of the scarf like a veil, to reveal a face streaked with multi-colored sunpaint. "I'm Sebasten-Januarias."

He sounds a little older than he looks, Heikki thought, and gestured for the boy to seat himself across from her. Is this Ciceron's idea of a joke? "Get yourself a drink, if you want," she said aloud, "and then have a seat. Ionas Ciceron mentioned you as a pilot."

"Thank you," the boy said, somewhat ambiguously, and slid gracefully onto the cushions opposite. "That's kind of him."

Interesting that he doesn't want the drink, Heikki thought. "You got my name?" she said, and the boy nodded.

"You're in salvage, I hear?" There was just enough of an upward lilt to make it a question.

"That's right," Heikki said. "I have a local contract, and I need a local copilot to back my main man, going into the 'wayback, probably along the Asilas into the massif."

"That cargo flight Lo-Moth lost?" Sebasten-Januarias asked.

"That's right. Is that a problem?"

"No." The boy's voice was confident, and when he did not continue, Heikki sketched out a quick description of the job, studying him while she talked. Sebasten-Januarias was definitely older than he looked at first glance, but not very old—maybe in his early twenties, Heikki thought, no more. Beneath the garish sunpaint she thought he was rather plain, strong boned, but ordinary. He frowned slightly as she spoke, and the frown deepened slowly, but when she had finished, he nodded to himself.

"Will you be taking a latac?"

"No, a standard jumper."

"Then I'm your boy—if you'll take me." He had an engaging smile, and Heikki smiled back.

"How long have you been flying?"

Sebasten-Januarias's smile widened, and he said, without rancor, "You mean, how old am I. I'm twenty-four, but I've been flying the 'wayback solo for eight years, and I apprenticed with my uncle before that, for two years."

"Sounds good," Heikki said, and meant it. If Sebasten-Januarias had been taking aircraft across the wayback since he was sixteen without an accident—and if he had had an accident, he would not be sitting here now; the wayback did not forgive even minor errors—then he was the sort of pilot she wanted. She curbed her enthusiasm abruptly. "Can you give me some references?" She kept her voice briskly professional, and, to her surprise, the young man did not bridle.

"Tom Tolek at the tower will speak for me, and Kameka Decker. I've worked for Lo-Moth, too. The field ops coordinator knows me."

"FitzGilbert?" Heikki looked up sharply.

"Yes." He seemed unsurprised at the question.

Heikki looked back at her noteboard. "I'll contact them, certainly. In the meantime, I'd like you to come to dinner, and meet the rest of my team. Are you free this evening?"

"Yes'm."

"Your full name?"

"Josep Laurens Sebasten-Januarias." His lips turned up briefly in a rather wry smile.

"What do they call you for short?" Heikki asked idly.

Before the other could answer, a voice called from the doorway, "I hear you're working, Joe-Laurie."

Sebasten-Januarias turned to face the tall man weaving his way through the tables, warning him off with a stare. "I might be, Uncle Cass, if you don't screw up the deal."

The tall man laughed without anger—he was three-quarters drunk, Heikki saw—and fetched up against the bar, his hand fumbling for the bell. Sebasten-Januarias turned back to her with an apologetic grimace.

"My *friends* call me Jan."

"Good enough," Heikki said, and stood. "I'll expect you at—" She hesitated then, remembering local traditions, and compromised between Loop and Precinct custom. "—at eight evening, at the corporate hostel in Lowlands proper. All right?"

"I'll be there," Sebasten-Januarias said, and stood with her. Heikki did not look back, unexpectedly pleased with her choice.

She settled herself back in the 'cat's cab, glancing at the side and rear mirrors. Nothing moved in the sweltering shadows except the trio at work in the repair shed, bending oblivious over a ho-crawl's opened fan housing. She engaged the engines and swung the 'cat slowly back around toward Lowlands' center.

The 'cat had a fairly up-to-date communications block mounted in the forward panels. Heikki eyed it for a moment, dividing her attention between its controls and the road ahead, then felt one-handed in her pocket

until she had found Alexieva's card. She inserted that
into the machine's read-slot, and touched keys until the
voiceline menu showed faint against the 'cat's windscreen. She touched more keys, and was rewarded at
last by the three-toned chime of a standard secretarial
program. She exchanged codes and a message with it,
expecting it to file the information and close down, but
to her surprise the machine chimed again.

"Dam' Heikki," a flat synthetic voice said abruptly.
"Dam' Alexieva requests the favor of a personal meeting, at map coordinates JP89.332/I12N, as soon as possible. If that meets with your approval."

Heikki reached for the map controls. The coordinates
were on the north side of the city, probably an hour's
drive beyond the Limit. She sighed, but triggered the
communications console again. "I can reach those coordinates in—" She glanced again at the map display.
"—seventy-nine minutes. I would be glad to meet with
Dam' Alexieva at that time."

There was another, shorter pause, and the secretary
answered, "That would be ideal. Dam' Alexieva will be
expecting you then."

This time, the air filled briefly with static before the
console's overrides shut off the speakers. Heikki adjusted the map so that the route pointer showed on the
windscreen, then fingered the communications keyboard
until she reached the hostel's concierge program. Djuro
and Nkosi had not yet returned, the urbane artificial
voice informed her; she left a brief message explaining
where she was going and asking Djuro to check Sebasten-
Januarias' references, and to ask about Alexieva's reputation, then switched off the machine.

It took slightly less than the projected time to work
her way around the city to the road indicated by the
map. The map's ghostly arrow steadied in her windscreen, directing her down a metalled road that ran
almost as straight as the arrow itself. This part of Iadara
had been settled for almost as long as First Town, she
knew, but she had rarely ventured out in this direction
when she was younger, keeping either within the Limit,

or riding crew somewhere deep into the wayback. It was unfamiliar land, an unfamiliar kind of land, farmland of sorts, but far more diversified than on most other worlds, the fields patched and banded in a dozen different shades of green and yellow. The farm buildings were crammed into what she assumed were the least fertile sections of the property, low-lying, cramped buildings whose walls were covered with gleaming white insulfoam panels. The roofs were bright with solar panels, so that the most distant houses flamed like stars against the green land.

The guidance arrow flashed sharply against the windscreen, and a string of translucent letters trailed across the plastic beneath it: DESTINATION APPROACHING. Obediently, she adjusted the throttle, slowing the 'cat almost to a walking pace, and looked around warily. She was almost exactly in the center of a cultivated area, one set of buildings just visible in a stand of trees a kilometer or two to the north, another, more distant, sprawling across an expanse of some low-growing vegetable. The arrow swung abruptly to the left. Heikki started to swing the control yoke, and stopped, looking for the road. It took her a moment to realize that the machine really was pointing to the rutted dirt track between the two fields. She grimaced, adjusted the 'cat's tracking, and turned cautiously onto the ill-made road. For a few minutes, the towering fronds of neocale hid everything to either side, and then the road turned sharply, to end in a dusty turnaround enclosed by thickly growing hedges. Another fastcat was parked there, next to an ancient treaded cultivator with a digging bar cocked up over its rear cowling like the tail of some enormous insect. Heikki pulled her 'cat to a stop next to the other, and pulled the canopy release. The roof folded back, whining a little in protest, and she pushed herself up until she was sitting on the back of the driver's seat, bracing herself against the top of the windscreen.

From that vantage point, she could see into the next field, beyond the hedge that marked its border. Several people were at work there, and a standard-model robosurveyor was trundling busily along an invisible guideline. Heikki raised a hand to wave, unsure if anyone was even looking in her direction, and saw one of the distant figures put a hand to its mouth. A moment later, the nearer of the other two—a wiry shape barely distinguishable as female at this distance—turned and waved back, then beckoned to her companion. They spoke for a moment, and then the woman started toward the turnaround.

"Dam' Heikki?" she called, as soon as she was within earshot.

"Yes. Dam' Alexieva?"

"We've only got one more baseline to do," Alexieva shouted. "Would you mind waiting?"

Heikki shook her head, and then, realizing the gesture was probably not readable at a distance, called back, "No, take your time."

Alexieva lifted a hand in acknowledgement, and turned away. Left to herself, Heikki leaned forward against the windscreen, watching the robot move across the field. At some point in the morning, the sky had clouded over, but the change had been so gradual she had not noticed. Now, however, the wind was picking up, tossing little swirls of dust across the turnaround. To either side, the neocale dipped and rose with the breeze. Heikki frowned slightly, and glanced to her left, toward the southeast. Sure enough, a bank of clouds was rising there, not as heavy as the previous day's storm, but still impressive. I hadn't realized it was afternoon already, she thought, and in the same moment realized belatedly that she was hungry. After a moment's thought, she searched her belt pockets until she found a crumpled ration bar, and ate it without really considering the too-sweet taste. The robot was moving in short arcs now, and she glanced at the sky again, hoping Alexieva would finish before the storm broke.

The first of the storm clouds were almost directly overhead when Alexieva recalled her robot and lifted a hand to wave the others in. She paused at the edge of the field to give some last-minute instruction to her people, then pushed through the hedge and came to stand at the fastcat's side. Heikki looked down at her, seeing the other woman's fine dark hair stir in the wind.

Alexieva pushed the loose strands out of her eyes, frowning slightly. "Dam' Heikki. I'm glad you were able to see me now."

"No problem," Heikki answered absently. Alexieva was a small, sun-weathered woman, dressed despite that in trousers and a worn shirt that left her back and wiry arms mostly exposed. There was nothing at all remarkable about her, except her lightless eyes. They were brown, Heikki thought, but darkly intense, and marked at the corners with fine wrinkles: not the eyes of someone who compromised easily.

"Shall we talk here?" Alexieva went on briskly, seemingly unaware of the scrutiny, and Heikki brought herself back to the matter at hand. "Or if you could give me a ride back toward Lowlands, we could save some time."

I'd forgotten Precinct manners, Heikki thought, with an inward grin. "No problem," she said aloud. "We might as well talk on the way."

Alexieva nodded dispassionately. "Thanks. I appreciate it."

Heikki nodded in return, and reached into the cab to pop the passenger door. Alexieva swung herself inside, glancing up at the sky as she did so.

"Better close up soon."

Heikki felt a stab of annoyance, but had to admit that the clouds were closing fast. She slid back into the cab, and manipulated the controls to close the roof, then almost in the same movement switched on the engine and the map computer. "Coordinates?"

"I can put them in, if you'd like." Alexieva's voice made her preference clear.

Heikki's eyebrows rose. "Go ahead," she said, with a mildness that would have warned her friends. Even Alexieva seemed to sense something, and she looked up from the miniature keyboard.

"I have an appointment at 0300. I can set shortcuts easier than tell you about them."

It made sense, Heikki thought, but I don't have to like your interfering. Nevertheless, she nodded, and touched the controls, easing the 'cat back out of the turnaround. "You got my message, then," she said aloud.

Alexieva nodded. "You got my name from Ser Ciceron, and you're looking for a guide to travel in the Massif, probably along the upper Asilas. Is that right?"

"Yes."

"Is this the Lo-Moth latac?"

"I've been hired to find the wreck, and salvage anything I can," Heikki answered, and darted a quick glance at the other woman. Alexieva was frowning, but whether it was answer or merely concentration was impossible to tell.

"You won't find anything," Alexieva said, after a moment.

"Why not?"

There was a fractional hesitation before the surveyor answered. "There's a native hominid, called an orc, that lives up on the Massif. If there were human remains, the orcs found them already—maybe ate them, if it was a breeding group that hasn't had contact with us before. Regardless, they'll have disturbed the wreck site. You'll have a hell of a time proving causes."

"My contract is primarily to find the crash site," Heikki said.

"Oh." Alexieva looked at her hands, folded too tightly in her lap, then looked up again as though she'd come to a decision. "Yes, I'd be interested in the job."

*But why go on about the orcs?* Heikki wondered. "The orcs didn't use to disturb machine remains," she said aloud, experimentally, and there was another little silence.

Heikki risked a sideways glance, to see Alexieva frowning warily at the blank communications console.

"Things've changed," the surveyor said at last, and Heikki frowned.

"How changed? And why?"

"Who knows why?" Alexieva shrugged. "Probably human intervention."

A good catchall explanation, Heikki thought, except that human beings don't go into the Massif on that large a scale. "Changed how?" she said again.

Again there was that slight hesitation, before Alexieva said, a fraction too loudly, "Nesting habits—they're moving into new areas."

"The orcs rear their young in caves," Heikki said calmly. "Of which there are a limited number on the Massif, giving the orcs a set of reasonably well-defined breeding grounds, each one of which is occupied by a single breeding troupe. Nesting habits outside the limited breeding area have always been widely varied, depending on the available terrain. Orcs will cheerfully attack human beings who become separated from their vehicles, but have always shown a distinct aversion even to non-functional machinery, until and unless provoked into a killing frenzy." She looked sideways as she spoke, and saw dull color rising under Alexieva's tan.

"They've become less shy of machines lately," Alexieva said.

*And I think that's a lie*, Heikki thought. *It's a statement I'll look into, at any rate.* "Then I take it you're not interested in the job, after all."

"I didn't say that." Alexieva looked up sharply, frowning. Her cheeks were still red under the weathered tan.

"You surprise me," Heikki said, and waited.

"I simply wanted to be sure you were aware of the variables," Alexieva answered. "No, I would be interested in the work—at standard Guild rates, you were offering?"

*But would I be interested in hiring you?* Heikki wondered. An interesting question. "Guild rates are a little steep, especially on a world where—forgive me if I'm blunt—you're unlikely to have the latest equipment."

There was a little intake of breath from the woman beside her, but when Alexieva answered, her voice was unexpectedly mild. "That's true. I might be able to arrange a rebate."

Startled, Heikki glanced sideways again. Alexieva's expression was determinedly neutral, only her dark eyes and a tightness about her lips betraying any anger. *And she should be angry*, Heikki thought. *I've insulted her professionalism where a Precincter's usually most sensitive, the technology gap between the Loop and the Precincts. She must want this job damn badly.*

"My intent was to offer half the Guild rate," she said aloud—which was only half true, in any case, but should give some room for negotiation. "Plus a percentage of any success bonuses, of course."

"You'll accept a formal bid?" Alexieva asked.

"Of course."

"I'll have one for you tomorrow morning."

"I'll be glad to look at it," Heikki said. Somehow, she was not sure how or why, the balance of the interview had changed; Alexieva seemed suddenly to want the job far more than was reasonable. *And maybe I'm being unreasonable*, she told herself. *Maybe she needs the money badly—it wouldn't be the first time competent people have been beaten down to cut rates out here. If all she's been doing is boundary surveys, then she probably does need the money. Still, I think I'll ask at Lo-Moth if there's anyone else, since Ciceron didn't want to name anyone, and see if Sten can turn up anything.*

"Ah." Alexieva leaned forward in her seat, pointed toward a low-roofed, nondescript building. "This is the place, here."

Obediently, Heikki pulled the 'cat to a stop by the unmetalled side of the road, and manipulated the door controls. "It's been a pleasure talking to you," she said automatically, and saw Alexieva scowl as though she'd intended irony. Even then, however, the wiry woman controlled her temper, and slid gracefully from the 'cat.

"You'll receive my bid in the morning."

"I'm looking forward to it," Heikki answered, but Alexieva had already turned away and was hurrying across the dusty ground toward the building's single entrance. Thunder growled in the distance, and Heikki hastily shut the 'cat's door. The rain fell just as the seal cut in.

\* \* \*

The downpour began to slow as she eased the 'cat into the last series of turns that led to the Lo-Moth hostel. She made a face—perfect timing once again— and swung the 'cat onto the ramp of the underground entrance. Water sheeted up to either side, and she found herself hoping that at least one of Lo-Moth's employees had been in range. She shook that thought away, and concentrated on finding the workbay that had been reserved for her equipment. It was well-marked, and surprisingly convenient, within twenty-five meters both of the main cargo lift and the entrance to the hostel itself. It was also empty, except for the diagnostic computer sitting against one wall. So Sten's not back yet, she thought, and slid the 'cat neatly into the smallest of the available spaces.

Somewhat to her surprise, there was no attendant in sight. She levered herself out of the 'cat, half expecting someone to appear at any moment, and busied herself hooking the charger cables to the 'cat's capacitors. I wish Sten were back, she thought, and glanced around the enormous space. Most of the other bays were empty; those that were not had an oddly suspended look to them, as though the 'cats and triangle-wheeled crawlers had not been used in some time. And still there was no one in sight. *I wonder*, she thought suddenly, *if they did search our crates.* Kasib had put them in the sealed storage area, at the hostel's lowest level; it would be the work of a moment to find out. She glanced around again, this time looking for nonhuman surveillance, and was rewarded by the sight of two palm-sized cameras hung from the ceiling grid. One was focussed on her bay, the other on the entrance to the hostel. Quite deliberately, she stepped out of the first camera's range, and a third glided into view almost at once, swivelling from side to side in search of any movement. Right, then, she thought, and started boldly for the cargo lift.

Before she reached it, an almost invisible door opened in the wall beside it, and Kasib appeared. "Can I help you, Dam' Heikki?"

Several remarks sprang instantly to mind, and none of them were helpful. Heikki curbed herself sternly, and turned to face him. "Yes. I understand this leads to sealed storage?"

"Yes, Dam', that's right." Kasib's eyes were fixed on her unblinking, one hand in the pocket of his shapeless coveralls, and Heikki felt a sudden chill of fear. *He has a blaster,* she thought suddenly, irrationally, and cast about for something to say that would distract him.

"Will there be pallets down there, or will we have to use grav-units?"

"There'll be pallets if you want, or you can use the units," Kasib answered, his expression easing slightly. He slipped his hand from his pocket, hooked it instead in the loop of his empty toolbelt. In spite of herself, Heikki let out a sigh of relief, and knew he saw.

"Anything else, Dam'?"

Heikki shook her head, irrationally annoyed at her own fear. "No, that'll be all." She made herself turn her back on him, though the space between her shoulder blades tingled all the way to the hostel entrance. She sighed again as the door sealed itself behind her, her fear giving way completely to anger. *I'm behaving like an idiot, an inexperienced coward, jumping at shadows; it was impossible he had a blaster, or—if he had one— that he would use it. . . .* She paused then, just inside the archway leading to the hostel's main lobby, anger draining away. *I am not a fool, I've been in bad situations before—and I think he had his blaster in his hand then, ready to use it. It could've been security, but I want to make damn sure Sten knows about it before he goes down to collect our things.*

The lobby was empty of human beings, though a robot cleaner hummed to itself as it polished the mosaic floor. The concierge clicked and sprang to life as she passed its column, too-perfect voice saying, "Dam' Heikki."

She stopped, turning to face its cameras. "Yes?"

"There is a message cube waiting in your suite. A private and personal message arrived for you on the fast mail."

"Thanks," Heikki said, and then, because that was not a response the program would understand, "Its arrival has been noted."

"Thank you, Dam' Heikki." The machine went dormant again, leaving her alone in the empty space.

The unnerving quiet continued as she made her way across the lobby to the second bank of lifts, and all the way up to the fifth floor. *I can't think when I was last in a place this empty,* she thought—*if I ever was. It's not natural. . . .* But then she had reached the suite, and the cube that waited in the center of the living room floor. It was a standard mailgram, a block of super-tough translucent plastic, each of its faces a quarter-meter square. Santerese, Heikki thought, her spirits lifting in spite of herself, and crossed to the workroom to retrieve her personal remote. After a moment's hesitation, she brought the minisec as well, and triggered its field. She knelt on the thick carpet beside the cube, feeling across its unmarked faces for the shallow depression that would receive the key. When she'd found it, she sat back on her heels, adjusted the remote to her private mailcode, and laid it into the keyhole. The mailgram glowed, and projected a hissing cloud of static. Heikki sighed, and reached through the swirl of light to touch a second codesequence.

The picture cleared then, and the hiss became a familiar voice, backed by the gentle sound of waves. Santerese stood on what appeared to be a low balcony overlooking a pale grey beach and a brilliant blue ocean, twin moons hanging in the daylit sky behind her shoulder. There were single-sail boards in the water behind her, sport craft rather than anything useful, and strollers in brightly colored impractical draperies moved along the beach below. Despite her surroundings, Santerese was scowling, and Heikki's eyebrows rose.

"Well, doll," the projection said, "I guess you can see I'm not at the seamine, nor am I likely to be there. You won't believe this one, but apparently PAMCo is also owned by Tremoth Astrando, and they have some kind of corporate policy about not hiring one company twice on a job like this. They've got some locals who say they can do the work—" Her voice was brisk and contemptuous. "—so they've paid the cancellation fees and transport, and as an apology they offered me and Corsell a five-day at the better of the two resorts—which they also happen to own, by the way. I've accepted, and so has Corsell, but I don't mind telling you I'm pretty pissed."

The image paused then, Santerese visibly trying to calm herself. She forced a smile finally, and continued. "This means I'll be available if you want me for Iadara— let me know asap, I don't have to stay here, darling, that's for sure. I suppose I shouldn't complain, but it's a funny way to do business, if you ask me." Santerese paused again, her smile more natural now. "The Tremoth people were pretty decent about it all, gave me a long apology and explanation-of-policy, and sent a higher-up to do that, complete with staff. Speaking of which, do you have any kin who work for Tremoth? The guy's liaison was also named Heikki, Galler Heikki."

There was more to the message, but Heikki did not hear. *Oh, yes,* she thought, her mouth slewing sideways to keep in a bitter laugh, *I have kin who works for Tremoth, a brother, Marshallin, named Galler Heikki. My twin—and, oh, God, I did think I was rid of him, would never have to see the son of a bitch again. And I'll bet you money he was responsible for your losing the job, the little bastard. He could—would—have guessed, from the name, who your partner was, it's not exactly a common name. . . .* She shook those thoughts away, forcing the memory back where it belonged, and reached into the image to adjust the projection. The image blurred briefly, and then reformed.

"—Galler Heikki. Anyway, no big deal, but it would be like you not to mention a relative. Do let me know if I'm needed for Iadara." Santerese gestured vaguely at the scene around her. "This is all very nice, but a tiny bit dull. Love you, doll, and keep in contact." The image fuzzed, and vanished.

Heikki reached into the cone of light and picked up

the remote. The mailgram shut down automatically, and she did not restart it. Sent by mailship, she thought dully. *I suppose the Marshallin's making sure she gets to spend some time at this resort*—but she could not muster either amusement or annoyance about something so unimportant. *So Galler's back,* she thought, *and on Pleasaunce and in contact with my partner. Well, I'll do whatever's necessary to keep him from getting any closer.* She reached out then with reluctant decision, and triggered the erase function, wiping Santerese's message from the mailgram's memory.

"You fucking bastard, Galler," she said aloud, and set the cube outside the door for the cleaning robots to retrieve.

Djuro and Nkosi did not return for another two hours. Heikki spent the time hunting for other surveyor/guides, and culled three possible names from the directories. Two did not respond to her message of inquiry; the third seemed curiously reluctant to bid on the job. Heikki did not press the issue, but left name and numbers with the firm's junior partner. She turned her attention then to extracting the meteorological data from the disks Lo-Moth had provided, and setting up a crude simulation of the missing latac's flight path. Her answers did not match FourSquare's projections, deviating four degrees north of their line, and pushing almost a dozen kilometers further into the wayback: if her projection was right, FourSquare's course would have taken them well out of range of any visible remains. She smiled at the results, but could not muster more than a dour satisfaction. She copied her final results to a transfer file, and triggered the communications function. When the concierge program appeared, she gave it FitzGilbert's codes, and leaned back in her chair to wait.

The media wall lit within minutes, FitzGilbert's heavy-browed face superimposed on the mess of charts. *So we're still getting the first-class treatment,* Heikki thought, and nodded in greeting. "Dam' FitzGilbert, it's good of you to see me."

FitzGilbert grimaced. "I've a heavy schedule today, so let's keep this quick, please. What can I do for you?"

The words were brusque, but not intended to be actively rude, Heikki thought. "You said we could draw on Lo-Moth's staff if we needed. I've run a rough simulation; I'd like your people to check it for me—you must have a supercomp on line for crystal design."

FitzGilbert nodded, her hands busy out of camera range. She glanced down at an invisible workscreen, and said, "We can give you eight hours tonight, it looks like, if you have the material set up for us."

"I can flip it to you now."

"Do that."

Heikki nodded, and touched the keys that would transfer the contents of her working file to FitzGilbert's diskprinter. "You receive?"

"Copy received," FitzGilbert said, almost absently. "I'll pass it to Simulations right away. Is there anything else?"

"One other question," Heikki said. "I may have mentioned, I wanted to hire some local talent, a backup pilot and probably a guide of some kind. I had a pilot recommended to me, and he gave your name as a reference. The name was Sebasten-Januarias, Josep Laurens Sebasten-Januarias."

For a moment, she thought FitzGilbert would deny knowing the name, but then the other woman sighed. "Yes, I know him. He's a good pilot, one of the best. He doesn't like Lo-Moth, particularly, but he did good work for us. That good enough?"

Heikki nodded again. "How about a surveyor named Alexieva? Do you know her at all?"

FitzGilbert's head lifted slightly. "Now her I can speak for properly. She's the best there is, knows the wayback better than anybody on the planet. If she'll take the job, you'd be a fool not to hire her."

"Thanks," Heikki said, startled. "That was all I wanted to know."

The brief animation died from FitzGilbert's face. "I'll flip you the sim results as soon as they're available."

"Thanks," Heikki said again, but the other woman had already broken the connection. Heikki sat very still for a moment, then began mechanically to shut down the workroom. *So why is she pushing Alexieva?* she wondered. *Is she really that good, or is there something else going on?* She shook her head, suddenly angry. *I'll check with Ciceron again, and maybe with people at the port, or Jock's contacts, if he knows anybody on planet. Then we'll see.* She punched a final button, switching off the media wall, and stalked back into the living room. Djuro and Nkosi found her there an hour later, staring at the printed maps that showed the possible courses, stylus and shadowboard discarded on the floor beside her. She looked up as the door opened, and nodded, but said nothing.

"The rentals are set," Djuro said, after a moment. "Do you want to look over the papers?"

Heikki roused herself painfully, making an effort to put aside her bad mood. "Yeah. What did you get?"

"A standard jumper, like you asked for, capable of hauling a skyhook and a jungle crawler—with grav assist, of course," Djuro added, and Heikki gave a twisted smile.

"What's that add to the fuel costs?"

"Twenty per cent," Nkosi said, and when Heikki scowled, shrugged elaborately. "That is the usual factor—"

"I know that," Heikki snapped, and bit back the rest of her comment, well aware of the glance the two men exchanged when they thought she wasn't looking.

"Figuring in the exchange rates, we came in about fifteen hundred poa under your maximum," Djuro said after a moment.

Heikki nodded, and forced a smile, knowing she was being irrational. "Good," she said, and managed to sound as though she meant it. "Did you have a chance to check those references I gave you?"

"We both did," Djuro said, and Nkosi spread his hands.

"Heikki, who is this paragon? All the pilots say he is the best, and ten years younger than I."

"More like fifteen," Djuro interjected, smiling.

Nkosi gave him a look of disdain. "Which would make him a mere child, a baby. There must be something wrong with him."

Heikki smiled in spite of herself. "We can find out tonight. I asked him to dinner, so you'd both have a chance to meet him before I made a final offer."

"That was kind of you," Nkosi said, grinning, and Heikki gave a rueful smile.

"Well, if you can't work with him, that's my problem, isn't it? But I want to know what you both think."

"What about the surveyor?" Djuro asked.

Heikki sighed. "It's another weirdness, Sten. She wants the job more than she ought, and FitzGilbert was really pushing her. Of course, Ciceron said she was the best, too. . . ." She let her voice trail off, then went on with more confidence than she actually felt. "I'm going to wait and see what her bid comes in at. If there's anything funny there, we'll try someone else."

Djuro nodded agreement.

"One thing more." Heikki fumbled on the floor for the minisec, switched on its field. "When I brought the 'cat in, I started to go down to the storage, check on our stuff, but that guy who handled it, Kasib, was waiting, and I'm pretty sure he had a blaster. I want you both to watch your step around him."

"I checked the crates when we came in," Djuro said. "They've been opened. Nothing's missing, nothing's disturbed very much, but I'm sure someone went through them pretty closely."

"What the hell could they want?" Heikki said involuntarily, and waved the question aside. "Never mind, if you knew that—"

"—we would know whether we should dump the job," Nkosi finished for her, grinning.

Djuro looked at her, his lined face very serious. "I took a full photo-record, and I have pictures from before, too. I have evidence of tampering that will stand up in court."

"Are you saying we should pull out?" Heikki asked,

startled in spite of herself. Djuro had always been a grumbler, but this was something more than his usual worrying.

Djuro shook his head reluctantly. "No, not yet. But with your permission, Heikki, I want to put this evidence somewhere very safe, and not part of Lo-Moth."

"Do that," Heikki said. "If there's a Lloyds or a SwissNet on planet, that might work."

Djuro nodded. "And I'll send copies back to the office." He shook his head. "Let's hope we don't have to use it."

"Amen," Nkosi murmured, the smile for once gone from his lips.

"Dinner's at eight, evening," Heikki said, and switched off the minisec.

The hostel boasted a 'pointer-style dining area on its ground level, complete with private terraces and a fleet of service robots supervised by a human overseer. Despite the apparent emptiness of the hostel, Heikki was careful to reserve a table through the concierge, and was not surprised, when she and the others made their way down to the ground floor, to find the dining area busy, perhaps half the terraces occupied by medium-level functionaries. Sebasten-Januarias was there before them, very conspicuous in the loose coat and brightly-patterned headscarf, the only Firster in the comfortable bay, and Heikki's mouth twisted.

"Expecting trouble?" Djuro murmured at her side.

"I don't know," Heikki answered, and moved forward to meet the young man. He rose to greet her, but the hostel's overseer deftly interposed herself.

"Dam' Heikki? Your places are set, and I believe your guest has arrived." There was a slight, insulting stress on the word "believe."

Heikki ignored the woman in her turn, held out her hand to Sebasten-Januarias. "Glad you could make it."

"Thanks," the young man answered, and, unexpectedly, smiled.

Heikki smiled back gratefully, and nodded to her companions. "This is the rest of my permanent crew,

Jock Nkosi and Sten Djuro." As the three exchanged greetings, she turned at last to the overseer. "I think you said our places were ready?"

The woman at least had the grace not to show her chagrin. "Yes, Dam' Heikki. If you would follow me?"

"Of course."

The dining area was almost as luxurious as the hostel's publicity claimed, with semi-private terraces ringing a central public space where the tables stood on islands in an artificial lake. Most of those public tables were filled: corporate politics often required that its practitioners be seen making deals. Heikki cast a rather wistful glance at the nearest empty table—the careful geometry of the islands and the stepping stones that gave access to each one was more to her taste than the lush greenery of the terraces—but followed the overseer along the pool's edge to the area reserved for her. The low table was already set for the first course, a long platter of vegetables so artistically cut as to be almost unrecognizable set in its center, a tray with wine and glasses set discreetly to the side. A service robot sat inert to one side of the terrace; the overseer frowned discreetly at it, and reached into her pocket to trigger a remote. Lights flickered across the machine's face, and vanished. The overseer nodded, satisfied, and bowed to Heikki.

"If there's anything else we can do for you, Dam' Heikki, please inform us."

"Thank you," Heikki said, though privately she longed to demand some utter impossibility. "That'll do for now."

"Enjoy your meal," the overseer said demurely, and backed away.

"For God's sake, let's sit," Heikki said, and forced a smile to cover her sudden irritability. "Wine, everybody?"

"Yes, thank you," Sebasten-Januarias said, sounding more than ever like a child on his best behavior before the grown-ups, and the other two echoed him. Heikki filled the glasses—real star crystal, too, probably grown and cut from the rejects of the crystal houses—and handed them around. Nkosi darted a single glance at her, and turned his attention to the Iadaran.

"I am told by Heikki that you have been flying over the interior since you were very young."

"That's right, ser Nkosi." Sebasten-Januarias sounded reserved, and still absurdly young, Heikki thought, but not entirely wary. She sipped at her wine—it was quite good, just light enough—and leaned back in the padded chair, content to allow Nkosi to do the talking. She was aware that Djuro was watching her, and smiled benignly back at him, then glanced back at the others, only half hearing their conversation. It was dangerous to allow herself to be so put off her stride—and by what? The mention of the twin she had not thought of in years? That was foolish: Galler was nothing to her any more, had no more claim on her than she would make on him. The fact that he had met Santerese was unfortunate—no, not even that, not even something worth regretting. It had happened; she would explain it to Santerese when they met again.

She became aware suddenly that the conversation was flagging, and recalled herself to her duties as host. The platter of vegetables had been well picked over— mostly by Sebasten-Januarias, she thought, though Nkosi had run a close second. "Are we ready for the main course?" she asked, and when the others murmured agreement, pushed herself to her feet. "Next course, please."

The service robot trundled forward to remove the emptied dish. It carried it off into the greenery, and returned a moment later bearing a stack of place settings. It dealt them out with stiff grace, and vanished again. Heikki untied the ribbon that fastened the interlocking dishes. They were ceramic and crystal, rather than the usual plastic lacquers—more a product of the planet's wealth, Heikki thought, than of pointer ostentation. She glanced at Sebasten-Januarias, and saw her guess confirmed by his matter-of-fact handling of the pieces. The service robot appeared for a final time, this time carrying an enormous platter in three of its arms. It was an all-in-one meal, of the sort very popular in the Loop, but made with far more meat than was possible even for the richest 'pointers. It had been prepared with delicacy and skill, and Heikki found herself sniffing its subtle spices with real pleasure. It was her place, as host, to serve, but that was one of the social skills she had never fully mastered. She nodded instead to Nkosi, saying, "Jock, would you?"

"Of course," the pilot answered. The service robot, attentive to words and gestures, trundled toward him. Heikki poured out the second bottle of wine. When everyone had been served, she said, "You may leave the platter, thank you. That will be all."

The robot did as it was told, and rolled back to the edge of the terrace. Sebasten-Januarias said abruptly, "I was wondering—I've always wondered. 'Pointers are so polite to robots. Why?"

Heikki, who had fallen into 'pointer mode without thinking, blinked at him in some surprise. Djuro said, "They'll tell you it's because a robot's standing in for some person somewhere, and you wouldn't be rude to him/her. But it's really because if you get into the habit of being rude to anything, you'll find it very hard to be polite."

"You are a cynic, Sten," Nkosi said.

Sebasten-Januarias nodded thoughtfully. "That makes a lot of sense."

"You said you'd always wondered," Heikki said. "I didn't know you'd had much contact with people from the Loop."

"Not a lot," Sebasten-Januarias answered. "I have worked with off-worlders, though, and it's the sort of thing you notice."

"Since we're already on the subject," Heikki said, "I hope you won't mind my asking a few more questions." As she spoke, she reached into her pocket for the minisec, then triggered its field and set it in the center of the table. They were now cut off from the service robot, as well as from any likely eavesdroppers, but she guessed that it would be no hardship.

Sebasten-Januarias shook his head, his eyes suddenly wary again.

"For one thing," Heikki went on, "I heard a lot of talk about you, when I was looking for names—all good, except for one thing. Everyone told me you hated Lo-Moth, wouldn't work for them on a bet, and I know by now you're not stupid enough to think that working for me isn't the same as working for Lo-Moth. So what's going on?"

Sebasten-Januarias shrugged rather self-consciously. "Look, when I said I didn't want to work for Lo-Moth, what I meant was I didn't want to take a full-time job with them, something like that. I like working freelance, it keeps my options open. But I'm good, and people from the company kept asking, and I kept saying no. I don't mind having a bit of a reputation, because it stops people asking, or most of the time, anyway."

That attitude was familiar enough from her own childhood for Heikki simply to nod in agreement.

"I imagine it'd pay a lot better to work for Lo-Moth," Djuro said.

"Pay's not everything," Sebasten-Januarias retorted. "I make enough to live on, and I like being my own boss."

"Are you able, then, to make enough money outside the company?" Nkosi began, and waved his hands in apology. "I am sorry, that was rude. I have no right to pry."

Sebasten-Januarias shrugged. "No problem. I do all right." He gave a lopsided smile, its self-awareness robbing his words of bravado. "When you're the best around, you get work. Besides—" He hesitated for an instant, then looked straight at Djuro, defying him to laugh. "If ever I get to go off-world, I want to have the freedom, not be tied down by some contract."

"A very wise decision," Nkosi agreed. "I did much the same myself."

Heikki glanced at Djuro, lifting an eyebrow in question, and saw the little man nod in return. Nkosi saw it as well, and said, "Heikki, I think you must do it, you should hire him."

"I intend to," Heikki answered. "If you're willing, Jan."

Sebastaen-Januarias nodded slowly. "You were offering half the union scale, plus an eighth of any bonuses?"

It was not precisely a question, but Heikki answered anyway. "That's right."

"Then I'll accept—assuming the contract doesn't have any surprises, of course."

"I'll flip it to you in the morning," Heikki said. "If you can give me a number."

Sebasten-Januarias fumbled in the pockets of his enormous coat, and finally produced a crumpled slip of paper. "This'll reach me. It's at the field."

"Good enough," Heikki said. She reached across to switch off the minisec, saying as she did so, "If it meets with your approval, I'd like to talk to you about our search plans. Can you come by tomorrow at one?"

"I'll be there." The young man nodded.

"Good," Heikki said, and pocketed the minisec. The service robot trundled forward as she did so, and she waved it away. Only when the dinner was over and Sebasten-Januarias had left in an ancient fastcat did she wonder why the young man had not bothered to get himself a computer linkup of his own. Probably doesn't want to pay Lo-Moth any more than he has to for power, she decided. Everything in FirstTown runs off the company grid. You don't even know if he does live in FirstTown, a small voice whispered, at the back of her mind. She pushed it aside, and reached into her belt for the card that controlled the lift. The lobby was very empty, most of the corporate functionaries having left long before; even so, she lowered her voice a little as she ran the card across the sensor face.

"What did you think of him?"

"I like him," Nkosi said immediately. "I can work with him, that is quite certain. I think this will be fun."

*Oh, wonderful*, Heikki thought. She had been on other jobs when Nkosi had had fun with his work. "Sten?"

"He seems to have more sense than most," Djuro

said. "He'll do." He saw Heikki's grin and added, "All right, he'll more than do. I'm pleased."

"Good enough," Heikki said. "Then we'll settle with Alexieva in the morning, and see if we can't schedule a first overflight for—say, the day after tomorrow?"

Djuro nodded. "We can do that."

"Right, then," Heikki said, and punched open the door of the suite. She was more tired than she had expected, she realized belatedly, and had all she could do to stifle a jaw-cracking yawn. A light was flashing on the monitor cube. She glared at it, then manipulated the controls to transcribe the message to a storage disk unheard. "I'll deal with it in the morning," she said, when Djuro raised an eyebrow. "It's bound to be Alexieva's bid." She closed her bedroom door behind her without waiting for an answer.

When she ran the disk the next morning, however, the message proved to be from FitzGilbert instead. Heikki leaned back behind her workboard, a cup of the hostel's excellent coffee in her hands, and stared at the face projected on the media wall. She ran the message again, then a third time, and then sat staring at her empty screen.

"I take it that wasn't Alexieva's bid?"

Heikki turned, to find Djuro standing in the doorway, a cup of tea in one hand and a fresh message block in the other. "No," she said, and triggered the message again. "Somebody from Tremoth Astrando's on planet, and I'm summoned to a meeting."

"With a strong suggestion that you'd better have a team put together for this person," Djuro agreed. He held up the message block. "*This* is Alexieva's bid. It's good for us, on the low side, but not unreasonably so. Somebody really wants her on the team, Heikki."

"You noticed that," Heikki said, rather sourly. She took the message block from Djuro, plugged it into the workboard's socket, but let the data reel by without really looking at it. "What do you think, Sten?"

"I don't like it," Djuro said bluntly. "I don't think you should hire her if she were the last guide on planet."

"That's really reassuring," Heikki muttered. She glanced again at the figures, and said, more loudly, "But if not her, who? The other names I've unearthed are strangely uninterested, or at best don't answer my call. Lo-Moth wants me to have a full crew picked out and hired—and I can see why, it gives Tremoth less chance to interfere in what's Lo-Moth's affair. And, of course, I don't want to take the chance of anybody interfering with me."

"You're going to hire her, aren't you?" Djuro asked. His tone was unreadable, and Heikki glanced warily at him.

"I don't see that I have any other good choices. Alexieva is at least supposed to be the best."

"That's true enough." Djuro did not sound convinced.

"If I offer a provisional contract," Heikki said slowly, her fingers moving with sudden decision across her workboard, "and she accepts it, then I can say to FitzGilbert, and to this person from Tremoth, yes, I've got my team picked out, thank you very much, and I don't need any help from you. And I can still dump her if it doesn't work out."

"It could work," Djuro said, and sighed. "I think you're being a little paranoid about Tremoth, Heikki. Why should they interfere?"

Heikki looked at him and said nothing. The little man sighed again.

"All right. You're the boss, Heikki."

Heikki nodded. "I won't be able to be here to meet Jan. Can you and Jock handle that? Where is Jock, anyway?"

"Asleep."

"Oh." Heikki glanced at her workboard, already displaying the bones of a provisional contract, and ran her hand across the shadowboard beside it to throw a set of program menus onto the media wall. "All right. We should be getting some weather and course simulations that I asked FitzGilbert to run. I'm also getting Ciceron to run the same set, just to see how they compare. When those arrive, you and Jock go over them. I've made some preliminary notes, which are in the files, but I'd appreciate anything you two can come up with. Talk to Jan, too, see if he can add anything. I'm going to work on this contract."

"Whatever you say, boss," Djuro answered, and disappeared.

Heikki grimaced at her screen, and settled herself in for a long morning's work. She finished preparing a provisional contract and flipped it to Alexieva's mailcode, then copied her earlier simulations into another transfer file and dispatched that to Ciceron. The meteorologist came on line himself an hour or so later to discuss fees; they haggled for almost half an hour before settling on the usual rate for his sort of work. Nkosi appeared briefly, left the disk of rental contracts on the desk, and vanished again. The simulations results arrived from Lo-Moth—the corporate technicians confirmed her general conclusions, Heikki saw with some satisfaction, but had made some minor changes. She logged those, then tied her console into Lo-Moth's main library. As she'd expected, there was a set of survey-satellite photos of the most likely area of the massif—raw data, mostly, only a few frames processed around the time of the crash in a vain search for the wreck. She pulled up a program of her own, and set it searching through the accumulated material, looking for changes in the forest cover that might signal a crash clearing. The program produced nearly three dozen possibilities, but after several hours' work with her own battery of programs, she was able to narrow the possibilities to six. She skimmed through her final compilation once, then left the disk for Djuro, and headed for the workbay and her fastcat.

The trip to Lo-Moth's main headquarters took her back out through town, outside the Limit on the spaceport side. This was crysticulture country on a grand scale, the scrubland fading into glittering sand as it approached the distant bay. Sifters moved across the shifting ground, following courses marked by brightly colored flags. Their massive scoops grabbed up the first ten centimeters of topsoil, funneling it into electrostatic screens where the usable minerals were separated from the surface impurities, which were vented from chutes at the sides of the machines. The land in the wake of the sifters looked darker, almost tarnished. Heikki shook away the image almost angrily: the next good blow—and there would be one, at least one within each planetary year; that was a certainty, given Iadara's weather—would stir the darkness back into the sand, drive the sea up onto the land until it reached the edge of the scrub and even beyond, churning the loose soil until it was fit to be harvested again.

The road curved north a few kilometers further on, leaving the sands behind. The land showed scrub growth again, low-growing, fleshy-leaved plants that gave way quickly to the lusher growth of the plains. There were houses now, attached to the road by newly-metalled turn-offs, ostentatious single dwellings screened from the road and from the neighboring dozen-unit complexes by carefully tended screens of highgrass. This was mostly corporate land, and corporate housing; between the settlements, sunlight flamed from the mirror-bright walls of the enormous crystal sheds. Neilenn had been right, Heikki realized. Production had doubled or tripled, at the very least, since she had last been on planet.

Lo-Moth's headquarters complex lay at the heart of a little town, its streets and open parks laid out with a studied irregularity that was more artificial than the corporate rigidity it sought to avoid. Heikki swore to herself as she worked her way through the maze, damning all architects and city planners, but at last fetched up at the entrance to the headquarters complex. The securitron on duty at the main gate informed her blandly that she was expected, and gave her the guide frequency that would take her into the executive parking bay. Heikki thanked him with equal blandness, and let the flashing arrow in the windscreen guide her around and then through the cluster of towers. The mirrored glass cylinders reflected her fastcat back at her, and then reflected its reflection; she looked away, dizzied, and concentrated on the guiding arrow.

Neilenn was waiting for her in the parking bay, his hand running nervously over the electronics pad set into the high collar of his 'pointer-style jacket. Heikki swore again, silently, glancing down at her own too-casual dress, but composed herself to greet him with 'pointer courtesy.

"Ser Neilenn, it's good to see you."

"And you, Dam' Heikki," Neilenn answered, unsmiling. "If you'd come with me?"

Heikki's eyebrows rose, but she allowed herself to be led through the tangle of corridors, each one embellished with plates of half-grown crystal—slag crystal, flawed in the earliest stage of growth, useless but beautiful—and brightly polished metal. They passed through a plant-and-stream lobby, and then followed a circular stairway up to the next level. Glancing back, Heikki was suddenly aware of shapes, people, and security devices, concealed among the greenery. And why should they be watching me? she wondered. There were a dozen obvious answers, most of them having to do with corporate politics, and she didn't like any of them.

"Dam' Heikki." Neilenn came to a stop beside a brass-paneled door, one hand resting on the security box set into the wall beside it. "Dam' FitzGilbert is waiting for you."

"Thank you," Heikki said, and could not keep a certain tartness from her voice. She drew herself up, wishing once again that she were wearing something other than her four-paneled shift and high boots that were her usual exploration gear, but put aside that fear instantly. It would do her no good to arrive feeling inferior—that was a lesson she had learned long ago, and learned too well to forget now. Neilenn touched buttons on the panel, and the door slid back. Heikki took a deep breath, and stepped into air suddenly chill. She shivered in spite of herself, and glanced around quickly. FitzGilbert, standing beside a massive executive desk, greeted her with a strained smile. She seemed to be feeling the cold, too, Heikki thought; the other woman was wrapped in an incongruously heavy jacket that was trimmed with some sort of feathery fur. Then she saw the stranger, sitting at the desk, broad shoulders broadened further by the cut of his expensive jacket. He was sweating visibly, despite the chill. Used to a colder climate, Heikki thought, but did not speak.

FitzGilbert cleared her throat, and took a step forward. "Ser Slade, this is Gwynne Heikki, of Heikki-Santerese, the salvage company we've hired to try and clear up this mess. Dam' Heikki, this is Daulo Slade, a troubleshooter for our parent company."

Heikki murmured a polite response, trying to keep her face expressionless. Troubleshooters were just what their title implied, the people who solved problems for the mainline, Loop-based corporations—except that most troubleshooters' idea of solving a problem was to create other problems for other people.

"Dam' Heikki." Slade had risen to his feet at her approach. Light glinted from a pin clipped to his lapel: a green circle marked with three gold "R"s. *A Retroceder?* Heikki thought. *Damn, he must be good, if Tremoth's willing to tolerate that visible an eccentricity.* Slade stood now, frowning slightly, the expression barely raising a line on his rounded face. "Heikki. That name's familiar."

Heikki's stomach contracted. *Galler,* she thought, but kept silent, looking at the big man with an expression as innocent as she could make it.

"That's it," Slade said, "I had a publicity liaison, oh, not long ago, whose name was Heikki. Galler Heikki." The frown vanished, to be replaced by an enormous and unsettling smile. "Would he be any relation of yours, Dam' Heikki?"

"No," Heikki said, instinctively and irrationally, and in the next instant could have bitten her tongue for that stupidity. There was no point in lying; records were too good, and too easily checked, to make it worthwhile denying Galler. She hesitated, looking for some way to recover the situation, and Slade shrugged.

"I see. Not that it matters. Let's get down to business, shall we?"

"Certainly," Heikki said, and FitzGilbert stirred again.

"Ser Mikelis planned to join us if we could raise the main link. Shall I see if communications has managed it yet?"

"I doubt they have," Slade said, pleasantly enough, but with an edge that stopped FitzGilbert in her tracks. "The plant has been down since yesterday, and—forgive me, but your technicians don't seem to be very efficient in their repairs."

"We could use more up-to-date equipment," Fitz-Gilbert murmured, and Slade smiled again.

"I see the shoemaker's child still goes barefoot."

FitzGilbert flushed, barely restraining some profane retort. Slade's smile widened, and he turned his attention to Heikki. "Now, Dam' Heikki, please forgive me for being blunt, but I haven't much time to spend on planet. Would you mind my asking your plans for the recovery of our matrix crystal?"

"Not at all," Heikki answered, and was pleased with the academic detachment of her own voice. "I brought our—the firm's—best technician with us, and a senior pilot with whom we've worked in the past. We've hired a local pilot and guide as well, for back up—"

"If you don't mind," Slade interrupted. "Could you perhaps just give me a summary?"

"Whatever you want," Heikki said, suppressing her own annoyance. "We've run some simulations of the latac's course, and have mapped out an area for a preliminary aerial search. We've pulled in satellite data on the area—standard orbital survey material, both from before and after the crash—and have identified six possible sites. Once we've found the wreck, and I think the odds are that we will find the crash site within that preliminary area, then we'll either bring in equipment to analyze the wreck *in situ* or we'll fly out the remains and look at it here in Lowlands."

"I assume Lo-Moth has already run this sort of program," Slade said. "What makes you think you can find anything new?"

Heikki suppressed an angry answer only with an

effort. "Because this is what I do for a living. Look, I have either modified or have had written half a dozen programs that look through your raw data for the few trivial bits of information that will help me find what I'm looking for. Once those programs are running, I have to make decisions within the program—what it's looking for, whether a certain variable that meets the search parameters really is relevant or just noise—and I make those decisions based on twenty years' experience. Your people don't have the experience or the programs to do what I do."

Slade nodded again, oblivious to her anger. "What would cause you to decide to remove the wreck from the crash site? I would have thought an on-site analysis would be far more valuable."

"Any number of factors," Heikki answered, fighting for control, and in the same breath, FitzGilbert said, "Orcs."

"Orcs?" For a moment, Slade looked puzzled. "Oh. Your resident hominid."

His tone was faintly contemptuous, and Heikki struggled to keep her own voice steady. "That's the most likely reason we'd want to move the remains. If the site were awkward for any other reason, though, I'd move—after obtaining a full holographic record, of course."

"Of course." Slade sounded almost bored now. "Tell me, do you think this is a matter for internal affairs?"

"He means, was it sabotage," FitzGilbert interjected.

"I have no idea at this point," Heikki answered.

"You must have made some assumptions," Slade murmured.

Heikki stiffened. "I assumed the job was as advertised, Ser, and therefore that this was probably a case of bad weather bringing down a flight that should have kept to the coastal route. If you have any additional information, I would of course be grateful for it."

Slade shook his head. "None, Dam' Heikki, I assure you."

"Then I'll continue to go on the assumption that it was a routine accident."

"What will happen if it proves not to be routine?" Slade asked.

"That's really up to my employers," Heikki answered. "I assume Dam' FitzGilbert can tell you more about that."

Slade waved the answer aside. "I didn't mean in terms of company policy, I meant in terms of what you can do for us. If, for example, the LTA's crew were part of some conspiracy, is there any chance you could still find the wreck?"

Heikki nodded. "Oh, yes. It would probably take longer, but I think we'd find it in the end. Even a commando demolition charge would leave some traces—a multi-ton chunk of fused metals, for one."

FitzGilbert grinned at that, but said nothing.

"Under those circumstances, we wouldn't be able to tell you much beyond the fact that there had been sabotage," Heikki went on, "but even that's something."

"Quite." Slade pushed himself slowly to his feet, signalling the end of the interview. He was a big man, bigger than Heikki had realized, but there was muscle under the unfashionable softness. "I hope I'll be on planet long enough to receive at least a preliminary report first hand, Dam' Heikki."

It was an order, despite the velvet phrasing. Heikki smiled, and said, "I can't make any promises." Slade frowned, but before he could say anything more, Heikki had nodded to him and to FitzGilbert. "Dam-i-ser, good day."

On her return to the hostel, Heikki's temper was not improved by the announcement that Alexieva had accepted the provisional contract. She did her best to keep herself under control, but despite her best efforts snapped at Djuro until the little man raised his hands in surrender.

"What did you expect her to do?" he asked reasonably. "If you didn't want to hire her, you shouldn't've made the offer."

Heikki took a deep breath. "I know. Look, I'm sorry."

"What happened with this person from Tremoth?" Djuro asked, after a moment.

Heikki shrugged. "I think—" she began, and broke off, frowning now in puzzlement. "I'm not sure what he wanted, precisely. To find out how we were going about the job, certainly, but I don't know why he'd care. And I think I made a bad mistake dealing with him."

"Oh?" Djuro sat quite still, neither consoling nor condemning. Quite suddenly, Heikki wished Santerese were there instead, but put the thought aside.

"Yeah. He asked me if I had a brother, and I told him no."

"So?" Djuro said, after a moment.

Heikki looked up, briefly startled, then managed a rueful grin. "I do have one, you see. And he used to work for this troubleshooter—"

"I don't mind not knowing you've got a brother," Djuro said, "but you might've told me we were dealing with a troubleshooter."

"Sorry." Heikki spread her hands. "You'd expect them to send one, if the matrix is as important as they say."

"True. So why'd you tell him you didn't have a brother?" Djuro's voice was patience itself, but Heikki could hear the annoyance under the neutral words.

"Because I cut all contact with my family twenty years ago, because if I had a choice I wouldn't have a brother, and because I think of myself as not having a brother." Heikki glared at the monitor without really seeing the lights rippling across its surface. "I know I should've explained that, but there wasn't a chance."

"I doubt it'll matter," Djuro said, after a moment. "If it comes up again, you can always tell him what you told me. It's a good enough explanation."

"Thanks," Heikki said, rather sourly, and took a deep breath, putting aside the whole subject. "So, did you get the results from Ciceron? And where's Jock, anyway?"

"He and Jan went to look at the fliers we rented," Djuro answered. "The sims are in the boards, and we've worked out a tentative course. I spoke with Alexieva just before you came in, so I've got her input as well."

"Great," Heikki said, and reached for the nearest workboard. She fingered its miniature keyboard to display the projected course, traced its progress from the Lowlands airfield up across the scrub and then into the wayback, following the winding course of the Asilas river. The map program Djuro had been using was very good: the topography that unrolled beneath her fingers was almost uncannily like the land she remembered from her youth. "When do you think we can leave?"

"The day after tomorrow," Djuro answered promptly.

"Good. Get in touch with the others, have them meet us at the airfield at—when's sunrise?"

Djuro pulled out his data lens, glanced sideways into its depths. "Five fifty-six."

Heikki closed her eyes, trying to remember the weather tables she had studied on the journey to Iadara. The normal morning turbulence usually burned off within two hours of sunrise. "Have them meet us at the hangar at eight; we'll plan to take off at nine."

Djuro nodded. "You're the boss, Heikki."

"I know it," she said, but to empty air. She sighed, not entirely displeased, and reached again for the workboard, recalling the map. *It shouldn't be too bad a flight*, she thought, and started for the workroom.

# CHAPTER 5

The two Iadarans were waiting at the airfield, just outside the entrance to the control tower in the fitful shade of a canvas awning. The same hot wind that tossed the canvas up and sideways, snapping it against its grommets, sent little swirls of dust across the hard-metalled field. Heikki saw Nkosi pause, assessing its course and strength, then nod to himself and go on.

Alexieva lifted her hand in greeting as they approached, but did not otherwise move. Sebasten-Januarias, who had been squatting on the paving to her right, rose easily to his feet, Firster coat resettling in folds around his thin body. He wore the headscarf, too, spilling loosely across his shoulders, and Heikki saw Alexieva's grim face shift slightly, unreadably, as the younger man came forward to greet them. *Oh, Christ,* Heikki thought, *not that trouble again.*

Nkosi had seen that change of expression, too, and nodded to both Iadarans. "Let's get the pre-flight, Jan, shall we?" he said, and drew the younger man into the building in his wake.

131

"Is this everything you need?" Heikki stared at the single metal strapped crate that sat at Alexieva's feet.

"My mapping console and my disks," Alexieva answered. "I figured you'd have anything else I wanted."

*Let's hope so,* Heikki thought. *I wouldn't want to rely so obviously on the kindness of strangers.* She said aloud, "Load it with our stuff, then, and we'll start loading the jumper."

Alexieva obeyed without speaking, and perched herself and the crate on top of the equipment already piled on the ho-crawl's tow. Heikki glanced at Djuro, who said, "I'll bring the jumper around to the ramp."

"Coward," Heikki said, under her breath, and surprised a wry grin from the little man. She swung herself into the cab of the ho-crawl and turned it cautiously toward the access road, one hand on the brake to compensate for the drag of the tow. In the side mirror, she could see Alexieva balancing on top of the crates, and wondered why the guide had chosen such an awkward position. But then, the woman seemed uncomfortable around other people; Heikki shrugged to herself, and concentrated on bringing the ho-crawl and its tow to a stop alongside the waiting ramp. It was ready for use, locking legs down, conveyor belt already pointing into the sky at what looked to be the proper angle. Heikki smiled, and cut the engine. Its shrill whine faded, to be replaced by the deeper pulse of the jumper's multiple power plants as it nosed its way out of the hangar. Heikki swung herself out of the cab again, pulling her cups over her ears, and saw Alexieva wince at the growing noise.

"Get in the cab," Heikki called, and pointed broadly. The other woman frowned for a moment, then did as she was told. Heikki walked out onto the hard-metalled strip, squinting a little from the dust and the sun, and stood hands on hips, watching the big machine's approach. Djuro handled it well, for all he was not primarily a pilot—probably better than I could, she admitted. He had only two of the engines going, the baby nacelles at the end of each wing, but even so the power they developed was more than he needed just to pull the machine along the ground. Heikki could hear the notes of stress under the engines' steady beat. She could just make out Djuro's face behind the wind-screen's tinted glass.

The jumper was coming in a little crooked. She pointed to her right, then, as the machine corrected its course, nodded approval and gestured for him to keep coming. Djuro was already slowing before she signalled the stop; the machine slid neatly into place with its belly hatch directly opposite the loading ramp. Djuro shut down the engines—Heikki could almost hear relief in the dying sound—then popped the canopy and slid down the jumper's side without touching the recessed handholds.

"What do you think, Heikki?" he asked, and there was a note of pride in his voice.

"The ship or the docking?" Heikki asked, and beck-oned for Alexieva to come out of the ho-crawl. Then she relented. "They both look pretty good, actually. What's the interior volume like?"

"See for yourself," Djuro answered, still smiling, and started up the side of the ramp to unlock the belly hatch.

Heikki stood for a moment, staring up at the jumper. It was a standard six-engined biplane, of a design long renowned for its stability as a survey platform and—not incidentally—for its ability to survive a crash landing. It was not a fast machine, by any means, but it was both efficient and practical: it would more than do, for this trip.

Djuro had the hatch open now. Heikki swung herself up the ramp after him, leaving Alexieva standing silent on the metalled ground behind her, and ducked through the hatch into the belly of the ship. The work lights were on, casting a dull orange light through the empty space, and a solid wedge of light fell into the hold from the clear-roofed pilot's bubble.

"What do you think?" Djuro said again, out of the shadows.

Heikki took her time answering, turning slowly on her heel to survey the compartment. It was a standard set-up, with anchor points for equipment and crew fittings jutting from the beige-padded walls.

"Looks good," she said. "Let's get our stuff aboard."

She and Djuro had fitted out similar craft a hundred times before, and Alexieva proved more than willing to take orders. They had all the crates aboard by the time Nkosi and Sebasten-Januarias returned from the control tower, and were already fitting the first of the control consoles into place against the forward bulkhead. With two more pairs of hands, the rest of the procedure went quickly, the other consoles, the main and secondary sensor suites, the topographical scanner, Alexieva's maps, even the seats and padded benches that would double as bunks slotting into place with expected ease. When they had finished, Heikki stood for a moment, surveying the changed cabin, and then nodded to herself.

"It looks good," she said aloud. "I think we're ready, boys and girls."

Sebasten-Januarias let out a cheer, quickly suppressed. He looked at Nkosi instead, and said, "Do you want to lift on hover, or will you fly her out?"

"Fly," Nkosi answered instantly. "Why waste the chance, when we have all this space just waiting for us to use it?"

He did not say, did not need to say, that the heavy jumpers were notoriously less stable under the restricted power of the two variable-function engines. Heikki nodded her approval, and seated herself at the master console. It was set almost against the bulkhead separating the pilot's bubble from the main compartment, so that both pilots had to squeeze past her to reach their seats. However, the position gave her an unimpeded view of the other consoles, and of the projection tank laid out on the floor of the compartment. When that was lit, it would give her a realtime image of the terrain in range of the jumper's scanners. She ran her hands across her equipment, watching the checklights flicker, and slipped on the filament mike that would be her link with the rest of her crew.

"Does everyone hear me all right?" she said, on the general frequency, and heard the answers in her earphones as well as in the air around her. "Then we're ready when you are, Jock."

"I am getting clearance from the tower now," Nkosi answered. There was a moment's pause. "And we are cleared. All secure in the bay?"

Heikki glanced around one final time, making sure that all the seals were complete, that no telltale flash of red or emergency orange betrayed an incomplete connection, then looked at Djuro and Alexieva. Both nodded, and she said, "All secure in the bay, Jock. She's all yours."

"Then we are off," Nkosi said lightly, and a second later the first of the engines coughed to life. The jumper was well-screened against the outside noises; even so, by the time the sixth engine wound up to speed, Heikki had to swallow hard, and was grateful even for the minimal protection of her light earpieces. In an hour or two, she knew, the noise would fade into the background of her consciousness, but until then, it was an annoyance to be endured. The jumper lurched forward, then turned slow and reluctant, trundling toward its assigned runway. Heikki adjusted her frequency control until she had the tower, and listened idly while Nkosi ran through the final checkout procedure.

"Goodbye and good luck," the tower said at last, sounding almost indecently cheerful, and its last words were swallowed in the sudden roar as Nkosi opened the throttles. The jumper started forward, swaying on its heavy wheels, jouncing along the metalled runway for what always seemed a dangerously long time. Even though she knew from years of experience just how long it took one of these craft to become airborne, Heikki found her hands growing white-knuckled on the arms of her seat.

Then, reluctantly, the jumper lumbered into the air. Nkosi's voice sounded in the headpiece, "Everything looks green from here. We are starting our flight plan now."

"Good luck," Control said again, and the headpiece hissed with empty static.

Heikki winced, and adjusted her controls. The jumper still had a distinct angle—Nkosi had not yet brought it to their cruising altitude—but she switched on her console anyway. "I'm going to start calibrating now, Sten, Alexieva—do people call you anything for short?"

Even across the dim compartment, Heikki could see the one-shoulder shrug. "Not really."

"All right." Heikki looked down at her board. "I'm lighting the tank."

"Sensor input ready," Djuro answered.

"Then let's go." Heikki touched keys and the floor of the jumper seemed to disappear in front of her, to be replaced by a fuzzy, tilted image of the land over which they were passing. She frowned in concentration, touching buttons, and slowly the picture became clearer, until she could make out individual trees and the occasional building. "How does this match your maps?" she said, to Alexieva.

The dark woman bent over her console, her expression unreadable. "It matches my map 5b," she said, and an instant later bright red grid lines popped into being, hovering over the apparent countryside. "Which is as it should be. Of course, you won't get such a precise fit once we get into the wayback."

*I know that,* Heikki thought, and barely kept herself from saying it aloud. "Enhancements, Sten?" she asked, instead.

"This is infrared," Djuro answered promptly, and the image shifted, the buildings standing out in stark contrast to the land around them. "Metal concentrations, ionization, subsoil minerals—" He ran down a list of options, the image shifting with each new possibility. "Composite."

Heikki blinked at the chaotic image, and said, "Everything looks good on my board."

"Same here," Djuro answered, and returned to the real light projection. After a moment, Alexieva echoed him.

"So now we wait," Heikki said. This was the worst part of any job, the interminable travel—usually by slow-flying jumper—to get from the main base to the place where she could do the actual work. She curbed her impatience easily—both the impatience and her control of it were habits now—and leaned back in her chair, stretching her legs out into the aisle. There was nothing to do but wait.

The ground crept by in the tank's image, the clumps of thick-leafed small-jades that dominated the area around Lowlands gradually giving way to stands of giant jade and tree-tall reed grass. There were fewer farmsteads here, what few there were huddled along the lakes, bright as silver coins, that dotted the landscape. Alexieva muttered to herself at the map console, identifying each one. The lakes were linked by a network of little rivers, barely visible from this height, but drawn on Alexieva's maps like a filigree fan. Gradually, the lines of the fan drew together into three thicker lines, more clearly visible from the air: the Three Rivers that flowed from the Asilas, spilling around the enormous outcropping of Castle Knob. Centuries of wear, of the Asilas's water rushing past, had done little more than chip the edges of the volcanic plug; rather than carving a hole through it, the river had split around it, forming three new channels. A light was flashing from the top of the knob, and Heikki could see a light on her own console flashing in perfect synchronicity. She was receiving the beacon at Weather Station Green perfectly. She touched keys, checking her own course plot, and was not surprised to see the numbers match precisely.

There was a stirring behind her, and Nkosi stepped off the ladder and into the instrument bay. "We are just passing Castle Knob Beacon," he began, and then broke off, looking at the tank. "Ah, I see you have it. Good."

"Who's minding the store, Jock?" Djuro called.

"Jan, of course," Nkosi answered, managing to sound regally surprised.

"I'm glad you trust him," Djuro retorted.

"He has been flying us for the past hour," Nkosi answered. "Do you have any complaints?"

"Not me," Djuro answered, and bent his head over the controls. Nkosi nodded, and started for the toilet at the back of the compartment, walking straight through the image in the tank. It was a startling effect, as though he'd stepped through an empty space. Even Heikki, who'd seen the illusion more than once, caught her breath as he stepped into apparent nothingness, walking through and over the image of the beacon and the verdant hills as though they weren't there. And of course they're not, Heikki thought, not really, but she could not help holding her breath until he was safely on the other side. At the map console, Alexieva shook her head slowly, but said nothing.

Heikki cleared her throat as Nkosi emerged from the little compartment, made herself not watch as the pilot waded back through the image. "We're coming up on our first marker," she said, on the general frequency, and Alexieva nodded in hasty agreement.

"Yes, the falls, where the Asilas comes off the massif."

Nkosi paused at Heikki's console, staring over the woman's shoulder at the shifting image. "We do not actually make a course change here, do we?"

Heikki shook her head. "No, this is just to calibrate my instruments and Alexieva's maps. We follow the river another three hundred kilometers or so—" She touched keys again. "Three hundred seven point five, actually, and then turn onto the new heading. We'll cross the latac's verified course about an hour after that."

Nkosi nodded, still watching the tank, and then turned away. "I will let Jan fly us for a while, then," he said, over his shoulder, and disappeared into the bubble.

Heikki nodded back, and bent her attention to her console. So far, at least, Alexieva's maps and the terrain below seemed to match with better than average precision. She checked the last set of numbers, then leaned back in her chair. "It looks good, Alexieva. Everything checks out perfectly."

Unexpectedly, Alexieva smiled, the expression transforming her rather grim features. "Thanks. I spent about three years in the massif, mapping." Her face clouded again. "I didn't get very far, though."

"Grant money run out?" Heikki asked, not quite idly, and Alexieva shook her head.

"No, Lo-Moth ended the project. They were really only interested in mapping the edges of the massif—still are, for that matter. God knows, I've tried to get them to sponsor a trip to the center! But they say their flights don't cross the core, so there's no point in spending money on a really detailed survey."

"That sounds damn shortsighted of them," Djuro said.

Alexieva shrugged. "They've been pretty reluctant to spend money, ever since the home office changed management."

"Home office?" Heikki said. "Do you mean Tremoth, or the higher-ups at Lo-Moth?"

Alexieva looked down at her console as though she regretted having said even that much. "Tremoth, I guess. I don't really know—I only worked for them the once."

Heikki did not pursue the point, saying instead, "You'd think somebody would put up the money."

Alexieva shrugged again, the same sullen, one-shouldered movement Heikki had seen before. "Who's got it to spend?" She fingered her keyboard. "I'm switching maps."

Which was an effective end to the conversation, Heikki thought. She said nothing, however, merely noting the shift in her own records, and settled back in her chair to wait for the next course correction. The Asilas, a silver band almost two fingers wide, wound past in the tank, seeming to curve in time to the rhythmic drone of the engines. There was a flurry of movement on her board as they passed the Falls, looking from the air like a plume of smoke, and the jumper banked slightly, following the river's northeasterly curve. Heikki checked her calculations again, matching her course with the latac's last three position readings. They would intercept the first of those in a little more than two hours.

She sighed then, stretching, and pushed herself up out of her chair.

"Keep an eye on things, Sten," she said, and Djuro nodded. Satisfied, Heikki turned forward, pulling herself up the short ladder into the pilot's bubble.

Nkosi had the controls, and sat slumped in his chair, hands loose on the steering yoke, his eyes seemingly fixed on nothing at all. Sebasten-Januarias, in the left-hand seat, had his head turned toward the side of the bubble, but the direction of his gaze was hidden by his dark goggles. Iadara's sky curved overhead, its brassy blue darkened by altitude, touched here and there by thin wisps of cloud. The trees of the massif formed a dense and dark green floor beyond the jumper's nose, looking from the air like a coarsely knotted carpet. A lake flashed like a beacon as the sun caught it, and then disappeared again as the jumper slid forward. Heikki blinked, blinded as much by the lush beauty of the scene as by the brilliant sun, then cleared her throat.

"How's it going?" she asked, as much to let the pilots know she was there as to hear an answer to her question.

Sebasten-Januarias turned toward her quickly, then looked away again without answering. Nkosi said, without turning his head, "Not badly at all. I do not like the look of those, however."

He nodded toward the southeast, where a line of clouds showed like mountains on the horizon. Heikki leaned forward against the back of his chair, squinting past his shoulder at the distant shapes.

"What do you think, Jan?" she asked, after a moment.

The younger man shrugged, the goggles effectively hiding any changes of expression. "It's hard to tell. We don't usually get rain in the afternoon in the massif, not like you get around Lowlands."

"Is Station Green saying anything?" Heikki asked, and was not surprised when Sebasten-Januarias shook his head.

"Not yet."

"If we have to fly through them," Nkosi said, delicately stressing the word "if," "it will make it hard to hold a low altitude search. Of course, we can always work through the clouds."

*I know that*, Heikki thought, scowling. She realized she was tapping the back of Nkosi's chair, and stilled her fingers with an effort. "Sten," she said, on the general frequency, "I know you're tapping into Weather Station Green, but I want you to see if you can pick up Station Red Six as well. There's bit of cloud in the southeast I want to keep an eye on."

"No problem," Djuro answered promptly.

Heikki stayed in the bubble for a few moments longer, lulled by the sunlight and the steady drone of the engines. The ground, darker and less defined than its image in the tank, slid past almost imperceptibly, without many breaks in the vegetation by which she could gauge their progress. To the southeast, the clouds hung steady on the horizon, while the occasional thread of cloud whipped past overhead, borne on the high air currents.

"Heikki?" Djuro's voice in the headpiece woke her from her daze. "I'm monitoring Station Red Six like you asked. They're showing a line of rain, all right, which they predict will pass us to the south."

"Good enough," Heikki said, and was aware of Sebasten-Januarias's slow stare. He would have the right to say he told me so, she conceded silently, but to her surprise, the younger man said instead, "About how much longer till we turn onto the latac's course?"

Heikki glanced at the chronometer set into the control board. "About another hour," she said, and pushed herself away from Nkosi's chair. "We'll let you know, don't worry. Yell if you need anything, Jock."

"I will do that," Nkosi said, tranquilly, not taking his eyes from the distant horizon. Heikki, satisfied, slid back down the ladder into the bay, and reseated herself behind her console.

The last hour passed excruciatingly slowly, until Heikki found herself rerunning tests that had been redundant the first time. At last the flashing light that marked their position steadied into an amber circle, and a warning tone sounded in her ear. She touched the frequency selector, tuning her microphone to the general channel, and said, "Time, Jock."

"I see it," Nkosi answered. "Coming up on it—now." The jumper banked lazily, the image in the tank flickering briefly before the machinery adjusted to the new angle. "We are now on the new heading, flying by your wire, Heikki."

"You can start the descent to the search altitude whenever you're ready," Heikki said, and felt the jumper tilt forward slightly even before Nkosi acknowledged her order. She bent over her console, slaving the sensor array directly to her console, following the craft's progress on her line map as well as in the tank.

"We're coming up on the last reported position," Alexieva announced, and an instant later, Nkosi said, "We are steady at optimum search, Heikki. Cross winds are minimal."

"I confirm that," Djuro said.

His instruments were more sophisticated than the pilot's. Heikki nodded to herself, and took a last look at the array of lights covering her board. "Start scanning," she said aloud. "Full array. Alexieva, let me know if we deviate from the projected course. Take visual, Sten."

"We're right on the line," the surveyor answered.

"Scanners are on," Djuro announced. "And we're recording. I have the sight display."

Heikki did not bother to answer, watching her board flip from the array of green to the spectrum of brighter colors that displayed the sensors' readings of the terrain below. From this height, they could cover about a kilometer of ground with better than eighty-five percent accuracy; readings on the fringes of the web could extend almost three kilometers from the source, and occasionally as far as five, but with sharply decreasing accuracy. She frowned a little, studying the familiar pattern, spikes of blues and greens and almost-invisible purples, and adjusted her controls to sharpen the focus. It was a typical pattern, changed only slightly by local conditions, the fleshy leaves and trunks and the loam-covered forest floor providing a good contrast for any metal readings. And metal there would be, if—when— they found the latac: even if the craft had landed deliberately, retracting its enormous envelope, there was still the metal-ribbed gondola to betray the site to the probing beams. And if it had not, if it really had crashed, there would be strips of reflecting foil from the envelope to guide them in. Delicately, she played her controls, hunting along the narrow bandwidth that would show metal, fine tuning the machines so that even the fringes of the web would work at optimum resolution. In the tank, the forest floor crept by undisturbed.

"Jock, we're sliding off course, half a degree, now one degree to the south southeast," Alexieva said.

"Correcting," Nkosi answered, and the jumper tipped slightly. "Sorry about that, Heikki."

"No problem." Heikki's eyes were still on her console, flicking from the main readout, with its spiked lines of blue and green, to the course display and the tank and then to the spot analysis as it flashed its next string of symbols.

"How's it going?" Sebasten-Januarias's voice in her headpiece sounded rather lost.

"Nothing so far," Heikki answered, and was surprised to see how far they'd come along the latac's projected course. Even as she thought that, Alexieva cleared her throat.

"We're coming up on the projected crash site."

That was an elipse perhaps four kilometers long and three wide, the computers' best estimate of the latac's position when the full force of the storm hit it. Without waiting for orders, Nkosi swung the jumper into a slow search pattern, spiralling out from one focus of the elipse. Heikki frowned, and adjusted her sensors again, sending the fine-scan ghosting ahead of the jumper to probe the forest.

"I don't see anything," Djuro said. "What about you, Jock? Jan?"

"Not a thing," Nkosi said. "There is not a break in the canopy for kilometers."

"Same here," Sebasten-Januarias said.

Heikki glanced at her chronometer. The warning light had just begun to flash above the current time: two hours to sunset. "I'm not inclined to waste the time going back to Lowlands and then flying back out tomorrow," she said aloud. "Alexieva, is there any place nearby that we could set down for the night?"

There was a momentary silence while Alexieva worked her console, and then the surveyor answered, "There's a storm clearing about a hundred-twenty-five kilometers to the north. The last flyby was three months ago, and it was clear then. You'll have to land on rotors, though."

"Jock?" Heikki asked.

"I would prefer to land in daylight, if possible. Since we have to go to the rotors, that is."

"Right." Heikki adjusted her controls. "Flip me the coordinates, Alexieva."

The surveyor complied without speaking, and Heikki stared for a moment at the numbers flashing on her screen. It would take them about an hour to reach the storm clearing, a patch of land deliberately deforested to provide a safe harbor for any craft caught by bad weather while crossing the massif. That left them perhaps half an hour's further search, allowing for a safety cushion. . . . She sighed, and keyed a new course into her machines. It would take them to the clearing in a series of arcs, covering as much territory as possible before they were forced to set down for the night.

"Jock, I've got the new course for you." Without waiting for an answer, she flipped the numbers to his navigation computer.

"Very good, Heikki," Nkosi answered.

The land beneath the jumper changed slightly as they made their way slowly north, the giant-jades that dominated the massif's rim giving way to taller, needle-leaved blackwoods. Their trunks were more solid, the scalelike bark impregnated with minerals leached from the soil. Heikki scowled as her readings shifted, little peaks of red flashing up from the background, and adjusted the sensitivity of the analysands until the red no longer showed. It was necessary, she knew, but it cut her effective range back to three kilometers from the source. Frowning still, she began to swing her most sensitive instrument slowly through three hundred sixty degrees, trying to compensate for the loss of the general scan. Her display screen copied the movement faithfully, a wedge bright with detail sweeping steadily over the cooler general readings.

For what seemed an eternity, nothing changed. The chronometer ticked slowly forward, the warning light pulsing more strongly as sunset approached. In the tank, the visual display took on an odd, distorted quality as the ground shadows lengthened, and Djuro adjusted his instruments to compensate. The wedge of the fine-scan swept around the screen, bringing momentary detail to the picture. Then, at the far edge of the screen, metal flashed. For all that she had been anticipating just that, Heikki's reflexes were slowed by the afternoon of waiting. The red peak, almost off the scale in that single pulse, vanished. She swore, and worked her controls until she got it back. The intensity had already faded, as though the object were already out of range. She swore again, but managed to fix the coordinates precisely before the signal failed.

"Got something?" Djuro asked, and did not bother to keep his tone casual.

"I think so," Heikki answered, busy feeding coordinates to her navigation program. "Something, anyway. Jock, can we reach this spot before nightfall?"

It had been a forlorn hope at best, and she was not surprised when Nkosi answered, "No, Heikki, not a chance."

"We'll hit it in the morning, then," Heikki said, and kept an iron control over her voice.

"Do you think it's the latac?" Sebasten-Januarias asked.

"I didn't get much of a reading on it," Heikki answered. "I can't tell." But it was metal, and a lot of it, concentrated in one small area. *Unless it's another wreck, I don't know what else it could be.* She curbed her enthusiasm sternly, forcing herself to pay attention to the console in front of her. Already, she had missed the chance to fine-scan a dozen kilometers. She made a face, and applied herself to the work.

As predicted, the jumper came in sight of the storm clearing with the sun still a few degrees above the horizon. It was not an especially inviting place, just a break in the trees barely large enough to land a latac. As Nkosi circled slowly, assessing the difficulties, the tank in the main bay showed thin shoots of new trees already breaking through the dark ground.

"How's it look?" Heikki asked, after what seemed an interminable silence.

"We can land," Nkosi answered. "On rotors, of course, as you said, Alexieva, but we can land."

"Go ahead," Heikki said, and heard the engine note change as Nkosi began the switchover. The servos whined shrilly as the outboard nacelles tilted to their new positions, and the jumper shuddered under the new drag. There was a heartstopping moment when everything seemed to go silent, and the jumper seemed to hang suspended, held up only by momentum, and then the harsher sound of the rotors cut in. Slowly Nkosi increased their power, until forward motion stopped and the jumper was hovering a hundred meters above the floor of the clearing.

"Anything on the sensors, Sten?" Heikki asked.

Djuro shook his head. "Nothing of interest. Very small, mobile life—"

"Gerriks, probably," Alexieva said.

"—but nothing any bigger."

"You can take her down, Jock," Heikki said.

To her surprise, it was Sebasten-Januarias who answered, "Going down."

There was no reason Sebasten-Januarias shouldn't land the craft, Heikki knew—he had almost certainly made this kind of landing a hundred times, and it was for just that reason that she had hired him—but she found herself holding her breath anyway, until at last the jumper came to rest with a gentle thump. Sebasten-

Januarias cut the engines, and announced, over the descending whine of the rotors, "Well, here we are."

After the steady noise of the engines, the silence was almost oppressive. Heikki pushed herself up from her console and stood stretching, trying to shake off the irrational sense of unease. She heard footsteps on the ladder behind her, and then Nkosi slipped past her into the bay. A moment later, Sebasten-Januarias followed, still smiling with the pleasure of having completed a tricky maneuver. Heikki smiled back in spite of herself, and looked at Alexieva.

"What do we need to do here to secure the camp?"

The surveyor shrugged, both shoulders, this time, a freer, more relaxed gesture. "You didn't pick up any orcs on the way in, and they tend to avoid the clearings anyway. I'd want to put out barrier lights, though, just to discourage creepers."

Heikki nodded her agreement, and Nkosi said, "I will help you, if you like."

Alexieva looked momentarily startled, and then as though she were seeing the pilot for the first time. "Thanks," she said, after an almost imperceptible hesitation. "The lights are at the back."

Nkosi followed her toward the jumper's tail, walking blithely through the image in the tank, frozen now in an off-balance picture of the clearing, and they both vanished into the shadows outside the main lights. Heikki leaned back to her console to seal the day's recordings, and a moment later the tank vanished as Djuro finished closing down the console.

"That's that," he said, unnecessarily, and Heikki nodded. "I assume we're sleeping in the ship?"

"Absolutely," Heikki said, and saw Sebasten-Januarias grin.

"Pop the hatch, please," Alexieva called, and came back into the light, moving stiff shouldered under the weight of the barrier light units. Nkosi followed, four more units wedged into his enormous hands. Djuro worked the release, and the belly hatch sagged outward; at his nod, Sebasten-Januarias hurried to push it fully open. The ramp extended automatically, and the two headed down it into the clearing.

The air blowing in through the open hatch was very warm, and smelled sharp and green. Heikki breathed deep, teased by a vague memory, the suspicion that she had smelled that scent before, in some unpleasant context, but the thought faded before she could track it down. She shook herself, and crossed to the hatch, leaning out into the warm evening air.

The sun was down now, and the sky was fading rapidly toward night. The wind hissed through the blackwood needles with a noise like a dozen women whispering together in a distant room. The thin grass had been blown into tangles by their landing, and lay in knotted whorls; beyond the area affected by the rotors downwash, it lay in sleek waves, shaped by the prevailing winds. There were flowers, too, slender dark orange blossoms that grew four or five together from a cuplike circle of leaves. One lay almost at her feet, snapped by the ramp. *Death-trumpets*, she thought, and that was the smell, too, that had tugged at her memory. *Death-trumpets, the lovely insect-eater, perfect example of form and function:* she could still remember a company biologist, a friend of her parents', extolling the plant's virtues over dinner. The idea had frightened her, though she had understood that the death-trumpets could not consume a human being; Galler had seen a weakness, and grown pots of them on his windowsill, until overfeeding—there were too many insects in Lowlands— had killed them. She could still remember the mix of pleasure and disgust with which she'd watched their leaves turn yellow, their strong verdant odor giving way to the sicky stench of decaying, half digested strawflies.

She pushed the thought away, angry at its irrelevance, and made herself walk down the ramp and into the clearing. She made a quick circuit of the jumper, forcing herself to concentrate on checking the external systems while the light lasted, then turned back toward the hatch. Nkosi and Alexieva were there before her, the surveyor squatting over a junction box while Nkosi looked over her shoulder.

"Watch your eyes," Alexieva called, and Heikki looked obediently toward the jumper, one hand raised to shield her sight. Light flared behind her, forming a solid-seeming wall around the jumper. Heikki winced despite her protecting hand. Alexieva grimaced, and hastily adjusted the controls. The worst of the brilliance faded, refocussed outward; now the jumper was ringed with light no more dazzling than a fire, a light that cast multiple shadows across the tangled grass.

"Pretty impressive," Sebasten-Januarias said. He was standing in the hatch, a portable stove in his hands.

"I think the rations are self-heating," Alexieva said.

Sebasten-Januarias shrugged and came on down the ramp. At the bottom, he looked around for a moment before finding an almost bare spot of ground, then kicked at the bits of vegetation until he'd cleared a space for the stove. Setting it down, he said, "So? It's nice to have a fire."

"That is certainly true," Nkosi agreed, and moved to help him collect bits of debris for fuel. Alexieva eyed them expressionlessly, Heikki saw with some amusement, then went to join them, catching up a handful of dry grass as she passed. Then Djuro appeared in the hatch, balancing a stack of steaming ration trays. They ate in an oddly companionable silence, sitting cross-legged on the ground or on the edge of the ramp, while Sebasten-Januarias' fire crackled and spat in the open stove. It was full dark now, but the barrier units provided more than enough light. Looking up, Heikki saw that they drowned all but the brightest stars.

She stooped and picked up her emptied tray, suddenly aware of her own exhaustion. "I think I'll turn in," she said, to no one in particular, and saw Djuro nod in answer.

"Me, too."

"I think I will stay out for a while," Nkosi said. Alexieva looked up silently, and looked away.

"Seal the hatch and put on the monitors when you

come in," Heikki said, and started up the ramp into the main bay.

Sebasten-Januarias was there before them, already curled into a light-weight sleeping bag on one of the benches, his face turned to the jumper wall. Heikki grinned—it was funny how often the youngest members of her teams were the first to surrender to sleep— and threaded her way past the shut down consoles to the narrow storage rack at the back of the bay. She reached for her bag, twisting it deftly out of the clamps, and glanced along the bay wall. The best of the bunks was toward the nose, partially shielded by Djuro's console. *Boss's privilege*, she thought, and unrolled the bag onto the narrow pad. Djuro turned his back politely as she stripped off her four-panel shift, leaving herself in the loosely concealing undershirt. She tugged off her boots, rolling them up carefully so that nothing would crawl inside overnight—hardly necessary, inside the jumper, but a precaution so habitual that she would not sleep if she omitted it—and slid into the sleeping bag. The thermopack purred softly at her feet, adjusting itself to her body temperature and her sleeping preferences. She fell asleep listening to its gentle hum.

The hiss of the ramp jacks and the blast of sunlight from the newly opened hatch woke her the next morning. She swore, blinking balefully into the brightness, and heard Djuro echo her curse from the bunk behind hers.

"So sorry," Nkosi said, with patent insincerity. Heikki struggled upright in time to see him vanish into the light. She muttered another malediction, and reached for her shift, wriggling it ungracefully over her head. She ran her hands hastily through her hair, pushing it into a semblance of order, and slid out of the bag.

"Rise and shine," she said, not without malice, and prodded the nearest still-occupied bunk. Sebasten-Januarias emerged, looking rumpled, scrubbing at his eyes like a schoolboy.

"Breakfast," Alexieva announced, too cheerfully, and held out a stack of trays. Heikki accepted hers in decent silence—the premade coffee, for once, smelled almost drinkable—and retreated to her bunk. By the time she had eaten half of it, Nkosi had returned, carrying the first of the barrier lights. Alexieva fetched the rest, and then collected the ration trays and fed them into the compactor.

"What is the plan today, Heikki?" Nkosi asked, perching on the edge of the map console. Alexieva gave him a look, but did not order him away.

Heikki crossed to her own console and switched it on, calling up the metal reading she had gotten at the end of the previous day. "We got one sharp echo yesterday, just before we set down. First thing, I want to check that out; if it's nothing, then we'll proceed with the original search plan."

"What kind of reading?" Sebasten-Januarias asked. Three cups of coffee, downed in quick succession, had restored his good humor remarkably.

"I can't really tell," Heikki answered, and beckoned him over to see for himself. The young man squinted at the reddish spikes, and shook his head.

"Doesn't mean a thing to me."

"Don't feel bad," Djuro said. "It doesn't say much. Just that there's something metal out there." He looked at Heikki. "Want to give odds?"

It was an old game between them. Heikki paused, considering, and shook her head. "I don't know," she began, and then, seeing disappointment on the little man's face, made herself think. "Two to one against? It'd be too damn easy, Sten."

"Two to one against," Djuro echoed. "Bear witness, all of you."

Nkosi laughed. "And what are the stakes, this time?" Heikki shrugged. Djuro said, "Dinner?"

"No, how can that be two for one?" Nkosi objected.

"Heikki pays food and drink," Djuro said.

"Done," Heikki said. They shook hands, the Iadarans watching stone-faced. Heikki felt strangely foolish, especially under Alexieva's faintly disapproving stare, and was glad when Nkosi drew the surveyor aside, saying, "Please, Alex, show me the approximate course."

It took little time to stow the remaining sleeping bags
and prepare the jumper for flight. Nkosi lifted ship, this
time, easing the jumper into the air on the whining
rotors. He circled the clearing once, cautiously, before
switching to the main plant, then swung the jumper
onto a course that would bring them into scanning
range of the metallic contact in little over an hour.
Heikki, for all that she had given pessimistic odds,
found herself holding her breath as they came up on
the contact site, hoping in spite of herself.

Red spikes lanced across her board, shooting off the
scale, and she hastily adjusted the scanner to a lower
sensitivity. In the same instant, Djuro said, "Contact—
Jesus. I think you owe me dinner, Heikki."

"Let's wait and see," Heikki said, more calmly than
she felt. She switched screens, watching the numbers
shift across her board: the contact resolved itself into a
large, relatively solid mass, and several larger but far
less massive objects. *I think you may be right*, she
thought, but a caution as ingrained as superstition kept
her from voicing the thought aloud.

"There!" Alexieva said, pointing into the tank, and at
the same time both Sebasten-Januarias and Nkosi said,
"Balloon fabric!"

The tank flashed like lightning as sunlight was reflected
off the shreds of the latac's envelope into the cameras.
Djuro adjusted his equipment, muttering to himself.

"Hold this position," Heikki said, sliding out from behind
her console, and swung herself up to the pilot's bubble.

"Go to rotors?" Sebasten-Januarias asked, as she arrived, and Nkosi hesitated.

"Heikki, what do you think?"

"You're the pilot," Heikki answered, and Nkosi looked
again at his controls.

"Go ahead, make the changeover," he said, after a
moment. Heikki waited until they had completed the
maneuver and the jumper was steady, hovering over
the first tattered strip of thinmetal envelope, before
asking the crucial question. Already, she could see—
they could all see—the break in the forest up ahead

that must mark the gondola's resting place. She nodded to it, saying, "See if you can set us down there, Jock."

"I will do my best," Nkosi said. The jumper swung slowly toward the new clearing, turning to use the wind to help hold the craft steady in the air, and now they could all see the second and third scraps of envelope snagged in the treetops, the edges browned and ragged as though touched by fire.

"Christ," Sebasten-Januarias said, his face very pale. "That looks. . . ." He let his words trail off as though he could not bring himself to voice his suspicions.

Alexieva said it for him, hard-voiced. "That's blaster fire did that."

"Heikki," Djuro said, cutting through the younger pilot's confused protest, "I'm picking up lifesign, a lot of blips—I think it may be orcs."

"Let me see," Alexieva said, and there was a silence. Heikki imagined her peering over Djuro's shoulder, judging the numbers and the vague shapes on the little screen. "I think it is orcs, Heikki. About two kilometers off, and milling around. Something's upset them, that's for sure."

Heikki made a face, but did not answer at once, looking instead at Nkosi. "Can you land here?"

The pilot's answer was reassuringly prompt. "And take off again, too."

"Alexieva, will sonics keep off the orcs?" It was a long shot, Heikki knew: the old sonics had never been enough, but there was a chance that the newer models might do some good.

"It's possible," Alexieva said, after a moment, and Heikki could almost hear the shrug in her voice. "It's worth a try."

"Drop a pattern," Heikki said, "and once they're down—" She touched Nkosi's shoulder lightly. "—bring us in."

Nkosi circled the clearing twice before they dropped the sonics, giving them all time to study the wreck. The gondola lay at the far end of what had been a natural break in the forest, its rounded nose half buried in the ground at the foot of a well-grown blackwood. The tree was canted at a forty-five degree angle, half of its root system jutting into the air; two other trees, barely more than saplings, lay snapped in the gondola's wake. The ground in the clearing itself was churned and muddy, disturbed, Heikki thought suddenly, by more than the crash.

"I guess they were trying to land and overshot," Sebasten-Januarias said. He was still very pale, but his voice was under control.

"It looks that way," Heikki agreed. "What are the orcs doing, Sten?"

"Still holding off," Djuro answered.

Heikki made a face, studying the ground below as they swung past again. "Inform Lowlands tower that we've found the wreck," she said slowly, "broadcast the map coordinates and our official claim number. Make sure it goes out on a wide band, Sten."

"You got it," Djuro answered, his voice neutral.

Nkosi risked a glance over his shoulder. "You are taking chances."

"Am I?" Heikki said, stonefaced, and then relented. "Look, if this was a hijack, I want to be very sure everybody and their half-brother knows we found it, just so nobody decides to try the same trick on us on the way home."

"Lowlands control has acknowledged our claim," Djuro said. "I did a quick aerial scan, there's nothing up here within range except a scheduled commercial flight."

It was nice to work with people who anticipated her orders, Heikki thought. "You took the words right out of my mouth," she said aloud, and took a deep breath. "Let's drop the sonics, Alexieva, and then we'll go down."

The surveyor answered indistinctly, and a few moments later a light flared red on the central status board.

"The chute's open," Alexieva announced, almost in the same instant, sounding rather breathless, and then added, "First sonic's away. Dropping the second. And the third."

Heikki studied the pattern blossoming on Nkosi's small-scale display, her imagination transforming the throbbing points of light into bright orange parachutes supporting the half-meter cubes of the sonic deflectors. She watched them down—Alexieva's aim had been good; the cubes landed in a ragged line across the end of the clearing, falling between the wreck and the orcs—and rested a hand on Nkosi's shoulder.

"No more movement from the orcs," Djuro reported.

"Take her down, Jock," Heikki said, quietly. "But don't shut down till I tell you."

Nkosi grinned, clearly enjoying the challenge, his big hands easy on the controls. He brought the jumper down slowly, easing it into the space between the wall of trees to the west and the debris of the wreck, so that the craft seemed almost to float toward the ground. The wheels touched at last with a barely perceptible thump, so that Heikki had to look at the contact indicators to be sure they were down.

"Nice job," she said, and saw her admiration reflected in Sebasten-Januarias's eyes. "We're here," she went on, more loudly, and looked at Nkosi. "Jock, I want you to stay at the controls. Keep the engines running and ready to lift, just in case the sonics don't work. Jan, Sten, Alexieva, you'll come with me. Rig the detectors to warn us if the orcs start this way, Sten, and patch that into Jock's console."

"Do we go armed?" Alexieva asked flatly, and Heikki paused. She hadn't really considered the question, had simply assumed that the wreck would be what it so obviously appeared to be, abandoned and empty—and that, she thought irritably, could've been a really stupid mistake.

"Yes," she said aloud. "See to it, Sten. And break out the full-scan cameras."

"Right," Djuro answered.

The whine of the rotos eased a little, steadying on a note half an octave lower than its normal pitch. "I have us stabilized," Nkosi announced. "Shall I open the forward hatch?"

"Yes," Heikki answered, "and close it again—leave it on the latch—when we're gone." It wasn't much protection for the pilot, but at least it should be good enough to keep out orcs—if it came to that. She put the thought aside, and scrambled back down the ladder to the main bay. Sebasten-Januarias followed silently, wrapping his headscarf around his face as if to hide his thoughts.

Djuro was waiting with the two full-scan cameras and the heavy gunbelts, Alexieva at his side. The surveyor was carrying a blast-rifle at portarms—*not part of my equipment*, Heikki thought, and glanced at Djuro. Before the little man could answer, Alexieva said, "I figured it'd be safer."

"All right," Heikki said. Like most salvage operators, she was not fond of heavy weaponry—too often, it caused the very trouble a glib tongue could easily avert— but in this case she had to admit that the other woman was right. She accepted her own belt, and fastened it around her waist, very aware of the warmth of the blaster against her hip. She checked the spare power packs automatically, then shrugged on the camera harness. Djuro plugged the leads into the power pack, and turned for her to do the same for him.

"All set," he said, and Heikki nodded.

"Let's go."

The downdraft from the rotos raised a low cloud of dust even from the heavy soil, and swirled what was left of the grass into twisted knots. Heikki ducked through the blasting wind, then turned slowly, letting the camera record the clearing and the jumper. The row of lights glowed green in her lens: all the systems were running, recording the scene at half a dozen levels. She nodded to herself, and switched the camera to automatic, leaving her right hand free for her blaster.

"Crawler tracks!"

Heikki looked up quickly at the sound of Sebasten-Januarias's voice. The younger man was standing to one side of the clearing, almost inside the range of the nearest sonic. He made an eloquent face, but he did not move away. Heikki moved to join him, wincing as she, too, came within the sonic's arc. The beam was inaudible, tuned as it was to affect a non-human nervous system, but she could feel the almost-vibration, an unpleasant pins-and-needles tingling, on her exposed skin.

"See? There," Sebasten-Januarias said, and pointed.

To his right, running from the forest into the clearing, the familiar marks of a track-crawler showed stark against the dark mud. Automatically, Heikki turned the camera on them, panning slowly along their entire length, then crouched to examine the tread patterns more closely.

"It looks like a standard machine," she said aloud, as much for the record as for the others' benefit. "An Isu, maybe, or a Tormacher."

"Lo-Moth uses both of them," Sebasten-Januarias said.

Heikki looked sharply at him. "What do you mean?"

The pilot shrugged. "The company uses them, and then sells them used. There's a lot of them on planet."

*No*, Heikki thought, *that may be true, but that's not what you mean. That I'm sure of.* She filed her questions, grimly determined not to let them go this time, and stood up, grunting under the weight of the camera. "We'll check out the gondola."

The metal teardrop lay crumpled against the half uprooted tree, the once-smooth curve of its nose smashed inward. Heikki made a face, dreading what she would find, but kept the camera running as she circled the tail and its broken rudders to the main hatch. The thin skin around it was scored by drill beams; the hatch itself dangled from a single exploded hinge.

"Christ—" Djuro began, and bit off whatever he would have said.

Heikki took a deep breath, a familiar coldness settling over her. She had dealt with sabotage before, with hijackings, violence, and death; it could be no worse than the job on Galilee, or the time on Kavanaugh when she'd had to kill the poacher. She swept the camera over the burn marks, lingering on each one, and then on the broken hatch, saying in a voice she hardly recognized as her own, "I note for the record evidence of forced entry, probably effected by means of a standard issue laser drill."

Behind her, she heard Alexieva say something choked and inarticulate, but ignored it. She braced herself instead, hooking her hand carefully over the rough metal, and pulled herself up into the gondola. The floorplates, left unsecured to allow access to the cargo and ballast in an emergency, had been jarred loose by the crash, and lay at crazy angles like smashed paving stones. She balanced herself on the solid plate just inside the hatch, and panned slowly across the compartment. This had been an ordinary cargo latac; she was standing in what had been the main hold, between the tanks that should have held the gas for the envelope. That meant the distillery was underfoot, in the lower curve of the hull. The tanks had not ruptured, despite the gondola's dented frame. She glanced at the dials, and saw her guess confirmed: both the tanks had been almost empty at the time of the crash. They must've been trying to keep the envelope inflated, she thought. With those holes burned in it, meters-long, they could run the distillery at full, and still go through both tanks in no time, and crash. . . . She stopped that train of thought abruptly. There was still no proof that the ripped envelope had been destroyed before the crash; it was just as possible that it had been destroyed to help hide any sign of the wreck.

"I'm going forward," she said aloud, hearing still the coldness in her voice. "Jan, see if you can find the matrix."

"What's it look like?" Sebasten-Januarias asked. He made no protest at being left behind, and Heikki was remotely grateful.

"It should be in a quarter-crate," she answered, and at the same time Alexieva sketched a shape a meter or so square. "It'll be heavily padded." Sebasten-Januarias nodded, and Heikki turned away, starting across the rocking floorplates before she could change her mind.

The midships hatch was intact, dogged open against the unbroken bulkhead. She studied it for a moment, then methodically turned the camera on it.

"You think it was opened after the crash?" Djuro said, coming up behind her.

"I don't know," Heikki answered. "The stress analysis will tell us." *But I'd bet it was*, she thought, and stooped to examine the hatch frame more closely. Sure enough, the dull beige paint was scuffed and chipped, as though the hatch had been levered out of its seating. She recorded those marks as well, and ducked through the hatchway.

The technical compartment was as empty as the rest of the ship, though the buckled floorplates and broken screens betrayed that the frame had been twisted out of true. The crews' seats stood empty, trailing webs of safety harness; papers had blown around the compartment like leaves, and lay drifted in one downhill corner. The only other sign of life was a canvas shoe lying beside the hatch that led to the control room. She bent to pick it up, curious, and saw the glint of bone and the purpling flesh still in it. She straightened, her emotions shutting down completely, and heard Djuro say, "Heikki, look at this."

She turned as slowly as a sleepwalker. Djuro held up two pieces of a safety harness. "This was cut."

"Record it," Heikki said, and turned toward the control room. Remotely, she dreaded what she would find there, and so she did not hesitate, leaning through the crumpled frame into what was left of the compartment. The windscreen, which should have formed a quarter-sphere above the twin pilot stations, was bowed inward, almost on top of the twisted chairs. The heavy safety glass was crazed to transluscence, but had not shattered: a very minor mercy, Heikki thought. There were marks of fire along the forward walls, and smears of yellowing foam from the automatic extinguishers that had put it out. Probably short circuits in the consoles, she thought, automatically adjusting the camera to capture as much information as possible. There might be bits of bodies in the crumpled metal, but nothing larger, and she did not look too closely.

"Heikki." Nkosi's voice sounded in her earpiece, and she turned away from the burn-marked metal.

"Yes, Jock?"

"The orcs are moving back toward the clearing. I thought you would want to know."

That was an understatement, Heikki thought. "Are the sonics having any effect?"

"They are still on the fringe of the effective zone," Nkosi answered, "but I would say not. They are still coming toward us."

"How long?" Heikki asked.

Nkosi's voice was carefully casual. "Unless they slow down considerably, they will be here in about half an hour."

"You waited a while before letting us know," Heikki said, and could almost hear the pilot's shrug as he answered.

"I did not see any point in worrying you before it was necessary. And I thought you should have as much time as possible in the wreck."

"Right," Heikki said, grimly, and turned back to the technical compartment. "You heard that?" she began, and Djuro nodded.

"We heard."

"I think the orcs probably got the bodies," Alexieva said, her face pale but composed. Sebasten-Januarias was nowhere in sight. *Still back in the cargo section,* Heikki thought. *I hope.*

"They can tolerate a certain amount of human flesh in their diet," Alexieva went on, staring at the shoe that still lay against the forward bulkhead, "and they seem to like the taste. It's happened before, a breeding group using a wreck site as a secondary food source. They'll be sorry later, though, the young generally have problems on a long-term diet."

She was talking to stave off the horrors, Heikki knew, but there was no time for that now. "We've got twenty minutes," she said, riding over the other woman's words. "We need to find the crystal matrix—or be sure it's not on board." She lifted her voice to carry to the cargo bay. "Jan, found anything?"

There was a moment's silence, and then Sebasten-

Januarias leaned into the hatchway. "I think you should see this." His voice was tightly controlled. *Oh, God, more bodies*, Heikki thought, and followed him back into the bay.

Sebasten-Januarias had levered aside half a dozen of the distorted floor plates, stood now on the edge of the opening, the beam from his handlight playing on something in the wreckage below. Heikki glanced at Djuro, and saw the same mix of fear and disgust in his expression.

"What've you got?" she said aloud, keeping her voice deliberately neutral, and unclipped her own light from her belt. Sebasten-Januarias did not answer, and she stepped up beside him, training her own light on the hole. Light flared back at her, glittering as though from a hundred, a thousand tiny mirrors. She blinked, dazzled, and then realized what she was seeing. Someone—and who else could it have been but the hijackers?—had smashed everything in sight, everything moveable, and swept the fragments into the lower hull on top of the distillery. She swept her light slowly across the glinting field, picking out bits that might have been part of the instrumentation, something that might have been a tape player, something that gleamed white as picked bone. . . . She swallowed hard, and swung the light away again.

"Sten, get your camera over here, too," she said flatly, and trained her own machine on the field of debris. "Jan, Alexieva, I need more light."

The others obeyed without speaking, and for a long moment there was no sound in the compartment except the faint whisper of the cameras. "Full reel, Heikki," Djuro said at last, and Heikki glanced at her own indicator in some surprise. Ten seconds of disk left, she thought, and kept the machine going until the very end. She lowered the camera then, just as Sebasten-Januarias said, "Heikki, shouldn't we, I don't know, bring some of it back—?"

Heikki shook her head. "There's no time," she said, and tried to speak gently.

"We'll be back," Djuro said, "probably lift the whole thing out, right, Heikki?"

"Probably," Heikki agreed, and glanced at her lens. Almost in the same instant, Nkosi's voice said in her ears, "Heikki, you had best come back right now."

"On our way," Heikki answered, and collected the others with a glance. "You heard the man. Let's move."

The clearing seemed deceptively peaceful, empty except for the jumper at the far end, its rotos beating steadily against the breeze. Alexieva threw back her head, unslinging the blast-rifle she had been carrying across her shoulders; as if in answer, a sound like a throaty cough sounded from beyond the trees to their left.

"They're circling around the sonics," the surveyor said, quite calmly now. "Go on, I'll cover you."

"Right," Heikki said, and waved the others forward. She drew her own blaster and started after them, checking the charge as she moved. Alexieva backed after her, the blast-rifle levelled. They had covered perhaps two-thirds of the distance to the jumper when there was a movement in the trees to the left.

"Damnation," Alexieva said, quite distinctly, and fired twice. The short bursts kicked up smoke and dirt at the forest edge—she had fired quite deliberately into the ground, Heikki thought, with a sort of remote surprise.

"Keep moving," Alexieva called, and the first of the orcs edged out into the open. It was deceptively thin-limbed, a gangling biped, covered in mottled grey-green fur only a little lighter than the trees around it. It didn't look very impressive, Heikki thought, lifting her own blaster, and then the creature coughed again, baring enormous yellow tusks. Alexieva fired again, still into the ground, but the orc hesitated only for an instant before slipping sideways past the little plume of smoke. It moved very fast, limbs blurring. Heikki fired twice, and missed both times. A second orc appeared, and then a third, fanning out to try and get between the humans and their ship. More shapes moved behind them, slipping between the trees. Alexieva took careful aim then, and fired twice more. The leading orc dropped. The survivors shrieked, enraged, and then the nearer of the two dropped to all fours beside the corpse, sniffing at the body.

Alexieva let out a sigh of relief. "Let's go," she said, not taking her eyes off the orcs. The second survivor was sniffing at the corpse now; with a snarl, the first cuffed it away and began to feed.

Heikki lowered her blaster, and sprinted for the hatch, Alexieva at her heels. Djuro hauled them both into the jumper, and dogged the hatch behind them. "Get us out of here, Jock," he ordered, and Heikki echoed him, "Yeah, do it."

The engines whined up to lifting pitch, the sound rising a little more quickly than usual. Heikki, starting to struggle to her feet, felt the jumper lurch into the air, and sank back onto the padded floor plates until Nkosi had stabilized the craft. The jumper shot upward, tipped at a slight sideways angle, and did not steady until they were well above the forest canopy.

"Is everything all right down there?" Nkosi said, after a moment.

"Just fine, Jock," Heikki said, rather sourly, and Alexieva said, "I'm all right."

"Good," Nkosi answered. Heikki sighed, only too aware that she was shaking, and was glad to accept Djuro's hand to help her to her feet.

"Back to Lowlands, Jock," she said, and was too tired to care if the others heard the revulsion in her voice. "Take us home."

# CHAPTER 6

The flight back to Lowlands seemed interminable, despite the fact that this time they took the most direct route. Heikki did her best to concentrate on the numbing task of editing the cameras' data into a preliminary report, but by the time they landed at the Lowlands airfield, gliding down through the last of the afternoon's rain, she had barely pulled together a crude precis. She shook her head, collected the disks, and followed Djuro from the jumper.

The field was sunlit again, despite the stray raindrops, light lancing through gaps in the slowly dissipating clouds. A warm wind ruffled the surface of the puddles, and set the jumper's wings creaking faintly against their braces. Heikki looked toward the tower, shading her eyes against the low sun, and frowned. A low-slung car was sitting in the tower's shadow, its windows blanked against the sun. A familiar figure—FitzGilbert, Heikki thought—stood beside it, her hands jammed belligerently into the pockets of her long overcoat.

"What the hell?" Djuro said, softly, and Nkosi said, from the jumper's hatch, "Heikki, the tower says that Dam' FitzGilbert is waiting to speak with you."

"I see her," Heikki said, without inflection. "Did the tower say what she wants?"

"Of course not," Nkosi answered. "Did you expect they would?"

It wasn't an unreasonable question, Heikki thought, irritably, but said nothing. She stared instead at the waiting car, chewing thoughtfully on her lower lip. The two Iadarans, emerging from the jumper, started to say something, and then fell silent, watching her. Heikki made a face, fully aware of the others' stares, and jammed her hands into the pockets of her shift. "Wait here," she said abruptly, and started across the hot-metalled strip toward the car, heedless of the wind that whipped the shift's free-falling panels around her boottops.

FitzGilbert came to meet her, scowling, hands still buried in her pockets. "We got your message," she called, as soon as her voice could be expected to carry across the space between them. Heikki raised a hand in answer, but said nothing until they stood almost face to face. FitzGilbert was wearing corporate uniform beneath the overcoat, the well-tailored high-collared jacket and loose trousers seeming oddly out of place on the airfield. Her hair was braided up and back, held in place by a filigree net, invisible except when the sunlight caught it. Heikki was suddenly aware of her own disarray, of the undershift she'd slept in and the crumpled, well-worn shift, and her hair held back by a twist of cloth. She put that old inferiority aside, and made herself speak briskly.

"Then you know we found the latac."

"So you said. Did you find the matrix?"

Heikki raised an eyebrow. "No. What do you mean, 'so you said'? Has Lo-Moth lost so many craft that it can't keep track of the wrecks?"

FitzGilbert had the grace to look abashed. "Our—principal—oh, hell, our parent company—wants to be sure it is the right craft before they spend the money. They're being overcautious, but that's their right."

It was as close as FitzGilbert was likely to get to an apology, but Heikki was not appeased. "The serial numbers match, the crash site is damn close to the projected spot, and probably the foot we found can be matched to somebody's medical records. I should've brought that with me." FitzGilbert grimaced, and Heikki's temper snapped. "Jesus, do you think we're stupid, or just criminal?"

"I don't think either," FitzGilbert retorted, goaded, and stopped as abruptly as she'd begun, glancing over her shoulder toward the car. "You said you didn't find the matrix?"

Heikki shook her head. "Whoever brought down the latac smashed everything moveable, but I think they took the matrix with them."

FitzGilbert made a face, a tight movement on her lips that might have started out to be a bitter smile. "Our principal is taking the position that your job is done, now that you've found the site," she said, her voice once more under tight control.

"My contract with Lo-Moth," Heikki said, "hired me to analyze the wreck as well. And I think you might need that, considering."

"What do you mean?" FitzGilbert's eyes narrowed suspiciously.

Heikki allowed herself a crooked smile. "Like I said, your latac was shot down, FitzGilbert. There were burn marks on what was left of the envelope, and on the gondola. Somebody ripped a hole in their balloon, and watched them crash, then went in and smashed everything, possibly including the crew. Or else the orcs got them."

FitzGilbert shot her a look that would have melted steel, and Heikki was suddenly ashamed of herself. There was no point in taking out the day's frustrations on FitzGilbert, no point and any number of reasons not to. She made a face, trying to frame an apology, and the other woman shook her head. "All right," she said. "Did you find anything else?"

Heikki looked curiously at her, not knowing what she wanted, and FitzGilbert made a face. "Tracks, anything? Any trace of who?"

"There was one patch that showed crawler tread," Heikki answered, trying by the honesty of her answer to match the other's capitulation. "It was a standard make, probably an Isu or a Tormacher, nothing I could ID any better just by looking. We may be able to tell more when we've had a close look at the tapes, and at the wreck itself."

FitzGilbert swore under her breath, and turned away. "That's just what you won't be able to do," she said, and turned back toward the other woman. "Tremoth wants you to hand over your data and go home."

Put so baldly, the sheer ridiculousness of the request struck Heikki dumb. She stared for a moment, unable to believe what she had heard, and then, when Fitz-Gilbert did not deny it, drew a slow breath. "Do you mean to tell me that we're being fired?"

"Our principal's position," FitzGilbert said, slowly and with irony, "is that you have fulfilled the requirements of your contract. They are willing to pay you in full for your work, and to pay the applicable success bonus. Our principal feels that this is an internal matter, and best handled by internal security."

"What the fuck are you up to?" Heikki asked, and FitzGilbert stared back at her morosely.

"I wish to hell I knew."

Heikki took another deep breath, making herself count to ten and then to fifty before she spoke. "So you want me to hand over all my records, and the coordinates, and let you go to it."

"That's right." FitzGilbert looked away.

There was no choice, and Heikki knew it. Lo-Moth—or Tremoth, it's Tremoth that's stage-managing this—was willing to pay everything the contract called for, and that willingness robbed her of any reason to complain.

Except, of course, she added silently, for professional pride. "Your people, your labs, aren't experienced at this sort of thing," she began, and let her voice trail off as FitzGilbert managed a bitter smile.

"That's not the point," she said. "Whatever the point is, that's not it."

There was no one to appeal to, nowhere to lodge a protest. Heikki steadied her voice with an effort. "If you're determined, then," she said, and FitzGilbert nodded.

"Our principal is determined."

"Then I will flip you our raw data in the morning," Heikki said. "I expect to get vouchers for our full payment as soon as you receive the disks."

"That I can manage," FitzGilbert said, and turned away. Heikki watched her back to the car, squinting a little in the slanting light, and saw the door open and a shape lean forward to beckon the other woman inside. Even at a distance, she recognized Slade's blocky figure. She stood watching as the car drove away, wondering what had gone wrong, what the troubleshooter had against them, what convoluted internal politics were involved, then shook herself, slowly, and walked back to the jumper.

"What the hell was that all about?" Djuro asked.

Heikki smiled coldly. "We're off the job, Sten."

"What?" Djuro's shout was made up equally of disbelief and indignation.

Nkosi said, "That is not right—it is not reasonable behavior, Heikki, under any circumstances."

"That's putting it mildly," Alexieva muttered. She looked at Heikki, her expression suddenly very serious. "Whose idea was this? Not FitzGilbert's?"

*And what do you know about FitzGilbert?* Heikki thought, but held the question in abeyance for the moment. "I'm told the decision was made off-world."

"They did say Lo-Moth did itself in," Sebasten-Januarias said, carefully not looking at Alexieva. The surveyor scowled.

"What do you mean by that?"

Sebasten-Januarias gave her a limpid glance. "It was common talk when it happened, that Lo-Moth was responsible for the crash."

"It would have been nice to know that two days ago," Heikki said sourly, cutting off Alexieva's angry response. "Whatever happens, we're getting paid in full." Djuro looked up at that, and Heikki nodded. "Oh, yes, and I didn't even have to scream about it. They've asked us to turn over the disks as soon as possible; I told them I could have them ready tomorrow morning. We won't bother doing any analysis, we'll just hand them the raw data."

"You're just going to do it?" Sebasten-Januarias demanded.

"I don't have any choice," Heikki answered, and cut off further protest, saying, "Look, Jan, technically we don't have any cause for complaint. They're willing to pay our contract in full, even though we haven't completed the work. What can I object to?"

"So this is it," Alexieva said.

Heikki looked at her. "That's right."

"What are we supposed to do now?" Sebasten-Januarias asked, "Just go home?"

"I'll send your voucher tomorrow," Heikki said. "Unless you don't trust me?"

Sebasten-Januarias shook his head. "Tomorrow's fine." He turned on his heel, and stalked off toward the terminal.

"I'll be going, too," Alexieva said. Her voice was utterly without expression, but Heikki thought she glimpsed an unbudging anger in the other woman's eyes. She watched the surveyor walk away, and sighed slowly, the tension that had sustained her draining from her.

"So you're thinking of fighting this," Djuro said.

Heikki looked at him, startled, then gave a lopsided smile. "I've been considering our options, yeah. How'd you know?"

"Putting the innocents out of reach," the little man answered dryly, and surprised a laugh from her.

"Well, it wouldn't be right to get them into trouble with the company, not when they have to live here."

"Is there anything you—we—can do, do you think?" Nkosi asked, and Heikki shook her head slowly.

"I don't know. I just don't know."

The hostel was very quiet on their return, even the faint electronic murmurings of the concierge seeming somehow muted. Heikki led them through the silence to the lift, saying nothing until they were inside the suite and she had switched on the minisec. Even then, she sat very still, staring at the monitor cube, and tried to think of something that would take away the feeling of failure.

"I will make drinks, shall I?" Nkosi said, after a while, his voice sounding very loud and cheery after all the silence. He disappeared into the suite's kitchen without waiting for an answer; Heikki and Djuro sat listening for what seemed a very long time to the muted whirring of machines, before the pilot returned, bearing an enormous pitcher and three stacked plastic tumblers. He filled the glasses with exaggerated care, then handed one to each of the others. "I would like," he said, "to propose a toast. Murphy strikes again."

Heikki chuckled in spite of herself, and lifted her glass in answer.

"Murphy," Djuro said, the same wry smile on his face. They touched glasses solemnly, and Heikki took a long drink. It was one of the elaborate—and extremely potent—sweet-sour concoctions that Nkosi usually reserved for his women-of-the-moment, and she couldn't help raising an eyebrow.

"It is all I know how to make, these days," Nkosi said, with a shrug and a smile that were more boast than apology.

"I'm surprised anyone can function after one of these," Djuro said.

There was a little silence then, and Heikki cleared her throat. "All right. I figure we have the following options." She held up her hand, ticking each one off on her fingers as she spoke. "First, we can do nothing—

hand over the data and go home with our pay. Second, we can refuse the money, keep the disks, and file an official protest, probably with the Contracts Board."

"They'd laugh us off the Loop," Djuro muttered.

"Probably." Heikki allowed herself another lopsided smile. "Third, we can play for time—turn over copies of the data, or maybe even turn it over in installments, and put Malachy onto the contract itself, see if we have any legal recourse."

"On what grounds?" Nkosi asked softly.

Heikki shrugged. "I don't know, that's what I pay him to find out. But, damn it all, I don't like being thrown off a job for no reason."

"So that's your decision, then," Djuro said.

Heikki looked at him, trying to guess the emotions behind the neutral voice. "That's my recommendation," she said, after a moment, and stressed the word. "I'm open to suggestions."

"I'd like to know why we were bounced, that's all," Djuro said. "I think it's important."

"So would I—so do I," Heikki said.

Djuro went on as though she hadn't spoken, his tone still scrupulously uninflected. "After all, this could have more to do with Lo-Moth's politics—or Tremoth's—than any intention of insulting us."

Heikki looked down at her drink. She knew perfectly well what Djuro was saying, but shook her head irritably in rejection. "They've been jerking us around since we took the job. I don't think they should get away with it."

"Damn it, Heikki, there's nothing we can do about it," Djuro said.

Heikki took a deep breath, controlling her anger. "I grant you, not directly. Fine, we have to hand over the data, and I'm willing to do it. But I also think, given how strange this job has been right from the beginning, that we should keep certified copies of every disk, and put Malachy onto the question."

"You are thinking of suing Lo-Moth to make them show cause for ending the contract?" Nkosi asked.

Heikki nodded. "That's right," she said, and looked at Djuro. "It's self protection."

The little man shook his head. "You're the boss, Heikki."

That's right, Heikki thought. She said, suppressing her impatience, "I think we have to know, for the sake of our reputation, if nothing else. If they want to keep things quiet, that's fine, but I don't want us to suffer for it."

Djuro made a face, but nodded reluctantly. "You're right," he said, after a moment, and nodded again.

It was more than she had expected, and Heikki dipped her head in unspoken thanks. "I'm going to contact the Marshallin as soon as possible."

"There is a direct line available into the Loop," Nkosi said.

"Probably monitored," Djuro said.

"Quite possibly," Heikki agreed. "However, we're not doing anything wrong, remember? We're within our rights to check this out."

"I know," Djuro said softly. "I just don't like it."

At least he didn't remind her that he had objected to the job from the beginning. Heikki stood, feeling the past days' work in every muscle. "I'm going to try and get the Marshallin," she said, and went on into the workroom.

To her surprise, Iadara and EP Seven were roughly congruent, and there was an opening in the transmission queue. She gave the synchronizer Santerese's mailcodes and then her own bank payment code, wincing a little at the cost quoted her. Then there was nothing to do except wait, pacing, for the connection to be established. Nkosi appeared in the doorway, offering more to drink; Heikki let him refill her glass, and returned to the communications station.

It took a little less than an hour to establish contact, an unusually short turnaround. Heikki settled herself in front of the room's cameras, waiting with a familiar impatience while the media wall lit and slowly focussed. The image flickered steadily despite the compensating enhancements as the transmission passed through the distortion of the open warp, but it was all too recognizably Santerese. Heikki smiled, the day's events momentarily forgotten in the sheer pleasure of seeing Santerese again, and saw the same delight in the other woman's grin. Predictably, it was Santerese who spoke first.

"Well, doll, I was expecting to hear from you, but not like this." Her tone sharpened abruptly. "What's up? I was on the verge of calling you myself."

"Murphy's law, according to Jock," Heikki answered, and saw Santerese's smile widen. "We've lost our job, too—not precisely lost it," she amended, "since we're getting paid, but the effect is the same."

Quickly, she outlined what had happened, first the job and then Lo-Moth's reaction, and finished, "So I was wondering if you could get onto Malachy for me, have him check out our legal position." She hesitated, then said slowly, "Do you remember Idris Max?"

"The transit cop you were living with when I met you?" Santerese asked.

"We were roommates," Heikki said, with some annoyance, and Santerese gestured an apology.

"Sorry, doll. Do you want me to talk to him, too?"

"I think it might be useful. I hear he's with the Terran Enforcement now; he might be able to tell us if there's anything we ought to know about Tremoth."

"I'll do that," Santerese said, her hands already busy on a shadowscreen.

"So what were you going to call me about?" Heikki asked.

Santerese hesitated, finally said, with unwonted seriousness, "You remember I asked you if you had a relative, doll? Named Galler?"

Heikki paused in turn, not knowing what to say. This was not the way she would have chosen to explain things to Santerese, at a distance and over a flickering ultima line, but there was no evading the question. "Yes," she said at last, and couldn't think how to continue.

"Yes what?" Santerese said, after a moment. "Yes you remember, or yes, he's related?"

"Both," Heikki said. "I had—have—a twin brother named Galler. We lost contact a long time ago, and frankly I'd rather not regain it."

"It may be a little late for that," Santerese said. "When I got back from Pleasaunce, there was a message cube waiting for you, and the sender's listed as G. Heikki. So, unless you're sending yourself letters. . . ." She let her voice trail off.

Hardly likely, is it? Heikki thought, but bit back the angry comment. There was no blaming Santerese for this, only Galler—and only herself, for allowing herself to be found. She said, her voice strictly controlled, "What does he want?"

Even on the cloudy screen, she could see Santerese's shrug. "I don't know. The cube's palm-sealed, love, no way for me to play it. Do you want me to send it on, or do you think it can wait till you get back?"

"Let it wait," Heikki said. She paused then, considering, and ran her hand over the shadowscreen. It would take physical mail almost a ten-day to reach them—the main Iadaran FTLship had just made planet-fall, bringing Santerese's cube; the next scheduled landing was almost a week away—and by that time she and the others would be on their way back to the Loop. There was really only one other possibility. . . . "You know as many shadow-sides as I do," she said abruptly. "What's the odds of their fixing the seal?"

Santerese made a face at her through the pulsing static. "That's illegal," she said firmly, in a tone that was intended to remind her partner of the open line. When Heikki did not respond, she sighed. "It's the new model cube, Heikki. I doubt it could be done."

"Then it'll have to wait," Heikki answered. "We'll be home in a ten-day anyway."

"Good enough," Santerese said, and smiled. "I'm looking forward to it, doll."

Heikki smiled back, looking for an excuse to prolong the conversation despite the expense. There was none, and she knew it; her smile twisted slightly, and she said, "I think that's everything."

Santerese nodded with equal reluctance. "Nothing else here."

"Then transmission ends," Heikki said firmly, and watched the screen fade.

It took less than a day to make the necessary arrangements for their return to the Loop. A cargo FTLship on a semi-scheduled run was due to land at Lowlands in a little under a local week; as Iadara was its last stop before swinging back to Exchange Point Three, the captain was only too happy to fill her otherwise empty compartments with paying passengers. Somewhat to Heikki's surprise, Lo-Moth made no objection to covering the additional costs for equipment transfer—she had more than half expected to have to have the heavy crates shipped on a fully scheduled corporate flight. Maybe it was the fact that she had made no official objection to ending her job and handing over unedited, unanalyzed data; or maybe, she thought, with an inward frown, it was someone's—Mikelis's?—oblique apology for the situation. She put the thought aside as unimportant, and flipped the voucher numbers to the captain's agents back in the Loop. An hour later, the receipt numbers and confirmation were flashing on her screen, and the transport chits were in her diskprinter's basket. Heikki allowed herself a sigh of relief—she had been worried, irrationally, she knew, but undefinably uneasy—and locked the disks into her travel safe.

That left them with nothing to do but to wait for the cargo ship to land. Lo-Moth, through FitzGilbert, encouraged them to remain at the corporate hostel. Heikki hesitated, but could think of no reason to shift their quarters: the hostel was the most up-to-date transient housing on-planet, and there was no point in subjecting anyone else to her own prejudices. That decision made, she was more than a little annoyed when Nkosi announced blithely that he had made arrangements to fly out to the South-Shallow Islands with Alexieva.

"May one ask just what you expect to do there?" she asked, and blushed at the big man's grin. "Oh, never mind."

"As you wish, Heikki." Nkosi's expression sobered. "Besides, Alex has promised me the chance to brush up on my wavetop flying. It has been a while since I have had the opportunity, and I want to keep in practice."

*I bet*, Heikki thought, but bit back any further direct comment. "Have fun," she said instead, and thought Nkosi looked at least momentarily abashed.

Djuro, too, had found business elsewhere, renewing contact with an old acquaintance now an engineer on the transport *Carnegie*. Left more or less to herself, Heikki passed the time by running the raw data from the wreck through her own analysis programs. As she had expected, the results were inconclusive: the machines she had brought with her, the ones that would leave no record in Lo-Moth's systems, were simply not powerful enough to give her any kind of definite answer, and she was still prohibited from tying in to Lo-Moth's mainframes. When she had finished the last frustrating datarun, she sat for a long moment, staring at the empty workscreen. There were ways to get into the system—there were always ways—and maybe even to get the answers she wanted without risking being accused of a breach of contract, at the very least ways of getting what she wanted and getting off-planet before the intrusion was discovered. . . . It was a stupid idea, stupid and dangerous, she told herself firmly. Whatever was going on was part of Lo-Moth's internal politics, and not worth risking Heikki/Santerese's license over. Once she was back in the Loop, and once Malachy had analyzed the legal situation, then she could finish the job. She leaned over the workboard, typing in sequences that brought the mall menus onto the main screen, and spent an hour browsing through Lowlands' only bookstore. She took a certain perverse pleasure in sending the hostel's messenger service to pick up the freshly printed copies.

The suite's tiny kitchen had been restocked every day since their arrival, but, after a moment's hesitation, she turned away from the bright packages and used the main room console to order fresh-cooked food from the concierge. She felt vaguely guilty, less for the expense than for the indolence, but put that sternly aside. There was wine as well, in the wall bar; she decanted a smallish jug, and took it over to the suite's main window, dragging the most comfortable chair with her. The books and the food arrived together on an autotable, which positioned itself beside the chair and then shut down, only a single red light on its tiny control box still lit to show its dormant state. Heikki unwrapped the package of quick-print texts, smiling a little at the sharp pleasant scent of the new ink, and settled herself into the long chair. Santerese would laugh at her, she knew with a sharp pang of homesickness, tease her both for the adolescent indulgence, food and wine and books, and for the books themselves. She preferred—Santerese said needed—the carefully structured disorder of the classic mystery, the ultimately passionless passions, especially the stories set in the Loop and its maze of obligation and subtly conflicting rules. And analysis destroyed her pleasure, though she would never be free of the awareness: she put those thoughts aside, and settled down to read.

When she looked up again, the novel finished and the rules restored, the afternoon's storm was rising beyond the window, the thick blue-purple clouds making the yellow grass seem even brighter. As she watched, lightning slashed across the bank of clouds, a distinct and delicate tracery, but she was either too distant or the hostel was too well insulated for her to hear the thunder. She had seen storms before, and bigger ones; even so, she stared in fascination as the clouds swept up toward the zenith and the light changed, imagining in that shift of colors the sudden cooling of the air that was the breath of the storm. The lightning was closer now, and thunder was audible, low rumblings not quite absorbed by the hostel's thickened walls. The first gusts of rain rattled against the window. Heikki blinked, but kept watching, until the sheets of water obscured everything except the hostel's lawn.

The storm ended as quickly as it had risen. Djuro arrived with the returned sunlight, drenched and out of temper, and vanished into his bedroom. Heikki hid her grin, and disappeared into her own room with the rest of her books.

The concierge's beeping dragged her awake far too early the next morning. She swore, and groped for her remote, fumbling with its buttons until she had triggered first the room lights and then the little speaker next to her bed.

"Yes, what is it?" She didn't bother reminding the machine that she had requested it to hold her calls: only something important—or someone with the right codes—could override that particular program.

"A call for you, Dam' Heikki, from Dam' FitzGilbert." The machine-voice held only its programmed politeness. "She apologizes for disturbing you, but she says it's urgent."

Heikki shook herself, trying to banish the lingering sleep. "Please tell Dam' FitzGilbert I'll take her call in five minutes—on the workroom main line." She didn't know if the last instructions were necessary, but it couldn't hurt.

"Very good, Dam' Heikki," the concierge answered. "I'll convey your message."

"Thanks," Heikki said, sourly, and swung herself out of bed. There was no time for a shower; she pulled on loose trousers and shift, and made a beeline instead for the miniature kitchen. The coffee was premixed; she touched buttons, and a few moments later took a filled mug from the rack beneath the spigot.

"Heikki?" Djuro's querelous voice came from the door of his room. "What's going on?"

Heikki turned carefully, balancing the too-full mug. "A call from FitzGilbert. I don't know what about yet."

"God damn—" Djuro broke off as though they were still on the Loop. "Is Jock in yet?"

Heikki frowned at him. "No," she answered slowly,

and then hesitation sharpened into suspicion. "Why, what didn't he tell me?"

"Nothing, that I know of," Djuro answered. "I thought—hell, I don't quite know what, accident, maybe, or something like that."

"I don't think so," Heikki said, with only slightly more confidence than she actually felt. "FitzGilbert wouldn't be calling; that's the planetary police's job."

Djuro nodded, rubbing his eyes, then ran a hand over his bald head. "You're right, of course. I'm just not awake."

"Get yourself some coffee," Heikki said, "then perhaps you should listen in on this."

The buzzer sounded from the workroom before Djuro could answer. Heikki gave him a last abstracted smile, and turned away, her hand already busy on the remote, setting the acceptance sequence she would trigger as soon as she was in range. The wall lit, a window opening to present an image perhaps a little larger than life-size. It was like looking directly into FitzGilbert's office, and Heikki rubbed her chin thoughtfully, wondering just what sort of an image she herself presented.

FitzGilbert, discouragingly, looked as touchily ill-tempered as she always did, despite the early hour. "There's been a problem with one of your people," she began abruptly, and Heikki's stomach lurched.

"Nkosi?"

"No." FitzGilbert frowned, more puzzled now than irritated, snapped her fingers twice as though the noise would trigger her memory. "The other pilot—Sebasten-Januarias."

"Not exactly 'mine,' " Heikki said, automatically, and then frowned at her own cowardice. "I hired him here, on-planet. What's the problem?"

"He straggled in out of the wayback this morning," FitzGilbert answered. "Claims somebody tried to kill him."

At her back, Heikki heard Djuro's soft hiss, mingled surprise and anger, and said with a coldness she did not feel, "But what does this have to do with me? My job's over, remember?"

FitzGilbert's frown deepened again. "Ser Slade would like to see you. At once."

Heikki's eyebrows rose. "I beg your pardon?" The anger in her voice had been real, instinctive; she matched it deliberately. "It's just past the fifth hour, Dam' FitzGilbert—not an hour at which I am accustomed to doing business. Jan—Sebasten-Januarias has been paid off, his employment with me is over. I repeat, what the hell does this have to do with me?"

FitzGilbert grimaced. "Sebasten-Januarias was shot down—surface-to-air missile, a seeker—while taking a routine private-mail flight for a friend. Ser Slade would like to discuss the possibility that this may be connected with the attack on our latac."

Put that way, Heikki thought, the inquiry was not that unreasonable. "I can be at the headquarters complex in one hour," she said, and FitzGilbert lifted a hand.

"We can send a ho-crawl—"

"Thanks, I have my own transport," Heikki said.

"As you wish." FitzGilbert looked down at a shadow-screen, out of sight beneath the camera's sightline. "I'll have someone waiting to escort you."

"Thanks," Heikki said. "In an hour, then." She broke the connection without waiting for an answer.

"Damn," Djuro said softly. "I wonder if the kid's all right?"

Heikki made a face, embarrassed by her own negligence. "He walked out, she said. That's something." She took a deep breath, putting aside guilt as something less than useless. "Raise Jock—I think it's still middle night over the South-Shallow, that may help—and tell him what's happened. They're to get back here at once, taking all precautions."

"You think this Slade may be right?" Djuro asked, but he was already moving toward the communications console.

"I don't want to take the chance," Heikki answered. "Once you're sure he's on his way back, I want you to get over to the airfield, and find out what's going on, see what people are saying about this."

Djuro nodded. "Do you want me to try to track down Jan?"

"Yes," Heikki began, and then shook her head. "No, on second thought, better not. If it is because of the latac, the less contact he's had with us, the better. Just find out what the gossip is. And get Jock home."

Djuro gave her a lopsided smile. "I'll do that, boss."

"Thanks," Heikki said, and headed back to her room to dress.

This time, she didn't bother with the clothes a 'pointer would consider appropriate. The securitron on duty at the main gate glanced uneasily at her hastily-tied turban and unstylish shift, but the mention of her name brought him instantly to attention.

"Oh, Dam' Heikki. Ser Neilenn will be out to escort you at once."

"Thank you," Heikki said, and resigned herself to wait. To her surprise, however, Neilenn appeared within a few minutes: clearly, he'd been waiting somewhere close at hand.

"Dam' Heikki," Neilenn said, and bobbed a sort of greeting. "I'm so sorry to have to disturb you so early. . . ." His words trailed off unhappily, though Heikki could not tell precisely why.

She said, "It doesn't matter. I assume Slade is waiting?"

Neilenn bobbed his head again, and there was a note almost of relief in his voice. "Yes, Dam' Heikki. If you'll come with me, Timon will take care of your vehicle."

*So they don't want my 'cat inside the security perimeter,* Heikki thought. *I wonder why?* She said nothing, however, and followed Neilenn across the hard-metalled road to the waiting runabout. The little man lifted the passenger hatch politely, and Heikki swung herself into the low-slung seat. To her surprise, Neilenn settled himself behind the controls and touched the throttle gingerly. The runabout eased forward, and Neilenn gave her an apologetic glance.

"I'm afraid my driver isn't on duty yet."

Heikki made what she hoped was a sympathetic noise, her mind racing. She did not for an instant believe that Neilenn lacked the authority to wake up someone as junior as a driver, no matter how early—or late—it was. *No,* she thought, *he's been ordered not to use a driver— but why? To keep my meeting Slade a secret?* That was the only explanation that presented itself, but it didn't make much sense. She shook her head, and put the question aside for later, concentrating instead on the meeting at hand.

Neilenn brought the runabout to a halt beside one of the smaller towers, under a sunscreening canopy that hid the entrance from any observers in the neighboring buildings. Slade was waiting for her inside, in a second-floor room that overlooked the outer perimeter. The thin, sunblocking curtain was drawn back from the main window, letting in the light of the rising sun; the same sunlight gleamed from the roof of a crystal shed a thousand meters away, a blindingly bright rectangle well outside the circle of terrestrial green that marked the headquarters perimeter. Slade was staring at the shed, eyes narrowed against the light but his face otherwise expressionless. Heikki had one fleeting glimpse of that stillness, and then the man was turning toward her, his face taking on an expression of welcome. He was still wearing the Precincter button, clipped to the low side of his collar.

"Dam' Heikki, it was good of you to see me on such short notice. And so early in the day, too."

*So my protest was relayed,* Heikki thought, murmuring a politely meaningless response. *Well, too bad.* "I was concerned to hear about Sebasten-Januarias's accident," she said. *Better to make the first move directly,* she thought, *or he'll spend an hour dancing around whatever it is he wants.*

"If one can call it an accident," Slade murmured, a slight smile quirking his lips.

*Touche,* Heikki thought. "A seeker missile doesn't usually fall into that category, I grant you," she said aloud, "but I don't know what else to call it."

"I'll be frank with you," Slade began, and Heikki mentally braced herself for trickery. "All we know is the police report that Ser—Sebasten-Januarias?—filed this morning when the patrol picked him up. He claims his craft—I forget the type, some heavier-than-air model—was fired on from the ground as he crossed the Asilas below the massif; he took evasive action and was able to avoid the main explosion, though it damaged the ship. He made a crash landing, and walked back toward the nearest farming station, where he called for help. The police picked him up there this morning, as I said."

It was plausible enough, Heikki thought. The most common aircraft on Iadara were wood-framed douple-wings, propelled by a light, cool running Maximum Morris powerplant—not an easy target for the usual small-brained seeker missiles to follow. And the douple-wings were extremely forgiving in a crash—that was why they continued in use on Iadara and dozens of other Precinct worlds. The light frame would collapse and crumple on impact, but much of the force of a crash would be absorbed in the process. You could walk away from a smash-up that would kill you in any other craft. She became aware, tardily, that Slade was watching her curiously, and managed a shrugging smile. "I don't quite know what you want of me. I can see that you might be concerned that this has something to do with your crash, sure, but I can't for the life of me see what." Abruptly, she wished she had used some other metaphor.

Slade frowned. "The wrecked latac. Were there any signs, for example, that it had been hit by a seeker?"

Heikki suppressed a surge of malicious pleasure, and answered, "I really couldn't say, Ser Slade. After all, we only made the one visual examination, and that under less than ideal conditions. If we'd been able to finish the analysis, of course. . . . But I'm sure your own technicians will have the answers for you in a week or two."

"What's your guess, as a professional?" Slade's voice was untroubled, not in the least annoyed by her jibe, and Heikki hesitated, newly wary.

"I wouldn't rule it out," she said, after a moment. "Certainly, if I wanted to bring down a latac, a seeker's cheap and relatively efficient—the bigger powerplant makes a latac a lot better target than a douplewing's, for one thing. And there was nothing at the wreck site that would suggest otherwise. But it could also have been an on-board explosive, or even engine sabotage." Slade opened his mouth to say more, and Heikki spread her hands. "I'm sorry, Ser, I simply can't give you a better guess."

Slade sighed. "Fair enough, Dam' Heikki. As you say, our people will bring in their assessment soon enough." He paused, staring out the window at the distant crystal shed. Heikki watched him uneasily, not quite believing in his sudden abstraction.

"I suppose," he said, after a long moment, "this could be some—purely personal matter of the pilot's."

"It doesn't seem likely," Heikki said in spite of herself, and instantly wished she'd kept her mouth shut.

Slade looked curiously at her. "Why do you say that, Dam' Heikki?"

*Because nobody except a corporate stooge settles a private argument with a missile*, Heikki thought. She said, slowly, not quite sure why she was playing for time, "Certainly he never said or did anything that would lead me to believe he had that sort of enemy."

"But not that he had no enemies?" Slade nodded, almost approvingly.

*That wasn't what I meant*, Heikki thought, *and you know it. But I can see it would be very convenient for you to explain it that way, at least until you can figure out what happened to your latac. And right now, I don't see any reason not to give you what you want.* She said, "All I know about Jan is his professional reputation—which is excellent. I don't know anything about his private life."

"So you would not rule that out? As an explanation, I mean."

"I couldn't, no," Heikki answered. She was quite certain that Slade had noticed the changed verb, but the troubleshooter gave no overt sign of it.

"Mm." Slade turned away again, back toward the window. The light was fading as the sun rose into a thin haze of cloud, the shed roof no longer flaming against the dull green of the distant hill. "There is one other question, which I must apologize in advance for asking. Is there any possibility that this account is a fabrication, that Ser Sebasten-Januarias is using this to cover up, say, navigational or general error on his part?"

*That's going a little too far,* Heikki thought. *I'm willing to go along with you if you want to declare there's no connection with the latac crash—no harm to me either way—but I'm not about to see the kid's reputation destroyed.* "No possibility at all. He's too good to have to lie like that."

"I'm relieved to hear it," Slade said. He did not sound particularly relieved, merely thoughtful, and Heikki hid a frown of her own. *I have a nasty feeling,* she thought, *that I've just defined all too precisely just how far I'm willing to compromise.* It was not a pleasant thought.

"Well, it was a possibility that had to be mentioned," Slade said, with sudden affability. "I'm glad you think it can be discounted. And since you don't think this is necessarily connected with our crash. . . ." He let his voice trail off. When Heikki did not respond to the invitation, he smiled and continued, "I don't think we need be concerned unless further evidence turns up."

It was virtually an order, and Heikki could not quite hide her frown. "As you say," she answered, but knew the other heard the insincerity in her voice.

Slade touched the shadowscreen that lay discarded

on his desk, and a few moments later Neilenn tapped discreetly at the door.

"Ser Slade?"

"Would you see Dam' Heikki back to her 'cat, please, Jens?" Slade smiled. "Thank you for being willing to see me on such short notice, Dam' Heikki."

Despite her best intentions, Heikki choked on the formula of polite response. "Not at all," she managed at last, and saw Slade's smile waver. It was only for a fraction of a second, but she winced inwardly. Slade had never been less than an enemy, of that she felt sure, but now she had pushed him into something more than mere passive opposition. Damn all 'pointers, she thought, momentarily all Iadaran, and then common sense reasserted herself. She had obliquely insulted him, true, but she had also obliquely agreed to back him in his desire to keep the planetary police from connecting the attack on Sebasten-Januarias with the downed latac. Even if she'd annoyed him, he needed her for that—*and that should be enough to hold him*, she thought, *at least until we can get back to the Loop*. Still, she was frowning as she followed Neilenn back to his runabout, and the sense of unease did not leave her as she restarted the fastcat and eased it slowly out of the compound, moving against the stream of traffic arriving for the day shifts.

Her uneasiness did not abate as she brought the 'cat into the underground workbay. There was no point in it, she knew—she could not change what she had already done—but she could not help wishing she knew more about what had happened, and why Slade cared. Well, maybe Sten's picked up something, she thought, and levered herself up out of the 'cat. The underground level was relatively crowded, she saw with some relief, perhaps half a dozen vehicles of various types drawn into the bays, each one attended by a driver or two in loose-fitting coveralls badged with company logos at throat and shoulder. One or two looked up as she made her way toward the connecting archway, but no one seemed to be paying any particular attention to her arrival. As she reached the arch itself, however, she was joined by a stocky, good-looking woman whose dark-blue coveralls bore a silver crescent at the neck. Heikki gave her a polite smile, and was remotely pleased when the woman smiled back.

"Dam' Heikki?"

Heikki hesitated, and knew by the look in the other woman's eyes that it was too late to deny the identification. "That's right," she said, and wished she were carrying the blaster that was locked in her personal safe. Her hand crept toward the slit of her shift, and the knife sheathed at her thigh.

"Jan asked me to give you this." The woman lifted her arm fractionally, moving from the elbow, palm turned toward the floor. Heikki held out her own hand, and felt a thin packet, about the size of a minidisk but lighter, slip into her own palm.

"Thanks," Heikki began, but the other woman had already lengthened her step, was striding away toward the lobby. Heikki's eyebrows rose, but she suppressed the temptation to examine whatever it was she had been given, slipping it instead into the inner pocket of her belt. By the time she reached the lobby, the other woman had vanished. Heikki sighed, and made her way back to the suite.

Djuro was gone, as she had more than half expected he would be, only a light flashing on the message cube in the center of the main room. Heikki picked up the remote she had left by the door, and triggered the message, sighing to herself.

"I contacted Jock and Alexieva," Djuro's voice began, without preliminary. "They are returning as soon as it's light, taking all precautions. Jock estimates they'll be on the ground in Lowlands by the fourteenth hour. I'm heading down to the field myself, you can reach me through the beeper if you need me."

Heikki nodded as though Djuro could see her, and switched off the machine. Jock was coming in, and Sten was linked to her by the standard emergency channels: now that they were accounted for, she could turn her attention to the message Sebasten-Januarias had sent. If, of course, he did send it, she thought suddenly, and paused with her hand just touching the tight little packet. She shook herself, dismissing the thought as too fantastic even under the circumstances, and pulled out the message. It was not a disk, as she had expected, but a much-folded square of paper. She unfolded it, and frowned over the labored handwriting. *Need to talk to you*, she deciphered after a moment's study. *Will be at Uncle Chan's till midnight*. The signature was even less legible than the message itself, but at last she recognized *Jan* and the interlaced S and J.

She leaned back in her chair, chewing at her underlip. Sebasten-Januarias had to be worried, to send a written message rather than a disk or use the existing communal lines—unless, of course, it was a forgery. She shook her head slowly, unable to decide. She had never seen Sebasten-Januarias's handwriting, except for his signature on their contract. She pushed herself to her feet then, and went into the workroom, reaching for the disk file. She rifled through them until she found the one she wanted, and fed it into the reader. Her desk screen lit, and she touched keys to summon up the file she needed. Sebasten-Januarias's rather baroque signature filled the display window. She studied it, glancing from it to the written message and back again, then, still frowning, dismissed the file. They looked close enough to her, but she was no expert, and knew it. She stood for a moment longer, staring at the empty screen, then turned away abruptly. She was tired of waiting, of calculating and of caution.

"I'm going," she said aloud, and turned to unlock the safe before she could change her mind. The machine beeped softly to itself, and then released the lock. She slipped her blaster into its boottop holster, and laid Sebasten-Januarias's message in its place. Then she relocked the safe, and returned to the main room.

"Sten," she said, and touched the record button on the message cube. "Sten, if I'm not back by the fifteenth hour, take a look in the safe." She released the button and swept from the suite before she could change her mind.

Like anyone who'd spent any time on Iadara, she knew Uncle Chan's Bar. It stood in the heart of First-Town, a low, windowless, pink building just off the main through road. It was the meeting place as much as anything that had made her decide to believe the message, she realized, as she swung the 'cat back out of its bay. Not even Lo-Moth could expect to get away with murder in Uncle Chan's. Always assuming, a small, rational voice reminded her sourly, that Lo-Moth—or someone—does want to attack you, and that they'll wait until you get to Uncle's.

Traffic was light through the city—most of the day workers were already on the job, and it was too early for the leisured classes to be out of bed. Even so, it took her the better part of two hours to reach First-Town, and another dozen minutes to find a safe place to leave the fastcat. At last she found a lot where the guard looked as though she wouldn't sell the vehicles for spare parts, and slid the 'cat into a space between two ho-crawls. She gave the guard the fee in local scrip—credit was non-existent in a place like this—and started down the main street toward Uncle Chan's.

Purely by chance, she had chosen clothes that blended in with the prevailing Firster styles. No one seemed to be paying any particular attention to her; she relaxed a little, but kept a wary eye on the passers-by. She did not turn off the main street until she was sure no one was following her.

The pink-walled building looked as blank and foreboding as it ever had in her youth, and Heikki had consciously to remind herself that she was now of age, a legal patron of the bar. She was smiling rather wryly as she pushed through the door, and stood blinking in the sudden red light. The main room was not particularly crowded. Most of the private cubicles stood empty, curtains laced back, and the central tables were equally unoccupied. There were perhaps a dozen people still sitting at the wide bar, hunched over glasses and falqs: workers from the night shift, Heikki guessed, finishing a last drink before heading home to bed. There was no sign of Sebasten-Januarias. She frowned, and started for the bar, when a voice said, "Heikki?"

It was Sebasten-Januarias, and Heikki turned to see him standing in the arch of the nearest cubicle, the curtain held back with one hand. There was a bandage around his other hand, and a shiny patch of synthiskin on his forehead. Heikki winced in sympathy, and turned to join him.

"Are you all right?" she asked, and at the young man's nod slipped past him into the cubicle.

"More or less," Sebasten-Januarias answered, and let the heavy curtain fall behind him. He seated himself on the banquette opposite, favoring his bandaged hand. "So you heard what happened?"

"Part of it, at any rate," Heikki said. "Tell me anyway."

Sebasten-Januarias managed a wry grin, though the synthiskin crinkled painfully. "There's not much to tell, I'm afraid. A friend of mine came down sick, he has a mail run out to a couple of the mid-size farms, and he asked me to take the flight for him. I owe him a favor, so I said I would, and when I was on the last leg—the longest one, up to the edge of the massif—someone fired a seeker at me." He shrugged. "I caught it on the scanners in time, looped out and away, so it wasn't a direct hit. It knocked out most of the systems, though, and the main powerplant—I think a chunk of the casing holed it—and I had a hell of a time putting it down. I ended up in the treetops, spent the night in the bush, and walked out. The bus's irrecoverable."

Heikki nodded, impressed. It took a damn good pilot to survive at all, and a confident one not to brag about his brilliance afterward.

"But that's not what I wanted to talk to you about," Sebasten-Januarias said. He reached for the almost-empty glass in front of him, and Heikki saw that his uninjured hand was shaking. "A couple of days ago—a couple of days before Antoan asked me to take over for him—a man came out to the Last Shift looking for me. He said he wanted to hire me to do some mapping flights—he said he was a private surveyor, working for one of the truck farms."

Heikki nodded encouragingly. The massif, and the lands below, were still imperfectly surveyed, largely unsettled. More than one medium-scale farmer had made his fortune by clearing a secondary tract in the lower forests.

"What he really wanted to know about the wreck, what we'd found." Sebasten-Januarias stopped, shook his head. "I thought at first he just wanted gossip, but then he got nasty, and I lost my temper."

"What do you mean, he got nasty?" Heikki interjected.

The other shrugged, rather painfully, and did not meet her eyes. "He started saying we hadn't done the job right, that—well, that you'd been bought off, like FourSquare. And, like I said, I lost my temper and told him to go to hell. That's what I think caused all this."

Heikki's eyes narrowed. "Just what did you say to him, Jan?" she began, and Sebasten-Januarias cut in quickly.

"I said I had half a mind to go back out there myself, before the corporate goons could start messing around with the evidence." He made a face. "I know, it was a dumb thing to say—" He held up his bandaged hand. "—I mean, tell me how dumb!—but he made me mad."

"And the first time you flew out of the Lowlands control perimeter, someone took a shot at you," Heikki said slowly.

"Yeah." Sebasten-Januarias looked embarrassed again. "I was going to take some time off, figured I owed myself a vacation."

"Are you sure your friend—Antoan, was it—was really

sick?" Heikki asked. There was a vague picture forming in her mind, the details fuzzy, but the outline unpleasantly clear.

"Yes," Sebasten-Januarias began, but broke off. "I didn't check. Why should I?"

Heikki didn't bother answering, staring instead at the menu displayed beneath the table top. It was too early to be drinking, but a part of her wanted a glass of the harsh local whiskey, and the false calm it would bring.

"Antoan's one of us," Sebasten-Januarias said, a little too emphatically. "He wouldn't set me up."

"Maybe not intentionally," Heikki said, her mind elsewhere, and Sebasten-Januarias swore softly.

"How couldn't he intend it?"

Heikki looked up, belatedly remembering her responsibilities, and said, "He wouldn't've been told why—if he did fake being sick, that is—just offered money to do it. If I were setting it up, I'd say something like I wanted to see what kind of a pilot you are, without letting you know I was interested in hiring. That would work."

The younger man nodded grudgingly, somewhat appeased. "I guess it could happen that way."

"More important," Heikki said, "is what you do now."

"I somehow didn't think this was the end of it," Sebasten-Januarias muttered. "I was thinking I'd hole up with my cousins, out toward Retego Bay—"

"How were you planning on getting there?" Heikki asked.

The pilot shrugged, and swore, clutching his ribs with his good hand. "Fly myself, or hitchhike. All right, it wasn't that great an idea, but you know what Lowlands is like. Nothing's a secret here."

That had been true twenty years ago, Heikki thought, and some things didn't change. The Firster community was a small one, and despite its ideology was intricately intertwined with the corporate world. People talked—you didn't keep secrets from kin, after all—and inevitably Lo-Moth heard. It took time for information to make its way through the crooked channels, perhaps even enough time. "Be careful, Jan," she said aloud, wishing there was more she could do. "Thanks for telling me."

"You're welcome." Sebasten-Januarias hesitated. "Look, there's something else you need to know, about Alexieva. First, I don't like her. I'm saying that up front so you won't accuse me of being prejudiced. She's hard to get along with, and I don't like her. But she's also very close to Lo-Moth, too close for an independent, and she gets a lot of jobs from them that maybe she oughtn't on balance to get."

"We were told she was the best," Heikki said.

"She may be," Sebasten-Januarias retorted, "but she's also expensive, and Lo-Moth doesn't like paying top money for anything. Not on their own planet, anyway."

That was true enough. Heikki made a disgusted face, and looked away. *I knew there was something wrong when Alexieva agreed to that contract,* she thought. *I knew it, and I didn't have the sense to investigate. Damn, I should've listened to my instincts and not hired her in the first place. She can't be the only surveyor on Iadara.*

"She may be the only good surveyor on Iadara," she began, and Sebasten-Januarias cut in.

"That's just it, she isn't. There's Axt, and Karast, and Charlie Peng, for that matter, all just as good. Oh, she's an incomer, and that helps—not being Firster, I mean. But she always gets the recommendations and then the big jobs from Lo-Moth." He broke off, grimacing. "All right, maybe I'm not being fair. She is good, and there's no reason the company shouldn't recommend her. But she's just too damn close to them, that's all."

"Ciceron gave me one name," Heikki said, then shook herself. "Damn, I should've thought. Well, that explains how a weatherman got to be the Guild rep here. Lo-Moth must've put him in place, to look after their interests." It made sense when she thought about it, too much sense for her to have overlooked it in the first place. Of course off-worlder contract labor would prefer to go to their own guilds to find local help, and, equally, Lo-Moth would want to be sure their temporary employees hired only reliable locals. "Christ, I've been stupid." *Poor Jock*, she thought remotely. *He won't be happy to find out his latest playmate's a coporate hack.*

"I appreciate this," she said aloud. "Look, is there anything—?"

Sebasten-Januarias grinned. "Don't worry about me, Heikki. I can manage."

"I hope so," Heikki said, and pushed herself up from the table. In the doorway, she looked back, but Sebasten-Januarias was already gone.

By the time she returned to the suite, Djuro was there ahead of her, sitting with arms folded in front of the message cube. He looked up as she came in, his light eyes angry.

"What the hell was that all about?"

Heikki waved away the question. "Later," she said, and touched the button that would erase the message she had left. "Did you pick up any news?"

"Later, hell," Djuro began, and Heikki sighed.

"Let it go for a minute, Sten," she said. "What did you hear?"

The little man grimaced, and ran a hand over his bald head. "A lot of nothing. The Firsters are mad as hell, but no one seems to have any idea of what really happened. I think I must've heard half a dozen different stories—I don't suppose you know what's going on?"

Heikki gave a twisted smile. "I might." Quickly, she outlined Sebasten-Januarias's story, not adding her own suspicions. When she had finished, Djuro sighed again, looking up at her from under down-drawn eyebrows.

"You didn't hear all that from this—Ser Slade?"

"No," Heikki agreed. For an instant, she toyed with the idea of not saying anything more, but common sense prevailed. "I spoke to Jan, at a bar in First-Town—that's what the message I left you was all about. He told me what had happened."

Djuro muttered something through clenched teeth, but not loudly enough to force her to take notice. Instead, she fished her lens out of her belt. The chronometric display showed almost noon, and she went over to the little kitchen to mix herself a stiff drink.

The message cube lit a little before the fourteenth hour, and Djuro sprang to respond, data lens in his hand as he bent over the little display. Heikki waited until he straightened before saying, "Well?"

"I asked the tower to call me when Jock landed," Djuro answered. "He's down and safe, and taking a jitney here."

"A jitney?" Heikki frowned. "Is that wise, under the circumstances?"

Djuro shrugged. "It would take a lot of reprogramming, not to mention leaving tracks everywhere, to subvert a commercial jitney."

Nkosi arrived not long after, rumpled and cheerful and smelling faintly of sea salts. Alexieva, at his heels, looked far less cheerful, and more rumpled. Heikki, who was all too well aware of the pilot's apparently inexhaustible energy and equally insatiable curiosity, could almost find it in her heart to feel sorry for the other woman.

"So, what is all this about?" Nkosi unwound himself from his voluminous coat—a Firster coat, Heikki saw without surprise; Nkosi always managed to adopt something from each world he visited—and tossed it onto the nearest chair. "Do you really think this has to do with us, and with our job?"

"Yes," Heikki said shortly, not wanting to go into the details just at the moment.

"Then there is a double reason for doing what I wanted," Nkosi said, and glanced back over his shoulder at Alexieva. "We are travelling by freighter, are we not?" Heikki nodded reluctantly, already seeing where this would lead, and Nkosi continued, "Then there should be no difficulty arranging for Alex to share my cabin. Any extra fees I will pay, of course."

Alexieva made a noise that might have been protest, but Heikki spoke more quickly. "Hold it, Jock. You're telling me you want to bring Alexieva with you? Why?"

Nkosi frowned. "I should think that would be evident, especially now—"

"Did you plan to ask her before you found out about Jan?" Heikki went on.

Nkosi's frown was deeper now, but he kept his temper well in check. "As a matter of fact, yes. I had hoped to ask her, that she would accept—and what business is it of yours, Heikki?"

There was a warning in his tone, and in Alexieva's glare, but Heikki continued in spite of it. "Are you sure it was your idea, Jock?"

"What the hell are you getting at?" Nkosi's voice was deceptively soft, and very dangerous.

Heikki took a deep breath, controlling her own anger. "Look, Jock, I'm sorry, but I've got every reason to think that your friend here is a whole lot closer to Lo-Moth than she let us believe, and I'm not real happy about it. And I'm not real eager to take her back to the Loop with us."

Alexieva stirred again, but Nkosi silenced her with an outflung hand. "Do you have any proof of this, Heikki?"

"Circumstantial evidence, yeah." Heikki lifted her head at Nkosi's whispered curse. "And you know me, Jock. I don't make accusations lightly."

"No." Nkosi's temper faded as quickly as it had flared, and he turned back to Alexieva. "Well, Alex?"

"Well, what?" The surveyor's anger sounded convincing. "It's about time somebody asked me what I had to say."

"Well, what do you have to say?" Heikki murmured, and Alexieva shot her a look of pure loathing. Then she saw Nkosi's eyes on her, and controlled herself with an effort.

"I can see how people might say I worked for Lo-Moth," she said slowly. "Yes, I get a lot of jobs through them, and I have friends in the company. But I don't—spy—for them, if that's what you're accusing me of."

Nkosi looked toward Heikki, not convinced, quite, but wanting to believe. Heikki said reluctantly, "What about FitzGilbert?"

Alexieva flinched at that, and they all saw it, an involuntary and betraying movement of her shoulders. Heikki saw Nkosi's expression change, and Alexieva saw it, too. "Yes," she said abruptly, "I've done some private work for Dam' FitzGilbert, and, yes, she asked me to take this job as a favor to her. So what?"

"Why did she want you to take the job?" Heikki asked.

Alexieva looked again at Nkosi, a glance so rapid as to be unreadable, and answered promptly, "She wanted to be sure there wasn't another debacle like FourSquare. She thinks something's going on, and she wanted to have an independent observer—someone she could trust—along on the search."

*That makes a certain amount of sense,* Heikki thought, *and it fits the facts. And for some reason, I think I believe her.* She glanced at Djuro, lifting one eyebrow in question, and the little man nodded slowly. Nkosi was nodding, too.

"If this is true—and I do think it is, Heikki—Alex is still in danger here. I think she should come with us."

"I would like that," Alexieva said, low-voiced.

"What about your business?" Heikki asked.

"I have partners." Alexieva looked up, her mouth twisted in a bitter smile. "And what the hell good is a business, if you're too dead to run it?"

Nkosi grinned, his usual good humor reasserting itself. "You have a point."

"All right," Heikki said. "I'll see if the captain will take another passenger—Jock, you and Alexieva can work out the payment however you like."

"Thank you," Alexieva said.

Nkosi nodded. "I appreciate this, Heikki."

"I hope so," Heikki answered, but managed a smile to take the sting out of the words. Nkosi laughed, and vanished into his own room, Alexieva following. The door closed behind them, and Heikki shook her head, the smile fading.

"I hope I'm doing the right thing," she said, to no one in particular, and looked at Djuro. "What do you think, Sten?"

"About what Jan said?" Djuro asked, and shrugged when Heikki nodded. "I don't know. He could be jealous, you know."

"Of Alexieva?" Heikki couldn't keep the surprise out of her voice.

"Sure. Jock's a fine-looking man." Djuro's voice softened slightly. "And you don't see things like that even when they're right under your nose, Heikki."

Heikki smiled rather wryly, but had to admit the truth of that. "Maybe so. All right, put it down to jealousy, and we'll take her back to the Loop—but she can keep her distance once we're there."

# CHAPTER 7

As Heikki had expected, the freighter's captain was not unwilling to add two more passengers to her manifest, though she did add up the surcharges with an unholy glee. She had not expected that Nkosi would agree so meekly to his share of the outrageous price, but could not complain about the lack of protest. They were able to bring the equipment aboard without interference from Lo-Moth, though Heikki was somewhat surprised by the ease with which she evaded Fitz-Gilbert's offers of help. The voyage itself was uninteresting, and Heikki spent most of the time in her cabin, trying to sort out the crash data recorded on her disks. She was able to get somewhat further than she had on Iadara, but the captain was unable to spare her enough computer space to run the full scale simulations Heikki wanted. Despite that setback, however, she was able to analyze both the tapes of the wreck site and of the exterior of the latac itself, and by the time the freighter had nosed into its dock on Exchange Point 5, she was certain the LTA had been the victim of a deliberate attack, and thought she could even name the missiles used. Her report might not convince a full court of law, she amended silently, as she thumb-sealed each of three copies, but the tapes would be good enough for any inquiry short of that. The law was, after all, notoriously demanding.

She left Djuro to manage the transfer of their equipment to the next startrain for EP7, and went looking for the nearest locator screen. Its bright blue console stood just outside the entrance to the tunnel that led down to the dock—set there, she knew, for the convenience of the arriving crewmen. The inquiry rates were higher than in the main volume of the station, but she ignored that, and keyed in her request. The machine considered for a moment, then chimed twice. She lifted her data lens to read the output: the nearest postal station was at the Pod's core, just outside the main traffic control station. She nodded to herself, dismissing the screen, and looked up to find Djuro watching curiously.

"I have an errand to run," Heikki said, forestalling any questions. "I'll meet you at the Station Axis in half an hour."

"It's three hours to the next train," Djuro said, expressionlessly, and Heikki started to swear. She bit back the oath with an effort, remembering where she was, said instead, "All right. We'll meet at the Club, then. We can get Jan in, can't we?"

Djuro nodded. "You'll let Jock take responsibility for Alexieva?"

"He certainly seems to want to," Heikki said, rather dryly, but nodded. "Absolutely. I'm still not sure we can trust her, Sten."

"Does that have anything to do with your errand?" the little man asked, and Heikki sighed.

"I—maybe. This whole thing is screwed—fouled up," she amended, too late, and the inquiry console flashed a plaintext warning. *Immodest language is not permitted within the Loop. Visitors are advised to remember local custom.* Heikki made a face at it, and moved away from the console's pickups. "I've been doing some work," she said, lowering her voice, "and I'd like to get the results on record now, just in case there's any questions later."

Djuro nodded again. "I think that's smart," he said, and Heikki found herself wishing, irrationally, that he'd derided her fears. "I'll take care of the unloading then, and the transfer. How do you want to handle the transshipment fees?"

Heikki grimaced, annoyed with herself for forgetting, and slipped one of the business's bankcards from her pocket. "This should cover it. I'll see you at the Club in half an hour."

"Right," Djuro said, and turned away.

Heikki looked away from him, too, along the broader corridor that led toward the center of the Pod. The pods that made up the docking shell were fairly standardized; the fastest path from skin to center would also be the most spectacular. *Typical of the 'pointers,* she thought. *They want you to be sure and admire what they've wrought—and it is admirable, what's been built out here, out of nothing and less than nothing—but they also know better than to delay a harried businessman.*

The corridor sloped gently upward underfoot. She slowed her steps to meet it, and to match 'pointer expectations: here in the dock shell, precinct behavior was more tolerated, but it was hard enough to move from one mode to the other. From the moment she set foot on an Exchange Point, she had to become 'pointer from head to toe, or she could never make the transition. She walked carefully, stride restrained, and kept her eyes politely averted from the other pedestrians, assessing them only with the proper, sidelong glance and the reserved and silent smile.

The corridor's slant became more pronounced, and it curved gently to the left. Heikki allowed herself an all too genuine smile, earning a glance of censure from an elegant man in a severe grey-blue coat, but kept her pace steady. There was a light ahead, very white, like the light of a young sun. Then the polished-bronze arch that ended the corridor loomed ahead, and through it Heikki could see the blinding curve of armored glass that was the wall of the Lower Ring. She suppressed her smile, and stepped through onto the padded tiles.

The transparent wall of glass bowed gently outward above and below a ledge of darkly gleaming glass—a data bar, Heikki knew, but she ignored it, and stepped up to the wall itself, trying to hide her pleasure. Below her lay transfer tubes and the pressurized parts of the docking pods, their interiors visible through the broad bands of armored glass that let in the light of the Exchange Point's artificial suns. Those long tubes lay overhead, and even with the heavy filters to protect her, Heikki was not tempted to look up. She looked down instead, watching machines as small as ants maneuver the enormous starcrates in and out of the FTLfreighters' holds. Almost directly below, a customs team was at work, conspicuous in their brilliant yellow coveralls. As she watched, the team leader conferred with the ship's captain and a woman in a neat, dark red suit—the cargo owner's factor, Heikki guessed—and then, with a practiced twist, popped the seal on the meter-long packing tube that lay on the bench in front of them. A little of the tube's cargo spilled, glittering, and the team leader upended the cylinder, pouring its contents across the scratched surface: pearl crystals, the crudest, cheapest, and in some ways the most vital product of any crysticulture firm. The factor cupped her hands to catch a few that bounced away, sparkling, and poured them back with the others. The captain did not move, his eyes on the team leader as he swung his wand slowly back and forth across the spilled crystals. Then the man nodded, resheathing his wand, and another agent moved to sweep the crystals back into their container. The factor extended her board, and the team leader signed it. Deliberately, Heikki turned away, reaching for the data lens in her belt.

Through its circle, the black emptiness of the ledge bloomed with letters: the ship in the dock below was the *Kubera*, under contract to Salmatagin Bros., Lo-

Moth's largest competitor, just in from Diava; the location code was CF12/145; the station time, 1099. It was the location which interested her, and she ran her hand along the finger-marked flange, the letters blurring and shifting at her touch, until she found the right spot and the diagram-map sprang into existence in the ledge before her. The postal station was not far at all, the corridor where it lay less than five degrees around the Lower Ring's immense circle. She blanked the screen out of habit, turned to her left, and started off along the curve of the Ring.

It did not take her long to reach the corridor, which led off the Ring at a slight upward slope. Ceiling-mounted signboards pointed travellers to the traffic control center that lay at the corridor's end, and an enormous notice board filled an entire wall of the center's small lobby. The postal station stood in the center of that lobby, a red-walled kiosk with an "engaged" sign flashing above its door. Heikki scowled, and walked around to the other side. The second cubicle was unoccupied. She fed the machine her mailcard and ID codes, and stepped inside.

The interior volume was small, but the various vendors were well-stocked. It took only a few minutes for Heikki to find and purchase the necessary packing materials, and seal the disks containing both the raw data and her most recent conclusions into a secure and well-protected package. She hesitated for a moment over the address, and then placed Santerese's personal mailcode on the seal, and paid the extra charge for security handling. Now only she would be able to retrieve the package from the postmaster's hands, and there would be precise records of the package's movements through the system. She worked the package through the acceptance slot, and shut down the machines before she could change her mind. This was probably all unnecessary, she thought, as she let the kiosk door close behind her—and if so, she'd wasted almost a hundred poa on the various handling charges—but she could not shake the feeling that Lo-Moth wasn't through with them yet.

And there was still Galler to deal with. That thought
froze her in her tracks for a brief instant, and then, with
an impatient headshake, she started toward the nearest
cross corridor. There would be time enough to deal
with him once she was home again, and had seen his
message. Until then, there was no point in worrying.

The others were waiting for her at the Club, Alexieva
wide-eyed at her first real glimpse of 'pointer life. Djuro
had ordered food, and Heikki accepted her share gratefully, sinking into the empty chair at the little man's
side. After Iadara's damp heat, the Exchange Point's air
seemed almost chill; she shivered, and drew her coat
more closely around her shoulders. Alexieva gave her a
rather wry smile at that, and Nkosi said, "So, what are
your plans for us now, Heikki?"

Heikki, her mouth full and grateful for the excuse,
glanced at Djuro. The little man said, "I have tickets for
us on the next train to EP7, which leaves in—" He
glanced at his own chronodisplay. "—a little less than
two hours."

Watching the others, Heikki saw a brief look of disappointment flicker across Nkosi's face, and the frown that
appeared momentarily on Alexieva's forehead. "If you
want," she said, "you're welcome to come with us. I'm
sorry I didn't make that clear. I thought you had other
plans, Jock."

The pilot had the grace to look away at that, smiling
rather sheepishly.

"I'd better see to getting tickets, then," Djuro said,
and pushed himself to his feet.

"I'll come with you," Nkosi said instantly, and Alexieva
stood with him. She was clearly determined not to let
the pilot out of her sight, Heikki thought, watching
them leave together. *I wonder, could she be just as
uncertain as I was, once upon a time?* The thought was
obscurely comforting, and she turned back to her food
with renewed appetite.

The others returned with the tickets within an hour,
but they stayed at the Club table until only half an hour
remained to boarding. Alexieva glanced nervously at

the nearest chronodisplay—not for the first time, and Heikki sighed.

"There's a priority tube from this level to the Station Axis."

The surveyor flushed, and Nkosi said easily, "She is right, though, Heikki. We should be on our way."

Heikki nodded, and pushed herself to her feet. Djuro touched the key that would route the table's final bill to the accounting programs—Heikki had already, after only an instant's hesitation, routed the charges to the company membership—and gestured for the others to precede him.

The priority tube was as crowded as ever, but there were, for once, enough free jitneys cruising the broad traffic lanes. Heikki lifted her hand in signal, and Nkosi, less inhibited, gave a piercing whistle. One of the signals attracted a computer's attention, and a passing jitney slowed inquiringly. Heikki held up two fingers, and the jitney slid neatly up to the platform. A moment later, a second joined it.

"Alex and I will take this one," Nkosi announced, and pulled the surveyor into the crook of his arm. She made no protest, though her rather grim expression did not change.

"Why am I not surprised?" Heikki muttered, and reached to pop the other jitney's door. "All right," she said, more loudly. "We'll meet you at the station, then."

The jitney slowed as they approached the Station Axis. Heikki glanced past Djuro, through the righthand window, and saw the fluted pillars that marked the entrance to the station itself. Between and behind them, she could just make out the broad dull grey band that was the edge of the airtight hatch that would seal off the area should the outer skin ever be breached. She shivered a little, remembering the stories she had read all her life about the disaster of EP1. When the fifth PDE had failed, its crystal apparently shattering, the collapsing warp had triggered a wildfire reaction in the generators that had blown a hole through the shell and sent a plasma plume racing the length of the axis. There had

been some survivors, even so, sheltered in the cars of
the train that had been ready for the second and third
tracks, and in the panic someone had tried to reopen
the hatches that had sealed automatically. The mechanism, already damaged, had opened just far enough to
breach the tube's integrity, and then the outer door had
collapsed as well. The same scenario had been repeated
throughout the station, despite attempts to preserve
discipline; in the end, only the docks and the two most
distant pods had survived undamaged. EP1's economic
development had been set back fifty years, shifting
power permanently into the Loop's Northern Extension, and consolidating EP4's position as the richest of
all the points. Heikki smiled rather bitterly to herself.
If anyone should put up a memorial to the disaster, it
was EP4. Still, despite the loss of life and property,
EP1 had, in the end, been very lucky: the new station
at the other end of the warp, the one that would have
been EP15, had been completely destroyed. Scientists
were still arguing whether it was the chain reaction
destruction of the station's crystal, and the resultant the
plasma plume, coupled perhaps with faulty safety equipment, or some as-yet-unidentified property of the warp
itself that had destroyed the station, but there was no
denying the fact of that destruction. FTLships still occasionally translated back into normal space near the site
of the abortive station, and brought back photographs of
the exploded spheres, their broken edges curling like
the petals of a flower, that were slowly compressing
into a new planet for that distant sun.

It was not a pleasant thought, and Heikki shook
herself unobtrusively as she reached to pop the door.
Fortunately, neither of the others had noticed her momentary preoccupation, and she swung herself out of
the jitney with her usual grace. Nkosi's jitney drew up
to the platform behind them, and the pilot levered
himself out, then turned back to help Alexieva from the
compartment. Heikki lifted a hand in greeting, and
glanced back to collect the others.

"Which track, Sten?"

Djuro held up three fingers. Heikki nodded her acknowledgement, and started for the entrance, the others trailing behind.

The station itself was crowded, and there was the usual confusion at the gates while travellers sorted out their tickets and their destinations. Heikki bit back a curse, and gestured with her free hand for Djuro, who held the tickets and had an unfailing eye for the fastest-moving gate, to go ahead of them. Out of the corner of her eye, she saw Nkosi put his arm around Alexieva's waist and pull her close. They negotiated the crowd without difficulty, and were checked only briefly at the gate. The attendant on duty in the overseer's box didn't even glance down while the computer scanned their tickets and then opened the padded barrier. They swept through in a group, and the barrier thudded closed again just in time to cut off a skinny girl in bright metallic facepaint. She gave them a cheerful leer, and swung away.

Alexieva frowned, staring after her. "Does that happen often?" she asked.

"Often enough," Nkosi answered, already turning toward the tunnel-like entrances to the platforms themselves, but the surveyor hung back, staring at the place where the skinny girl had become lost in the crowd.

"But what if she gets through? Does somebody lose their ticket?"

"Sometimes," Nkosi answered briskly, "but more often not. They—the free riders—always pick on people who don't know the Loop, so the railroad is willing to give them the benefit of the doubt."

"It can make you miss your train," Heikki said dryly. "I think we'd better hurry."

"You are right," Nkosi said, contritely, and swept Alexieva ahead of him toward the tunnels.

The sign above the righthand entrance was a steady yellow, the destinations and departure time spelled out in black against it: the string of capsules was at the platform, but passengers were not yet allowed aboard. Heikki led the way through the final arch, past the green-glowing security eyes, and then out onto the platform itself. The capsules lay comfortably in the gravity field, rocking only as the moving air hit them. Heikki glanced at the wall board, reconfirming the standard symbols, and then moved along the platform until she found the section of the train that was marked with the familiar symbols that meant the cars would not be unsealed until they reached EP7. One capsule would hold them all, and she led them past several groups of travellers until she found an unclaimed car.

"We seem to be early," Nkosi said, with a grin.

"Better that than late," Heikki retorted, and the big man laughed.

"True enough. Shall I fetch supplies for the trip?"

Heikki glanced at the chronodisplay in her lens—fifteen minutes still to boarding—and then manipulated the bezel to find the schedule she had downloaded to the lens' memory. The entire trip would take several hours, what with the intermediate stops and transfers, and she wished she had thought to download the files from her newsservice. "Go ahead," she said aloud. "Would you get me a copy of the lastest techfax, if it's in?"

"Of course," Nkosi answered, and looked at the others. "May I fetch anything for the rest of you?"

"Piperaad," Djuro said, naming a favorite snack. Nkosi nodded, and headed off to intercept the slow-moving sales van that was making its way along the length of the platform.

The others stood for a moment in silence, idly watching the pilot's progress, and then Alexieva cleared her throat. "I was wondering," she said reluctantly. "About that girl. If she'd gotten onto the platform, how would she have gotten on the train? Don't they check the tickets again?"

Heikki shrugged, but before she could give her answer—that the automatic scanners were easily foxed— Djuro said solemnly, "Ah. Well you asked."

Alexieva gave him an inquiring glance, and Heikki frowned. "Sten," she began, but the little man was hurrying on, his face crinkling into an expression that Heikki knew to be one of sheer mischief.

"If she could get on the train, of course, she'd take it—and there're plenty of ways of foxing it—if you get a disk of the right material, reflex or tattrun, and stick it under the scanner, that'll usually work. But if it doesn't. . . ." He paused then, his voice becoming sepulchral. "Then you got two choices. You can either give up, or you can try riding free."

"Sten," Heikki said again, but she couldn't keep the amusement completely out of her voice. Djuro heard, and darted her a quick, evil smile.

"Riding free?" Alexieva said. From the sound of her voice, Heikki guessed she suspected she was being teased, but couldn't quite see how. She sighed, and Djuro hurried on before she could interrupt again.

"Yeah. You only see part of the train here in the station, there's a few dozen more capsules, cargo capsules, on a secondary platform beyond the firewall." He nodded toward the head of the train, and the barrier that closed off the runway. "You've probably heard they send any cargo through first, just to be sure everything's working right?"

Alexieva nodded, her expression still wary.

Djuro went on, "Now, you see that hatch there, left of the barrier at the end of the platform? Five'll get you ten the lock was jimmied a long time ago, and the securitrons haven't fixed it. That hatch gives access to the cargo platform—it's meant for the baggage handlers. If you can get through there, you can get into one of the cargo capsules."

He paused, expectantly, and Alexieva said, "What about the loaders?" Her voice was less disbelieving than it should have been, and Heikki shook her head at Djuro.

The little man ignored her. "They're pretty busy, and anyway, they leave the area before the run-up starts— that whole area's too close to the warp, once the train gets under way. So you've got maybe ten minutes to slip aboard. Or you could bribe somebody," he added, after a moment's thought. "It might well cost you less than a ticket. But it's not hard to get into one of the capsules."

He stopped then, waiting. Heikki was suddenly aware that Nkosi had returned, and that the pilot was waiting just as eagerly. She frowned at him, ready to tell both of them to stop their nonsense, and then saw Alexieva's face. The surveyor was certain she shouldn't listen, but she believed all the same. The temptation was overwhelming. Heikki swallowed her reproof, and slipped her hands into the pockets of her shift.

After a moment, Alexieva said, as though she grudged the question, "Isn't that dangerous?"

At her side, Nkosi grinned, and as quickly wiped the expression off his face. Djuro said, "Oh, yeah. The capsules aren't screened, you see. Why should they be? After all, it'd be a waste of money to protect inanimate cargo. So you go through the warp without the shielding."

There was a moment of silence, and Heikki shivered in spite of herself. Even though she knew better than to believe Djuro's story entirely, the picture was a frightening one: to be exposed to the unimaginable forces that could tear open the universe and then hold it open, to face a chaos that wasn't chaos, but an order beyond any description except the most approximate of mathematics. . . . She shook the thought away.

"Oh, for Christ's sake, Sten," she said, more roughly than she'd intended, and Nkosi shook a finger at her.

"Language, Heikki."

"You know perfectly well that isn't true," Heikki said, without turning to look at the pilot. "Stop telling old wives' tales."

Djuro grinned. "It's all perfectly true, and you know it," he protested, but without conviction.

Alexieva blushed furiously red, and looked even angrier as she touched one hot cheek. "So what about that girl?"

"Persistent, isn't she?" Djuro murmured.

Heikki frowned at him, and said, "Well, half of what Sten said is true, anyway. Those kids, station rats, free riders, do hide in the cargo capsules—but the capsules are solid, even if they don't carry the same shielding as the live transfer ones. When people get killed, it's usually through lack of oxygen. Somebody suffocates in a loose cargo."

"Or they forget to open the cock," Djuro began, and Heikki glared at him.

"Give it up, Sten. You've had your fun." The chimes sounded, releasing the cars for boarding, and Heikki was grateful for the interruption. "All right, everybody on board."

She held the capsule door for them, shaking her head at a stranger who would have joined them, and the others filed inside, Alexieva darting a single distrustful glance at the barrier ahead before ducking into the little car. It was, Heikki thought, a sweet—if petty—revenge, and she allowed herself a faint smile as she closed the capsule door behind them. Djuro passed their tickets under the capsule's scanner; the machine clicked to itself, then flashed a steady green bar: *passage confirmed.* Heikki settled herself against the cushions, glancing around the compartment, and took the single sheet of folded thermoprint that Nkosi held out to her. The warning sounded, and the train slid smoothly forward, picking up speed as it approached the opening barrier. In spite of all the times she'd ridden the trains, Heikki braced herself, and saw, out of the corner of her eye, the others doing the same. The train lurched once as they passed over the threshold of the barrier—Alexieva turned as white as she had been red—and then the capsule seemed suddenly to pick up speed at an impossible rate.

"Now," Nkosi said softly, one big hand closing over Alexieva's clenched fist, and then they were into the warp itself. For a moment that seemed horribly endless, they hung in non-space, outside of space, and then reality returned, and the string of capsules was coasting up to the platform on EP3.

Alexieva murmured something that might have been

a curse, and shook herself free of Nkosi's hand as though she were angry at her own frailty.

The rest of the trip was uneventful. Heikki, watching covertly over the edge of her newssheet, was surprised and reluctantly impressed to see that Alexieva, while she avoided looking at the screen, managed to face the rest of the trip with surprising equanimity. *But then,* Heikki thought, *I knew she was brave enough. I just wish her courage were all I had to worry about.*

And then at last the capsule slowed to a halt at the inbound platform of EP7. Heikki reached for the door controls with more eagerness than she'd admitted feeling, and felt her cheeks grow hot as she fumbled with the latch. The door slid open, and she stepped out onto the platform, glad that the others were busy with their own belongings.

"Where away?" Nkosi asked cheerfully, folding the last newssheet into his jacket's capacious pocket.

"Baggage claim first," Heikki answered, "and then— I'm heading for home. What you do is up to you, but you're all welcome back at the office."

"Thank you," Nkosi said, and looked at Alexieva. "But I think we had better find a place to stay, first. My usual flat only has housepacks for one."

"I want to stop by briefly," Djuro said, "but just to pick up my pay."

Heikki gave him a smile of thanks, as much for the tact as for the offer itself, and said aloud, "Whatever suits you, people. Just—keep your mailcodes current with us, please? After all the strangeness of this contract, I'd like to be able to get in touch with you if the lawyers have any questions."

"You're not thinking of suing?" Alexieva asked.

"Not yet," Heikki answered. "But—as I've said all along—this way of terminating a contract doesn't make me look good."

They made their way through the first set of gates to the baggage windows, and Nkosi volunteered himself and Alexieva for the tedious job of waiting for the crates to appear. Heikki, genuinely grateful, dug a handful of transfer slips out of her belt pockets and gave them to him.

"I will not need all of these," the pilot protested, halfheartedly, and Heikki shrugged.

"Send your own stuff wherever it's going, and if you haven't used up the credits, flip me the excess sometime." She glanced over her shoulder, and saw an unexpected and familiar figure standing at the entrance to the transport concourse. Santerese lifted a hand in exuberant greeting, and Heikki felt her own heart lift. "Keep in touch, Jock," she said, and tried not to turn away too quickly.

"Oh, I shall," Nkosi called after her, laughing. "We have not yet completely settled accounts, after all."

Heikki turned back, flushing in embarrassment, and Nkosi waved her on. "Which we will do when you have settled your contract, I know. I will contact you tomorrow, all right?"

"Right," Heikki agreed, relieved, and made her way through the crowd to Santerese. Djuro was there before her, but Heikki ignored him.

"Marshallin," she said, and the two women embraced.

"Lord, doll," Santerese said, heedless of modest language, and held her partner at arms' length. "It's good to see you back."

"It's good to be back," Heikki said, aware both of the foolish inadequacy of her words and of Santerese's impish acknowledging smile. "How're things?"

"Well enough," Santerese answered, but there was a note in her voice, a hint of restraint, that made Heikki look sharply at her. Santerese shook her head once, and said, "Let's get back to the suite, and get Sten fed—"

"That's not necessary, thanks," Djuro interrupted, with a slight smile. "I just want to get a draft, if I can, and then I can be on my way."

Heikki saw Santerese's almost imperceptible sigh of relief, and knew Djuro had heard the same restraint in her partner's voice. Thank you, Sten, she said silently, and opened her mouth to suggest they take a floater across the stations's central volume, when Santerese said, with an almost perfect imitation of her usual breezy tone, "As it happens, Sten, I can save you the trip. I brought a voucher here, if you can bear to take LloydsBank."

Djuro lifted an eyebrow. "I'll take what I can get, Marshallin." He paused, hazel eyes darting from one to the other as he took the slim card from Santerese, visibly considering further questions, but in the end said only, "I'll be in touch." The words were as much a threat as a promise.

He started away—toward the common transport tubes, Heikki saw without surprise, but she could not muster amusement at the little man's habitual frugality. "What's wrong, Marshallin?"

Santerese made a face. "Nothing's wrong, precisely—or nothing's wrong, yet." She shook her head—annoyed with herself, Heikki knew, and offered a tentatively consoling hand. Santerese accepted it with a smile, but the response was abstracted. "Let's get back to the suite," she said, "and then we can talk."

As bad as all that? Heikki thought, chilled, but let the other woman draw her away toward a waiting jitney. Santerese was unusually silent on the long ride back through the station corridors to the suite of rooms that served as both office and living quarters, and Heikki found her nervousness contagious, so that she barely noticed the familiar landmarks passing outside the jitney windows. At last the machine drew to a stop at the end of the corridor that led to their pod, and Santerese popped the canopy with a sigh of relief, saying, "I was beginning to think we'd never get here."

*So was I*, Heikki thought. She followed Santerese down the twisting corridor that led to the stairs, nodding to the securitron on duty at the head of the stairway, and then rode the movingstairs down the three levels to their suite. The staircase seemed slower than ever, and it was all Heikki could do to keep from breaking modesty and start striding down the stairs at twice the stair's sedate pace. She shifted uneasily from one foot to the other, and Santerese gave her a wry glance, but said nothing until they were finally inside the suite.

Even then, she didn't seem eager to begin, but glanced instead toward the kitchen alcove. "I'll start some coffee—"

"Marshallin," Heikki began, but the other woman did not seem to hear.

"—and that tape I told you about, the one you thought was from your brother? It's on the desk in the workroom."

"Screw my brother," Heikki said, and Santerese gave her a flickering smile before she sobered again. "Marshallin, what's going on?"

Santerese sighed, her mobile face suddenly grave. "I think maybe a drink's better than coffee," she said, and palmed open a wall storage space to produce a bottle of amber liquid and, after some search, two glasses. Heikki accepted what was poured for her, but stood waiting. Santerese sighed again. "Since you asked, I had Malachy ask some questions about the contract, and I spoke to Idris Max about Tremoth. It was just checking, all the lightest feelers, nothing more. . . . But somebody took it all wrong. The answer—well, take away the legalese, and Lo-Moth's lawyers, pardon me, Tremoth's, it's them who're handling it, *not* Lo-Moth—" She seemed to have lost the thread of her sentence, and paused to recover it. "Take away the legalese, and they're threatening to go to the Board, accuse us of illegal procedures, archaeology—failure to report antiquities, improper handling and so on."

"What?" Heikki's hand tightened painfully on her glass, and she loosened it with an effort. "That's ridiculous—we've been triple certified, and everything."

"They hint they have evidence. Nothing so direct as a threat, of course, but they do drop hints," Santerese said. She sipped her drink, and gave a tight smile. "Which they won't use, as long as we don't pursue this contract."

"Galler," Heikki said, with a decisive venom that surprised even herself. "That son of a bitch."

Santerese was looking at her in some surprise, and

Heikki bared teeth in an angry grin. "This is just the sort of thing he'd do. Where's the cube?"

"In the workroom," Santerese answered, her voice a little wary now. "Heikki—"

"What?"

Santerese seemed to swallow what she had been going to say. "What makes you think he's responsible?"

Heikki laughed. "This is the sort of thing he'd do, the sort of thing he always did do. Haven't you noticed that we haven't had a bit of luck since he showed up again?" Santerese's eyebrows lifted, but Heikki stalked into the workroom before the other woman could say anything. After a moment, she heard Santerese call after her.

"Why don't you bring that cube out here?"

Heikki swore to herself, unreasonably unwilling to follow any suggestions, but then curbed her temper and hefted the message cube. It was heavier than it looked, and she stared at it with loathing, almost ready to blame that, as well, on Galler's machinations. The irrationality of that brought her back to her senses a little. She laughed, with a touch of real amusement this time, and went back into the main room.

Santerese was waiting exactly where she had left her, her glass still held a little above waist level, her face, its only expression a sort of polite neutrality, turned toward the door. Heikki, recognizing the signs, set the cube on the nearest table, and said, with an effort, "All right, 'Shallin, I'm overreacting."

Santerese's expression did not change. "Yes, you are."

"You don't know my fucking brother," Heikki retorted, stung, and then gestured an apology. "He's more trouble than you can imagine, always has been."

Santerese did not answer, and Heikki shrugged to herself, reaching for the tag that contained the thumbprint seals. *If that's how you want to be. . . .* she thought, and studied the little tab. There was no movement from Santerese. Heikki's lips tightened, and she set her thumb firmly on the bright orange dot. The tag considered the imprint, comparing that to the pattern in its memory, and then, reluctantly, the dot faded from orange to green. Heikki took a deep breath, twisted it away, and used her thumbnail to pry open the little door that covered the controls. They were the standard set, but she pretended to study them for a moment before she could bring herself to trigger the tape.

A funnel of light flared from the machine's projector, filled at first with static, and then with a sort of visual noise that slowly resolved itself into an image. For an instant, Heikki didn't recognize the face that stared out at her, but then the long chin and the undistinguished nose, so like her own, resolved themselves into her brother's once-familiar face. He had aged, she thought vaguely—but then, so had she. In a wicked mirror image, the same lines bracketed their mouths, fanned delicately from the corners of their eyes. *If anything,* she thought, *we look more alike now than ever we did.*

"You didn't tell me you were twins, you know," Santerese observed.

"I did—" Heikki began, and the first words of Galler's message cut across whatever else she would have said.

"Heikki," said the voice—her own voice, if deeper; the same tricks of phrase and the same flat vowels. And then the image smiled in the old way, sweetly malicious, and Heikki's thoughts steadied. "Gwynne. I apologize for troubling you, but I could use your help—which, of course, I am willing to pay for, as I realize old affection doesn't stretch nearly that far. These codes are current; contact me as soon as possible." The image smiled again. "For old times' sake," it said, and dissolved into static.

"I'll see you in hell first," Heikki murmured, and switched off the machine.

Santerese whistled softly, and stepped forward to examine the codes inscribed on the plastic tag. "What is all that about, darling?"

"I don't know," Heikki said, flatly, staring at the cube without really seeing its flat grey surface. She was sorely tempted to do nothing, to ignore the message—but if she did, Galler would find some way to force her to do what he wanted anyway. *I wonder,* she thought sud-

denly, *is everything that's gone wrong his way of proving to me just how far he can go?* She shook the
thought away as unproved, if not unfounded, and said
again, "I don't know. I suppose I'll have to make contact."

Santerese lifted an eyebrow. "What's between the
two of you, anyway? He sounded like he was in
trouble—he said he needed your help, anyway."

"That's just like him," Heikki answered. She took a
deep breath. "You don't know Galler. He always did
get into trouble, and then drag me into it after him, just
so I could get us both out." Santerese was looking at
her oddly, and Heikki managed a sideways smile. "And
if you're wondering why I didn't just leave him, he
usually managed to involve me in spite of myself, so I
didn't have any choice but to help him if I was going to
save myself."

"What kind of trouble?" Santerese asked slowly.

"Oh, you're right, nothing too serious," Heikki answered, and with an effort held onto her smile. "The
usual stuff, staying out after curfew, borrowing sail-
boards, things like that. But one of his schemes got me
in bad with some people I really cared about, and—"
*I've never forgiven him for it.* She bit off the words
unspoken, perfectly aware of how ridiculous it sounded,
to hold a grudge against your own brother for twenty
years, and over a long-dead friendship; said instead,
"We were always opposites, anyway. I said black, he'd
say white to spite me, and vice versa. I only went by
Heikki to prove the name was mine, I never minded
Gwynne, but he kept digging up proof that in the old
days it wouldn't've mattered that I was older, he would've
gotten the name because he was the male." She'd said
too much, she knew suddenly, and shrugged and fell
silent, not looking at Santerese.

There was a little silence, seemingly interminable,
and then Santerese said, "How come you never told me
any of this, in all these many years, doll?"

Heikki shrugged again. "It didn't seem to matter. I'd
left home, cut the ties—I never expected to have to
deal with him again."

"So what are you going to do?" Santerese nodded toward the message cube, still sitting on the table where Heikki had left it.

Heikki stared at it, loathing mixed with resignation filling her. "I suppose I'll have to contact him," she said, and saw the approval in Santerese's nod. *Not for the reasons you think, Marshallin*, she thought, but accepted the other woman's embrace. *You'd do it because he's family, you with your cousins and god-cousins scattered all over the settled stars. Me, I'll do it because it's dangerous not to, because I know him, and I know he'll hurt us if we don't.*

She looked again at the contact codes, peering over the curve of Santerese's shoulder. "But not until tomorrow," she said, with some relief. "Those codes are for EP4."

Santerese laughed softly. "All right, tomorrow, then." And then, when Heikki did not relax in her arms, she tilted her head back and sideways to look into the other woman's face. "You do hate him, don't you?"

Heikki kept her cheek against the warm curve of Santerese's neck, rubbing against her like a cat for comfort. "No," she said after a moment, because it was expected of her—you don't hate your siblings, not blood-sibs and most especially not your twin—and felt Santerese's arms tighten quickly. "I guess not." She heard the lie in her own voice, but, blessedly, Santerese did not seem to notice. "Tomorrow," she said, with an attempt at briskness. "I'll deal with him tomorrow."

# CHAPTER 8

The public trunk lines between EP7 and EP4 were among the busiest in the Loop, and it took Heikki almost an hour to find an operator who could give her a place in the transmission queue. Even so, it was over an hour's wait before her slot would arrive. Heikki growled a curse at the empty screen, and pushed herself up from the workstation, punching a last series of keys to set her remote to pick up the incoming operator's signal. She started for the suite's main room, but paused in the doorway, hearing familiar voices.

"—this new woman of yours?" That was Santerese's voice, cheerful as always, and Heikki started to pull back into the workroom, not quite ready to face such determined good humor.

"Heikki doesn't like her," Nkosi answered, and lifted a hand in greeting.

Fairly caught, Heikki came on into the main room, nodding to Nkosi. At least Alexieva was nowhere to be seen. Santerese emerged from the kitchen carrying a tray of steaming mugs, and smiled when she saw Heikki.

She set the tray on the low table, gesturing for the others to help themselves, and said, "Why not?"

Heikki shrugged, uncomfortable, and busied herself with the plate of spices. Nkosi said, not entirely playfully, "I do not think she trusts her."

Heikki sighed, keeping control of her temper with an effort. "That's true, I don't, not entirely."

"You can't just leave it there," Santerese said.

Nkosi smiled. "I admit, Marshallin, I do not—entirely—trust her. Not entirely."

Santerese scowled, and Heikki said, "She wanted the job too badly, 'Shallin, and she admits she works for Lo-Moth, or for Electra FitzGilbert, which to my mind is much the same thing."

"*That* I am not certain of," Nkosi murmured. "She said that she worked for FitzGilbert."

Santerese's frown was growing deeper. Hastily, Heikki outlined the circumstances of Alexieva's hiring, and then her own suspicions. When she had finished, Santerese made a face. "Lord, doll, you sure can pick them."

"Which, jobs or people?" Heikki asked, sourly, and Santerese touched her shoulder.

"Both and neither." She looked at Nkosi, the smile fading from her face. "So if you don't trust her either, why are you bringing her along?"

"Well, there are two reasons," the pilot began, and Santerese glanced at him.

"I could stand to hear the short version, Jock."

"As you wish." Nkosi did not seem in the least abashed. "First, she is attractive, and when you are not growling at her, Heikki, she is good company. Second, or was that two already? No matter. The other reason, the last reason, is that I would rather have an eye on her than leave her out of sight."

"There's something I've been meaning to ask you," Heikki said slowly. "Did you suggest her coming back with you, or did she ask you first?"

"Ah." Nkosi gave her a rather sheepish smile. "I would have said I asked her, but I have been thinking,

Heikki, and I believe she was hinting for such an invitation all along."

Santerese looked from one to the other, and shook her head in disbelief. "It sounds to me like you did just what Lo-Moth—or FitzGilbert, or whoever's running her—wants. She's watching us, Jock, not the other way around."

"The thought," Nkosi said, "had crossed my mind." He looked at Heikki, and then back to Santerese. "I am sorry. What do you want me to do about it?"

"Nothing," Heikki said abruptly.

Santerese gave her a startled glance. "You've changed your tune."

"No, look." Heikki put down her mug. "We know she's watching us, so we don't let her see anything, right? And we still have a connection with Lo-Moth if we need it."

"That makes a great deal of sense," Nkosi said. "And I will not pretend I am sorry to have to keep an eye on Alex."

*I bet you're not*, Heikki thought, but a soft beeping from the remote cut off her next remark. "My call's gone through," she said instead, to Santerese, and looked at Nkosi. "Excuse me, Jock."

"Of course," the big man said, and Heikki retreated to the workroom.

A string of lights rippled across the communications display, now projected on the media wall. Heikki studied it, her fingers already busy on her workboard, finetuning her receivers' frequencies to match more closely the numbers displayed below the flickering lights. The string steadied, became a solid bar, and the monitor system said, in its artificial voice, "Local station tuning within acceptable limits. System connect offered, system connection made. You may enter your contact codes when ready."

Heikki had already hit the keys that transferred Galler's codes to the system. A light flashed green below the bar, and then turned red. The monitor said, "Codes not valid. Please reenter."

Heikki swore to herself, knowing she'd been overeager, and hit the keys again. The light flashed briefly green, then went back to red.

"Codes not valid," the monitor announced. "Please reenter."

Frowning now, Heikki reached for the tag she had taken from the message cube, and keyed the numbers in directly, reading them over twice before she pressed the button that flipped them to the communications system.

"Codes not valid," the monitor repeated.

"Please reenter," Heikki snarled in chorus. "I know." Despite the expense of the connection, she hesitated, hands poised over the workboard. The codes Galler had given were no longer good, that much was obvious—and how typical of him, she thought, then pushed the complaint aside as less than useless. She could disengage from the system now, and would only have to pay a nominal fee; the local databanks should be able to give her any updates to Galler's code listings. Still, she thought, there was no guarantee they'd have the most recent books from the other stations, and this was clearly a very recent change. Before she could think too much about the expense, she triggered the codes for EP4's main directory service. The screen faded, shifted, and at last displayed a scratchy system prompt. She flipped it Galler's codes, and waited. The system was silent for a long moment, the wall showing only the standard "processing" symbol, the speakers hissing faintly. Then at last the symbol faded, to be replaced by a dozen lines of closely-spaced printing. The last dozen letters were highlighted, and Heikki copied them into her own machine. A moment later, a chime and a second symbol indicated a successful transfer. She sighed, and touched a button, turning control of the communications system back over to the workroom's operating system.

"End session," she said aloud, and saw numbers begin to stream across the wall too fast for a human eye to follow as the automatics took over. She settled herself in her chair, staring at the codes that now filled her workscreen. Galler's contact codes were listed—the new set—along with his present place-of-employ and his residence code. The date-of-last-revision was listed as well: less than thirty hours before.

*You must want my help real bad,* she thought, *changing your codes like that at the last minute. The least you could've done was flip me an update—one thing I do know is that you have my codes.* She studied the numbers for a moment longer, a slow smile spreading across her face. *Never mind the mail system,* she thought, *never mind whatever stupid games you're playing. I've got your residence number, and I'm going to show up on your doorstep—and I don't care if it's a corporate pod, or maybe I hope it is, and you have to explain my very unpointer presence—And, by God, when I get there, you're going to tell me exactly what is going on.*

That decision made, she touched keys, calling up departure schedules and a fare table. There was a train for EP4, a one-stop, that left in an hour. She ran her hand across her board again, transferring money, and reserved a seat. The diskprinter chattered, and spat a set of ticket foils; she left them in the basket, and ran her hand across her board, pulling chunks of data from the past hour's work and melding them into a single reference file. When it was finished, she slid her lens from her pocket, and fitted it carefully into the read/write socket. As she touched the sequence that would transfer the file to the lens' memory, Santerese spoke from the doorway.

"What do you think you're doing?"

Heikki gave her a guilty glance, but said, "I'm going to EP4 myself."

"Was that what he wanted, your brother?"

"I couldn't get him. He'd changed his codes."

Santerese's eyes narrowed. "So why are you going to EP4?"

"Becasue I don't intend to put up with this runaround any longer." The transfer light flicked off, and Heikki freed and pocketed her lens. "He chose to change his codes after he'd asked me for help. That's fine, except that he's been screwing around with my—our—work. He said he'd pay for my help, and, by God, he is going to pay for my time and trouble, even if I have to beat it out of him myself."

"I don't think this is a good idea," Santerese began, and Heikki rounded on her.

"Do you have a better one?"

"Several," Santerese said, drily, but Heikki had already pushed past her into the main room. "Heikki—"

Nkosi was staring at them, open-mouthed, but Heikki ignored him, swinging around to stare at Santerese. "This is the last time that little bastard interferes in my life. You can't stop me, Marshallin. Don't try."

Santerese closed her mouth over whatever she had been going to say. After a moment, she said, "All right, if that's the way you want it."

"That's the way I want it," Heikki agreed, too angry to analyze the complex emotion in the other woman's voice, and started for the storage wall. Nkosi's voice floated after her.

"Perhaps it would be well if I came with you?"

"No." Heikki tapped the nearest cell's latch with more force than was necessary, got herself under control with an effort. "Thank you, Jock. But I want to deal with this myself."

It didn't take her long to pack a change of clothes, and throw that and her kit into a single carryall. The others were still standing in the main room, Nkosi frowning and worried, Santerese with her face tight with anger. The sight made Heikki pause, letting the carryall slide from her shoulder.

"Marshallin," she said, slowly. "I have to do this."

"Oh, I see that," Santerese agreed, with angry emphasis. "This is stupid, Heikki."

"I'm not going to be pushed around any more." The flat finality of her own voice startled Heikki; Santerese seemed to hear it, too, and looked away.

"All right," she said, shaking her head. "If you have to. But be careful, damn it."

"I will," Heikki said. They embraced, quickly, **and**

Heikki pulled away. "I'll try to get a jitney at the stairhead—"

"I called one," Santerese said. "It'll be waiting." She shook her head again, but said nothing more, and Heikki turned away.

The jitney was waiting at the stairhead as promised, and reached the Station Axis with time to spare. Heikki made her way through the crowd at the inner arches, not bothering to leave her carryall at the baggage window, and took her place on the platform, waiting for the signal that opened the capsules for boarding. The platform was crowded, and by the time she had worked her way up to the train, all of the capsules were occupied. She found one that had only one other passenger, and took the seat opposite him, barricading herself behind an otherwise unwanted newssheet. She sighed, wishing she had been able to find an unoccupied car, and guessed from the rustling of faxsheets that the stranger was thinking the same thing. *At least,* she thought, a brief smile tugging at her lips, *we don't have to worry about unwanted conversations.*

The trip itself was uneventful. At the customs barrier, Heikki handed over her ID disk. "Purpose of your stay?" the securitron asked.

"Business," Heikki answered, and wondered if there had been less than the usual boredom in his voice.

"You're cleared for entry, Dam' Heikki," he said, and only the routine politeness colored his tone.

Heikki murmured her acknowledgement, sweeping her ID back into her belt, and passed through the now-open barrier into the volume of EP4's Entrance Pod. Like everyone else on the Loop, she had always known that EP4 was the richest of the Exchange Points, not excepting EP/Terra, but she could not help recalling that fact as she stepped out into the plaza. Underfoot, the broad flat-grey squares of tile fragmented and changed color, deepening first to a dark, moonlit blue, and then to the rich black of interstellar space as the tiles reached the center of the plaza. Across that background were scattered tiny points of light, diamond-like tiles no bigger than a child's thumbnail, swirling across the darkening tiles until they formed a two-dimensional sketch of the galaxy, spread out across the plaza floor. At the center, where the galactic core should have been, a star-fountain bloomed, shaping a hemispheric haze of blue-white light. Overhead, meters overhead, beyond the crystal latticework that crossed and recrossed the open space, carrying the distance-shrunk forms of passers-by, a plane of silver flecked with blue and black reflected in negative the pattern of the floor. Almost in spite of herself, Heikki found herself tracing the curve of one spiral, following it in toward the central fountain; she shook herself hard, and made herself walk straight away, across the bands of diamond, toward the trilobed arch that gave onto the Transit Concourse.

Things were less breathtakingly beautiful here; there was a roar of voices, and the constant snarling counterpoint of the jitneys that slid up to the well-marked kiosks to discharge one set of passengers and pick up another. A half-dozen Retroceder protesters stood under their green banner beside an information kiosk, but securitrons were already converging to move them along. Most of the travellers' societies had branches here, ranging from elaborate clubs to a single information cubicle. Glancing to her left, Heikki could see the simple gold-on-black logo of the Explorers' Club flaunting below a mirror-windowed bay, but she turned instead in the opposite direction, taking her place in the line of people waiting to use the standard station directories. It had been an instinctive decision, not at all rational, but it made a certain sense, she thought, tapping her fingers impatiently against the strap of her carryall. Why draw attention to herself by going to the Club, when her inquiry would be all-but-invisible among the hundreds of thousands of requests the system must process every day?

At last the light turned green above the nearest cubicle, and a stocky man in a neat 'pointer suit stepped out, politely holding the door for the next user. Heikki took it from him, and stepped inside, carefully sealing

the door behind her. The fittings were spartan, but
adequate, and included a socket for transferring data
directly to her lens. She spent a moment studying the
charges, then fed a single hundred-credit voucher into
the cash slot. The machine hummed to itself as though
surprised, and then unlocked the keyboard. Heikki
smiled sourly, watching the credit number tick away in
the upper left hand corner of the display, and began
punching in her requests. Galler's address and contact
codes remained unchanged, as did his listed place-of-
employ. She used the machine to plot the easiest route
to his residence, downloaded it to her lens, and then
glanced again at the credit number still displayed above
the readout. Sixty-five credits remained. She smiled to
herself, and typed more codes, transferring the set of
general station maps into the lens' memory. The low-
memory warning was flashing in its depths by the time
the transfer was complete, but the information was
there, and accessible. She closed down the machine,
accepted the twenty-credit voucher the credit meter
spat at her, and stepped from the cubicle.

The nearest free-transit station was one level down,
on the secondary Lower Concourse. She found it without difficulty, and settled herself to wait for the proper
omnitram, watching the crowd from under her lashes.
It was a different group, all right, poorer than the
pedestrians who wandered the Grand Concourse or the
businesspeople who waited for jitneys and corporate
shuttles on the Transit Court, and there were even a
few spacers, conspicuous in their low-collared coats and
jackets, waiting for the tram that ran to the distant
docking pods. There were no neo-barbarians or protesters here: the securitrons, wandering in pairs along the
well-marked rows of tramstops, made sure that the less
desirable transients remained in the docks where they
belonged.

A tram, marked on every available surface with the
five-digit route code, slid up to the stop. Heikki pushed
herself up off the bench, and took her place in the
forming line. She felt out of place among the range of

corporate workers, mostly machine clerks and data handlers, found herself almost unconsciously adopting their stance, head down, eyes on nothing in particular.

The tram was almost full by the time Heikki was allowed aboard, and she had to climb to the upper deck to find a seat, squeezed in next to a thin, tired looking man whose broken-nailed hands betrayed him as a keyboarder, and a green-eyed girl who looked to be barely twenty and had not yet learned to suppress an urchin's grin. The tram lurched into motion, throwing her against the keyboarder, who pressed his lips together and said nothing. Heikki suppressed a sigh, and tucked her heavy carryall under her feet. The girl darted a glance in her direction, but looked away as soon as their eyes met.

The tram wound its way slowly along the Low Concourse, then turned onto one of the spiral ramps that led to the nearest connector, picking up speed as it went along. The corridor walls blurred into an indistinct smear of color, and Heikki looked down at her carefully folded hands.

The tram slowed at last as it approached the spiral leading down to Pod Twenty-Eight, and Heikki allowed herself a sigh of relief. It slowed further in the turns of the spiral, and by the time it reached the Pod's transit bay was moving at what even Heikki had to admit was a reasonable pace. It slid up to the double-levelled departure deck, and attendants moved to swing back the heavy hatches. Heikki filed off with the other passengers, bracing herself for possible questions. If the mid-level residence pods of EP4 were like their counterparts throughout the rest of the Loop, those attendants would have security responsibilities as well. Somewhat to her surprise, however, no one questioned her, and she followed the rest of the passengers through the station's massive double doors. She did not pause, however, until she had turned a corridor corner at random, and was out of sight of any lurking securitrons. *At least, I hope so*, she thought, and reached for her data lens.

According to the plan she had retrieved from the station directory, the Pod's layout was non-standard.

The usual quadrangles that held individual flats and the small, necessary clusters of service merchants had been broken up into smaller, asymmetrical units. Maybe as compensation, the corridors were unusually well marked, walls subtly color-coded, each junction displaying a central rosette like an ancient compass rose that named the corridors shooting off in each direction. It was easy enough to figure out the quickest route to Galler's flat by comparing the numbers at the last intersection with the names in the map, but even so Heikki kept her data lens closed in the palm of her hand, a ready reference if needed.

Galler's apartment was one of four that lay off a cul-de-sac off one end of a corridor of service shops. It was late in the day, by EP4's clock, and most of the human-monitored stores were closing; only a few people, mostly midlevel employees by their uniforms, stood in the vestibules of the robot vendors, choosing the night's dinner. Heikki made her way slowly past the row of shops, pausing once to pretend to study the service menu displayed outside a small service broker's. The menu's polished surface reflected the corridor behind her: no one seemed to be paying the least attention to her. The precaution had been automatic, as automatic as her refusal to use her club's facilities, and she was frowning to herself as she turned away from the little storefront. There was no need to take such care, no need that she could rationally see, and yet, instinctively, every time. . . . She put the thought aside, frowning, and turned toward the cul-de-sac.

The alley was closed a meter from its mouth by a security grill. There was a call box on the wall to one side, however, and Heikki crossed to it, adjusting the bezel of her lens as she did so. Galler's home contact code flickered in the lens's depths, and she quickly punched those numbers into the call box's tiny keyboard. Lights flashed across the tiny display plate, but there was no answer from inside the grill. Heikki's frown deepened, and she repeated the codes, this time adding the standard emergency numbers. Still nothing happened.

"Come on, Galler," Heikki said, between her teeth, staring at the call box as though she could force a response by sheer will. Could he still be at work? she wondered. It didn't seem likely—it was a point of status to be able to leave on time, and Galler had always been punctilious about taking every advantage of his position.

"Oh, are you looking for Galler?"

The light voice came from the mouth of the alley. Heikki controlled herself with an effort, and turned to face the stranger, schooling her face to an appropriate neutrality.

"Yes, I was. Do you know if he's out?" It was a stupid question, she realized instantly, and hid her annoyance.

"I think he's moved." The voice belonged to a woman of indeterminate age, the childishness of her tone and mannerisms belied by the fine lines at the corners of eyes and mouth. Her suit, high-collared and softly tailored, was not quite a uniform. "Or been transferred."

"Thanks," Heikki said, through clenched teeth. "I'll try the directories again."

She swept past the other woman, out of the alley toward the distant free-transit line. A part of her saw that the stranger did not reach immediately for the palm-lock, but stood watching, until she turned the corner and passed out of sight. *Moved again, have you?* she thought, the words matching the rhythm of her steps. *Not changed the codes? Then, by God, I'll go to Tremoth, and see how you like that, your sister showing up on your doorstep, and I'd like to see you try to explain that away—*

She stopped abruptly, only peripherally aware of the free-transit station's arches looming ahead of her. This was not the time to approach Tremoth, or the mood in which to do it—if nothing else, she needed to control her own anger, if she was going to have any hope of dealing with Galler. And that meant getting a room for the night—at the Club, probably, or in one of the better hotels, she added silently, pushing away the first picture that thought had conjured for her, of the anonymous transient pods that collected in the spaces around the docks. There was no need for such caution—no need to make herself uncomfortable. She took a deep breath, and continued on through the arches, heading for the tram that would carry her back to the main pods and the better hotels.

Even without prior notice, it was not hard to find a room in one of the exchange point's moderately priced hostels. Heikki told herself she was glad of its comforts, but could not shake her feeling of unease, and by the next morning, she was more than ready to leave. She curbed her impatience, however, and made herself wait until the morning meetings would be over before settling her bill and calling a jitney to take her across the Ring to the pod where Tremoth kept its adjudications department. That, at least, was the office Galler had listed in the directory; Heikki smiled slightly, anticipating the corporation's response. If Galler were no longer with that group, and right now that seemed more than likely, she would simply have to make whoever was on duty there tell her where he'd gone—*which might be a struggle*, she added silently, *but I think it's one I'll win.*

The jitney drew up at the entrance to the pod's main lobby, a double-finned "airlock" badged with Tremoth's trefoil logo. The doors opened ahead of her as Heikki crossed the sensors' invisible line, and a disembodied voice said, "Please state your business and your employee number, if applicable."

Heikki did not look up, said instead to the young man who sat behind the ring-pedestal, "My business is with Galler Heikki."

The young man's hand moved on controls hidden behind the pedestal's edge, and the overhead speaker cut out with a sigh. "I'm sorry, Dam'—?" He let the words trail off into a question. When Heikki did not answer, but remained smiling politely, he went on, "How may I help you?"

"My business is with Galler Heikki," Heikki repeated. To either side of the broad lobby, she could see the corporate touts eyeing her from behind the raised side of their collars, murmuring into the voicepads sewn into the stiffened fabric.

The young man touched his controls again, the movements as well as the results hidden from sight, and said, quite politely, "Who may I say is calling?"

"My name is also Heikki. Gwynne Heikki."

"Yes, Dam'." The young man did not look up from his hidden screen. "May I ask your business?"

"It's personal," Heikki said, and bared teeth in a smile.

The young man pondered his screen for a moment longer—too long, surely, Heikki thought, for a simple inquiry. "Is Galler in?" She allowed her voice to sharpen slightly, and was rewarded by a swift glance from under the young man's lashes.

"I'm very sorry, Dam', I can't seem to get a precise answer from his department. He seems to be out of his office. . . ." His voice strengthened slightly. "They say, if you'd care to go to the inner lobby, they'll have an answer by the time you get there."

Heikki frowned, and one of the touts stepped up to the pedestal. Probably, Heikki thought, in response to a private signal, and she eyed him discouragingly.

"If you'd follow me, Dam', I can show you the way." The tout smiled ingratiatingly, showing good teeth.

It was too late to draw back now. Heikki smiled more moderately, and nodded. "Very well. But I hope they'll have found him by then. I wouldn't want to take up any more of your valuable time."

The young man behind the pedestal nodded back, but the tout's smile widened. "No trouble at all, Dam', in fact, a pleasure."

Heikki murmured some proper response, suddenly wary. This was not the way the major corporations generally treated miscellaneous visitors, especially ones who could not claim to be on the usual admittance lists. She followed the tout across the lobby, and past a discreetly armed securitron into the maze of corridors that made up the office complex. As they passed more security stations, her suspicion hardened into certainty. The man she followed was more than a mere tout; the securitrons were too respectful for him to be anything except one of their men. The ordinary workers, keyboarders, data clerks, and so on, were even more respectful, and Heikki could feel a cold knot of fear growing in the pit of her stomach. She put it aside as best she could, all too aware that she had made a mistake in coming here to find Galler. If anything ever wanted discretion, she began, and shoved self-reproach away as well. There was no time for that now; what mattered was to get out of this with as little fuss as possible. She glanced to either side, painfully casual, trying to memorize the twists and turns of the corridors, but knew with a sinking sensation that she would never be able to retrace her steps unaided.

The tout brought her at last to one of the circular inner lobbies, this one presided over by a young woman in a severely cut suit. She looked up at their approach, her thin face at once wary and annoyed, and the tout said silkily, "Good morning, Shen. Dam' Heikki here is looking for Galler. Is he about?"

The young woman's face did not change as she looked down at her board. "I believe Ser is mistaken—" She broke off abruptly, a faint line appearing between her brows. "I beg your pardon, dam-i-ser," she said, after a moment, and there was an odd reluctance in her voice. She looked at Heikki, still frowning slightly. "The secretary has gone to get him—he's out of his office right now. If you'd be so good as to wait. . . ?"

Heikki nodded, and the young woman smiled directly at the tout. "And there's a message for you, Ser. Tynmar would like to see you directly."

That was unequivocal, Heikki thought, and glanced sideways just in time to see the tout smooth a frown from his face. "Thank you, Shen. I'll leave Dam' Heikki in your capable hands."

"Of course, ser," the young woman said demurely, and looked down at her console.

Heikki waited until the lobby door had closed behind

the tout, then, doing her best to keep the edge of fear from her voice, said, "Can you tell me if Galler's here, please?" She heard the sharpness in her tone anyway, and hoped Shen would take it for a businesslike haste.

"One moment, please," the young woman answered, her fingers busy on her keys. She looked up then, her work complete, all traces of the polite mask wiped from her face. "Galler isn't here. He's vanished, about a week ago." She looked at her screen again, and shook her head. "They've called security, all right. Oh, don't worry, I've put on the privacy screen."

Heikki started to swear, then swallowed the words unspoken. There was no time for that, only for the right question, and then, maybe, a way out. "Why are you telling me this?" It could be a trick, after all, a part of her added silently, that would be very like the corporations. . . .

"I worked for him for three years," Shen answered, her expression old behind the heavy paint. "He was a good boss. I don't know what happened, but he knew something was going wrong, and he told me I might expect you."

Heikki's mouth twisted, but she bit back her automatic response. *He always knew how to punch my buttons.* . . . She said instead, "You said security's on its way. Is there another way out?"

Shen hesitated, then reached for the keyboard of a secondary screen. "Maybe—there's always the fire tubes, but they're alarmed. I don't think I can cut them from here."

"How far?" Without waiting for an invitation, Heikki came around the barrier desk to look over the other woman's shoulder. Shen shifted her screen, pointing to a red line on the suite's plan.

"The entrance is through the inner office, opposite the media wall. It comes out on the fourth level piazzetta, near the shopping concourses. But it's all alarmed—"

"How much time do I have?" Heikki interrupted.

"Ten minutes, no more." Shen gave a crooked smile.

"They figure I can keep you busy that long, and they won't have to alarm the rest of the office."

"Sa." Heikki tugged at her lower lip, studying the plan. The Exchange Points maintained a standard escape system in case of fire, but the alarms that monitored unauthorized use were less standardized. There was a chance she could fox those alarms, if they were of the simple models she understood. . . . Not that there was any other choice. She smiled, briefly and without humor. Under any other circumstances—if anyone else had been involved—she would have chanced a private arrest, refused to answer questions and protested it to her lawyers, maybe even filed a harrassment suit of her own. But there were too many unknowns here, too many ways she could hurt not just Galler, but herself and Santerese as well. Malachy's advice had been to stay well away from Tremoth until the situation had settled a bit—*and I wish to hell*, she thought, *I'd followed his advice.*

Almost without conscious volition, her finger was tracing the course of the fire tube. As Shen had said, it debouched onto one of the busy shopping squares. It would not be difficult to lose herself in the crowds once she'd left the tube, not difficult in fact to get out of the tube—if she could deactivate the alarms. And even if she couldn't, the crowds and the panic that any alarm would set off would help cover her escape. Odds on, she thought, this could work. She glanced at the data lens she still clutched in the palm of her hand, triggering the chronodisplay: seven minutes left.

"You said you didn't know what happened to Galler," she said, and held up her hand when the other woman would have agreed. "Do you know where he is, or how to contact him?"

"No." Shen shook her head. "The only thing I know is, he annoyed some higher-ups over some contract job. Something outside the usual channels. There's a man named Slade, a troubleshooter—he's the one Galler was really worried about."

"But why?" Heikki said involuntarily, and made a gesture of apology when Shen shook her head again.

"I'm sorry, Dam' Heikki—"

"Sorry, talking to myself," Heikki interrupted. She looked around the lobby again. "Where's the nearest tube entrance?"

"Through there," Shen said, and pointed to a half-closed door in the wall behind her desk. She smiled again, lopsidedly. "That's—that was Galler's office. I'll tell them you wanted to wait there, that way I won't get into trouble."

"Thank you," Heikki said, and started past her.

"He was good to work for," Shen said, so softly that Heikki could pretend she didn't hear. She pushed through the door and into the dimly-lit space. It was smaller than she had expected, most of the space taken up by the media wall and its peripherals, and by an enormous data block. Lights were still flickering across its multiple faces, and Heikki hesitated for an instant, glancing at her lens. Four minutes left—not enough for a search, damn it, she thought, and without thinking reached for the block controls. There were disks in nine of the twenty drives; she popped them all, and stuffed the disks into the pocket of her belt. Only then did she turn her attention to the emergency exit.

The heavy door, an airtight hatch more like an airlock's outer seal than something you'd find in an expensive office suite, was hidden behind a painted screen. Heikki pushed that aside impatiently, and bent to study the lock. It was a type she recognized, and her spirits rose for the first time that day. The lock mechanism was designed to operate separately from the alarm, to allow for inspection; the trick was to find the codes that disabled the trigger. She frowned over it for a moment, then fished the data lens out of her belt, adjusting the bezel to an analyst setting. It was designed to pick up callcodes from the communications system, "reading" the tones as the system itself would, and translating them into numbers—not precisely an illegal function, Heikki thought, setting the lens against the box above the tiny number plate, but one the use of which required a certain amount of discretion. She studied the mechanism for a moment longer, then took a deep breath and pressed all the numbers in rapid succession. She hit the cancel button before the signal could go through—the alarm gave a gasping rattle, and subsided—and lifted the lens away. As she hoped, four numbers glowed in its depths: the key to the system. Or so she hoped. She smiled to herself, wry-mouthed, and pressed the four buttons. There was a moment of silence, and then an orange light flared above the lock. The system was disabled.

Heikki sighed, and depressed the latch, swinging back the heavy door, but paused long enough to pull the screen back across the opening. With luck, that would buy her a minute or two more, she thought, and tugged the door closed behind her.

The escape corridor was dimly lit, the lights amber and spaced several meters apart. Heikki blinked hard, and stretched out one hand to the wall, feeling her way along the padded surface until her eyes had adjusted to the light. According to Shen's plans, the tunnel ran directly along the firewall that formed the edge of the office suite, with only one sharp bend just before the exit into the piazzetta. She kept her hand on the wall as she increased her speed, her footsteps dulled by the thick flooring, looking for the turn that marked the exit. She did her best to move quietly, straining her ears for any sign of pursuit, but the only noise was her own steps, and the rasp of her breathing. Then at last the tunnel turned, and ended abruptly in another heavy door.

There was no lock box on this side. Heikki swore under her breath, and crouched to examine the mechanism more closely. Sure enough she could just see the wires that led through the sealant into the release bar, but there was no way to reach them from this side of the door. And why should there be, after all? she thought, and reached under her skirt for her knife. This part of the system would be tested from the outside, not from within. She pried at the seal, scraping for the wires, but the opening was too narrow. Then, distantly, she heard a voice shout something indistinct: Tremoth's securitrons had figured out where she'd gone. There was no time left for finesse. She sighed, sliding the knife back into its sheath, and depressed the lock release. Instantly, the alarm wailed, a strident, two-toned siren, loud enough to hurt the ears, and the door swung outward, letting in a wedge of bright blued light from the piazzetta's artificial suns. She blinked, blinded, but stumbled out onto the harder tile, blinking hard to clear her sight. Green clouds danced in front of her, obscuring all but the vaguest shapes; from a distance, she heard someone shout, and then the shrilling of a securitron's whistle. She swore, 'pointer manners forgotten, turned blindly to her right, where the maze of shops should begin, and felt someone grasp her left arm just above the elbow. She turned instinctively into the hold, her right hand coming up in the proper counterblow, and that too was blocked and held.

"My," a too-familiar voice said in her ear, "haven't you made a mess of things."

# CHAPTER 9

Heikki let herself be drawn away from the whooping
alarm and the confused shouts, stumbling on suddenly
uneven tiles. Then she was pushed through a door into
darkness, and then through a second door into the
subdued lights of a side tunnel. A hand snatched at her
turban, pulling it loose, and Galler said, "Must you
wear precinct clothes? You stand out like a sore thumb."

"I work in the precincts," Heikki said, and grabbed
back the strip of cloth. Her sight had cleared now; they
stood in one of the deliveryways that ran between the
blocks of shops, the passage empty now except for
neatly flattened and stacked piles of used packaging.
She folded her turban as small as possible, grimly aware
that Galler was right, her clothing was conspicuous, and
then, changing her mind, wound the strip of cloth
around her waist in imitation of a fashionable nuobi. It
would help hide her own belt, with its many pockets,
too. She shook her head vigorously, then ran her fingers through her tangled hair, trying to shape it into
something resembling a style. Galler frowned, and fum-

bled in the pockets of his well-cut jacket until he produced a length of black ribbon. Heikki glared, but took it, and bound her hair into a short tail, then stooped to fasten all the clasps of her shift. That closed the walking slits, narrowing the skirt to a fashionable sillhouette, and Galler nodded grudging approval.

"Better, anyway," he said, and glanced over his shoulder. "Come on." He started down the deliveryway without looking back.

Heikki made a face, but followed, enough in control of her temper to recognize necessity. "What the hell were you doing there?"

Galler glanced back, a cherub's smile playing on his lips. It was an expression that rarely failed to drive Heikki to attempt homicide. This time, however, she controlled herself with an effort, and repeated her question.

Galler's smile broadened. "Waiting for you."

"And if you knew I was going to be there," Heikki said, her voice thin with anger and the need to suppress it, "why did you let me run myself into that trouble?"

Galler shrugged. "I needed to. Did you, by any chance, pick up the disks that were in my machine?"

Heikki's jaw dropped, and then she closed her mouth firmly over her first response. He had known she would do it, he had known—had assumed, after twenty years of almost no contact between them—that she would take the time to steal his disks, and, worse, he had been right. "No," she said deliberately. "Are you crazy? Why would I do a thing like that?" She was savagely glad to see his face fall.

"It would have been useful—" Galler began—betrayed, Heikki thought, into an unguarded utterance?—and then cut himself off. He said, with an attempt at his earlier manner, "Oh, well, I suppose it doesn't matter. You always were too honest, Heikki."

"Not a family fault, I see," Heikki murmured, and was rewarded by a single angry glance before Galler had himself under control again.

"But profitable, you must admit." They were almost at the end of the deliveryway, and he took a deep breath, stepping out onto the main street.

Heikki followed, grateful for the crowd of pedestrians that swallowed them instantly. This was one of the major markets, specializing in gems; the pedestrians were uniformly well-dressed, the professional dealers in expensive, casual clothes mingling with and deliberately indistinguishable from the tourists who moved slowly along the promenade, stopping now and then to gawk at the merchandise displayed on the shops' window screens. There were corporate hacks as well, but not so many of them, and most of them wore their uniforms with a difference that suggested they were of sufficient rank to ignore the house rules. *A bit above my usual company,* Heikki thought, automatically matching her pace to that of the people around her.

"What now?" she said under her breath, and smiled blankly at her brother.

"We catch a jitney at the end of the plaza," Galler answered, and Heikki frowned.

"Not here—?" she began, and realized her mistake almost as soon as she had spoken.

"Traffic restricted," Galler answered. "They're worried about crime, want to cut off the escape routes." He took her arm in what seemed to be a polite gesture. The grip bit hard, and Heikki suppressed a curse. "Don't look back."

Heikki did as she was told, her mouth setting briefly into an ugly grimace. Obeying the pressure on her arm, she slowed before a display of jewelry, cage-coronet and bracelets and heavy collar, set with flawed PDE crystals. Even in the imperfect reproduction of the window, the crystals flared blue and white, strikingly beautiful against the black metal mesh that formed both backing and setting.

"The mesh is an energy damper—lavanite, I think," Galler said. "Otherwise there'd be a danger of random discharge injuring the owner or his or her companions."

*I do know that,* Heikki thought, irritated, and then

realized that they were within earshot of another couple. She smiled sweetly and said, "One wouldn't want that, of course. Just think of the insurance."

Galler's lips twitched—as much in surprise, Heikki thought, as in amusement—but he answered with commendable steadiness, "No, the liability would be high."

The stranger couple had moved away. Heikki kept her smile as she said, "What's going on, Galler?"

"Securitrons," her brother answered tightly. "Behind us, coming up the street." He turned away from the window, his hand still linked lightly, urgently through her elbow, drawing her on up the street. Behind them, Heikki could hear exclamations and the shrill peep of a whistle, and fought down the urge to run.

"What in the world—?" a strange voice exclaimed, quite close by, and Galler drew Heikki into the relative shelter of a shop entrance.

"Robbery?" he called over his shoulder, and a moment later they were joined by a well-dressed man whose face, close up, was a little too hard for his fine suit. A carrycase was slung over one shoulder, apparently idly, but then Heikki saw his knuckles go white on the strap. A jewel courier, she guessed, and made herself look anywhere except at the case. On the street, pedestrians scattered to either side of the main travelway, tourists' voices rising in immodest alarm as they tried to crowd against the shop windows and entrances. The merchants had locked their doors at the first hint of trouble. Heikki could see a frightened face staring through a peephole almost level with her shoulder. Then the securitrons swept by, a dozen of them riding two-man hoverfans, a dozen more on foot. Heikki stared in genuine astonishment—all this for me? or for him, she added silently, certainly, and could not help glancing at Galler. On her other side, the jewel courier whispered something that might have been a curse.

"What is the name of—?" someone else began, and remembered belatedly where she was.

And then the procession had swept past out of sight,

whistles shrilling again to clear the intersection. Heikki allowed herself a soundless sigh of relief, and looked at Galler, who silenced her with a pressure of his hand. All around them, voices rose in worried speculation, here and there a voice demanding petulantly or in genuine fear to be taken home at once. Only she and Galler and the courier were silent, and she saw the courier eyeing them sidelong, the hard eyes narrowing.

She pitched her voice high, aiming for the fashionable squeal she found intolerable. "What could that have been about?" she cried. Galler gave her an irritated look, but the jewel courier looked away, his suspicion visibly easing. "I think we should leave, right now."

The look of annoyance faded, and Galler managed what might have been a nod of approval. "Of course, at once."

Most of the other pedestrians seemed to have had the same idea. It was easy to lose themselves among the crowd streaming toward the end of the street, but once they had reached the round plaza where the jitneys were swarming, Galler turned left again, doubling back toward Tremoth's offices.

"Are you crazy?" Heikki asked under her breath, and Galler darted an annoyed glance at her.

"Not entirely. We're more likely to pick up a jitney here, before they get to this mob."

There was logic to that, Heikki admitted silently, and made no further protest, though she sighed with relief when they turned station-north again, back toward the center of the Exchange Point. As Galler had predicted, the streets were less crowded, and jitneys streamed past them, summoned by the central computer to the scene of the sudden demand. Galler did not signal one until they were well away from the jewelers' district, and Heikki had to approve the tactic. There was no sense in allowing themselves to be connected in any way to the disturbance they had just left.

At last, however, Galler lifted his hand as a jitney

turned down the street toward them, saying in the same moment, "I hope you have some cash slips?"

"Typical," Heikki said, bitterly. "Yes, some." *And I'll be damned if I tell you how much I'm carrying*, she added silently.

"Well, I hope it's enough," Galler answered, and opened the jitney's passenger compartment.

"Probably," Heikki said, with equally false good humor, and the jitney said, "Destination, please?"

Galler's face stilled, all trace of banter vanishing. "Pod Twenty-One, level six, fourth court. The traffic circle there," he added, forestalling the next question.

"Acknowledged," the jitney answered, and slid smoothly away from the curb.

"Where—?" Heikki began, and bit back the rest of her question.

Galler, however, did not seem disturbed, but leaned back against the seat cushions. "Home. Or what passes for home these days."

Was that wise? Heikki wondered, but could not bring herself to question her brother further. Still, it wasn't like Galler to be less than devious.

She had her answer quickly enough. They changed jitneys three times before Galler finally seemed satisfied, and directed the last machine to take them to the Samuru Court in Pod Fourteen. This was on one of the lower levels, where the semi-transient populations, the people who worked in transport or trade rather than in the prestigious sedentary jobs, tended to live. Heikki glanced surreptitiously at her lens, and saw that the area was shaded pale green, a mix of light commerce and housing.

The jitney deposited them on the edge of the Court, and Galler led them slowly around almost the full circle, watching their reflection in the shop displays to see if anyone was following them. At last he nodded to himself, and cut directly across the Court, dodging the anemic fountain. He was headed for side street eighty-two, Heiki thought, but then he changed direction as abruptly as before, and ducked into an ungated door between two shops. She was caught wrong-footed, stumbled and swore, and Galler hissed at her to be quiet.

They were in what seemed to be a machinists' service alley, a dark cul-de-sac between the buildings, with hatches in the walls to either side that probably concealed the shops' utility panels. Heikki frowned, and Galler said, to the apparently blank wall at the end of the alley, "Apartment Five. And one guest."

*Oh, I see*, Heikki thought, and wondered if she could afford to be amused. This was a "privacy flat," the sort of place rich businesspeople hired for unapprovable lovers. *I wonder if my little brother is renter or beneficiary? Probably the renter*, she decided, with some disappointment, *and probably for political rather than sexual reasons.*

At Galler's words, the wall slid aside silently, revealing a tiny entrance hall and stairway quite at odds with the just-respectable shops that ringed the Court. The walls were painted a pale and dusty rose-red, and a pattern of wave-like whorls had been etched into the surface; the carpet—and it was carpeting, not plush tiling—echoed that pattern in darker shades. Heikki mouthed a soundless whistle, and Galler gave her an almost embarrassed look.

"It serves its purpose," he said, and started up the stairs.

"And what is that?" Heikki asked, following. Galler pretended he hadn't heard.

Galler's flat was on the third level—*which reassures me a little*, Heikki thought. At least he wasn't paying premium rents, not if he actually had to walk all that distance. She grinned to herself, but the smile faded as Galler unlocked the flat's door.

The place was tiny, only two miniscule rooms, plus bath cubby and the wall kitchen only half hidden by a folding screen, but it was perfect, the sort of luxury Heikki herself had only dreamed of.

"You do all right for yourself," she said involuntarily, and winced, hearing the envy in her voice.

Galler heard it too, and smiled as he waved her

toward the couch that dominated the tiny main room. He said nothing, however, busying himself instead with the touchpad set into the wall beside the door. Security systems, Heikki guessed, and, moved by an obscure impulse, kicked off her shoes on the mat by the door before settling herself not on the couch but on the meter-tall pillow that was the room's only other chair. Seen up close, the room was less impressive, the furniture not of this year's, or even last year's, style, the single flower—a pseudo-orchid as big as her head, fushcia edged in black, vivid against the discreet cream walls—fabric and wire rather than a live blossom. *Even so,* Heikki thought, *it still proves a corporate salary's better than mine.* She had not needed the reminder, and the annoyance soured her voice as Galler turned away from the wall panel.

"So what's going on, little brother?"

"Well you should ask." Galler seated himself on the couch and moved aside a concealment panel to touch buttons on a hidden remote. A bar set-up, complete with bottles and fancifully molded ice, rose from the floor in front of him. He reached for a glass, began to fill it, and then belatedly remembered his manners.

"Help yourself, please." Heikki shook her head, and Galler went on, "Trouble and more trouble, that's what's going on. What did you find on Iadara?"

Heikki laughed without humor. "Oh, no, you first."

Galler grimaced, the ice snapping in his glass as he poured ink-blue liquor over it. "I've worked for Tremoth almost twenty years," he began, and then shook his head. "No, let's not descend to self-pity. What's going on. . . . I'm not completely sure, Heikki, but if what I think I've figured out is right, we're not just going to get sued, we're going to get lynched."

"Who's we?" Heikki asked pointedly, and Galler laughed.

"Tremoth, Gwynne. All of us."

"Not me," Heikki said. She shook her head. "You got in touch with me, Galler. You asked for my help, and got me into a lot of trouble in the bargain. Give."

Galler stared into his drink for a long moment. "The crystal matrix you were hired to find," he said at last. "Apparently the structure was derived from research that Tremoth did about a hundred and fifty years ago. I found that out—it's part of my job, checking up on things like that, just so no one can sue us for stealing ideas—and when I told my boss, he hit the roof."

"Why?" Heikki asked. "Lo-Moth's practically part of Tremoth. It's not like they were stealing it from you—is it?"

Galler shrugged. "Normally, no. When our techs have a good idea, it usually gets farmed out to the appropriate subsidiary. It's just logic, they have the facilities and a lot more hands-on experience than we do. But this time . . . This time, my boss threw a fit, started me hunting who'd passed the matrix codes, and then who had access to the relevant files, all of that. I found it, all right—it was old data, back in the historical files, so I assumed it was something that had been proved unworkable, and passed all that along to my boss. Two weeks later, I was transferred to a different division." He managed a rather strained smile. "Which was something of a shock, as I'd thought I was doing rather a good job."

"Just who was your boss, Galler?" Heikki interjected quietly.

"A man named Daulo Slade." Galler smiled again. "As you knew, and it gets better. He was a rising man, he seemed a good person to get in with, even if he is a Retroceder—" He broke off, shaking his head. "Which isn't important. Anyway, all of this aroused my curiosity, of course, and I kept an eye—a discreet eye, I thought—on the Lo-Moth project. The next thing I heard, the matrix had been lost in an LTA crash on Iadara."

"Which wasn't what you normally think of as a crash," Heikki murmured. Galler lifted an eyebrow, and Heikki allowed herself a slight smile. "Somebody shot it down. They went through the wreck pretty thoroughly, too."

"Did you find the matrix?"

Heikki shook her head. "They must've taken it. We were pulled off the job before I could do anything about tracking them. The trail was pretty old, anyway." She looked at her brother. "Did you pull us out, Galler?"

"No."

*For once,* Heikki thought, *I think I believe you.* One corner of Galler's mouth twitched upward, as though he'd read her mind.

"Did you have a chance to do any work at the site?"

"Of the crash? No, the orcs were swarming. All we had time to do was take tapes." Heikki matched her brother's twisted smile. "Which Lo-Moth—or more precisely, your ex-boss—took from us."

"Slade was there himself?" Galler's hand, which had been idly swirling the ice in his glass, froze suddenly. "That I didn't know—it wasn't in the networks I had access to. He was supposed to be on personal leave."

He was looking expectantly at Heikki now. "So?" she asked. "I don't—"

"You don't understand," Galler interrupted. "I'm supposed to have full access to all of that information, supposed to be able to find anybody, of any rank, anywhere and any time. That's part of being a liaison, finding people—and knowing when not to find them, of course. But the point is, I should've known." He put his drink aside. "Do you have copies of those tapes you took?"

Heikki hesitated, and Galler waved his hand impatiently. "Of course you do. Oh, damn it, why didn't you have the sense to pick up those tapes I'd left in my office?" He stopped abruptly, fought himself under control. "Gwynne—Heikki, I have to see the tapes you made."

"Why?"

"Because it's the only way I can save myself, and you, and your Santerese and maybe a lot of other people."

*Since when did you ever care about anybody except yourself?* The words trembled on her tongue, but there was something in Galler's voice that silenced her. She said instead, "Why don't you finish the story? What happened to you—why were the securitrons waiting for me at your office?"

Galler waved an impatient hand. "Politics, partly, and of course I'd read the files. But I don't have a lot of friends in the company. Anyway, someone started fiddling with my personal records, especially finances, slipping in backdated deposits I hadn't made—purchases, too, just to balance things. Shen—you met her, my secretary? She alerted me, I looked over the books, and realized there wasn't anything I could do to get out of a probable embezzlement charge, at least not quickly enough to do any good. So I called you."

"What did you expect me to do about a charge of embezzling?" Heikki asked, almost with resignation.

"Nothing, directly. But I knew you'd've kept the survey tapes, and I thought I might be able to make you mad enough to steal my disks—I can't believe you didn't—and that would give me enough data to prove my charges."

Heikki was very aware of the disks jammed into her belt under her ribs, but made no move to betray that pressure. She said, slowly, not sure she wanted to hear the answer, "What was in those files you read, Galler?"

Galler looked back at her, his expression suddenly old. "I think—I can't prove, but I think—that the EP1 disaster wasn't caused by trying to fit another generator into the stability. The crystals—the core crystals—were flawed. Maybe deliberately so."

There was a long silence. Heikki shivered, though the room was warm enough. If that was true, then Galler was right, this would not merely ruin Tremoth as a business, but half the galaxy would be after blood. "Why?" she said at last. "Why would they do that?"

Galler shrugged. "EP4 is the biggest of the stations on the Loop, just because there are four railheads here. The Southern Extension was slated for development next, and EP1 was getting five railheads. EP4 would probably have lost its primacy. Tremoth has a lot invested in EP4."

Heikki shivered again, cold fear creeping along her spine. All that, all that destruction, the lives lost and an entire habitable system abandoned, its one possible Exchange location choked now with debris that was too massive to remove or destroy, and all for money, for abstract numbers in the system computers. "They wouldn't've been poor," she said almost to herself. "They'd still have been the main connector to the Northern Extension, still had all those profits, and Tremoth would've been handling it still—they wouldn't've been poor." She looked at Galler. "They just wouldn't've been first."

Galler nodded slowly. "These things matter, Heikki."

Heikki shook her head in pointless denial. "They damn well oughtn't," she said fiercely, and knew even as she spoke that the words meant nothing to her brother. "Tell me," she said instead, "would you have said anything, done anything, if they hadn't tried to do you in?"

"Are you crazy?" Galler looked almost annoyed, as though the retort had been surprised out of him. "What good would it have done? The disaster was a century and a half ago. Their great-great-grandchildren are old now, the people who died then. No, if I'd been left to myself, I would've buried the file, manufactured a good reason for Lo-Moth not to pursue the crystal pattern, and left it all strictly alone."

*If you were paid enough*, Heikki thought. Something of her disbelief must have shown in her face, and Galler's chin lifted. "It could only hurt everybody, bringing it up now. It should've stayed well buried."

"But now you're willing to bring it out into the open?" Heikki asked.

"I'm not willing to go to prison for them," Galler answered. "Not now."

*But you would've been*, Heikki realized, *if they'd asked right, and then none of this would've happened.* She was suddenly very tired, tired of the whole miserable business and of her own involvement, even of her own anger. Galler was right, nothing good was going to come out of this, even though a part of her wanted to see the proper persons blamed, a measure of justice served, late as it was for that storybook ending. And once again, her brother had left her no choice at all.

She shook herself, and leaned forward to the drinks tray, made herself take her time mixing a stiff drink, pouring the liquors, then adding ice in shapes like seastars. She sipped it thoughtfully, wondering what they could do now. *Get off EP4 for a start,* she decided, *get back to EP7 and Santerese—back to EP7,* she corrected herself sternly, *where you are a known and respected businessperson, and your word will be worth something against even Tremoth Astrando. My tapes are there, too, and maybe a proper analysis will show us something useful.* Galler's disks might be useful, too, and she leaned forward a little to feel their edges digging into her ribs. She became aware that Galler was watching her with hooded eyes, an expression she remembered from their childhood.

"What I'd like to know," she said slowly, and saw Galler lean forward fractionally, "is why they kept any record at all." Galler frowned, and Heikki elaborated. "Records of the crystal pattern, I mean. If Tremoth did cause the disaster, why not destroy everything that could possibly reveal that fact?"

Galler shrugged. "I don't know. Maybe the original recorders were afraid that destroying files would tip off the people who'd actually worked on the project, make people remember things." His mouth twitched again. "In fact, I bet they handled that the way they should've handled Lo-Moth, just quietly dropped the project as though it hadn't worked out." He leaned forward to pour himself a second drink, and Heikki saw for the first time that his hands were trembling. "What really concerns me right now is what to do next."

Heikki allowed herself a second of exultation, but kept her face sternly expressionless. "First thing, we need to get off EP4. Tremoth has entirely too much influence here."

"I'll agree with that," Galler muttered.

"I say we go to EP7," Heikki continued. "I have friends there, and the authorities know me." Belatedly, she remembered the charges Santerese had mentioned, but suppressed the thought. One thing at a time, she told herself, and went on as though nothing had occurred to her. "Plus we can analyze the wreck tapes there. That will give you a bit more ammunition when you go to the Authority."

Galler grimaced, but nodded. "They'll be monitoring ticket sales, you know."

"Depends on how closely," Heikki answered.

"Probably very," Galler muttered, touching keys on his remote, and looked at the chronodisplay that blossomed on the far wall. "It's too late now—there won't be enough traffic in the networks to hide me. I'll test the waters in the morning, all right."

"All right," Heikki said. "How secure is this place, anyway?"

Galler grinned. "Nobody from Tremoth is going to come near us."

Heikki's eyes narrowed. "How can you be so sure?"

"The president of Tremoth herself keeps her latest boyfriend in the flat below us. Nobody from the company would dare come around here, just in case they had to notice something."

Heikki woke to the spattering of a keyboard in the main room. She pushed herself upright in the massive bed—Galler had offered to sleep on the couch, and Heikki had not felt chivalrous enough to insist on accepting that hardship herself—and cocked her head to listen. Sure enough, beneath the steady clicking she could hear the sound of a synthesized voice turned low, and the humming of a portable screen. As promised, Galler was testing the waters, she thought, and swung herself out of bed, reaching for the clothes she had discarded the night before. Shirt and shift were both sadly crumpled; she smoothed the fabric ineffectually for a few minutes before giving up and starting out into the main room.

Galler's media suite was a miniature console set into the far wall, its controls and screen usually hidden behind a folding screen that matched the kitchen divider. He glanced back at her approach, but did not lift his hands from the keyboard.

"There's coffee on the hob, and stuff in the cooler."

"Thanks," Heikki said, dryly. She drew herself a mug of coffee, shuddered at the array of sweets on the cold shelves above the microcooker, and came to lean over her brother's shoulder. "Any luck?"

"Depends on what you mean by luck," Galler answered. He typed a final command and leaned back, studying the screen. Heikki frowned at the array, but could make no sense of the unfamiliar corporate codes.

"What am I looking at?" she asked.

"I accessed the low-level maintenance programs that security uses to carry out some of its sweep/scans," Galler answered. "These are the trigger codes, things that will be automatically reported to a human operator, in descending priority."

"So tell me what it means," Heikki said, and sipped her coffee.

Galler smiled without humor. "Basically, the system's set to pass any ticket purchase for EP7 to a human operator, or any of my listed credit numbers, or any of your cards." He touched a section of the screen, and highlights sprang up beneath his finger. "Unless you've got some that aren't listed?"

Heikki studied the numbers, shook her head regretfully. "They've even got the private accounts, not just business, and my Club numbers."

"I thought it was too much to hope for," Galler said. He lowered his hand, and the highlighting vanished.

"What about a roundabout route, say EP4 to EP3 or EP1, and buy tickets there for EP7?" Heikki asked.

"Possible, if we used cash," Galler answered, "and if this program didn't catch us." He touched keys again, and a new set of codes appeared on the screen. "They've set up a watch at the station axis, tapped into the regular security cameras—with the Authority's permission, I might add—with a program that matches photos of us with images from the passenger scan, and rings all kinds of bells if there's a match."

"Exactly what happens?" Heikki asked.

Galler made a face. "All right, they don't send every goon on the Point to the station axis. But the images do go to human operators, and they make a decision."

"Damn," Heikki said softly. So much for plan one, she added silently. Security camera images were notoriously fuzzy; it would have been easy enough to find someone, some drunk or druggie down on its luck, willing to go to the station and trigger the alarms for them, letting them slip past in the resulting confusion.

"How much cash do you have, anyway?" Galler asked.

Heikki shrugged. "Not enough for a ticket, but I can sell something, pawn something."

Galler shook his head. "They're watching that, too."

"God damn," Heikki said again. This was the first time in her adult life that she had been cut off from the financial networks, regular and irregular, that linked the points of the Loop and even the Precinct worlds into a coherent whole. It was a bad feeling, frightened and helpless together, and she summoned anger to block out the rising fear. "Who the hell do they think they are?" she began, and Galler grinned.

"The richest corporation on this Point, Gwynne."

Heikki glared at him. "So?" She looked back at the screen before he could answer, and mercifully he said nothing, leaving her to her thoughts. They were cut off from the usual means of travel, all right, she thought, which leaves us—what? FTLship, conceivably, though that was even more expensive than the trains, but neither EP4 nor EP7 are regular FTLports. Even if there were a ship or two in, the docking facilities were so limited that it would be easy for the securitrons to monitor all traffic in and out. "There's one last possibility," she said aloud, and saw Galler's eyebrows rise. "We ride free."

"Absolutely not," Galler answered flatly.

"Do you have a better idea?"

After a moment, he looked away. "No. But it's still too dangerous."

"What do you suggest, then?" Heikki asked, with as much patience as she could muster. "Waiting around until the securitrons relax their guard?" In spite of her best intentions, sarcasm tinged her tone. "Bearing in mind that most of what's looking for us is computer-based, and doesn't get tired, need a lunch break, or go off duty at 2100—"

"No." Galler sighed, and touched keys to begin extricating himself from the system supervisor. "I suppose you're right, at that. I just hope you know what you're doing."

*So do I*, Heikki thought, but knew better than to let her doubts show in her face or voice. "It's going to take a little time," she temporized. "And I need some information. Can you get me a detail map of the Axis, especially service corridors?"

"In a minute," Galler answered absently, most of his attention on the screen.

"Then I'll want a schedule of freight runs, and the cargo carried, for the next few days—as far in advance as you can get me," Heikki went on.

"That could be difficult," Galler said.

"As much of it as you can," Heikki conceded. "But I need some information." Her mouth twitched upward into an involuntary smile, and she was glad Galler could not see her. He did not need to know that she would be doing this for the first time, based on Sten Djuro's two-minute scare story for people new to the Loop. *Come to think of it*, she added silently, *it doesn't make me feel any too confident, either.*

"I suppose you want all this without alerting any of the watchdogs?" Galler said.

"Of course."

"I'll do what I can. Go take a shower or something, I'll let you know when I have it." He looked over his shoulder then, visibly assessing the crumpled skirt and shift. "There's clothes in the left-hand wall that might fit you."

Heikki grinned, and did as she was told. As she had more than half expected, the clothing—presumably belonging to Galler's most recent lover; on second glance they would suit the secretary Shen quite nicely—was of neither a style nor a shape to compliment her own angular body. It was, however, clean and unwrinkled, and after some searching she found a not-too-fitted shift and a straight-bodied overvest that would not look too much as though she had rifled a younger sister's wardrobe. The shoes were impossible, and even if they had not been painfully small, would have been hopelessly impractical. Heikki shook her head at the thought of trying to slip unseen into a cargo crate while wearing bright red heels at least eight centimeters tall, and slipped her feet back into her own flat station shoes. The plastic knife in its .thigh-sheath presented the greatest problem. The shift's walking slit was cut too low for easy access, and in any case the overvest prevented a quick draw. In the end, Heikki wedged the knife and sheath into the vest's front pocket, and hoped she wouldn't have to use it.

By the time she returned to the main room, the hard printer was chattering to itself in one corner, and Galler was studying yet another screenful of information.

"I wish I knew what you were looking for," he said without turning, and Heikki hid a grin. *So do I*, she thought, and then Galler swung around to face her. "Well, at least you look less frumpy."

"Thank you," Heikki said, with a sweetness she wished would poison. The printer had stopped, and she crossed the room to pick up the folds of recyclable paper.

"That's just the first installment," Galler said, "and the inquiries are scattered. The rest will be coming in over the next few hours."

Heikki nodded absently, scanning the closely printed listings. It was more secure to do things that way, even if it did make her job more tedious. Still reading, she felt her way to the couch and settled herself there, reaching into her belt for a marker.

"You're welcome," Galler said, with a sweetness that matched her own. Heikki glanced up, momentarily abashed, but managed a shrug.

It took her most of the day to work her way through page after page of freight listings. Most were obviously unsuitable—the cargo was either too valuable not to be carrying the most advanced electronic seals as well as the standard railroad locks, or carried loose, like grain or seed crystal, or toxic enough to make riding with it impossible. By the end of the day, however, she had marked a dozen or so cargos that might be suitable, and flipped back through the pages to study them more closely. Two she eliminated at once: both left the station just after a shift change point, when the loaders would be entirely too alert. Three more were crossed off when she noticed that the shipper was either Tremoth itself or one of its subsidiaries. Another five were hard-pack cargo, each item packed in its own individual inner crate. *Possible*, she thought, *but hardly comfortable. Still, with any luck that sort of sacrifice won't be necessary.*

She sighed, scanning the remaining listings. All were acceptable, and she lacked the experience that would help her pick out the most likely. Two left at mid-shift, the other three closer to the end of the time: that's as good a way as any to decide, she thought, and flipped through the pages again. One, bolt fabric on the last leg of its journey from the mills on Jericho to manufacturers on the Loop, was scheduled to load and leave at about the time the loaders should be taking their mandated break. *If I know dockers*, Heikki thought, *they'll see the point in hell before they'll give up one nanosecond of their personal time. That's the run we want.*

"Galler?"

"Yes?" Her brother appeared with an alacrity that belied his bored tone of voice.

"I think I've got one." Heikki held out the sheaf of papers, folded now so that the freight run she had chosen lay at the top. "This is what we want."

Galler took the pages from her, studied it dubiously. "If you say so."

*I do say so,* Heikki thought. She said, "It leaves tonight, too, late but not so late we won't have a crowd to cover us going into the Station Axis."

"Well and good," Galler said, "but what do we do once we get there?"

Heikki grinned, enjoying her brother's uneasiness. "Leave that to me."

They left for the Station Axis toward the end of the third shift, when the mid-class shopkeepers were closing down their operations and the mainline data clerks were ending their eight-hour day. They fit in well with the slow-moving crowds, Heikki thought, boarding the omnitram, last of three, that would take them into the lower levels of the Axis. Her pale overvest and shift matched the clothes worn by a dozen other women sitting on the tram's lower deck, and Galler's moderately tailored suit did nothing to call attention to them. Even so, it took all of Heikki's concentration not to glance around at every stop, scanning for securitrons. She fingered the toolkit Galler had tucked into her pocket, and hoped it would be more use than her knife. At her side, Galler bent over a lapscreen, data lens to his eye as though busy with last minute work. At the second stop, Heikki frowned, and then leaned over to murmur in his ear, "It would be more convincing if you turned it on."

Galler looked up, startled, then blushed deeply. He flicked a switch, and the status light came on in the machine's side panel; he adjusted the screen image with a sweep of his hand, and returned to his apparent industry. Heikki controlled the desire to giggle, and stared instead out the tram's nearest window.

The crowd changed as the tram drew closer to the Station Axis, partygoers, amateur and professional alike, mingling with higher-status businessmen on their way to the trains. There were still enough midrange workers to hide them, Heikki thought, and saw Galler frown.

She glanced over her shoulder involuntarily, and saw nothing, but her brother was still frowning. She jostled him deliberately then, and leaned forward as if to apologize.

"What's wrong?"

Galler made a face. "Nothing. I thought I saw someone I knew, that's all."

*I hope you're wrong,* Heikki thought, and leaned back in her seat. In spite of her best intentions, she could not keep her eyes from roaming around the car, scanning each unfamiliar face for some sign of recognition. She saw none, and relaxed against the hard plastic just as Galler said softly, "No."

Heikki looked at him, and he shrugged slightly, head down as though he were concentrating on his lapscreen. "It is him."

"Has he seen you—recognized you?"

"I don't know." The frustration in Galler's voice was barely under control. "I don't—I can't tell."

"So pretend you don't see him," Heikki said, and wished with all her heart that she had more effectual advice to give.

Then, at the next-to-last stop, Galler gave a sigh of relief, and Heikki looked sideways past him to see a tall man with thinning hair making his way down the tram's narrow steps. "Is that him?" she asked, and Galler nodded.

"So he didn't see you," Heikki said, and in that moment the stranger glanced back toward them, his eyes fixing briefly on Galler before he turned away and lost himself in the crowd. *Or did he?* she wondered, and said aloud, "Who was he?"

"Another liaison for Tremoth," Galler answered, and Heikki made a face.

"So we have to assume he did see you. What then?"

Galler shrugged, annoyed, and Heikki waved the question away. *Of course he couldn't answer, not in this crowd,* she thought, *and anyway I don't really need him to tell me. There's not a lot of places we could be going on this tram except the Station Axis, so we have to assume the securitrons will be alerted when we get there. And that means following plan two. Wonderful. I just hope half of what Sten said—was it only three days ago?— was true.*

The tram slowed, grinding to a halt against the worn bumpers of the lower Axis platform. This was the lower-class section of the Station, the transit platforms that served the employees of the railroad and of the companies that served it. Most of the people filing off the tram would be night clerks, Heikki thought, handling freight. The others would be heading for the cheap but trendy—and often dangerous—clubs that lay below the main Axis, or simply going on a walk through the entrance plaza, dreaming of wealth they would almost certainly never achieve. She let herself be carried along with the crowd toward the wall of transluscent mosaic that formed the exit, as always a little surprised by the sameness of the people here and on all the other Exchange Points. She was aware that Galler was close behind her, his lapscreen closed and slung now over one shoulder, but she did not look back until they had passed through the automatic doors into the Rotunda.

Overhead, an immense lens of pressure-tested triglass admitted light from the artificial strip-suns of the entrance plaza, its color transmuted by the lens to an oddly amber shade. It was a stormy color, vaguely unnerving, and people did not linger in its circle, pausing only long enough to find their direction on any one of the dozen display kiosks before setting off decisively. Heikki stopped just outside the ring of strongest light, pretending to study a kiosk displaying a gaudy series of nightclub advertisements, and waited for Galler to join her.

"Such taste and discernment," her brother's voice said at her shoulder, and Heikki did not bother to hide her grin.

"I thought one of them might be to your taste."

"No, thank you," Galler answered, with austerity. "Now what?"

Heikki glanced up toward the triglass lens, feeling

the familiar vertigo as its shape distorted distance as well as light, giving the illusion of far more height than could possibly be there, then looked away. "Follow me." Without waiting for an answer, she turned toward a cluster of unnumbered corridors that led off to the right.

"Those are employee access corridors," Galler said uneasily, and held his lapscreen more tightly.

"I know," Heikki answered, with what she thought was commendable nonchalance. She slipped her hand into the pocket of her vest, however, loosening the plastic knife in its sheath. The back corridors of any train station were always dangerous, filled as they were with any station's least skilled, and most exploited, workers; anyone who wasn't part of one of the rail unions was considered fair game. "If your friend saw you," she said aloud, "he'll have alerted the security upstairs, right?"

"He may not have recognized me," Galler said, halfheartedly.

"Do you want to take the chance?" There was no answer, and Heikki nodded. "Right, then. Come on."

The access corridor was filled with the hard blue light that dominated any 'pointer working space. Heikki blinked in its brilliance, and slipped her data lens from her belt left-handed, her right hand still on the hilt of her knife. She held the lens to her eye, fingers awkward on the bezel, but at last triggered the map she wanted. Access to the loading areas was further on, through a series of feeder tunnels that sloped up from the warehouses five levels below their feet. This particular corridor joined a secondary feeder a hundred meters on, and that secondary tube would take them into the main feeds. The only trouble, she thought, trying to walk, to move as though she had business in this part of the point every day, is that those areas are bound to be busy now. Djuro's advice had been to enter the loading platform itself, going directly to it from the passenger platform. Unfortunately, Heikki thought, that was no longer possible.

"Hey, you."

The voice came from a side passage. Heikki turned to face it, lifting an eyebrow in her best 'pointer manner. "Are you talking to me?" she demanded, and heard Galler's sharp intake of breath behind her. *Don't screw this up, Galler,* she prayed silently, *just play the flunky and everything will be fine*—

"Yeah, you." The speaker was a big-bellied man, a dozen union badges dangling from his belt, some almost hidden by the swelling stomach. "What are you doing down here?"

"I have business here," Heikki answered, and withered him with a look, doing her best to read the badges in that same brief glance. They were mostly engineers' codes, making him one of the elite crew that handled the tuning and maintenance of the warp itself—but that also means, Heikki thought, that he doesn't know the dockside work at all. Or I hope he doesn't, she added, and waited for the next question.

"Yeah?" The man's expression was not as disbelieving as his tone. "What's the name?"

"Gallatin." She heard Galler gasp again, but did not dare look back to glare at him. Gallatin Cie. was one of the Loop's largest shippers, and its principal was a woman of Heikki's age and status, a woman Precinct-born, who did not bother with publicity. She held her breath, and hoped the union man had never seen any of Gallatin's infrequent interviews.

The engineer's eyebrows rose, though he held onto his sceptical expression. "Where you heading?" He managed not to add the honorific, and Heikki mentally gave him points for it.

"I've got a cargo going on the platform in twenty minutes," she said. "I want to watch it through."

It was a common enough precaution, and the engineer shrugged. "The platform riser is that way," he said, and pointed down the corridor.

Heikki nodded, not daring to believe that they'd gotten away with it, and started off in the direction indicated. Galler followed, clutching his lapscreen to his side in a plausible imitation of a private secretary's protective gesture. Heikki did not look back, but she was very aware of the engineer watching them. Then, to her relief, a woman's voice called from a side corridor, and the man turned away.

"You were lucky," Galler said, under his breath.

I know, Heikki thought, but said only, "Take the left-hand corridor."

This one was less well-kept than the main road, its rounded, tunnel-like walls covered with much-scarred padding, the floor tiles scored with deep parallel grooves from the robo-pallets. There would be no explaining their presence here, Heikki knew, and quickened her step until they were almost running, at the same time straining to hear over the soft slapping of their own footsteps. Broad, shallow alcoves lined the walls: safety cells, Heikki realized after a moment, for the human crews' use when the pallets were too wide to let them pass.

They had covered perhaps a third of the distance to the first feeder tunnel when Galler said, "Christ!"

He pointed to a cell perhaps fifteen meters ahead, where the tunnel lights dimmed slightly. A single leg protruded into the corridor. Heikki bit back her own fear, and said, more roughly than she'd intended, "Keep your voice down."

She flattened herself against the wall, and waited. Nothing moved in the corridor ahead of them. Galler copied her movement, holding the lapscreen now as though it were a shield. The leg did not move, and Heikki made herself take several slow, deep breaths. Well, she told herself, with a bravado she did not feel, either it's dead, or too stoned to care, and eased herself away from the padded wall. She heard Galler make a little noise of protest at her back, and waved impatiently for him to be quiet. She moved forward, as soundlessly as she could, and was suddenly aware that Galler was at her back, the screen held now like an ungainly club. Heikki felt a stab of surprise and annoyance, and angrily suppressed both feelings.

The leg did not stir as they came closer, and Heikki paused again to survey the corridor. There was still no sign of movement, nor any signs of blood or burning, just the single coveralled leg protruding into the walkway. Drunk or drugged, Heikki thought, but did not relax her grip on the knife. Slowly and still cautiously, she made her way up to the cell and looked in. The man who lay there, sprawled uncomfortably against the padding, had a young face, but his hair was already greying. A plastic case half the size of Heikki's palm lay on the floor beside his outstretched hand.

"Christ," Galler said again, and Heikki looked back at him, her own emotions shutting down just as they had done on Iadara, at the wreck site. "Shouldn't we—?"

"What?" Heikki asked. She started to turn away, and then, grimacing, kicked the stranger's leg back out of the main passageway. The man did not stir, or make any noise. He moved like a man already dead, and Heikki winced. "There's nothing more we can do," she said, as much to convince herself as for Galler's benefit, and turned away.

"Not without betraying ourselves," Galler said. Heikki did not answer, and he followed without fruther protest, looking back only once.

They had covered most of the distance to the feeder tunnel when Heikki heard something in the tunnel behind them. She stopped, lifting her hand for silence, and then recognized the noise of a robo-pallet's wheels on the compressible tiling.

"Heikki," Galler began, and Heikki nodded.

"I hear it. There's a cell ahead of us, get in it."

"Can't we outrun it?" Galler asked, quickening his step.

"Are you joking?" Heikki said, and bit back the rest of her comment. "No, we couldn't outrun it—these things move, Galler—and besides, they don't usually carry human operators." They were at the alcove's edge, and she stepped inside, flattening herself against the near wall. Galler wedged himself in beside her, swearing under his breath, and she hissed at him to be quiet. The noise of the pallet was already louder, the crunching sound now interspersed with the shriek of an unoiled bearing. Heikki winced, but hoped that meant there were no human attendants. Surely no one would endure that when all it takes is a minor adjustment, she thought, but did not move from her place against the wall. Beside her, Galler made a face, and covered his ears as the machine drew closer. Heikki winced, tilting her head against her shoulder, but did not let go of her knife.

Then the pallet was alongside them, the thin screech of the bearing painful in their ears. The narrow ledge beside the guidance box was empty, and Heikki released the breath she had not known she had been holding. As the machine swept past, she leaned forward, trying to read the numbers stenciled on the tags that dangled from each of the crates piled high on the cargo platform.

"5G," she said, when the noise had faded enough to allow conversation. "We're in luck, for once."

"What do you mean?" Galler asked, rather irritably.

"You weren't cut out for adventuring," Heikki said, unable to resist the temptation.

"No, I wasn't," Galler answered. "Nor did I ever wish to be." He shook his head. "What did you mean?"

This wasn't the time to tease him, Heikki told herself sternly. "Those are the last numbers on the routing slips, the load slot numbers. 5G is the standard code for the last items to be loaded—I've seen it often enough, there's a discount for shipping in that spot, so we ship our equipment that way, unless there's going to be a disaster if it doesn't arrive. Class five stuff is the stuff that gets left, if there're any delays." She was already moving in the pallet's wake, heading toward the feeder, and Galler followed reluctantly.

"I still don't see how that's lucky."

"It means we don't have to wait so long before the platform empties out," Heikki answered. They were almost in sight of the first feeder tunnel now. She paused, glancing at the chronodisplay in her lens, then twisting the bezel to display the maps she had downloaded from the Point's main directory. "We keep going," she said aloud. "The next tunnel's not far, and there should be a safety cell just past it where we can wait."

"Whatever you say," Galler said morosely. Heikki laughed, but did not look back.

The entrance to the first feeder tunnel was closed and sealed according to regulations, lights glowing above the grill of the tonelock. Galler paused to stare for a moment at the mechanism, then hurried after his sister.

As the map had indicated, there was a safety cell set into the wall of the main corridor just past the entrance to the second feeder tunnel. From the cell's location, Heikki guessed that the tunnel had been added after the completion of the docks, probably when the Northern Extension had finally opened and traffic through EP4 really took off. *Whatever the reason, I'm glad it's there*, she told herself, and rested all her weight against the padding. Galler gave her a wary look.

"Now what?" he asked, and lowered the lapscreen to the floor at his feet.

"We wait," Heikki answered, and frowned, trying to remember what Djuro had told her. "They clear the cargo platform about ten minutes before the run-up actually starts—they're close to the warp there, and there isn't as much shielding. We'll see them go, let them get clear, and jinx the door ourselves. There's a cargo of bolt fabric going to EP7, four or five capsules' worth—I showed you the documents—and we'll jinx the capsule seals and crawl in with the bolts."

"We'll have to work fast, won't we?" Galler said.

Heikki lifted an eyebrow. "Well, of course—"

"No, I mean because of the warp." Galler gestured impatiently. "Look, if the powers-that-be clear the platform, it's not just out of concern for their people's health. The effects must be pretty serious, if they're willing to waste ten minutes of work time."

Heikki curbed irritation born of fear. "You're right, we'll just have to work fast."

Galler did not answer. Heikki rested her head against the wall, willing herself to relax. Anger did no good, nor did fear; one could only be calm, become calm, and be ready to act when the time came. . . .

Warning chimes, signalling that the locks on the feeder hatch had been released, interrupted her private litany. Heikki straightened, fear stabbing through her, and felt Galler stiffen beside her. She forced what she hoped was a reassuring smile as the noise of the pallets' power plants grew suddenly louder, and knew she had failed miserably. The noise grew louder still—the squeaking bearing, she noticed, was muted, had been crudely repaired, and then was annoyed with herself for the irrelevance of the thought. Most of the machines seemed to be leaving from the first two hatches, and she congratulated herself on her foresight. Then the noise of wheels seemed suddenly to surround them, and a pallet swept into view, coming from the last feeder tunnel joining the corridor above them. It was too late to be afraid; she stood frozen, seeing in a split second the tall woman on the driver's ledge, her hands lazy at her sides, and the two young men sprawled in the empty cargo bed, laughing at something someone had said. And then it was past, and no one had raised the alarm.

Heikki stayed very still for a long time, even after the sound of the machines had faded to a distant mutter, until even that seashell noise was gone and the tunnel was silent. Galler stirred beside her. "Shouldn't we be going?"

"A little more," Heikki said, automatically contrary, then shook herself. "No, let's go."

The feeder hatch was locked again, the telltales glowing above the sensor grill. Heikki studied it, frowning, and Galler said, "I assume it's some kind of automatic? A unit on each of the pallets with a trigger signal?"

Heikki nodded. "Let me see your lapscreen."

To her surprise, Galler shook his head. "Let me do this." At Heikki's look of surprise, he made a face. "What do you think I've been doing for most of my adult life? Half a liaison's job is to get into places he's not supposed to."

Even as he spoke, he was fiddling with the controls, his eyes darting from the miniscreen to the telltales, and back again. Heikki watched with grudging admiration as patterns formed and reformed on the little screen.

"Got it," Galler said abruptly, and touched a key. For a split second, nothing seemed to happen, and then Heikki heard something, a sound so high and shrill that it was hardly a sound at all, more a shiver in the air around her. The lights flashed wildly above the lock, and then turned green. Galler smiled, and gestured grandly for Heikki to do the honors. Heikki smiled back rather sourly, and pushed open the hatch. It was heavy, designed to be operated by one of the pallets, and she had to throw all her weight against it before the thick metal would budge. It swung back at last, the hinges groaning, and Heikki stepped through onto the cargo platform.

The lights were dim, cut back to emergency levels, and she swore under her breath, wishing she had a handlight. Behind her, she heard Galler say something indistinct, his tone questioning, but she ignored him and started for the capsules lined up at the platform. The first two, the two closest to the entrance to the passenger platform, carried expensive double locks as well as the railroad's soft sealing. She ignored them, and moved forward along the train, bending close to read each of the tags stuck to the capsule's smooth surface just above the wads of sealant.

"I don't think we have much time left," Galler said quietly.

Heikki looked up, startled, and in the same moment felt a strong vibration deep in her bones. She had been feeling it for some time now, she realized abruptly, but it had been too familiar to draw notice: the thrumming of the PDE running up to full power. To her right, the pressurewall that contained the warp seemed to shimmer slightly. It's your imagination, she told herself, but there was no denying that the light on the platform was slowly growing brighter.

"You start looking, too," Heikki ordered. "You know the code—TTJ8291 slash 929K. Ignore the first half dozen capsules, we don't want to ride in them anyway."

Galler nodded, and started up the line. Heikki put him out of her mind, concentrating on the strings of numbers embossed on the half-meter square stickers. The codes blurred as she went, numbers and letters running together; she wanted desperately to check her lens, see how much time she had until the warp opened and the train pulled out, but she did not dare. Not much, she knew, and maybe not enough, but— And then she saw it, the code on the sticker beneath her hand matching the numbers she had memorized less than a day before.

"Got it," she called, and reached into her pocket for the toolkit. The seal was nothing complicated; she had jinxed its like before. Frowning, she selected a thin probe from among the array nestling against the clingcloth, and inserted it into the spongy material of the seal itself, running the probe's tip under the lower edge where the insertion mark would be least likely to be noticed. She checked the setting a final time, and pressed the button at the end of the probe. There was a flash of light, and when she touched the seal again, the material had gone rigid, held in stasis until she released it. She freed the probe, and used a spade-headed key to pry the seal away from the lock. That mechanism was uncomplicated. Behind her, Galler cleared his throat, but Heikki ignored him, and punched in a set of numbers. The lock considered, and then snapped open. Heikki allowed herself a quick grin, and hauled up the capsule's loading hatch. She searched along the inner wall below the latch mechanism until she found the vent control. She turned the cock to full open, then straightened again.

"Help me move the bolts. Stack them to the side, I think there's room."

Together they hauled at the bolts of fabric, slippery in their protective wrappings, wedging them up against the top of the crate until they'd cleared two rectangular spaces. The openings looked unpleasantly like new-dug graves, but Heikki pushed the thought away. "Get in," she said, and swung herself sideways into the nearer space.

Galler did as he was told, his expression one of resignation. "Two questions," he said, tucking his lap-board between the bolts beside him. "Are you sure you can close it, and how are we going to get out again?"

Heikki had swung around on her knees, reaching for the lid above her, but allowed herself a sour smile. "Yes, I can close it," she said, and braced herself for the effort. "There's an emergency release on the inside of the latch—standard precaution, ever since a worker was trapped in one. Ready?" Without waiting for Galler's answer, she brought the lid down, balancing awkwardly on knees and elbows until she heard the lock catch. She sprawled on her stomach then, unable comfortably to turn over in the confined space. Nothing to do now but wait, she thought, and tried to make her breathing slow and even. The air in the capsule already smelled hot and stale. Imagination, she tried to tell herself, there are vents and you opened them, but her body was not fully convinced.

"Heikki?" Galler's voice was muffled—by the crowding bolts, Heikki told herself, and not by fear.

"What?"

"How the hell did you open the lock?"

Heikki grinned in the darkness. "This isn't high security. Almost everybody who ships by rail codes the capsule lock to the date and time of the shipment. I punched that in, and, sure enough, it opened."

There was a moment's silence, and then Galler swore. "How can they be so stupid?"

"Write them a memo," Heikki suggested. The capsule lurched suddenly, and she swallowed her laughter. The copper taste of fear was in her mouth; she dug her fingers into the plastic covering the bolts to either side, wishing she had never listened to her brother, this time or any time. The capsule swayed again, carried by the lifting field, then bounded forward a meter or two.

"What the hell?" Galler said again, and there was enough of a note of hysteria in his voice to force Heikki to answer.

"The passenger train just linked up," she said, and hoped he believed her. It was a plausible enough explanation, anyway, whether or not it happened to be true. Then the capsule lifted a final time, the movement steadier, more controlled, and slid forward toward the warp. Heikki braced herself, staring into the darkness, and felt the gentle bumping as the capsules began to slide into the warp. Their capsule lifted, and her with it, her body rising into a silent explosion filled with indescribable color, colors that did not, could not exist in anything approaching reality. She felt her body floating, then streaming away, as though the unimaginable forces of the warp were sweating the last atom of flesh from her bones. She clasped her hands in denial, felt the touch of skin on skin, but the sensation of melting, of dissolution continued, more real than the thin pain of finger against finger.

And then, mercifully, it was over, ending with an abruptness that left her dizzy, mind still reeling in non-space. The capsule slowed, bumping to a stop, and Heikki forced herself to move, feeling in the darkness for the raised letters that marked the emergency release. There was less time on arrival; the loaders would appear all too quickly. . . . She found it at last, and slammed her palm against the release button. The lid did not budge, and she hit it again, harder, bruising the heel of her hand painfully, her breath catching in a gasp that was almost a sob. This time, the release worked, and the lid rose majestically, letting in the dim light of the cargo platform on EP7.

Even that seemed bright, after the cave-like darkness
of the capsule. Heikki blinked away tears, and pushed
herself up onto her knees, forcing herself to hurry.
"Come on, damn it," she said, as much to herself as to
Galler. "Come on."

Galler groaned, and pushed himself up into a sitting
position, both hands at his temples. Heikki swore, and
reached for him, but he batted her hand away, and slid
out of the capsule on his own. He reached back for his
lapscreen, slinging it shakily over his shoulder, and
said, "I don't think much of your cheap flights, Gwynne."

Heikki, hauling at the bolts they had pushed aside,
did not bother to answer. Light flared above them
then, flooding the platform with a hard blue glare.

"Leave that," Galler said, with sudden urgency. "The
loaders are coming."

"I know," Heikki snarled, and slammed the capsule
shut. She could see, at the far end of the platform, the
red-painted door that was the emergency exit to the
passenger platform. She pointed to it with one hand,
the other fumbling in her pocket for the seal she had
removed from the lock. "Get going, go on."

"But—" Galler bit off whatever protest he had been
about to make, and started for the emergency exit at a
trot.

Heikki slapped the seal back into place, and drew out
the molecular probe again, frantically twisting the dial
until she had the setting she wanted. She slid the probe
back into the hole she'd originally made, and triggered
the button. In the background, she thought she could
hear the snarl of a robo-pallet's power plant, but dismissed it as imagination. Light flared, and the stasis
field vanished, the seal resuming its original spongy
composition. She withdrew the probe with hurried care,
certain now that she heard pallets approaching, and
sprinted for the emergency exit. *I hope to hell Sten was
right and the lock's been jinxed already*, she thought,
and knew it was entirely too late to be worrying about
that. Galler was at the door already, beckoning wildly.
Behind her, Heikki heard the thudding as the first

hatch was opened, and then she was at the emergency door. She slapped the release bar hard, no longer caring if she triggered all the alarms on the station, and saw Galler gaping at her, mouth and eyes wide as if in protest. The door swung outward easily, without alarm or even the shriek of hinges, and Heikki barely managed to catch it before it swung too far. And then they were through, staring at the crowd streaming out of the passenger capsules toward the main exit. Heikki closed the emergency exit gently behind them, hardly able to believe she was here and safe, and saw the same disbelief on Galler's face.

"We made it," he said, foolishly, and Heikki could not stop herself from laughing.

"We made it," she agreed, and started toward the main exit, walking like a woman in a dream.

# CHAPTER 10

They passed through Customs' usual cursory check without difficulty, without even attracting the full attention of the young man on duty at the residents' gate. After the struggle to get off EP4, Heikki found it hard to muster the strength for fear, and could see from Galler's face that he was feeling equally numb. The sights and sounds of the main concourse roused her a little, let her shake off the lethargy that had closed around her, and she caught at her brother's arm to hold him back from the jitney line.

"Let me call Santerese first," she said.

"You're expecting trouble?" Galler asked, and Heikki shook her head.

"No, but there's no harm in being careful." She hesitated, but could not resist adding, "You stirred up enough trouble on EP4; it may have spread by now."

Galler made a face, and did not deny it. Heikki left him slumped on a bench in the orbit of one of the concourse's grand mobiles, staring at the intricate exposed clockworks that sent tuned spheres bouncing through a maze of nuglass and chiming crystal, and went in search of a public combox.

She found an empty one at last, half a level below the main concourse, on the mezzanine overlooking the floater platforms. She settled herself in the booth, latching the door behind her, and fed her personal card into the machine. The system considered it for a moment, matching numbers and credits, and flashed a clear screen. Heikki punched in the callcodes, and waited.

It took a few minutes for Santerese to respond to the summons—an unusually long time, Heikki thought, and sat up straighter on the hard bench, frowning at the screen. Then the picture cleared, and Santerese's broad face looked out at her.

"Heikki." There was something in her tone that was not quite right, and Heikki's frown deepened.

" 'Shallin. I'm back, with what I went for." The evasion came out smoothly, almost without thought. "How're things at home?"

"All right." Again, there was an unfamiliar note in Santerese's voice, a hesitation that was not normally there, almost, Heikki thought, as though she were choosing her words for an offscreen listener. "I'm glad you were successful, doll. We've had—a bit of a time here."

"What do you mean?"

Santerese grinned, but it was a shadow of her usual smile. "I told you there were questions about our working methods? Well, the investigation is official now—nothing's showed up, nor is it likely to, but it's been expensive, and a hassle. I'm glad you're back."

"So am I," Heikki said. The story was plausible enough, and would certainly account for Santerese's harried look, but. . . . They had set up codes, check phrases, long ago, the first time they had worked apart on a politically restless planet; over the years, the system had come in handy more than once. "What does that do to the Morgan job?"

There was a moment's pause before Santerese answered. "I thought we could hand it over to Penninzer, if worst comes to worse."

That was the countersign, the signal that everything was all right. Heikki relaxed, and said, "Good enough. But I hope we won't have to."

"Me, too," Santerese answered. "Are you coming straight here?"

Heikki nodded.

"Take a jitney," Santerese said, with a ghost of her usual manner. "This is no time for you to be cheap, Heikki."

"I'll do that," Heikki said, relieved, and broke the connection. The screen faded to neutral gray, waiting for her next command, but Heikki sat still for a moment longer, staring past the screen at the floater platforms half a level below. Even as she watched, one of the bubbles rose past her, carried on the invisible beam, its riders distorted shapes against the transluscent plastic. She fixed her eyes on it as it rose out of sight, then waited until it began its leisurely descent toward the receiving station on the far side of the station's open central volume. It was not like Santerese to be so quiet, not like her to worry—in fact, Heikki thought, it would be more like her to be fighting back, with suit and countersuit. Something simply wasn't right. Heikki shook herself then, annoyed with her own imaginings. She had asked the code question, and Santerese had answered: nothing could be wrong. No one else knew their system, not even Djuro. Nothing was wrong.

A prompt question had been flashing on the screen for some time now, Heikki realized suddenly. She touched the keys that closed down the system and retrieved her card, and then levered herself out of the narrow box. Nothing is wrong, she told herself again, but caught herself looking over her shoulder more than once as she returned to the concourse where she had left Galler.

"What kept you?" Galler looked up from his lapscreen, scowling irritably.

"It took me a while to find an empty box," Heikki answered. "Come on, will you?"

Galler's eyebrow rose in a mocking question, and

Heikki glared at him, daring him to speak. After a moment, it was Galler who looked away. Heikki allowed herself a grim smile, and took her place in the line of people waiting for jitneys.

Most of the crowd from their train had already found transport, and it wasn't long before a jitney pulled up to the platform. Heikki fed it her cashcard, wondering morosely just how much this rescue was going to cost her before it was over, and gave the machine her address. The canopy sprang up instantly, and Heikki climbed in. Galler followed, tugging the canopy closed behind him, and the machine slid smoothly away from the platform.

EP7 had only one major connector, a massive corridor known as the Artery that ran along the central spine of the station. The jitney swung wide around the open volume at the center of Pod One, then turned onto a spiral ramp that carried it up and into the traffic of the Artery. It was not crowded at this time of the Exchange Point's day, and the mix of traffic, mass carriers on the lower levels, private vehicles, jitneys, and the like in the upper lanes, was moving almost at the permitted maximum. Heikki's mood lifted a little, seeing that: not long, she thought, not long at all until we're home and we can finally start fighting back.

The jitney deposited them at the top of the stairwell that led down into Pod Nineteen. Heikki stopped at the security booth to identify Galler to the bored-looking securitron, then led the way past the lowered barriers and down the spiralling stairs to the suite of rooms that was both office and flat. As she stepped off the stairway, she noticed that the heavy curtains had been drawn across the narrow window. Stepping closer, she saw that the red bar was lit above the concierge plate: *Business closed.*

"I would've thought your partner would be working today," Galler said, at her shoulder.

Heikki shrugged. "Things happen." She turned toward the alleyway that led to the private entrances, and Galler caught her shoulder.

"This isn't right, Gwynne. There could be something wrong."

Heikki made a face, debating whether she should tell him, then shrugged. "Ever since we stopped working for Lo-Moth, people have been asking questions about our past methods. The Marshallin says we're under investigation. That's why we're closed."

"Damn." It was unlike Galler, 'pointer to the bone, to swear, and Heikki stopped to look at him, startled. He gestured apology. "I'm sorry. But if they've started to investigate you—what is it, illegal procedures, things like that?"

Heikki nodded.

"Then I don't see how you can help me," Galler said. "I need supporters who are above reproach."

Heikki took a deep breath, and caught her brother's shoulder, spinning him back to face her. "Get one thing straight, little brother. I am above reproach. We are professionals, we do not break laws, and we don't cut corners. The Licensing Board, or even the cops, can investigate until doomsday, and they won't find anything that isn't faked—obviously faked. Is that clear?"

Galler nodded, but did not look particularly convinced. Heikki turned away, angry with herself for losing her temper, and unlocked the grill that barred the private entrances. The door to the flat opened before she could lay her hand against the lock, and Santerese beckoned her in.

"I heard you yelling outside," she said, with a shadow of her normal smile.

"I'm sorry, Marshallin," Heikki said, and stepped into the familiar room, Galler at her shoulder. A drinks tray was resting on the side table, two filled glasses waiting. A third stood half-empty on the monitor console, and a fourth—also half-empty—on the sideboard beside the door to the workroom. Heikki's eyes narrowed, but before she could say anything, an enormous figure poked its head out of the doorway. If he had been a little smaller, and darker, he could have been Nkosi's twin; as it was, he bore an uncomfortable resemblance to one of the shaggier terrestrial bears. He looked like a clown, Heikki thought, torn between laughter and shrieking fury, and drew breath to say something she would certainly regret. Before she could speak, however, the big man said cheerfully, "Good to see you, Heikki. And you, ser, must be the lady's all too elusive brother." His tone changed abruptly. "You are Galler Heikki?"

Galler hesitated, and Heikki said, flatly, "Yes, this is Galler." She looked at her brother. "And this is Idris Max, who last time I knew him was with the Transit Police."

"Oh, I've been promoted since then," Max said genially. He always had been impervious to insult, Heikki remembered. She looked at Santerese.

"I thought you told me everything was all right."

"As far as I knew, it was." Santerese looked at Max. "Unless you've changed your plans?"

Max smiled. "Not at all. But there is a query out for him."

"Which is not the same thing as an advice of arrest," Galler murmured, just loudly enough to be heard.

"Very true," Max said. "However, I am obliged to ask you a few questions."

Heikki looked again at Santerese. "Marshallin, why don't you tell me what's going on?"

Santerese made a face. "Doll, I wish I knew. When I got word that a formal investigation was being launched, I put Malachy on the legal aspects, and—since I had to admit you were probably right about Lo-Moth screwing us on this one—I started to work on the tapes you sent me. I also got back in touch with your ex-boyfriend here." She nodded to Max, who bowed.

"He never was," Heikki said.

Santerese grinned. "Whatever you say, doll. Anyway, I figured if anybody had the connections we needed, it would be him. So here he is, and here you are."

"What did you find on the tapes?" Heikki asked.

"Now that," Max interrupted, "was the most interesting thing about all of this mess." He lumbered over to the drinks tray, and scooped up one of the glasses. He passed it to Heikki, who stared for an instant in fascination at the delicate goblet clutched in the enormous paw before accepting it.

"It's that bad?" she said aloud.

"The crystal matrix was destroyed at the wreck site," Santerese said.

Heikki swore, and did not bother to apologize. That was, in her opinion, the least likely of all the possible results—but on the other hand, if Galler was right, if Lo-Moth's new matrix wasn't new at all, but was derived from the same research that had produced the flawed crystal that had destroyed EP1. . . . What else could the pirates do with it? It couldn't be sold, and it certainly couldn't be kept—and the pirates couldn't've been the usual run of hired thugs, she realized abruptly. They had to be company men, trusted men, because otherwise there would be too many opportunities for blackmail. . . .

"This is making sense to you," Max said, and the buffoonery was gone from his voice. "Give."

Heikki took a deep breath, marshalling her thoughts, but before she could say anything, Galler spoke. "Wait a minute, Gwynne." His voice was brittle, amused. "Before you start talking to the—authorities—I think there are a couple of questions you should be asking."

"Ask away," Max said.

"First, what's the status of this investigation of yours?" Galler glanced at Heikki. "You see, I'm not entirely selfish. And what's my status—ser?"

"Commissioner," Max said affably. Heikki lifted an eyebrow. The change in title represented a considerable promotion since the last time she had seen Max. "The investigation is proceeding—though right now I'm more interested in *why* we were put on the job than in the trumped-up 'violations' we've been shown." He smiled at Heikki. "Not at all your style, Heikki." He looked back at Galler. "As for you, ser. . . . As they say, that depends in large part on how you choose to answer my questions."

"I see." Galler managed a wry smile, and reached for the last drink left on the tray.

Max seated himself on the largest of the chairs and leaned back, still smiling benignly. "Now, as I said, this all seems to make sense to you two. Why don't you explain it all to me?"

Heikki looked at her brother, unable to keep an unholy joy from her face. "Galler knows so much more," she said sweetly. "I think he'd better explain this one."

It took perhaps half an hour for Galler to outline what he had found in Tremoth's files and Slade's reaction to his discoveries. When he had finished, Heikki spoke, explaining her contract with Lo-Moth and the work she had done on Iadara. Max sat quietly through it all, eyes hooded, leaning back comfortably as though he were listening to children's tales. When they had both finished, he sat quietly for a moment, staring at nothing, then shook himself, looking up with an abstracted smile.

"So sorry, but I was just thinking, this might explain a couple of bodies that turned up one one of the lower levels of EP10 last week—Tremoth employees who'd broken their contracts and gone underground. Or so their bosses said, even though the grieving widows claimed they were company men to the last molecule."

"The hijack crew?" Heikki said.

"By coincidence, they were last seen on Iadara," Max said. "Oceanic survey work, officially."

Definitely the hijackers, Heikki thought, but said nothing. Iadara's oceans were effectively useless for any of Lo-Moth's products; they weren't even terribly useful as a food supply. She shook the memory away, and said to Max, "So now what?"

Max shook his head. "You tell me. It might interest you to know, by the way, that Slade's been giving money to Retroceder politicians and action groups."

"I thought he was a Retroceder," Heikki said, and Galler made a little noise of satisfaction. Max pointed a finger at him. "You claimed you had information from Tremoth's files. Where is it?"

Galler made a face. "It was in my office, in the reader

there." Max raised an eyebrow in polite disbelief, and Galler said, stung, "Well, in my experience, no one ever looks at the tapes *in* the reader, they search the files and the strongbox and all that. It was the safest place I could think of on short notice. I was planning to recover them, anyway, take them back to my pied-a-terre, but things moved a little faster than I was expecting. I set things up so that Gwynne—"

"Gwynne?" Max said, chortling. Heikki waved him to silence, all too aware of the color mounting in her cheeks.

"—so that Heikki could collect them," Galler went on, "but she didn't do it." He shrugged. "So I don't have any proof. I have to admit, I wasn't able to tell her they were there, but—" He broke off abruptly, staring at the circles of plastic Heikki was pulling from her belt pocket. Heikki allowed herself a single smile, one smile of triumph for all those years of rivalry, and leaned forward to pass the disks to Max.

"What's on these, anyway?"

Galler closed his mouth, blinking. After a moment, he said, "You had them all along."

Heikki nodded. "What are they?"

"Why—?" Galler began, then shook his head. "No. Not important." He took a deep breath, focussing his attention on Max. "Those disks contain the information I pulled from our files on the original crystal project, including schematics. There are also records of Daulo Slade's actions after I informed him of the overlap between the historical documents and Lo-Moth's latest project."

"Very nice," Max said, tranquilly, and tucked the disks into his jacket. "But not exactly conclusive." He held up his hand, silencing Galler's automatic response, and looked at Heikki. "Heikki—your name's really Gwynne?"

Reluctantly, Heikki nodded, and Max shook his head. "I was expecting something really awful, after all the fuss you made about not using it. Can you reconstruct the crystal matrix that Lo-Moth lost from the information on the tapes?"

Heikki looked at Santerese, who said, "It was pretty well fragmented, and the fragments were mixed in with a lot of other debris. It looked like they swept it down into the hold."

"I remember," Heikki said, softly. There had been a mass of wreckage, objects crushed almost to powder, a powder that glittered in the beams of their handlights. . . . She shook the thought away, said aloud, "I don't know. It depends on how big the fragments were, and how many of them we can find on the tape. And, of course, how good the tape is."

Santerese said, "We can try. But do you really want us to do it, Max? We're—interested parties, to say the least."

"Oh, don't worry," Max said, with a smile that showed a disconcerting number of teeth. "Copies of your tapes are already in my main labs. But you are the best, Marshallin, you and Heikki. You'll do it?"

"Of course," Santerese said, with a quirky smile, and Heikki said, "I don't see you've left us a choice, Idris."

The tapes from the wreck site were already in the workroom. Heikki settled herself at her console, frowning, and called up the menu of tools she had available for this sort of job. At the console opposite, Santerese bent over her keyboard, reloading the raw data. "Was the composition of the matrix standard?" she asked, and Heikki shrugged.

"Galler?"

"What?" Her brother appeared in the doorway, Max looming behind him.

"Was the matrix of standard materials, do you know?"

"I think so," Galler answered, frowning. "Why?"

Max laid a hand on his shoulder, drawing him away. "Let's let them get on with it, shall we?"

Heikki was hardly aware of his departure. She stared at the list of programs displayed on the workscreen, tugging thoughtfully at her lower lip. She touched keys to load the restoration program—*no question I'll need that one*, she thought—then added the more sensitive of the two modelling programs. After a moment's hesitation, she added a second construction program, and leaned back to let the three spool into working memory.

"I'm sorting the debris by apparent composition now," Santerese announced. "Or trying to, anyway. God, I hate working with tape."

Heikki nodded her agreement. Even with the most sophisticated programs, you were still working with a computer's best guess, and if that guess was wrong, it was usually catastrophically wrong, so that you thought you were looking at diamonds, and were actually dealing with ground glass. She put the thought aside. After all, the computers weren't often wrong. Her eyes still on the filling screen, she said, "So what do you think of my brother, Marshallin?"

Santerese looked up from her screen in some surprise. "I've hardly seen enough to judge." Heikki said nothing, waiting, and Santerese shrugged. "Got his eye on the main chance, hasn't he?"

Heikki grinned. "That's a polite way of putting it."

"You don't like him at all, do you, doll?"

"No," Heikki said, "I don't." She became aware, tardily, of the disapproval in Santerese's tone, and looked away. "I'm sorry if it bothers you, Marshallin, but that's the way it is. It's a little late to change."

There was a brief silence, and then Santerese said, "I think you're overreacting, just a little." Her screen beeped before Heikki could think how to answer, and Santerese said, "I can flip you the raw feed now."

This was not the time to discuss Galler, Heikki knew. She touched keys on her board, and said, "Ready to receive." Numbers streamed across her screen, and she pushed the keyboard aside to make room for the more sensitive shadowscreen. The flow of numbers stopped at last, and a single icon pulsed in the center of the screen. Heikki took a deep breath, once again remembering the wreck site, and touched the shadowscreen.

The icon vanished, to be replaced with a strange, washed-out image. There was a scattering of brighter shapes along the bottom of the screen. Heikki frowned for a moment, then realized what she was looking at.

This was a processed image of the latac's hold, looking down onto the field of debris that had been swept onto the distillery. The highlighted pieces would be the bits the computer had decided probably belonged to the crystal matrix. She ran her fingers along the sensitive edges of the shadowscreen, shrinking that image and opening a new window above it, then began painstakingly to transfer the highlighted pieces from the original image to the window. They hung there as though suspended in space, strange three-dimensional shapes that showed odd rifts and fracture lines.

"I don't think that's all of it," Santerese said.

Heikki looked up, startled—she had not seen Santerese leave her console to come and lean over her shoulder— but looked at the screen again. She had already moved more than half of the highlighted pieces to the working window, and even allowing for the remainder, there was not enough to make up a complete matrix. "I agree," she said quietly.

"Do you want me to run the program again on what's left?" Santerese asked, and Heikki shrugged.

"You might as well. I don't know if it will do any good, though."

Santerese nodded, and returned to her machine. Frowning, Heikki finished removing the last highlighted images from the lower screen, then ran her hand along the edge of the shadowscreen to shrink the image even further. The pieces isolated in the upper window swelled until they almost filled her screen.

Those fragments weren't enough to make up a complete matrix, that much was obvious. Heikki studied them for a moment longer, head tilted to one side, then ran her hands across the shadowscreen again, shifting the pieces. Several of the larger shards looked as though they would fit together, and she ran her hand across the shadowscreen, lifting and rotating them until the broken edges meshed and melded. It was a start, she knew, but resisted the temptation to do more. Instead, she called up the first of the reconstruction programs, and let it work while she waited for Santerese to finish the second survey. As she had expected, it displayed "inconclusive" across its tiny window, and when she touched the override, produced a vaguely dodecahedral shape. Most of the lines flashed blue, indicating serious uncertainty. Heikki shrugged, and banished the program.

"How's it coming, Marshallin?"

"Almost done," Santerese answered. "The probability is lower, though, by about ten percent. You'll want to bear that in mind."

Heikki nodded. A few moments later, her screen flickered, and Santerese said, "I'm flipping you the new figures."

"Thanks," Heikki said. "Ready to receive."

The image at the bottom of her screen disappeared, and was replaced a moment later by another, this one larger, with a rather sparse collection of highlighted images spread across the lower part of the window. They were concentrated in the center, where the debris field had been deepest, about what Heikki had expected. She nodded to herself and began transferring those images to the larger working screen.

When she had finished, the fragments looked somewhat more promising than they had, almost, she thought, as though there might be enough for the computer to work from. She triggered the construction program again, and this time the machine went to work without immediate complaint. After a few moments, a shape—still dodecahedral, but more clearly faceted, more recognizably something functional—appeared in the working window. A moment later, a second image, a crude cross section, with more lines flashing uncertain blue, appeared beside it, and then a third, this one a rotation of the first.

"Analysis?" Heikki said aloud.

The program considered for a moment, then responded, *Function unclear. No recorded parallels of statistical significance.*

Heikki had not expected anything else. She sighed, and leaned across the console to fit a disk into the room's recording system.

"No luck?" Santerese asked, and pushed herself up from her console.

"Nothing conclusive," Heikki answered, shrugging. "It's handwork from here on in."

Santerese grinned, and brought her chair around so that she could sit beside her partner. "I've seen worse."

Heikki nodded, still staring at the screen. This was the trickiest part of any reconstruction, especially when they had only the tapes to go on, not actual samples of the debris. The reconstruction and restoration programs had taken things as far as they could; now she and Santerese would have to evaluate the machine's work, and use their informed judgement to add to the computer's construct. "Switch on the recorder, will you?" she said aloud, and Santerese did so. "Report—" She glanced at the string of characters that appeared at the bottom of the workscreen, labelling the work by date and time and session number. "—229.1631.2, Gwynne Heikki and Marshallin Santerese, for Heikki/Santerese Salvage, private report. Data is drawn from tapes 214.1426.a, 214.1426.b, and 214.1426.c, taken under contract to Lo-Moth, of and on Iadara. Data has been processed using Loppi Standard Analysis, and modified Forian Reconstruction and Restoration programs. We are now proceeding under the assumption that the recovered fragments were part of a crystal matrix, deliberately destroyed by hijackers." She nodded to Santerese, who adjusted the recorder's setting.

"This machine is now set for sound-activated recording," Santerese said, "and for real-time recording of all on-screen and in-memory activity."

Heikki nodded again. "Then let's begin."

It took them another four hours of slow, painstaking work to finish reconstructing the crystal. At last, however, Heikki leaned back in her chair, stretching, and said slowly, "I think that's all I dare do. I can't really justify adding anything more."

Santerese glanced at the secondary screen, which displayed schematics for half a dozen different types of standard crystal. "It's pretty obvious what it was, doll. That was a matrix."

Heikki nodded her agreement, and reached across her partner to touch a button on the recorder cabinet. "Work is completed on report 229.1631.2. This recording ends." She flipped off the recorder, and said, more normally, "And that proves it wasn't an ordinary hijacking."

"Not that you ever thought it was," Santerese murmured.

"Well, what hijacker in his right mind would destroy the thing he came to steal?" Heikki asked, and pushed herself up out of her chair. She was stiff from the hours of work, she realized belatedly, and winced as she moved to the door. "Max?"

The commissioner had been asleep, sprawled on the couch, his feet propped up on the monitor box, but he opened his eyes at the sound of his name, contriving to look instantly aware. "Yes?"

"We've finished the report," Heikki said. "I'd like you to see the results, and seal the disks." She looked around the room. "Where's Galler?"

Max pointed down the hall toward the bedrooms. "Asleep, I expect. I'll take a look at your disks."

Trust Galler to have settled in comfortably, Heikki thought, but there was less malice in the thought than there would have been before. That was not an entirely comfortable realization, and she put it aside, saying, "We're almost certain it was a matrix—"

"Almost?" Max cut in, and Heikki gave a reluctant smile.

"I'm certain. The almost is there for the courts and the statistics."

"Good enough," Max said. He maneuvered his bulk past the banks of machines to perch cautiously on Heikki's chair. "Show me."

Obediently, Santerese triggered the media wall, throwing the final projection onto its central field. "This is the complete reconstruction," she said. "We made a full recording of all procedures used, of course, but this is what we got."

Max stared at the slowly rotating crystal, his face without expression. It didn't look like much, Heikki admitted to herself, just a rough cube, its corners sawn off to create smaller planes, and those corners sawn off as well, creating smaller and smallers facets. She leaned past Max to touch keys on the nearest workboard, throwing a second, similar image onto the wall beside the reconstruction.

"That's a simulated core crystal from a class-5 freighter—just a sample of the approximate form, not a real one." She touched keys again, and produced a third image. "This is a schematic of the type of crystal used in the Exchange Points' PDEs."

"All right," Max said again, "they're obviously very similar. What did Lo-Moth tell you this one was, again?"

"A matrix for a possible universal center crystal seed," Heikki answered.

"Mmm." Max returned his attention to the media wall. He reached into the pocket of his jacket, and drew out the disks Heikki had given him. "Can you copy these?" he asked, not taking his eyes from the screen. "And then play back the copies?"

"I thought you'd never ask," Santerese said. She took the disks, slid them one by one into a diskprinter, then fed the copies into her workboard. Max tucked the originals back into his jacket. He had never taken his eyes off her during the entire process, Heikki realized abruptly, and wondered if she should be insulted.

"Put it on the big screen, Marshallin?" she said instead, and Santerese nodded. Another window opened on the media wall directly below the slowly rotating crystals, and filled with text that flickered past at an almost blinding rate.

"This is just the record of Slade's movements," Santerese translated. "I'm looking for the data on the original crystal." The text, mixed now with strings of numbers and flashing images, flickered past for a few minutes longer, and then Santerese said, "Got it."

The flow of data slowed, and then stopped, a delicately drawn schematic filling a quarter of the image. Santerese adjusted her controls, and the schematic expanded, until it had pushed the last bits of text out of the window. It looked surprisingly familiar.

"Bring up the schematic we created, would you, Marshallin?" Heikki said slowly. Santerese smiled grimly, and did so. The two diagrams were very similar.

"So," Max said, almost to himself, sounding satisfied.

Heikki reached for her own controls, adjusting the images until the two schematics overlapped. There were minor differences, of course, there always would be between plan and actual crystal, but the main lines merged impeccably into one. "So Galler was right," she said aloud, and Max leaned back to look at her, a crooked smile on his face.

"That's assuming you're right, Heikki, in your reconstruction." He held up his hand, forestalling her automatic protest. "Don't get me wrong, I agree with you—but please remember, I have to go to the courts with this, and Tremoth's lawyers are—well, experts is the politest word I've heard used. This is nice, but I'd like to have something solid in evidence to back it up."

"What about the records of Slade's movement, this stuff?" Santerese asked. "And his politics?"

Max shrugged. "Again, useful, but not conclusive. The source is tainted, after all."

He was right, of course, and Heikki looked down at her workscreen, not really seeing the array of figures it displayed. By now, Slade would have covered his tracks, both within Tremoth and on Iadara. Though it might be more difficult on Iadara, where a substantial local population hated Lo-Moth, and not all of Lo-Moth supported its parent. . . . She frowned. FitzGilbert, in particular, had disliked Slade, and, more to the point, she'd lost people of her own when the latac was shot down. She had not approved of Heikki/Santerese being taken off the job—and even putting all that aside, Heikki thought, with an inward grin, she's the likely scapegoat if Slade decides to dump the blame on Lo-Moth. All of which just might make her willing to cooperate with the authorities.

"Max," she said, "what if I told you there was someone on Iadara, in Lo-Moth, that just might be able to come up with the hard evidence you need—if you approached her the right way, of course."

Max eyed her warily. "If it was true, Heikki, I'd be very happy, naturally. What makes you think anyone in Lo-Moth would have anything useful, even if they were willing to give it up?"

Heikki took a deep breath, marshalling her thoughts. "My contact on Iadara was a woman named FitzGilbert. She's the operations director on-planet—it was her latac that was shot down, and her people who were killed." There was a faint look of amusement in Max's eyes, and Heikki said, stung, "Yes, people still take that sort of thing seriously in the Precincts, Max."

Max waved a hand in apology. "Go on."

"I think she suspected something of what happened, and she wasn't happy when we were pulled off the job. Plus she doesn't like Slade at all, or at least she didn't seem to." Heikki paused, pulling herself back to the main line of her argument. "As director of operations, she has to know a good deal about the crash, and about Slade's behavior immediately afterward. She might have what you're looking for."

"I've tried to contact Lo-Moth personnel," Max said gently. "In fact, I have spoken to some of them. But I haven't been able to pry any of them loose from their company-appointed lawyers—they don't want to be pried loose, most of them—and I'm not going to get anything useful from them under those circumstances."

"Ah." Heikki could not restrain a smile of sheer pleasure, and then laughed aloud as Max's brows drew together into a frown. "You are a suspicious sort, Max." She sobered quickly. "Max, a woman named Alexieva, Incarnacion Alexieva Cirilly, rode back to the Loop with us, she's staying with Jock Nkosi right now. She is, or at worse was, FitzGilbert's agent while she was on

Iadara. If anybody could get you a private conversation with FitzGilbert, she could."

"But would she?" Max said, and Heikki smiled again.

"I think you could persuade her."

Max nodded, and pushed himself away from the console with renewed energy. "But you'll make the call, Heikki, just in case." He smiled, and this time there was no humor in it, just the predator's bared teeth. "I don't care what company secrets he was trying to protect—I don't even care if Tremoth crystals did cause the EP1 disaster. That was a hundred and fifty years ago. You don't kill, what is it now—the latac crew, and the hijackers—almost a dozen people, for a stale secret." His smile shifted, went lopsided and wry. "And if you ever repeat that, Heikki, I'll reveal your first name to the Loop."

"No one would ever mistake you for an idealist," Heikki said, her voice more gentle than her words. She was tired, her eyes gritty from staring at the screen, but forced herself to stand upright. "I'll make the call."

To her surprise, Nkosi was both in and accepting contact, though he did not switch on his cameras. Heikki could hear someone moving in the background as she made her appeal, asking him and Alexieva to come by the office suite as soon as possible, and hoped it was the surveyor. There was a moment of silence when she had finished, and then Nkosi said, a faint note of surprise in his voice, "But of course, we will be there within the hour."

"Thanks," Heikki said, but the pilot had already broken the connection.

"Will he come?" Max asked.

"Jock doesn't break his word," Heikki said, but privately she was not quite so confident. Nkosi she trusted, knew she could trust, but Alexieva remained an unknown quantity. She massaged her temples, digging her fingers hard into the pressure points in a vain attempt to drive away some of the aching tiredness.

"Why don't you lie down for a while?" Santerese said gently. "This hasn't exactly been one of your better days."

Heikki nodded in reluctant agreement. "I'll do that," she said. "Wake me when they get here."

Santerese looked as though she would protest, but Max said, "Of course."

Heikki nodded again. The bedroom was cool, and very quiet, the air lightly touched with Santerese's perfume. A single light faded on as Heikki entered, the room sensors reacting to her movements, but she waved it off again, and stretched out on the bed without bothering to undress. It seemed only a few moments before Santerese was touching her shoulder.

"Jock's here, and Alexieva."

"Oh, God." Heikki sat up slowly, blinking away sleep. The brief nap hadn't helped at all—if anything, she thought, *I feel worse than I did before.*

Santerese gave her a sympathetic smile, and held out a single dark red capsule. "Try this."

Heikki swallowed it without question, grimacing at the bitter taste. "Pick-me-up?" she asked, and Santerese nodded.

"You'd better come on," she said. "Alexieva's getting difficult."

Heikki swore under her breath, but levered herself up off the bed. "What do you think of her, Marshallin?"

Santerese shrugged. "I don't know her. I don't think I like her, but I don't know her. And these aren't the best of conditions for making those decisions, doll."

"True," Heikki agreed, but could not help feeling rather pleased that Santerese shared her own opinion of the Iadaran. The thought buoyed her up as she made her way back into the suite's main room.

The others were waiting there, Alexieva seated on the long couch, her face set in an expression at once stubborn and remote. Nkosi loomed protectively behind her, scowling at Max, who seemed completely unaffected by his stare.

"Ah, there you are, Heikki," the commissioner said affably. There was a choked noise from the wall behind him, and Heikki glanced curiously in that direction to see her brother smothering a laugh. "I've explained the situation to Dam' Alexieva, and what we want from her, but she's a little uneasy. She wants assurance from you."

*From me?* Heikki thought. *What can I give you— what can I promise you that Max can't?* She said nothing, however, but looked at Alexieva.

"What I want," the surveyor said clearly, "is your word—which Jock tells me is good—that Dam' Fitz-Gilbert won't be harmed by this."

Heikki hesitated, knowing just how much was riding on her answer. At last she said, "Damn it, I can't tell you that. I can't predict the future. All I can do is give you my word that it isn't our—his—" She pointed to Max. "—intention that FitzGilbert be hurt in any way."

It was not, she thought remotely, a particularly convincing speech, but to her surprise, Alexieva looked away. "That was what I meant," the surveyor said, after a moment. She glanced up at Nkosi, then looked away, shrugged. "All right. Yes, I will contact Dam' Fitz-Gilbert, and ask her to contact me here, through secure channels."

"But will she do it?" Galler murmured, loudly enough to be heard.

Alexieva glared at him. "She will."

"Then let's get on with it," Max said, interrupting Galler's response. "Dam' Alexieva?"

There was no refusing the invitation. Alexieva pushed herself to her feet, looking suddenly very tired, and followed Max into the workroom. Nkosi pushed himself away from the couch, shaking his head.

"You had better be right about this, Heikki," he said, and followed the others into the workroom.

Heikki looked at Santerese, a wry smile tugging at her lips. "I do hope so," she said softly, and Santerese grinned.

"Like the man says, you better be."

They sat in silence for the better part of an hour before the others emerged from the workroom. "Well?" Santerese said after a moment, and Max shrugged.

"I left the message," Alexieva said—rather defensively, Heikki thought.

"What message?" she asked.

"We have a whole code," Alexieva said impatiently. She looked at Max. "Dam' FitzGilbert will contact me."

"It would be helpful," Max said dryly. "Preferably before entropy sets in, however."

Alexieva looked as though she wanted to spit at him, but Nkosi laid a restraining hand on her shoulder. "She has done all that she can," he said quietly, but with a note of gentle menace that might, Heikki thought, have given even Max pause. "All we can do now is wait."

The commissioner, however, did not seem impressed. "True enough, but I'll have to ask you to do your waiting here."

For a moment, it seemed that Nkosi might protest further, and Heikki said softly, "Jock. . . ." The pilot looked at her then, and sighed.

"All right. We'll wait—here."

FitzGilbert did not respond for almost twenty hours. Heikki spent most of that time drowsing on the couch, the events of the past few days finally catching up with her. She roused long enough to eat at some point late that night, station time, when Max allowed Nkosi to send out for dinner, but soon fell asleep again. The next morning was better, however, and by the time she'd finished the second pot of coffee she felt almost ready to face whatever FitzGilbert's call might bring.

The chimes sounded a little after station noon, bringing Max bolt upright in his chair.

"Incoming transmission," Santerese said, unnecessarily, and started into the workroom. Heikki followed her, and heard Max call behind her, "Alexieva!"

The surveyor appeared a few minutes later, Max looming behind her like a jailer. "Are there any special codes?" he asked, and Alexieva shook her head.

"No. It should go through."

Heikki seated herself at the main console, watching numbers shift across her board as the machines on Iadara and on EP7 struggled to match frequencies pre-

cisely. At last, the connection was made; the media wall
lit and windowed, FitzGilbert's face framed in the apparent opening.

"Dam' Heikki."

The Iadaran's voice was almost less surprised than
angry, Heikki thought, and her own brows drew together into a frown. "That's right," she said, and knew
she sounded inane. "I need to talk to you."

"You and someone else, I see," FitzGilbert said, and
Heikki realized that Max had stepped into camera range
behind her.

"Yes," she said, and Max cut in smoothly.

"My name is Idris Max, commissioner, Terrestrial
Enforcement. I have some questions to ask you about
this lost crystal of yours."

FitzGilbert frowned. "I've already spoken to the Enforcement at some length, and I really don't see what I
could add to that." She looked directly at Heikki. "As
for you, Dam' Heikki, I remind you that Lo-Moth had a
confidentiality clause in its contract with you, which I
suspect you are in breach of already."

"Confidentiality clauses can't be used to hide criminal actions," Max began, and Heikki said, "Shut up,
Max. FitzGilbert."

The Iadaran looked at her warily, her expression
without encouragement.

"It's about the latac," Heikki went on, fumbling for
the words she needed to convince the other woman.
"Tremoth, Slade's people, they didn't come up with
anything of use in tracking the hijackers, did they?"

After a moment's pause, FitzGilbert shook her head
silently.

"That's because he, Slade, was responsible," Heikki
said. "I have proof." She reached for the tapes she had
made, but Max caught her wrist. Before she could
protest, FitzGilbert said, "Why? It makes no sense. . . ."
Her tone was less convinced than her words, and Heikki
struck at that uncertainty.

"Because Lo-Moth got its idea, and most of its plans
for that crystal out of Tremoth's back files, didn't they?

It was just your technician's bad luck he/she got the wrong set. Those plans were supposed to stay buried forever, lost in the system, because that was the crystal that destroyed EP1. But your techie found them, passed them along, and you grew a crystal, grew a matrix—a flawed matrix—before he even knew it was in the works. And by the time he did find out it was too late to stop you any other way except by destroying the matrix and then taking over and burying your research. You'd already set up a test facility for it, hadn't you?"

FitzGilbert nodded, her expression very still. "Slade did this personally—killed my people?"

"He hired the men who did it," Heikki answered.

FitzGilbert's face was grey even in the link's flattering reproduction. "So what do you want of me?"

"You may have information," Max began, and Heikki said again, "Shut up, Max. Slade pulled me off the job you hired me to do before I had the chance to complete it, and did his best to ruin my professional reputation, just in case I happened to put the pieces together. And that's nothing compared to what he did to you. I want his head, FitzGilbert. And so should you."

There was a long silence, and then FitzGilbert said, in a sleepwalker's voice, "Slade told me you had a brother who worked for Tremoth, that you were working with him to ruin the company."

Heikki laughed. It was a harsh sound, without humor. "My brother used to work for Slade, yes. I hadn't spoken to him for twenty years—I wouldn't have spoken to him if Slade hadn't tried to ruin me."

"What do you want from me?" FitzGilbert said again.

"Anything you have," Heikki answered.

There was another silence, this one longer than the first. Finally FitzGilbert said, "Yes—no, wait. There's one thing you don't know."

Max stirred slightly, and Heikki flung out a hand to silence him. "Well?"

"Those crystals—the plans, I mean, for the matrix. It was Slade himself who gave the schematics to Research."

"Why the hell would he do that?" Heikki said, almost

to herself, and then stopped, appalled. Slade was a Retroceder, everyone had said so—he wore the party's green badge openly even inside the corporation. If the Loop were destroyed—and the defective crystals would do that—he would be in a position to take up power in the Precincts, could probably have his choice of planets, backed by his fellow Retroceders. God knows, she thought, he may have become a Retroceder only to make use of their ideals, their politics, to make this entire maneuver possible. It would explain why the original data had never been destroyed. "He was going to use the crystals—sell them?"

FitzGilbert nodded, once, but then her face hardened. "Which I will deny, publically and in the courts."

"Why—?" Heikki began, but FitzGilbert was talking on, staring now at Max.

"All right, Commissioner. Yes, I have information that would be of use to you, information that ought to help you convict that bastard, but I want guarantees first."

"I can't promise anything," Max said, and FitzGilbert laughed harshly.

"Oh, you can promise this. You will, or you don't get what I have." She waited, and when Max made no further protest, went on, "Try him and welcome, but only for the latac. That's enough, seven people dead, but leave EP1 out of it. Christ, do you know what would happen if it was known that somebody'd made a bad crystal that could get past all the tests? That that was what caused EP1, and that somebody had tried to do it again? It wouldn't just ruin Lo-Moth, and Tremoth, it'd destroy the Loop." She paused then, searching their faces. "There are enough fringe groups that distrust the railroad, the Retroceders are just the loudest and the most organized. Give them a cause like this, and the whole system will go down. You give me that promise, Max, or you get nothing from me."

There was another long silence, broken only by the faint hissing of the open communications channel. Heikki sat very still, staring at the trees beyond FitzGilbert's window, and the bright reflection from the roof of a crystal shed. The Iadaran was right, there were entirely too many extremists who disliked the Railroad, some out of economic jealousy, some out of an irrational fear of the technology itself—which turned out not to be entirely irrational after all. She shook her head, and saw, out of the corner of her eye, that Max was nodding slowly.

"Wait a minute," she said. "What about these flawed crystals? How're you going to keep this from happening again?"

"I think something can be worked out," Max said, with a cynical smile.

FitzGilbert's lips twisted into an expression that might have been intended as a smile, but looked more like a grimace of pain. "I will see that the specifics of the design go to our heads of research, with an appropriate simulation of what might happen if such crystals were put into use. They can then compare all subsequent core crystals with that schematic—it can become a regular part of the inspection process. Will that suffice, Commissioner?"

No, Heikki wanted to say, it's not good enough, damn it. Max was already nodding.

"I can accept that, Dam' FitzGilbert. Now, about the data you said you had—"

"What about your promise?" FitzGilbert answered.

Max sighed. "I can give you my word that Ser Slade will only be charged with the deaths of the latac's crew, and with attempted fraud in regard to Dam' Heikki here, and her brother—and whatever else I can catch him on that does not reveal that the EP1 disaster was caused by these flawed crystals. Is that acceptable?"

There was a long pause, and then FitzGilbert sighed. "All right." Her hands moved on a workboard in front of her, out of the cameras' line of sight. "Are you ready to receive my data?"

Heikki did not answer, still overwhelmed by the turn of events, and Max reached impatiently over her shoulder to touch the necessary keys. "Ready to receive," he said.

"Transmitting." The machines squealed thinly, just at the edge of hearing. Heikki ducked her head in spite of herself, wincing, and then green lights flashed above the diskprinter.

"Transmission complete," FitzGilbert said, in almost the same moment. She looked suddenly very grim. "But if you break your word, Commissioner, you're going to find that that's worse than useless. End contact." Her image vanished in a flare of light. Heikki began to shut down the system, her hands moving almost without conscious volition.

"I hate it when people threaten me," Max said quite placidly, to no one in particular, and reached over Heikki's shoulder for the disks. He slipped them into the nearest workboard, tuned it to a private frequency, and began scanning pages through his data lens. Heikki released the last console from the local system and leaned back in her chair, watching as a smile spread over Max's face.

"I assume it's good news?" she asked.

"It's what I was hoping for," Max agreed. "This should be the last piece." He looked at Alexieva, waiting all but forgotten in the doorway, Nkosi still hovering at her side. "Thank you for your help, Dam' Alexieva."

"Then we may go now?" Nkosi asked, his face hard and watchful. Max nodded, and Nkosi transferred his stare to Heikki. "I will be in touch, Heikki."

"Right," Heikki answered, but the pilot had already withdrawn, pulling Alexieva with him. A moment later, Heikki heard the suite's outer door open and shut behind them.

"Now," Max said brightly, tucking the disks into his jacket pocket, and stepped out into the main room. Heikki pushed herself up from the console and followed, gratefully aware of Santerese's presence at her back.

"Galler Heikki," Max said, still with that alarming good humor, and Galler rose warily from the couch. "You, ser, will have to come with me. We'll want your evidence."

Galler smiled then, a bright, malicious smile, and Heikki shook her head. "You'll enjoy that, won't you?"

Her brother looked at her, his expression suddenly serious. "He tried to destroy me, Heikki, don't forget. Yes, I'll enjoy it. So would you."

Heikki opened her mouth to deny it, but could not muster the energy. Suddenly their old quarrel no longer seemed important—she no longer cared, she realized abruptly, whether she had the last word. "Maybe," she said, and looked at Max, who was waiting impatiently in the main doorway. "Make sure nobody strangles him, will you?"

"Why, Gwynne," Galler murmured. "I never knew you cared."

"I don't," Heikki said, but not until the door had closed behind them. Santerese touched her shoulder gently, comfortingly, and Heikki shook her head. "I really don't, not about any of it."

"If you didn't care," Santerese said, "you wouldn't be angry."

It was true, Heikki knew, but it didn't help. *I want justice,* she cried in silent protest, *not just for the latac crew, but for EP1 and the people killed—murdered— there. There ought to be some restitution made—except that FitzGilbert was right, justice for them, telling that old truth, could well destroy the railroad and the stations that depended on it. Where was the justice in that?* She shook her head, tired of the uncertainty, wanting only to have it over. *Did I do right, even remotely? I did the best I could.*

"I'm too old for this," she said aloud, and Santerese took her in her arms.

"Aren't we all, darling, aren't we all?"

# THE MANY WORLDS OF
# MELISSA SCOTT

*Winner of the John W. Campbell Award
for Best New Writer, 1986*

**THE KINDLY ONES:** "An ambitious novel of the world Orestes. This large, inhabited moon is governed by five Kinships whose society operates on a code of honor so strict that transgressors are declared legally 'dead' and are prevented from having any contact with the 'living.' . . . Scott is a writer to watch."—*Publishers Weekly*. A Main Selection of the Science Fiction Book Club.

65351-2 • 384 pp. • $2.95

## The "Silence Leigh" Trilogy

**FIVE-TWELFTHS OF HEAVEN (Book I):** "Melissa Scott postulates a universe where technology interferes with magic. . . . The whole plot is one of space ships, space wars, and alien planets—not a unicorn or a dragon to be seen anywhere. Scott's space drive and description of space piloting alone would mark her as an expert in the melding of the [SF and fantasy] genres; this is the stuff of which 'sense of wonder' is made."—*Locus*

55952-4 • 352 pp. • $2.95

**SILENCE IN SOLITUDE (Book II):** "[Scott is] a voice you should seek out and read at every opportunity." —*OtherRealms*.

65699-7 • 324 pp. • $2.95

**THE EMPRESS OF EARTH (Book III):**

65364-4 • 352 pp. • $3.50

**A CHOICE OF DESTINIES:** "Melissa Scott [is] one of science fiction's most talented newcomers. . . . The greatest delight of all is finding out how she managed to write a historical novel that could legitimately have spaceships on the cover . . . a marvelous gift for any fan."—*Baltimore Sun*    65563-9 • 320 pp. • $2.95

**THE GAME BEYOND:** "An exciting interstellar empire novel with a great deal of political intrigue and colorful interplanetary travel."—*Locus*
55918-4 • 352 pp. • $2.95

---

To order any of these Melissa Scott titles, please check the box/es below and send combined cover price/s to:

**Baen Books**  Name _____
**Dept. BA**
**260 Fifth Ave.**  Address _____
**NY, NY 10001**  City _____ State _____ Zip ___

THE KINDLY ONES ☐        FIVE-TWELFTHS OF HEAVEN ☐
A CHOICE OF DESTINIES ☐  SILENCE IN SOLITUDE ☐
THE GAME BEYOND ☐        THE EMPRESS OF EARTH ☐

BAEN BOOKS

# WHAT OUR READERS SAY ABOUT

## LOIS McMASTER BUJOLD

"I read [THE WARRIOR'S APPRENTICE] very carefully with an eye on making criticisms based on my experiences as a former military officer, but each time I found something, you repaired it. . . . I could find nothing to fault in the story. It was well done and well written."
—Kevin D. Randle, Cedar Rapids, Iowa

"I am reading Lois Bujold's THE WARRIOR'S APPRENTICE for the third time. . . . The girl [sic!] plots intricately. I love her writing, and will buy anything she writes."
—R.C. Crenshaw, Eugene, Oregon

"You may be off on a new Space Patrol with the Dendarii Mercenaries. It will strain my purse, but I should cut my eating anyhow!"
—John P. Conlon, Newark, Ohio

"I have been recommending [SHARDS OF HONOR] to my friends, telling them that the book is about personal honor, love, duty, and the conflict between honor, love and duty. I am looking forward to your next novel."
—Radcliffe Cutshaw, Boca Raton, Florida

# AND HERE'S WHAT THE CRITICS SAY:

## SHARDS OF HONOR

"Bujold has written what may be the best first science fiction novel of the year."
—*Chicago Sun-Times*

"A strong debut, and Bujold is a writer to look for in the future."
—*Locus*

"An unusually good book."
—*Voice of Youth Advocates*

"Splendid . . . This superb first novel integrates a believable romance into a science fiction tale of adventure and war."
—*Booklist*

## THE WARRIOR'S APPRENTICE

"Highly recommended for any SF collection."
—*Booklist*

"Bujold continues to delight."
—*Locus*

"Bujold's first book, *Shards of Honor*, was called 'possibly the best first SF novel of the year,' by the *Chicago Sun-Times*. *The Warrior's Apprentice* is better."
—*Fantasy Review*

# ETHAN OF ATHOS

"This is Ms. Bujold's third novel, and the consensus of opinion among those who enjoy watching the development of a new writer is that she just keeps getting better."     —*Vandalia Drummer News*

"An entertaining, and out-of-the-ordinary, romp."
     —*Locus*

"I've read SHARDS OF HONOR about twenty times; THE WARRIOR'S APPRENTICE not so repeatedly but I'm working on it. If [Ms. Bujold] can maintain the quality she'll rank with Anne McCaffrey and C.J. Cherryh."
     —Aeronita C. Belle, Baltimore, Md.

"I just finished your book SHARDS OF HONOR. It was so good I almost don't want to take it back to the library.... Keep up the good work."     —Jan Curtis, Delaware, Ohio

---

Order all of Lois McMaster Bujold's novels with this order form. Check your choices below and send the combined cover price/s plus 75 cents for first-class postage and handling to: Baen Books, Dept. BA, 260 Fifth Avenue, New York, N.Y. 10001.

SHARDS OF HONOR * 320 pp. *
  65574-4 * $2.95                                     ☐
THE WARRIOR'S APPRENTICE * 320 pp. *
  65587-6 * $2.95                                     ☐
ETHAN OF ATHOS * 256 pp. *
  65604-X * $2.95                                     ☐

## AN OFFER HE COULDN'T REFUSE

They were functional fangs, not just decorative, set in a protruding jaw, with long lips and a wide mouth; yet the total effect was lupine rather than simian. Hair a dark matted mess. And yes, fully eight feet tall, a rangy, tense-muscled body.

She clawed her wild hair away from her face and stared at him with renewed fierceness. Her eyes were a strange light hazel, adding to the wolfish effect. "What are you *really* doing here?"

"I came for you. I'd heard of you. I'm . . . recruiting. Or I was. Things went wrong and now I'm escaping. But if you came with me, you could join the Dendarii Mercenaries. A top outfit—always looking for a few good men, or whatever. I have this master-sergeant who . . . who *needs* a recruit like you." Sgt. Dyeb was infamous for his sour attitude about women soldiers, insisting that they were too soft . . .

"Very funny," she said coldly. "But I'm not even human. Or hadn't you heard?"

"Human is as human does." He forced himself to reach out and touch her damp cheek. "Animals don't weep."

She jerked, as from an electric shock. "Animals don't lie. Humans do. All the time."

"Not *all* the time."

"Prove it." She tilted her head as she sat cross-legged. "Take off your clothes."

" . . . what?"

"Take off your clothes and lie down with me as *humans* do. Men and women." Her hand reached out to touch his throat.

The pressing claws made little wells in his flesh. "Blrp?" choked Miles. His eyes felt wide as saucers. A little more pressure, and those wells would spring forth red fountains. *I am about to die. . . .*

*I can't believe this. Trapped on Jackson's Whole with a sex-starved teenage werewolf. There was nothing about this in any of my Imperial Academy training manuals. . . .*

**BORDERS OF INFINITY by LOIS McMASTER BUJOLD**
**69841-9 • $3.95**

# TIMOTHY ZAHN

## *CREATOR OF NEW WORLDS*

"Timothy Zahn's specialty is technological intrigue-international and interstellar," says *The Christian Science Monitor*. Amen! For novels involving hard-edged conflict with alien races, world-building with a strong scientific basis, and storytelling excitement, turn to Hugo Award Winner Timothy Zahn!

---

Please send me the following books by Timothy Zahn:

\_\_\_\_ COBRA, 352 pages, 65560-4, $3.50

\_\_\_\_ COBRA STRIKE, 352 pages, 65551-5, $3.50

\_\_\_\_ COBRA BARGAIN, 420 pages, 65383-0, $3.95

\_\_\_\_ TRIPLET, 384 pages, 65341-5, $3.95

\_\_\_\_ A COMING OF AGE, 320 pages, 65578-7, $3.50

\_\_\_\_ SPINNERET, 352 pages, 65598-1, $3.50

\_\_\_\_ CASCADE POINT, 416 pages, 65622-8, $3.50

Send the cover price to Baen Books, Dept. BA, 260 Fifth Ave., New York, NY 10001. Order soon, and as a bonus we'll also send you a copy of *THE WHOLE BAEN CATALOG*, which lists and describes all Baen titles currently available.

---